Praise for W

Eton Rogue

'A delicious tale in which class, politics, and a toxic press all jostle'
Tunku Varadarajan, *The Wall Street Journal*

Palace Rogue

'This charming tale of secrets and love is a must for royal fans.'
Hello Magazine

'A plump and cheerful romp through royal corridors and bedrooms.'
Tunku Varadarajan, *The Wall Street Journal*

'This rom com is packed full of love, laughs and scandals, and is well worth a read.'
Hampshire Chronicle

'A right royal romp through one of Buckingham Palace's shadier moments.'
Shaun Bythell, author of the international hit *Diary of a Bookseller*

The Eton Affair

'Charming, moving, uplifting. Why can't all love stories be like this?'
Tunku Varadarajan, *The Wall Street Journal*

'This is a charming and uplifting book.'
Piers Morgan

'An outstanding debut novel. A wonderful story of first love. Few male authors can write about romance in a way which appeals to women – but Coles has managed it quite brilliantly.'
Sunday Express

'Elegantly structured, tinglingly evocative of the passion and brutality of first love – a wonderful read.'
LOUISE CANDLISH

'What a read! Every schoolboy's dream comes true in this deftly-written treatment of illicit romance. A triumph.'
ALEXANDER MCCALL SMITH

Dave Cameron's Schooldays

'A cracking read... Perfectly paced and brilliantly written, Coles draws you in, leaving a childish smile on your face.'
NEWS OF THE WORLD

'A fast moving and playful spoof. The details are so slick and telling that they could almost have you fooled.'
THE MIRROR

Mr Two-Bomb

'Compellingly vivid, the most sustained description of apocalypse since Robert Harris's Pompeii.'
THE FINANCIAL TIMES

ETON ROGUE

WILLIAM COLES

Legend Press Ltd, 51 Gower Street, London, WC1E 6HJ
info@legendtimesgroup.co.uk | www.legendpress.co.uk

 British Library Cataloguing in Publication Data available.

Print ISBN 9781915643315
Ebook ISBN 9781915643322
Set in Times.
Cover design by Kari Brownlie | www.karibrownlie.co.uk

William Coles has been a journalist for 30 years and has worked for a number of papers including *The Sun*, *The Express*, *The Mail* and *The Wall Street Journal*.

William's novel, *Palace Rogue*, is the prequel to *Eton Rogue*, and was published in 2023.

Visit William at
wcoles.com

and follow him
@WilliamColes1

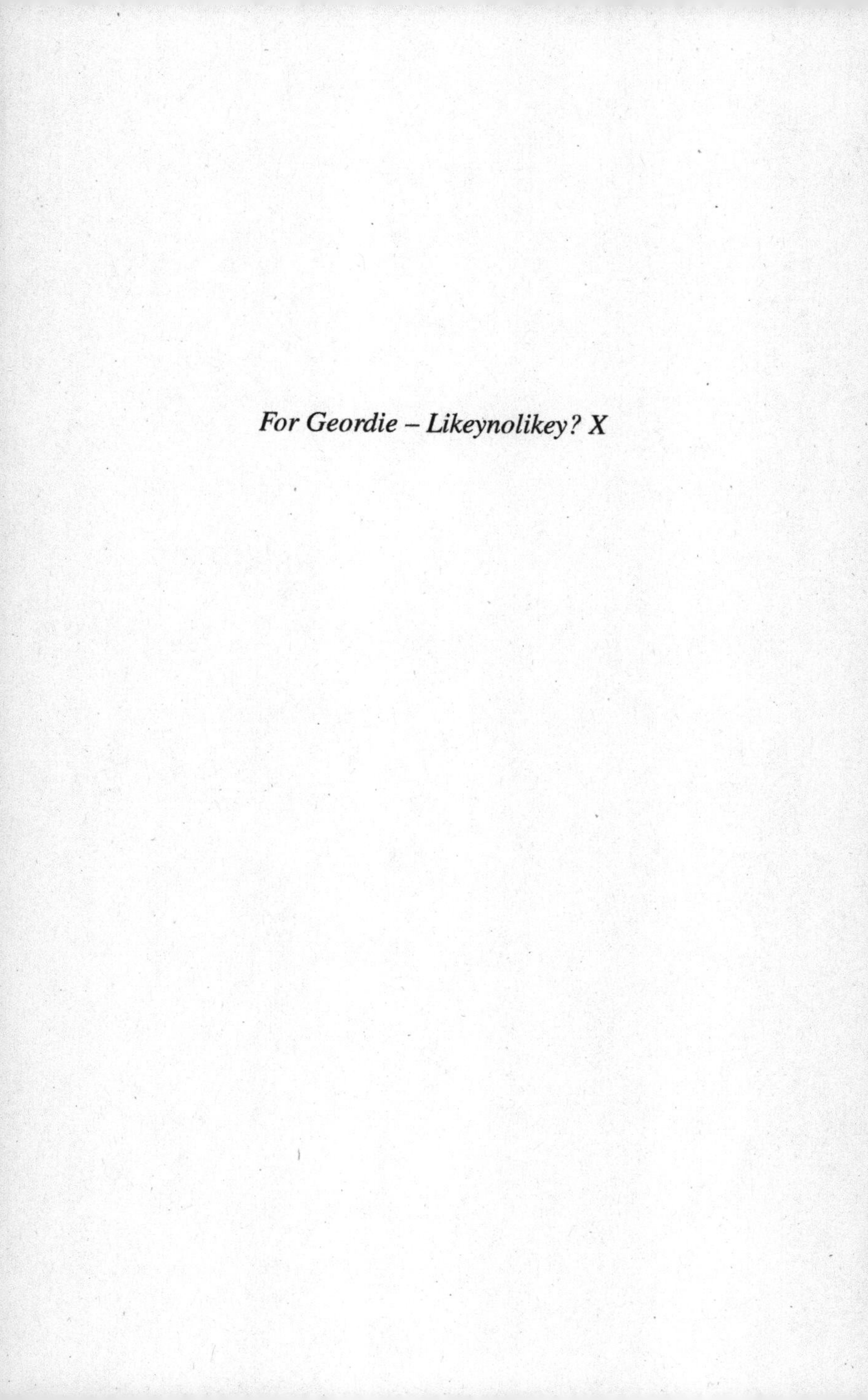

For Geordie – Likeynolikey? X

Though this story is a novel, it is very much based on real events. The basic rule of thumb is that the more outlandish a scene, the greater the likelihood that it actually occurred.

Names have been changed to protect the guilty – save one. In this story, The Sun *newspaper's Eton mole is called 'Agent Orange'; that was indeed the codename of* The Sun*'s rogue Etonian.*

CHAPTER 1

We are in the school hall of the world's most famous school, Eton College. Such a sea of black tailcoats, hundreds and hundreds of them – and in amongst this swirling blur of boys in black, there is one delicious dot of red. You can pick her out quite easily from the balcony, as all else is either black or white. But Lily, sitting right in the middle of the hall, has decided to wear red today – because she can, because she's the only girl in the school, and because she's fed up with wearing muted blues and blacks and greys in the vain hope that it'll help her blend in with her schoolmates. Over half-term, she had an epiphany: she's never going to blend in. And that's because she's a girl – the only girl amongst 1,300 boys.

Her father had hoped that bringing Lily to Eton would be no more cause for comment than, say, a beak taking his dog to class – unusual, yes, but the boys would get used to it soon enough. But the boys can't get used to it, and the boys will never get used to it – and though Lily's father might have fondly imagined these Eton boys would eventually get used to it, they haven't. She becomes ever more alluring. And now that, for the first time, she has decided to wear a red dress, the boys can't help but sit up, and nudge, and stare, and whisper, and dream.

Aside from Lily, there is not a single girl within two miles of Eton, so there's a lot of weight bearing down on this doughty girl's shoulders. For the past six weeks, since she started at Eton, it's felt like she's been a weird zoo animal – not necessarily cooped up in a cage, but nevertheless relentlessly gawped at. Wherever she goes in Eton, she is watched. She is watched, she is admired, she is commented upon. Initially, for a while, she scuttled along Eton's streets with her head down, not making eye contact, new leather briefcase braced like a shield, nothing to look at here. But that, of course, is a complete impossibility – she's the only girl in the school, not an Etonian but an Etonienne, and whatever she does, whatever she says, and certainly whatever she wears, will be analysed and dissected in the most minute detail.

A few days ago, Lily had a conversation with Miranda, the Dame at Farrer House, and this conversation has fluttered and sputtered in her mind and today has finally taken wing.

'You're the only girl in the school,' Miranda said. 'You should own that. If you're comfortable in blues and blacks, that's fine. But if you want to wear something a little more edgy, then… Go for it!'

That same afternoon, they'd gone shopping in Windsor. The result: the red dress. And now – well, here she was, head high, golden hair for once loose about her shoulders, and those damn boys could slobber and nudge all they liked. She didn't give a damn. She looked down, not out of shyness, but to admire her shoes. Along with her red dress, she'd bought new shoes – and she'd certainly never bought a pair of shoes like these before. Converse HighTops, black with white laces; she rolled her heel to admire the logo. She'd dithered in the shop, but Miranda had insisted, and Miranda had been right. With the red dress, they were terrific.

Lily laughed as she looked round the hall, wondering if she'd be able to see him. The reaction, when she looked round, was instantaneous. Everyone who'd been looking at her suddenly averted their gaze. And that made her smile too; what a great day, what a great day to be alive – she was wearing her new dress, her new shoes, and that afternoon, after a full week apart, she would be seeing him. Then to do… that which had to be done.

Right at the back, leaning against a pillar, she could see Mr McCreath, the school's head of security, like an old heron, just watching, waiting, biding his time. But the one person she wanted to see she could not see. He'd be there, she knew it, and he'd love it that she was wearing red – and later, and unless she was very much mistaken, he would soon be easing her out of her red dress... She all but blushed at the thought.

The Headman, the bristling Mr Moffatt, had come into the School Hall, and, like some old wolfhound that's been rousted out of its basket, the boys shook themselves down and got to their feet and the rumbling mutter of voices stuttered and stopped. And then she saw him, just a little taller than the rest, a glimpse of blond hair and a smile. He sort of jerked his head, as if to say... see you outside afterwards. And why not? Seeing him in the afternoon at The Project would be nice; nicer still to be kissing him in ten minutes.

Mr Moffatt trotted briskly onto the stage, a little terrier of a man, a no-nonsense man who prided himself on always knowing what was best for his boys and best for the school. Though, when he got to the lectern in the middle of the stage, he did this funny thing that he'd started doing about a month ago. He did nothing. He fiddled with his notes. He stepped back, looked to the organ behind him, looked dead ahead at the boys in front, looked to the balcony, looked up to the lofty barrel ceiling. And then started fiddling with his notes again.

Lily supposed he was trying to build up a tone of tense expectation in his audience, but most of the boys just looked bored, picking at their spots, scratching at their stubble, scrubbing at the stains on their tight black waistcoats. Some of the boys had given up altogether and begun to whisper.

Finally, after thirty, forty seconds of foreplay, Mr Moffatt tapped the microphone on the lectern.

'There is here, amongst us now, a rogue Etonian,' he said.

Lily sighed. Of late, this had become a fairly well-worn theme for Eton's Headman – and now here he was, once again firing them up for another diatribe about The Rogue.

'Since Prince William started at Eton six weeks ago, there has been a steady stream of stories about the school appearing in *The Sun*!

'I believe,' continued Mr Moffatt, 'in fact I know, that these stories are being sold to *The Sun* by an Eton schoolboy. More than that, I believe that that boy is in this hall now.

'And I ask you now – why is this boy selling stories to *The Sun*? Why does he think so little of his school, his teachers and his peers that he wants to drag Eton's name through the gutter?'

Mr Moffatt paused and rocked back on his heels.

'I will tell you why this boy is selling stories to *The Sun*! He is doing it for the money! This rogue boy is making thousands – thousands and thousands of pounds from *The Sun*. They are paying him in hard cash. He is literally selling his school down the river.

'And what I would like – and what I am requesting from you – is the name of this boy. And for this name, I am offering an amnesty. I am offering a substantial cash reward. I will pay whatever it takes to catch *The Sun*'s Eton mole. And if you are *The Sun*'s spy, then hear me now: your days are numbered.'

The harangue continues, though Lily has stopped listening. She smooths her dress, slim hands stroking down her thighs; what if they were his hands? The daydream is broken as she becomes aware that the boys are lumbering to their feet again. Mr Moffatt rattles down the steps and leaves the hall, though even before he's left the room, the boys are chattering – who is the mole? Who could he be? Who is this snoop who is being paid these astronomical sums of money? And is there any chance at all that he might spread the love?

As the boys drift out of the hall and onto the street, Lily remains in her seat. She flicks through the school's Fixtures book, bides her time, waiting, waiting with this glorious sense of anticipation until the hall is all but empty. Then she gets up. She heads not for the exit but for one of the doors next to the stage. She walks into a cool, dark passage, where just a couple of boys are ragging at the far end. She ignores them, and heads to the further recesses of the hall, with its rehearsal rooms and conference rooms and cloakrooms and, though she doesn't yet know what she's looking for, she's sure she'll know it when she sees it.

She follows the corridor as it leads around the back of the hall. On the back stairs, leading up to the tiered benches behind the stage, a white rose has been placed on a bannister. She takes the rose. It's one of those old-fashioned roses, with real thorns. It smells just heavenly. She wends her way up the stairs. Will he be lurking behind the organ?

She arrives at another corridor, narrower, gloomier, lit by a single light bulb, doors to the left, doors to the right, and another staircase leading up to the top floor. A white handkerchief winks at her from on top of a fire extinguisher. She picks it up and continues down the corridor. She can hear a tune being picked out with a single finger on a piano. It's a song from South Pacific, 'I'm Going to Wash That Man Right Out Of My Hair'. The effect is instantaneous – goosebumps. He's here. He's waiting for her.

Lily can see it long before she gets there. A white bow tie has been tied onto a door-handle, tied with the most perfect bow. She opens the door – and there of course he is, in all his most handsome glory, standing by an upright piano in a lime green room. He smiles at Lily, pulls her into his arms and gives her a kiss that is more than good enough to make up for a week, a month, of lost kisses.

'You,' he said.

'Are you the Eton rogue?' she asked between kisses.

'I am the boy who is quite literally selling his school down the river.'

'I hear there's a pretty sizeable reward for you.'

'What – this big?' From the pocket of his tailcoat, he produced an inch-thick wad of £20 notes, slowly riffling them in front of her love-drunk eyes.

Lily sized it up; in the past month, she'd become quite

the connoisseur of used banknotes. 'Looks like 3K to me,' she said.

'To the penny!' he said. 'I picked it up from Kim while I was going through London yesterday.'

Lily started to unbutton the silver buttons of his black waistcoat. 'There was also mention of an amnesty, whatever that means,' she said.

He laughed. God, how she loved him. 'I think it means you can break any school rule you like – with total impunity.'

'What about…' Taking his hand, she led him past the piano and over to the armchair in the corner. 'Making love in the School Hall?'

'I'll bet that's not even covered in the school rules.' He kissed her cheek, her neck, hands riding her thighs. 'It wouldn't have even occurred to them!'

She peeled off his shirt. 'They might add a new rule just for me.'

'What an honour!" he said. 'One rule just for you – Lily must on no account make love. I love your dress, by the way.'

The dress lay discarded on the piano stool. 'And my shoes?'

'Keep them on.'

'Hey,' she said, picking up the wad of twenties. 'You know we're never going to spend any of this money?'

He chuckled, stroking her fondly, remembering a very slight disagreement, their only disagreement, a month back. 'I do.'

'Just once, I'd love to make love on it – so that one day, when I'm an impoverished crone, I can remind myself that I once made love in a shower of cash.'

'Like Zeus seducing Danaë in a shower of gold?'

As Lily lay back in the armchair, he tossed the money into the air and the notes fluttered onto the floor, and onto her dress, and onto his back, and onto Lily's head and her hair, with one particularly impudent note staying stuck on the slick sweat of her stomach.

In short order, and like star-cross'd lovers the world over, they are renewed and reacquainted.

'How do I look?' she said. Red dress back on, she gave him a twirl.

'You look far too happy,' he said. 'You're just back from half-term. You should be scowling.'

'Like this?' She glowered. 'I learned it from the Headman.'

'A human gargoyle!' he said. 'More hideous, even, than the real thing!' He popped a stud through the front of his starched stick-ups and deftly tied his white bow tie. 'You go now, I'll pick up the loot.'

'Anyone'd think you'd robbed a bank!' The room was quite littered with £20 notes. She gave him a kiss. 'See you in The Project this afternoon?'

'I can't wait.' He was already stooped to the floor and picking up the notes.

Lily was singing to herself when she breezed out of the School Hall, a young girl in love – and for a moment, she let her guard down. Because she wasn't just any girl in love. She was the only girl in the school, and wherever she went, she was watched.

By chance, perhaps, Mr McCreath, Eton's head of security, is taking his ease by The Burning Bush, a Victorian streetlight, very florid Gothic, that's just next to the School Hall. The Burning Bush is Eton's hub, from which all its spokes radiate, so that it doesn't matter where you're going in the school, at least twice, three times a day, you'll walk past this street lamp – and it is here, in his tweed suit and his deerstalker hat, that Mr McCreath likes to ponder. He likes to lean against the lamp's Portland stone base and watch and listen, and it's here, more often than not, that he can pick out the mischief-makers. He has a nose for them. Not that, quite yet, he has discovered the identity of *The Sun*'s Eton mole, but of one thing he's certain: he most assuredly will.

Mr McCreath's wizened eye was drawn naturally, obviously, to Lily as she skipped down the School Hall steps; she was even singing that song from South Pacific, the one that had been used to so effectively humiliate the Headman last month.

Mr McCreath looked after her as she strolled off down Judy's Passage. Now there was a young woman in love. And not that Mr McCreath was a betting man, but if he had been so inclined, he might have had a modest wager that that girl, Lily, had just been kissing her boyfriend.

A boy eased out of the School Hall's heavy metal doors – a remarkably cheerful boy, rather dashing actually, with his slightly rumpled hair.

'Morning, Mr McCreath,' he called as he trotted down the steps.

'Good morning, Cary,' Mr McCreath said. 'You appear to have lost your buttonhole.'

Cary patted his empty lapel. 'So I have,' he said. 'I'll find a dandelion instead.' He sauntered through Cannon Yard, tailcoat fluttering in the breeze as he returned to The Timbralls.

Mr McCreath watched and mused. Funny to think how, six weeks earlier, on almost this exact same spot, he'd seen one of the most astonishing spectacles of his life.

On the far side of the road, by the entrance to Cannon Yard, had been The Press. Though those two words didn't remotely do justice to the complete scrum of reporters and photographers and film crews that had descended on Eton for two days. They were, in fact, representatives of The World's Press, with hundreds of reporters and photographers from all over the world, row upon row of them, all lined up in stands that had been specially erected on the pavement. At the front of the stands, in a vain attempt to keep the mob at bay, Mr McCreath's team had even put up a flimsy metal fence.

On the other side of Common Lane had been Prince William – happily posing with his parents when he'd arrived, and then the next day, his first full day at Eton, again posing for the mob, though now in his school uniform, black tails, black waistcoat, black pinstripe trousers, and starched white collar taut around his neck.

Mr McCreath had watched the whole sorry circus from the steps of the School Library, just next to the School Hall – and had had a revelation. That free-for-all on the first day of term was supposed to be one final sop to The Press, one last bone for them to chew on before they were sent on their way, never to darken the College again. Under a unique deal that had been hammered out with Buckingham Palace, The Press had unanimously agreed to leave off Prince William for the duration of his stay at Eton. Whatever the 13-year-old Prince did at Eton, however many scrapes he got into, however many exams he contrived to fail, The Press wouldn't run a word of it.

But on that first day, as he'd stood by the library and as he'd watched Prince William being hosed down by the photographers, it had slowly dawned on Mr McCreath that Eton College was itself now very big news. The papers might not be able to run any stories about the young Prince. But there would still be a limitless appetite for any stories at all about Prince William's schoolmates and his teachers.

The one thing that had never occurred to Mr McCreath, had never crossed his mind, was that the first story, the very first Sun royal exclusive, would happen on the first day of term.

CHAPTER 2

And so to begin at the beginning: Prince William's first day at Eton, September 6, 1995.

But while The World's Press devoured the young Prince, there were three boys, at least, who could not give a fig for any of this ridiculous royal hoopla, and who had hied themselves off to the school pub, Tap. Tap was like a gritty North Yorkshire bar with high wood panels and low cobwebbed ceilings; grimy. But unlike the bars of North Yorkshire, the voices were just that little bit more crystal cut, and the clientele were mostly wearing not tweed but tailcoats and neck-chafing collars. At the age of 16, the boys were allowed to drink a couple of pints in Tap, the better to learn how to hold their drink.

It was a blissfully balmy afternoon and these three tearaways were celebrating the start of their final year by going on the most epic bender. They were Bruno the German and Viktor the Russian, and the last of the three was that young man who, when last we saw him, was throwing a great wad of £20 notes over his beautiful lover: Cary the hero.

They were wearing jeans, T-shirts and trainers, perfect dress-down clothes for Eton – and also, as it happens, the perfect clothes for being chased by an armed policeman.

Bruno sighed as he spied the beleaguered barman surrounded by a crush of tailcoats. 'I feared this,' he said. His father was German (the UK ambassador, no less), his mother Spanish, and Bruno spoke the most precise English of any boy in the school.

'Why did you bring us here, then?' Viktor said, tetchy. For the past fortnight, he had been denied all alcohol; some horseplay gone wrong, the family cat strangled.

And Cary just smiled. He was so happy to be back at Eton and back in Tap with his friends. He was also inordinately happy to be away from his parents; he'd spent the whole of the summer holidays with them, without surcease. Eton had never seemed more inviting.

'Do not trouble yourself, Viktor,' Bruno said. 'I foresaw the queue. I have brought a small flask to help pass the time.'

'How small?' Viktor said.

'This small.' Bruno brought out a stainless steel hip-flask, the size of a bed-pan. 'And I have glasses! The embassy's finest!' Three cut-crystal schooners were produced from his rucksack.

Cary held the glasses and Bruno poured three tots, casually slopping some of the black liqueur over Cary's fingers.

Cary laughed and licked them. 'I like it,' he said. 'Coffee and something?'

'It is my father's favourite drink, coffee tequila,' Bruno said, taking a glass for himself and passing one to Viktor. 'I needed five bottles of his Café Patron to fill my, my… no it is too big for a hip-flask, my bum-flask. It is not only delicious, it is deliciously expensive. Prost!'

'Cheers!'

'Though I should warn you this tequila is 35 per cent proof. We will soon be, as my grandmother so liked to say, fusionless with drink.'

'Is that a problem?' Viktor said.

'Not for me,' Bruno said, raising an eyebrow to Cary. 'But then I am neither a scholar nor a Popper. This school expects nothing from me!'

Cary shrugged – because there could, actually, be quite a lot of problems with getting drunk on the first day of term.

But the problem is never just about getting drunk.

It's about the subsequent scrapes.

'I'm in,' he said.

And that's the way life works. You have all your plans, your grandiose dreams, and you may even have tactics, strategy and grand strategy, and yet the single event that turns your life on a sixpence is deciding to get drunk with your friends on the first day of term.

Nevertheless… this was how it all started for Cary; it was the start of the stories, the lies, and the astronomical sums of hard cash; it was the start of his life as *The Sun*'s rogue Etonian; and, best of all, and without which there would be no tale whatsoever to tell, it was the start of a love that would last a lifetime.

The queue surged round the bar.

Bruno staggered. 'Let us away to the fireplace.'

Viktor carved a path through the melée of tailcoats and planted himself square by the empty fireplace. Bruno placed his monster bum-flask on the mantelpiece. Just above their heads, hanging so very enticingly from the ceiling, was a dusty quart glass.

'In my entire life, I have never seen so many journalists here for this Prince William,' Bruno said, again topping up their glasses, and again slopping Café Patron over Cary. 'Two hundred of them – three hundred!'

'I think I will be on front pages tomorrow!' Viktor said, knocking back his tequila. He never sipped. 'When the Prince come out, a girl walk out of library. Pretty!' He helped himself to more tequila. 'Very pretty! She must be new girl, master's daughter! I saw her and tripped on Hall steps,' Viktor continued. 'All my books - everywhere! Paper – everywhere! It very funny!'

'The Headman must have been unhappy,' Bruno said.

'Headman not unhappy – Headman furious!' Viktor chortled. 'He help me pick up paper, but it blow everywhere, into road, down pavement. The girl, Prince William, they all pick up my paper!'

Cary studied the beautiful tracery that had been etched into the bowl of his schooner. A youth was chasing a girl through a field of vines, her long hair flowing behind her, and Cary could even make out the smiles on their faces – though as Cary turned the glass round, he saw that the pair were equidistant, so perhaps it was the girl who was herself chasing the youth.

Bruno stretched up for the quart glass that was hanging from the ceiling. 'The Long Glass,' he said. 'I have never done it, you know.'

'You're going to try it after the tequila?' Cary said, still just about hanging onto some last vestiges of common sense.

'In Tap, we are allowed to drink two pints of beer,' Bruno said. 'I would like to take my two pints from the Long Glass. Will you not join me?'

'Yes!' Viktor said.

Cary nodded, tingles of disaster.

Bruno returned from the bar with six pints of beer on a tray. He poured two pints into the Long Glass, just over a foot long, fluted, with a bulbous end. Word spread.

'I shall go first,' he said. 'Let me show you how.' Bruno raised the Long Glass to the humming circle of tailcoats. 'This glass that I hold now is Eton's famous Long Glass. It was given to the school by the Duke of Wellington, and has been touched by the lips of countless Prime Ministers, not to mention writers, actors, churchmen, musicians – and rogues. And now, it is my turn to take my place in this illustrious line of Etonian topers!' He bowed to the cheers and took a small sip from the Long Glass. 'Nectar!' he said.

Bruno drank smoothly and slowly, taking his time, breathing easy, gently twirling the glass in his fingers, and after a minute, and a slight belch, and to tepid applause, he was done.

'Give me the glass!' Viktor said. 'In Russia, we do it with vodka. Nostrovia!' The Long Glass was emptied in under 30 seconds easy, as if Viktor had been pouring it down the sink.

And last, of course, was Cary, and Cary was very dubious indeed about drinking two pints of beer on top of a pint of Café Patron. But he couldn't back down – not after his friends had done it, and not now that the whole pub was thumping on the tables and stamping on the parquet floor.

Cary took the glass, smiled. 'My friends,' he said. 'This will be my first and only attempt at drinking the Long Glass. I would like to apologise in advance if it ends badly, as it most assuredly will. For your own safety, please stand well back.'

He took a sip of the beer, Directors, not much to his liking, but drinking two pints of lager would have been impossible. He'd only had three more sips before he'd had enough. He paused for a moment wondering what to do next.

He could have carried on drinking, or he could have handed the Long Glass to somebody else to drink, but where was the fun in that? And then, brightly, he realised he could give all these boys exactly what they'd been waiting for. He lifted the Long Glass up high, much too high, took one more pull, and then down it came, the bulbous end of the glass suddenly releasing its contents and sousing Cary with beer, flooding his face and soaking his T-shirt. An instant roar of approval. Cary received more back-slaps and more handshakes that afternoon than he'd ever had on the athletics track.

They continued with the tequila.

'This young Prince who has joined us,' Bruno said, speaking even more precisely now that he was completely pie-eyed. 'Will he be going over to Windsor to have tea with the Queen?'

'Might do,' Cary said.

'I think we should go and see her,' Bruno said.

'When?' Viktor asked blearily.

'Now,' Bruno said. 'This afternoon. We shall see her! And we shall drink her health!' He topped up the three glasses with the last of the Café Patron. 'To the Queen!' He downed the tequila and hurled the glass into the fireplace. It exploded against the brickwork.

'To Queen!' Viktor said, also throwing his glass into the fireplace. He laughed as it shattered into a thousand shards. 'Feels good!'

'To the Queen,' Cary said. 'But this glass is lovely. I don't want to smash it.'

'But Cary, you must,' Bruno said. 'Now that we have toasted Her Majesty, these glasses cannot be used again.'

'Smash it!' Viktor said.

'I'll keep it,' Cary said.

'You must smash it!'

'It is the tradition, Cary, you must smash the glass,' Bruno said.

'I'm not smashing it,' Cary said. 'I'll keep it. Every time I drink from it, I'll think of you.'

Bruno sighed. 'I fear, Viktor, that Cary does not get the same pleasure from smashing things that we do.'

'Sorry about that.' Cary tucked the glass away into the top pouch of his own rucksack. 'It's the most beautiful glass I've ever seen.'

Now – the next bit Cary was not so very sure about. One moment they had been in Tap, and the next, barely without setting foot on Eton's High Street, they were in the private grounds of Windsor Castle. And again, he was never too sure why they'd decided to go into the Castle grounds to see the Queen, rather than just, say, going in via the main entrance and politely asking if Her Majesty had a moment for three of Prince William's new schoolmates.

But somehow, they'd broken into the private grounds of Windsor Castle, and now, hands in pockets, they were drunkenly blundering around the parkland. Bruno stopped by an old oak to have a pee.

Cary was admiring the Round Tower with the Royal Standard, which was being run up the flagpole; the Queen was now in residence. He was the first to spot the problem. 'Do you see the camera in the tree?'

Bruno looked up. 'I think it looks like a dummy, no?'

'If it's a dummy, it's a pretty good one. It's moving. It's looking right at you!'

Bruno stared glassily into the camera. 'Who would put a camera in a tree?'

'Maybe the guys who are paid to look after the Queen?'

'Scheisse!' said Bruno, reverting to German. He furiously zipped up, nearly doing himself a mischief.

Two men in suits loped towards them. One was talking into a radio.

The three boys should, of course, have stayed where they were, taken their medicine.

But the boys followed their teenage instincts. They ran.

The boys had no idea where they were heading. But with another black suit appearing in front of them, they were fresh out of options. They ran towards the Castle's outer walls; there was a thicket of trees where they could hole up. When you've got over a pint of Café Patron swilling inside you, you don't tend to over-analyse these things.

Viktor was the first to be caught. He plain ran out of puff – stood there, hands up, I surrender. He was ordered face down onto the ground.

Bruno was holding his own against the armed security men, not gaining, but not losing ground either.

But Cary… Cary was a runner. He was the school's 400 metres, 800 metres champion, he was a discus thrower, a shot-putter, a long-jumper, he was the complete athlete and, next summer, would, unless there was some shocking, shocking event, not only shatter various running records but would again be crowned Eton's Victor Ludorum, the Champion of Champions. He was tall, he was rangy, and even from a distance, and even with a pint of coffee tequila swirling in his guts, you could tell this was a guy who could run.

So as Cary tore down that majestic green sward in the Queen's private grounds, there were a lot of thoughts going through his head – but chiefly he was just thinking, 'Shit!' Not that he much liked Eton, and not that he much disliked it either, but this year, he'd actually rather been looking forward to being back at school. His bedroom at The Timbralls had stupendous views out over the playing fields where, or so they say, the Battle of Waterloo was won, but more fascinating by far was that his room had once belonged to Ian Fleming. To think of it – James Bond had been born in Cary's room, possibly in that exact same bed.

But the chief reason Cary had been looking forward to getting back to Eton was the sheer blessed relief of being able to get away from his rather pushy parents, who expected so very much from their boy; not just A-grade exams, but an Oxbridge degree followed by a highly lucrative career. Despite Cary being on a full bursary, Anthony and Penny had had to scrimp and save over the last few years to send their boy to Eton. It didn't help that Cary was their only child, and that it was he alone who carried all the weight of their own crushed dreams.

Other thoughts joined the expletive as Cary continued running with effortless ease. How on earth had he let Bruno talk him into coming to Windsor – to see the Queen? Expelled on the very first day of term! At very best, he'd be demoted from Pop, not to mention rustication – temporarily being sent back home – where Anthony and Penny would turn into twin dentist drills, grinding into his head from dawn till dusk.

Cary looked back, wondered if he could dummy the men who were trotting down towards him. He was definitely good enough. He'd have had a chance, but even if he succeeded, they'd probably just call for back-up.

Into the thicket of trees it was, with Bruno not far behind him. Bruno busied himself trying to hide in some bramble bushes, diving to the ground and crawling inside.

Cary ran till he had to stop. He had come up against a high flinty wall; if he'd had his pole, he could have vaulted it, but then if his aunt had had wheels, she might have been a tea-trolley. Filled with this heady mix of terror and adrenalin, Cary did the only thing left to him. He climbed a chestnut tree. The trunk itself was too thick for a handhold, so instead he snatched at one of the lower branches, swinging himself up before clambering to the main trunk.

Cary idly watched as one of the security men seized Bruno by the foot and bodily hauled him out of the bramble bush. Bruno was frisked and cuffed.

Two of the security guards were now at the foot of the chestnut. They watched their quarry disappear into the foliage. But though these security men could run, and shoot, and though they excelled at unarmed combat, climbing was not their strong suit. They could have attempted the same route as Cary, but it looked risky, even dangerous, and besides, they were not being spurred on by visions of Anthony and Penny nipping at their heels.

So instead, they resorted to that age-old tactic that has been used by hunters since the dawn of time.

'Come down!' called one. 'We'll be a lot easier on you.'

The second security man tried another tack. 'Give up! You could kill yourself.'

But just because the outlook was bleak, it was not in Cary's nature to give up. As the security guards settled in for a long wait, Cary continued to climb the chestnut tree.

CHAPTER 3

While all this stramash is going on at Windsor Castle, we turn to one of the more modern Eton houses, Farrer, where Lily, our 16-year-old new girl, is facing several dilemmas, of which the chiefest is this: how to politely yet firmly tell a one-time swain that she is no longer even remotely interested.

Lily was utterly diligent at her schoolwork, did exactly what she was told to do, but what dreams she had, and when she unfurled her tight ponytail, you caught a glimpse of the raw, energised woman that lurked beneath. Her father – formally known by his initials MTC, informally known as Arctic, because he was indeed a freezing Empty Sea – was the housemaster at Farrer, and had pulled Lily out of her state school so she could spend two years studying for her A-levels at Eton. Why did he do that? Because he had always dreamed of sending his son to Eton – and when Arctic didn't father his longed-for son, and when his wife Tor gave birth to a not-quite-so-longed-for daughter, Arctic immediately resolved to send her to Eton regardless.

Lily didn't have much say in the matter, nor was even allowed a farewell party with her friends. She sucked it up, just as she always did with the tempestuous Arctic. She had said farewell to her old friends, and now, ever optimistic, she was looking forward to making some new ones.

But there was a problem, quite a large problem, and anyone but the blinkered Arctic and his wife Tor would have seen it a mile off. The problem was this: Eton had around 1,300 pupils and Lily was the only girl in the entire school. Already on the first day of school, as she'd walked with her new leather briefcase from one div to the next, she had been spotted and commented upon and, by lunchtime, the electric news was all but being shouted from the rooftops: Lock up your sons – there's a girl in town!

Some girls would have revelled in the attention, but studious Lily did not enjoy being a head-turner, for that was what she had literally become.

The College itself has no walls or boundaries. Its classrooms and its 25 houses are dotted all over the town, and what an upmarket little town it is, with even its own branch of Coutts, the Queen's bank.

On her first day, Lily was doing a lot of walking – all of her divs seemed to be at least half a mile apart! And wherever she walked in Eton, boys gawked, boys stared, and boys turned their heads as they wistfully dreamed.

She tried to ignore all the attention when she sat in the College Chapel for the first time that morning, but it wasn't easy. Every single time she looked up from her hymn book and tried to take a surreptitious glance at her new schoolmates, she could sense a score of eyes watching her. She touched her hair – the boys stared. She scratched her nose – the boys whispered. She was blushing even as she strolled out of the Chapel at the end of the service and, aware she was being watched by this beast with a thousand eyes, she suddenly lost the ability to walk, somehow clipping her toe on the back of her heel, and it was the choirmaster himself who lunged to catch her. She couldn't recall much of what happened, save for the sound – a wave of noise, a collective gasp, just as you hear at the circus when a tightrope walker slips but manages to right herself.

Lunch was in the Farrer dining room with all 50 boys from the house. Farrer was one of the newest Eton houses, brick-built and a full 500 years younger than the original College. The dining room was handsome, lofty, with a broad window looking out onto tarmac, though it had a tinge of gloom, perhaps due to the chilling effect Arctic had on his boys.

There were three long tables; Arctic at the head of the middle one, his wife Tor with the junior boys, and heading the third table was the Dame, Miranda, who mothered the boys when they needed mothering.

Lily sat on Miranda's table amongst the ten 16-year-olds who had also just started studying for their A-levels. The boys were much, much chattier than they'd normally have been during a school lunch, but then they were all doing their best to entertain – for Lily was not only very pretty, she was also sharp, and she laughed at their jokes. And all those 16-year-olds were dreaming the same absurd dream, that one day, if they played their cards right, they might become the most envied boy in the whole of Eton, by notching up a genuine girlfriend, with kisses and hand-holding, not to mention that completely absurd fantasy of night-time corridor creeping to sneak into Farrer's ice-cold private quarters and into the bed of Arctic's teenage daughter.

These, then, were the dreams of the 16-year-olds in Farrer, but there was one 17-year-old boy in the house who had high hopes of turning this dream into a reality. His name was Maxwell, a brawny rower, and unlike any other boy at Eton, he had actually kissed Lily.

They'd met two months before at a summer party in London. Maxwell had, of course, known precisely who Lily was and had known also that she'd be joining him at Eton the next term. But the cunning reptile feigned complete ignorance, so that after they'd been introduced, and after Lily had told him of her plans, he could express disbelief followed by delighted surprise.

'Arctic's your dad!' he'd said. 'We'll be schoolmates!'

Lily, being a little tiddly as well as naturally thinking the best of everyone, was thrilled to have made such a powerful ally. Maxwell was the captain of sport at Farrer and rowed for the school, and though he didn't seem overly cerebral, he had high hopes of rowing for Cambridge.

A makeshift disco had been set up in the dining room. Maxwell had already plied her with three glasses of Pimm's and had asked her to dance. Almost before she knew it, they were slow-dancing, Maxwell's arms around her waist, and this bit she really didn't remember at all, but how it sort of happened was that Maxwell kissed her neck, kissed her cheek, she turned her lips and, the next moment, they were kissing.

Though it was not a very nice kiss. Lily had kissed a few boys before, and those kisses had tended to start more delicately, pecking and titillating rather than lustful tongue lashings, but Maxwell was living up to his rowing motto – 'Let's take it to the Max!' – by pretty much sticking his tongue straight into her mouth. Revolted, Lily had recoiled. Besides, if she was going to be doing any kissing, she'd prefer a little privacy, as opposed to snogging on the dance floor in front of 20 other teenagers.

They left the dance floor, Maxwell gave her his coat, and they walked outside to the candlelit greenhouse. Maxwell apologised profusely, claimed that he'd never had much practice. Lily forgave him, like the lovely girl she was, more kissing ensued, though this she really couldn't remember much about, but what she certainly could remember was Maxwell fumbling at her bra-strap and pawing at her thigh.

'Thank you for a lovely evening.' She got up and did the smartest thing she'd done all day, which was to leave. 'I look forward to seeing you at the beginning of next term.'

'You mean half?' said Maxwell, tilting back on his chair against the side of the greenhouse, lazy smile on his face.

'Are we in Eton?'

'I look forward to giving you your colours test.'

'I think I'll skip it,' she said, and with a little wave, and with a great feeling of relief, she departed. Now, it was difficult to say why Lily left so abruptly, but it was probably just female intuition. She may not have been able to put her finger on why, but she already had a sense that Maxwell was bad news.

That, then, was two months earlier, and now at the Farrer lunch on the first day of term, Lily had seen Maxwell again. He was much bigger than she remembered, looked like he'd been bulking up at the gym. He was on the top table, sitting one down from her father. He kept trying to catch her eye. Without success.

At the end of lunch, Lily's father stood up and the boys followed his lead. Arctic said a brief grace, 'Benedictus benedicat,' and then marched out of the room, followed by his wife. Lily didn't really know what to do next, so she just stayed in her place. The boys flooded out and she eventually followed her parents through to their private quarters.

'Well, that went well,' said Arctic, carefully hanging up his gown. 'How were the F-tits, darling?'

'A little shy. They'll come on.'

'Good, good,' he said, not listening to a word of what his wife was saying. He stalked off to his office to attend to the queue of boys who would be waiting to see him.

Lily thought it a little odd that he hadn't even looked at her, let alone talked to her, but perhaps that was the way of things, now he'd become her official house tutor. Couldn't have any favouritism at Farrer, least of all for your own daughter.

She went upstairs to her room and it was a room that most definitely did not belong to some flibbertigibbet teenager. No pop star posters, no speakers, no makeup to speak of, and certainly no mess; just four framed prints, Picassos and a Mondrian, a lot of books, and a generous window with views out over the Farrer garden. Her desk was immaculate, as was her 3/4-size bed with crisp white duvet, a much-loved lamb, Lamby, and a grizzled monkey, Babs, who were tucked in the bed with their heads on the pillow. She gently moved Lamby and Babs to the side, threw herself onto the bed, exhaled loudly, stared at the ceiling, and, not to put too fine a point on it, wondered what the hell she had gotten herself into. Leave her old school and her old friends for this? To be surrounded by over a thousand boys and not a single girl in sight; no girlfriends to confide in, no girlfriends to laugh with at this river of witless boys in black, and not only stuck with these boys but stuck with them for a two-year stretch, with not a single day off for good behaviour. Though perhaps, thinking of it, you might get quite a long time off for **bad** behaviour! What a thought!

She picked up a well-thumbed novel. If there was one single thing she'd learned from her mother, it was that a book is solace for any kind of heartache. She'd picked the book from her mum's bookshelf. It was Jilly Cooper's Riders, probably not a book on any of the Eton reading lists, but a cracker for all that.

Lily had never ridden a horse, but within just a few pages, she was ensnared in Jilly's web and all her saucy stories of girls and riding and rutting in Rutshire.

There was a knock on the door, and a moment later, Arctic came into the room; it might have been more courteous to have given her a few seconds.

He stood in the doorway, slightly ill at ease. He was a tall man, a one-time rower who now coached the house team. He was a Geography teacher and, once upon a time, used to pride himself on knowing not only the capitals of every sovereign state in the world, but also their currencies.

'Ah, Lily,' he said. 'Almost forgot you're one of my pupils now. How is it, being the new girl?'

Where on earth to begin?

'It's been lovely, thank you, Daddy.' She drew her knees up under her blue pleated skirt.

'Good, good.'

Arctic wandered into the room, took a look out of the window to admire his garden, would have liked to make some small talk, but couldn't think of anything to say. It suddenly struck Lily that her father was a dead ringer for Desperate Dan, the cartoon cowboy from the Dandy. He had a shovel jaw which, even at three in the afternoon, bristled with steely black stubble. She smirked at the thought. She'd never be able to see her father in the same way again.

'Seen anything of the young Prince?'

'I saw him posing for the photographers.'

'He'll be on the front page of every paper in Britain tomorrow.'

'Poor boy.'

'True – but it'll be the last story The Press can write about him for the next five years, thank God!' Arctic saw the book by her side. 'What's that you're reading?'

Lily flashed him the cover. 'Just something I picked up from Mummy's shelves.'

'Jilly Cooper!' he said. 'You're at Eton now, my girl, and you are really going to have to start raising your game.'

'Yes, Daddy.'

'Here at Eton, we have the finest library of any school on earth,' he squawked. 'It has thousands, tens of thousands of books! We have more first editions than most schools have books – we have the Gutenberg Bible! And yet you choose to read Jilly Cooper's Riders!'

'I thought it looked quite fun,' she said, before adding with a touch of asperity, 'Certainly, Mummy's read it enough.'

'Your mother is not studying at Eton for her A-levels, and nor did your mother get into Cambridge University.'

Had Lily possessed a slightly more tart tongue, she could have made a number of ripostes – not least that her mother, Tor, had had no interest whatsoever in going to Cambridge University because she had instead earned a place at Britain's premier art school, Central St Martin's.

She let it ride. 'You're right, Daddy.'

Unaware of the wind he was sowing, and the whirlwind that soon enough he would be reaping, Arctic began to thaw. 'That's my Lily.'

Lily put the book down, vowing to herself that she'd not only finish it by the end of the week, but that, by the end of the month, she'd have read every single one of Jilly's Rutshire Chronicles.

'I think I'll just pop out,' she said.

'Off anywhere?'

'I'm going to Windsor, to see if I can help out at The Project.'

'It all counts for your Duke of Edinburgh.'

He stepped aside and, as Lily walked out, she wondered if it was just hers, or whether all fathers turned into quite such uptight sticklers. Probably not, she decided – though becoming an Eton housemaster hadn't helped.

Outside Farrer House, there was one last piece of unpleasantness to be dealt with. Maxwell had been watching out for her, and the moment Lily left the house, he tore down the stairs and trotted after her. He'd spent some time on his outfit, and had eventually plumped for his rowing gear, tight shorts and tight singlet, the better to show off his formidable physique. He ran past her, glanced, glanced again, and then turned and stopped.

'Well, hello, stranger,' he said, arm stretching towards her, as if to give her an 'old friends' hug.

'Oh – hello,' she said.

He touched her on the shoulder, moved in to kiss her on the cheek. Lily recoiled.

'I'd rather not,' she said.

'Has your father read you the Riot Act?' he asked. 'There is to be no touching of Eton schoolboys, and in particular, there is to be no cheek-pecking with old friends?'

'Old friends?' Lily said. 'I don't know if I'd call you that.'

'Well, let's just call it friends.' He was now standing arms akimbo, but he was standing way too close to Lily; he didn't know the first thing about personal space.

Lily steeled herself. She'd run over this conversation only about a dozen times in the last week, and now it was upon her. But even though she knew the words she had to say, now that this gargantuan boy was standing in front of her, it wasn't so easy to spit them out.

'We had a kiss two months ago, Maxwell,' she said. 'But I'm here now to make the most of Eton and to get my A-levels. And if we do eventually become friends, then great. But on the first day of term – half, then – and when there are eyes everywhere, I'm certainly not going to be hugging a guy I once met at a party.'

'Of course,' said Maxwell, dreams momentarily crushed. No matter – he'd just have to be in it for the long haul. 'I'm sorry I've been so pushy, but, you know, I just really, really like you. You're so refreshing, I've never met a girl like you before, and one day I hope you'll see that there's a little more to me than a rough kisser.'

Lily was so nearly shot of him, but now, because she was kind, and also because she still hadn't even begun to plumb his hideous depths, she let Maxwell off the hook.

'Yeah, your kissing technique could do with a little improvement,' she said.

Maxwell realised that, for the moment, this was as good as it was going to get. 'I'm a fast learner!' he said, jogging off to the boat house.

'We'll see about that.' Not a come-on; but then not a put-down either. Maxwell's dreams flickered back to life.

In one respect, Lily had been spot-on the money. Eton was awash with spies, and a 15-year-old Farrer boy, Freddie, or Fredster as he liked to call himself, had not only seen Maxwell with Lily but had managed to earwig a little of the conversation. He may not have got the whole of it, but he certainly got the gist – Lily had got it on with Maxwell at a party. And now it seemed that the lumbering lout had been turned over. Couldn't have happened to a nicer chap.

Lily walked down the Eton High Street, over Windsor Bridge, and on towards her only safe haven, The Project – entirely unaware that news of the Maxwell Canoodle was spreading far and wide, and that by bed-time that evening, even her parents would have played their part in this monstrous game of Chinese Whispers.

CHAPTER 4

Lily's woes were but a gnat bite compared to those of Cary, still stuck up a chestnut tree in the Queen's private grounds at Windsor and still facing the swift demise of his stellar career at Eton. But even as he sat in a crook of the chestnut, and even as the branches creaked and the wind sighed through the leaves, he couldn't help but laugh to himself. Booted out of Eton on the same day Prince William arrived there! It'd be mortifying – but, in time, hilarious.

The security guards were still mumbling into their radios at the bottom of the tree, and still occasionally yelling at him to give himself up. He wondered if he should do just that. He wondered what he'd do if they sent somebody up after him. Probably just keep on climbing up the tree until he was clutching at twigs and his head had poked out of the canopy. But he did have the ken to realise that, if they did chase him up the tree, and he fell off the top and ended up in hospital or perhaps even the morgue, it might just be a little uncomfortable for them. Heavy-Handed Palace Guards Chase Eton Scholar To His Death! In which case… they'd probably just sit tight at the bottom of the tree and continue to squawk into their radios.

At least he didn't have to worry about Bruno and Viktor. They might have been caught, but they'd never squeal, he'd stake his life on it. In West Point in America, or so he'd heard, they had a ludicrous Honor Code, where cadets were obliged to turn into whistle-blowers. But the Brits, so much more civilised, had an unspoken Code of Honour – you never grassed anyone up.

So, for a little while, Cary allowed himself to nestle against the thick tree trunk and admire the gorgeous views of the river and Eton beyond. As he squinted down, he could just make out a boy sculling on the Thames, and that amused him too – Cary had a ripe sense of humour; it was probably the braying Maxwell meathead.

Rather more pressingly... How to get out of this wretched chestnut tree? Preferably without being caught. He closed his eyes, breathed in deeply, and, imagining himself in his bedroom in The Timbralls, and infusing himself with the spirit of Ian Fleming, he asked himself one simple question: What would James Bond do?

He thought it was the wind, but when he listened more closely, he realised that Fleming was whispering to him. 'Listen to me, boy.' It was a patrician voice, gravelly from all the thousands of cigarettes, but merry with it, as if the old sod was delighted to find Cary in such a fix. 'I don't know yet what James Bond would do – but I'll tell you one thing Bond would never do. He'd never give himself up! Bond surrender? Impossible!'

Cary heard the click of a cigarette lighter and a long rasping inhale.

'You're never going to get out of this tree unless you're closer to the ground. Maybe wait till dark, climb out on one of the branches, make a run for it.'

'Good thinking,' said Cary. 'Thanks.'

'You're welcome. You could beat those stiffs any day of the week.'

Cary sinuously started to climb down. Through the tangle of leaves, he could just make out the shaven head of one of the security men. He caught a whiff of Fleming's cigarette smoke and he liked it.

Cary tried to be analytical about the problem. If James Bond had been stuck up this tree, then there'd absolutely have to be a way down, because Fleming would never leave his hero stuck like this. Bond might get stuck up a tree, but he'd never stay stuck.

So since there had to be a way down, and since he didn't have the time to wait till dusk, Cary started to explore the only other available option: the wall.

'Good lad,' came a gravelly whisper.

Maybe… maybe he could walk out on that overhanging branch, keep his balance by holding onto the one above. Then let go, two smart steps, leap into the abyss like it was nothing more than the long-jump pit, land on the wall and scrabble down the other side. With one bound, Bond would be free!

'It's only a ten-metre drop.'

Cary dithered. Even ten metres seemed quite a long way.

'Come on, Cary – man or mouse?' He noticed Fleming's high amusement.

He edged out onto the branch, hands high as he held onto the branch above him. A twig snapped. He didn't need to look down. The security men had already spotted him.

'He's on the move.'

Teetering to the edge of the branch, both hands clutching onto twigs and leaves. The lower branch has dwindled to nothing, barely the width of Cary's wrist. He isn't even sure if this tiny launch-pad will take his weight.

Breathe in, breathe out.

'Be Bond, boy!'

Let go of the cluster of leaves, the lower branch juddering, the first step is solid, but with the second step, he all but misses the branch, nothing for it now but to make a sort of hop with his trailing foot, gets a slight bounce, gives him a feather of air, but now that he's free of the tree, he sees that the wall is a lot further away than he thought – and a lot lower.

He's going to miss the top completely, just crash into the wall and then tumble to the bottom, a bag of shattered bones. In thrilled desperation, he stretches out his long sinewy body, arcing from toes to fingertips, and by some astounding miracle, his left hand hits the top of the wall. Not solid, but it's enough, and Cary knows what's coming next: he's going to face-plant the wall at about 20mph. He turns to the side so it's only ribs and legs that are slamming into the flints. He all but loses his grip, but with a squeal, lunges up with his other hand, good contact. Feet pedalling, hands scrabbling, he hauls himself astride the top of the wall.

But not nearly out of trouble. The drop down to the street on the other side is colossal, a leg-breaker.

'Come on, lad, final hurdle.'

The top of the wall is only about a foot wide, but Cary takes it at a trot. Down below, he can see the security men following him in the Castle grounds. They haven't thought to send anyone outside to wait for him. But from the barks on the radio, that error is about to be rectified.

He's aiming for a rooftop about 200 yards off, and from there... well, something will turn up. A scramble over the rooftops, scuttle down a drainpipe. Anything has to be better than being stuck up the chestnut. But from far off, way down the street, he can just make out another guy in a suit sprinting towards him.

He hadn't wanted to do this. But then there wasn't really anything else he could do.

He didn't even pause, just continued to run along the top of the wall and then launched himself headlong into the abyss, just like those textbook tackles that he'd been forced to practise on the rugby field, before he'd – thankfully! – given the game up. Sweet, solid contact. He plucked at one of the arms of the Victorian lamp-post, swung forward, swung back, and in a moment, he was down that lamp-post quick as a fireman's pole.

Fleming laughed. 'Always knew you could do it.'

Finally, a proper pavement beneath his feet, roads to run down, alleyways to hide in, and the nearest security guard at least 50 yards away. And maybe these guys thought they'd be able to chase him down, but whoever they might have chased before, they'd never chased a runner.

He was much too canny to go on the direct route back to Eton over Windsor Bridge, but instead looped down through the woods at Frogmore, before crossing the Thames at Datchet, and then he was on the home stretch, and though he felt absolutely euphoric, he was also worried about Bruno and Viktor, and the exact sort of punishment that would be coming their way.

But though he'd just pulled off the escape of his life, and though he'd just been introduced to Ian Fleming, there was one other thing to mull over. It was as he'd been running through downtown Windsor. He'd been coming up to what was probably his favourite place on earth, had even waved at a couple of the old-timers, Renton and Fergie, who'd been nursing mugs of tea on the pavement bench. He knew them both, had known them for over two years, ever since he'd ducked out of the Eton Rifles after one week to have a try-out with the school's Community Services. Had tried it. And had absolutely loved it.

'In a hurry?' called Renton.

'I am!' he yelled over his shoulder.

'Well come and see us tomorrow!'

'I've got a lot to tell you!'

But it wasn't the old boys who had caught his eye. Sitting next to them on the bench, and sipping her own mug of builder's tea, was the most remarkably pretty girl Cary had ever seen. He'd only caught a glimpse of her long, bare legs, a blue pleated skirt, hair that had been turned by the sun into a burnished halo, and then to cap it all, an intoxicating smile. And because he was obviously a friend of her friends, she'd given him a little wave. But who was she – and what was she doing with those lovable down-and-outs at The Project?

CHAPTER 5

It is night-time after Prince William's first full day at Eton and, as the young Prince says goodnight to his bodyguards and to his new friends, and as Cary winces as he rubs lotion on his bruised ribs and bruised thigh, and as Bruno and Viktor are having a tense time of things as they await the next day's interview with the Headman, we find Lily alone in her bedroom.

She'd joined the boys for a light supper, and then for prayers, but after that, and while the rest of the Etonians could lark as they pleased, she was all alone in Farrer's private quarters. Her father was doing the rounds of the house, popping into the boys' rooms, seeing that they were all settled in, and her mother had probably gone off to play bridge, and all that Lily could see stretching before her was a lot of lonely nights with just homework and reading, and more homework, and not a single friend to talk to. This, mark you, was the middle of the 1990s, the very last days of this Stone Age world, with payphones and pen and ink letters hanging on by their very fingertips as they were gradually replaced by mobile phones and that geeky gadget called the internet.

Lily certainly does not have a mobile phone, and nor do any of her old friends, so though she would love to talk about the day's just extraordinary goings-on – the only girl in the Chapel, in the house, in the entire school! – there is no-one to talk to. Instead, she makes do with her diary, just a black hardback A4 notebook she bought from Alden and Blackwell.

She has kept a diary for two or three years, and she instinctively cherry-picks – but how ever to pick from this huge basket of Eton cherries, when every single thing that happens to her is just extraordinary! There are only a handful of girls in **history** who could have experienced anything like it.

So down it all goes, everything right from the heart, since if it's not from the heart, it's not worth a damn. And as she looks back on that day of days, she lingers on one brief moment. She helped out at The Project, did some cleaning and some ironing, and stopped off for a break with Renton and Fergie. The irony of it rather tickled over. She's only been working at The Project for two months, since the start of the summer holidays, and now almost all of her friends are vagrants and winos. How happy that would make her father.

She'd been sitting on the bench outside the front door, basking in the sun with Fergie and Renton. Renton, an old Scottish banker, done for fraud and fallen on hard times, was the first to spot him. A young man was running down the street towards them. Not just jogging down the street, but really running – running like he was catching a train. Or perhaps… insane thought!... like he was being chased.

'That looks like young Cary!' cackled Renton, wiping the spittle off his bristles.

'It is young Cary!' said Fergie, a one-time hack who'd given it all up to become a novelist, writing loads and loads of unreadable door-stoppers until the misery of his unending failure had finally driven him to drink.

Lily couldn't quite remember what Renton had said – something jokey, something about asking him if he was in a hurry.

And the guy, young Cary, had just yelled that he really was in a hurry, and had carried on tearing down the street, but as he'd run past The Project, they'd locked eyes, and she didn't know why, couldn't even put her finger on the fact that there was a 'why', but in that single heartbeat, she sensed the distinctive snap of a spark.

'He was going like the clappers!' crowed Renton.

'So who's Cary?' said Lily.

'Cary? He's a lovely lad, the very best,' said Fergie. 'Come to think of it, you might like him. Pop in tomorrow and you'll see—'

Renton trailed off. Two men in black suits were running towards them, one yammering into a radio. The pair, beet-red, flecked with sweat, ran past, easing up as they reached the junction. They looked left, looked right, stopped.

'Do you think they were after young Cary?' Lily said.

'We didn't see a thing, Lily,' said Fergie. 'We never see anything at all in The Project. And if we should happen to hear anything in The Project, or sense anything in The Project, then we never talk about it.'

'I like that,' Lily said.

Lily paused her diary writing. Anything more to add? Could she be bothered to write about the lumpen Maxwell? Not really – so she'd kissed him and so what? She merely contented herself with writing, 'Alcohol + Boys = Trouble'. Maxwell wasn't worth another word.

A knock at the door, and her father came in – unusually, he was wearing his full Eton regalia: gown, grey suit, starched stick-ups and a white bow tie. Did her father consider such stiff dress regulations a perk of the job?

'Hello, Daddy.' She closed her diary and put it into her desk drawer; later on, she'd tuck it into its floorboard hideaway.

Arctic coughed, couldn't look her in the eye. 'Er, Lily, I wondered if you could come to my study.'

'Why?'

'I'd rather hoped that we wouldn't be having this conversation at all, let alone on your very first day here.' He was shifting from side to side, itchy feet. 'I'm your father and I am also now your house tutor, and that means that regrettably, I am going to be the first port of call when it comes to matters of school discipline.'

She laughed. She! Far and away the most diligent girl at

her previous school, she had never even received so much as a detention – and now she was about to be disciplined!

'What am I supposed to have done?'

'I would prefer it if we went to my study.'

'It can't be that bad, Daddy! I haven't done anything today apart from go to chapel and lunch and three lessons!'

'Divs, you mean.'

'Divs, then.'

He held the door open. Lily got up and led the way down to Arctic's study, with its dented globe, its OCD desk, not a pen out of place, not a pencil left unsharpened, and, hanging in state above the mantelpiece, a pair of dusty oars from Arctic's two Boat Races. The room was, as always, freezing. Arctic never put the radiators on, believing that his icy office was not just good for the circulation but good for the soul.

'Take a seat.'

Lily perched on the edge of the brown leather sofa. She never liked actually sitting on it – the sofa was tautly overstuffed, the leather cold and brittle and about as comfortable as a bag of bones.

'It has, ahh…' He tugged at his tight collar. 'It has come to my attention that you have, ahhh, formed a relationship with a boy at this school, and that, further to that, you have been… copulating with him.'

'What??'

'You heard me.'

'And who is this boy with whom I've been… copulating?'

'I understand it is a boy in my own house – Maxwell.'

'Maxwell?' She laughed. 'What a complete load of rubbish!'

'You deny it?'

'I absolutely deny it. I met him at a party a couple of months ago, and I spoke to him for a minute in the street this afternoon, but you'll be pleased to hear that I'm still very much a virgin.'

'Ahh.' Arctic was perplexed. 'But you didn't just meet him at a party, did you?'

'I kissed him, if that's what you mean.'

Arctic found it easier to pace the room rather than sit at his desk.

'Lily, dear Lily, you must understand surely that you're in a unique position at this school – you're the only girl here —'

'I had observed.'

'And that it is not seemly for you to be conducting a relationship with another pupil at the school – let alone a boy in this house.'

'I'm not in a relationship with anyone!'

Her father stood in front of the fireplace, which never had a fire, and which was instead filled with a large pot of dusty dried flowers, withered husks of the blooms they'd once been. He stared at his oars, etched with the names of his rowing-mates; stout fellows, every one of them. How much simpler life had been then. You trained, you rowed, you ate like a horse and drank a gallon of beer a day – and the next day, you did it all over again. Not – necessarily – that he'd have preferred to have had a son. But life might have been easier, simpler, if Lily had been a boy; Arctic certainly wouldn't be facing problems like this!

'I understand the attraction, Lily, really I do. He's a rower—'

'Rest assured, Daddy, there is no relationship with Maxwell, and nor will there ever be.'

'Methinks she doth protest too much—'

'It happens to be true!'

He turned, looked at her for the first time. 'Can we just say then that things will be a lot easier for you if, for the duration of your stay at Eton, boys are off limits?'

Now she was riled. 'All boys – or just Etonians?'

'Why are you making this so hard for me – so hard for yourself? You must see that it's an immense privilege for you to be at Eton. But with that privilege comes—'

'Responsibilities. Yes, I know.'

'All I want is the best for you.'

'I'm sorry that you think so little of me. Copulating? With Maxwell? Yuck! Where did you hear this foul rumour?'

'It is the talk of the school.'

'Oh my God!'

'I was quite as shocked as you are.'

Lily got up from her perch. 'I'm going to bed.' She left the room without giving her father his customary night-time kiss on the cheek.

Thoughts spiralling, Lily trudged up the stairs, where there was a homely presence waiting for her on the landing. Miranda, the Dame, stood by the door to her apartment. She was in slippers and night-gown and with an old rug round her shoulders. Her hair may have been grey, but she had the skin of a much younger woman, and she had had so many laughs in her life that her mouth now automatically crinkled upwards.

'Come and have a cup of tea, dear.' She put a consoling arm around Lily's shoulders.

Miranda kept her sitting room as snug as a hot-house, curtains drawn and gas fire blazing. Radio 2 chirped in the background. Lily settled into a sagging, much-loved armchair, while Miranda made the tea.

'I've got something stronger, if you want it,' she said. 'Tot of Navy rum? Might cheer you up.'

'Tea would be lovely.'

It dawned on Lily that, in the past five years, since Arctic had taken over Farrer House, Miranda had become more of a mother to her than her own mum, Tor. She certainly knew this room, with its souvenirs from all over the world, better than she knew her own mother's office.

'Where's the new addition from?' She pointed to a picture of a flower, far more exotic than anything she'd ever seen in real life, brilliant orange dotted with vivid blues and reds.

'That – some Batik art from Bali, in Indonesia. Picked it up a month ago. While you were having your annual pilgrimage to the Peak District.'

'It would be quite nice to go somewhere different.'

'I think one walking holiday in the Peaks would be quite enough for me – besides, going to the same place every year means you can't go anywhere new. And that, horrors, means that the number of countries you've visited will never be more than your age.'

'Should it be?' Lily accepted her cup of tea.

'Undoubtedly! You're 16, so you should have been to at least 20 countries by now!'

Lily quickly totted up. 'I've been to five – and that's if you include the Channel Islands. How many have you been to?'

'I'll be able to live to 154 and I'll still be ahead of the game!' Miranda poured a slug of rum into her tea. 'One of the perks of being a Dame, dear, is that I get a lot of holiday. And one of the joys of being a spinster is that I can do as I please!'

'I might just get a job as a Dame!'

Miranda chuckled. 'Not you, Lily – you are destined for something much bigger than just being an Eton Dame.'

'Just? It sounds wonderful!'

'I don't know about that.' Miranda leaned forward to massage her calf, looked up, smiled at Lily. 'But I do know you're going to do something that's absolutely extraordinary.'

'I'm glad you're so optimistic. From where I am now, it seems like I'm on a five-year treadmill. A-levels, a degree. And then… who knows what the next grindstone will be?' Lily stared into the gas fire and pondered that question we all ask, and to which we all dread the answer – how will it all turn out?

'I heard that idiotic story of you and Maxwell. I told your father it was completely impossible, but he'd have none of it, said he had to have it out with you. I daresay he means for the best, but like all these Eton housemasters, he's never learned the correct route across a square.'

'I didn't know there was an incorrect route.'

'The correct route across a square, dearest Lily, is by three sides. But housemasters always prefer to take the most direct route across a square, which I suppose has the advantage of being efficient, but it lacks finesse. It has no subtlety. And as far as I can see, in most dealings with Etonians, not to mention Etoniennes, the correct route across a square is not just by three sides but should, in fact, be by five or even seven sides. He's got to be canny.'

'I'm not sure Daddy does canny.'

'Anyway, dear – in my official capacity, I am the Dame of this house. But don't forget that for you, at least, I am a lot, lot more.'

'You are?'

'I've got your back.' Miranda was about to top up her cup with tea but thought better of it and instead poured more rum.

'Thank you.'

'You'll be giving your father conniptions, I'm sure of it.'

CHAPTER 6

In the mornings, Cary undertakes a strange ritual that no other Etonian has ever done before. Rain or shine, and while all the house is fast asleep, Cary gets up at 4am, slips on his running gear and clears his head with a six-mile run. For the past four years now, Cary's housemaster, a bachelor called Ormerod, cheery and avuncular, has gently encouraged this boy's mild eccentricities.

It started on Cary's very first day at school, when Cary said he liked early morning runs. On Cary's second day at Eton, the 13-year-old announced that he was no team player, that he did not enjoy ball sports, and that he'd much rather be turning himself into an athlete. And then on his third day at Eton, the 13-year-old Cary made his boldest move yet – he told Mr Ormerod that, if at all possible, he'd like to help out in the house kitchen.

Mr Ormerod had never come across such a strange request before, but if the boy wanted to help out in the kitchens, then why not let him – just so long as the cook, Mrs Parker, was happy with the arrangement. And as it turned out, the fearsome Mrs Parker and her slightly less terrifying sous-chef, Mrs Webber, as well as the two giggling maids, Minty and Jazz, were just thrilled to buttons to have this particular Etonian in their kitchen. Within weeks, days even, the atmosphere in the kitchen had been transformed from a gruelling workhouse into a jolly house party, such that, one morning at 6am, as a 14-year-old Cary prepared the porridge, and as Mrs Parker and Mrs Webber sat at the table drinking coffee, Mr Ormerod heard one of the most extraordinary sounds he had ever experienced: the sound of Mrs Parker and Mrs Webber both absolutely guffawing with laughter. Not that Mrs Parker didn't still occasionally express her extreme ire, but when Cary was in her kitchen, all was as tranquil as a tropical beach in an azure sea.

And what delighted these two cooks most about Cary was that he had an insatiable hunger to learn new techniques, new recipes. Within two years, he was as brilliant with a knife as with a saucepan. Just give him the ingredients and he could rustle up anything you wanted; and he was fun, interesting and knowledgeable – and frankly, quite a hard act to top, such that, when Minty and Jazz compared their own boyfriends to the young lad who worked in the kitchens, their boyfriends always ended up falling short. (They were not Cary fans, obviously, and after a few weeks of raving about the new kitchen wonderboy, Minty and Jazz soon learned it was wisest not to mention Cary to their menfolk.)

And now Cary is 17, and after four years in the Timbralls kitchens, he has become an excellent cook, and he is Mrs Parker's pride and joy.

This morning, he's already been for a six-mile run along the river, and it's felt like he is the only man alive. He stops by a white rose growing wild on the riverbank, and buries his nose into the bush, inhaling the sweet scent. He's about to carry on running but snaps off three roses and carefully tucks them into his pocket.

He showers, shaves, and now, wearing just tracksuit bottoms and a T-shirt, he positively glows. It is 5.30am, and while the house yawns and rolls back over to sleep, Cary bounces into the kitchens.

'Mrs Parker, good morning, Mrs Webber, good morning!' he says, giving them each a rose and a kiss on the cheek. The third rose, which he'd planned to use for a buttonhole, he tucks behind his ear – and then promptly forgets about it. 'Let me get you both a coffee.'

It's difficult to tell exactly how old these ladies are. They could be in their sixties, but if you'd told Cary they were in their eighties, he'd have believed you. Mrs Parker is small and wiry, a pugnacious terrier, while Mrs Webber is a little taller and a little less lined; there is no need for her to bark, because Mrs Parker does more than enough barking for the pair of them.

In the years Before Cary, preparing breakfast was rather a stressful time of things for the two cooks – making the porridge, making the cauldron of tea, cooking the eggs, the bacon, the sausages. And now, as if some genial Rumpelstiltskin has come into their lives, they sit at the good solid table and read the papers while Cary tinkers around them. He first puts on his butcher's apron, then switches on the oven and Classic FM, rubs his hands and washes them and the Cary Show is about to begin. He knows exactly what he's got to do and when he's got to do it, pouring good Scottish oats and milk into the pot, with just a moment to pour the ladies their coffee, before he slams 50 sausages and 50 rashers into the oven and starts frying up the eggs.

'We're fairly going to miss you next year, you know, Cary,' Mrs Parker says.

'I'll come visit you,' he says. 'Check that standards aren't slipping.'

Mrs Parker sips, sighs. Soon enough, it will all be over, and the Cary years will seem like the most outrageous dream. 'I don't know what you do with the coffee, Cary, but it always seems better than the stuff I make at home.'

'A pleasure, Mrs Parker,' says Cary, before casting the most perfect fly. He's cast this fly many times over Mrs Parker, and she has never once failed to take the bait. 'I've always fancied a go with one of those Gaggias.'

'The best coffee I ever had was from a Gaggia. Double Espresso with a spoonful of brown sugar.' She sighs and stirs in more sugar. 'We were outside a little café in Florence.'

'The fact that you were on honeymoon had nothing to do

with it,' says Mrs Webber. 'You've spent more time talking about that holiday than you ever spent in Florence!'

'Wishty!' Mrs Parker laughs. She's been widowed now for 15 years, and though her honeymoon was a trailblazer, she probably prefers things as they are.

Mrs Webber leans forward to inspect her copy of *The Sun* more carefully. The whole of the front page is devoted to a picture of Prince William, but along with the story, there is a byline she recognises.

'Listen to this!' she announces. 'This front-page story was written by our Kim!'

'Your Kim?'

'His byline thing says he is — and I quote – *The Sun*'s Very Own Old Etonian Toff!'

Mrs Parker looks at the paper, laughs. 'Kim! So that's where he's turned up!'

'Did you know Kim?' Cary says.

'He was in this house about 12 or 13 years ago,' says Mrs Webber. 'He was another of Fleming's boys – just like you.'

'What's that?'

'Ian Fleming's boys are quite different from the others. They go their own way—'

'Scamps, all of them.'

'Yes, there was that talk of Kim and his piano teacher – she was a good six years older than him! It doesn't surprise me in the slightest that he's ended up at *The Sun*.'

'And you, Cary, are a Fleming boy through and through. Fleming didn't do any of the team stuff either. But you know what he did do?'

'I'm sure you're about to tell me.'

'He was a super athlete. Won the Victor Ludorum in 1925 – exactly 70 years ago. Won it again the next year. Sensing a connection now, are we, Cary?'

Cary chuckles to himself. 'Of course he was an athlete.'

Like all Etonians, Cary has his own room, and because he's in his last year, he has one of the best rooms in the house, on the third floor. On one side of The Timbralls, the rooms overlook New Schools Yard, which is not much more than an upmarket car park surrounded by Victorian schoolrooms. But on the other side, Cary's side, the rooms have the best views of any house in Eton, looking out onto the playing fields of Sixpenny and Mesopotamia, as well as the famous wall that is such an intrinsic part of that incomprehensible Eton tradition, The Wall Game.

You would not have guessed it from the way that Cary generally shambles round the school in his tracksuit or in his jeans, but he is one of Eton's prefects, or Poppers, and, unlike the rest of the Eton rabble, who have to content themselves with tailcoated monochrome, Cary's uniform is so swish that he could walk straight into a Society wedding: sponge-bag trousers with black and white houndstooth check, beautiful braid piping on his black tailcoat, white bow tie with starched wing collar, black socks, black Oxfords, and, luxury of luxuries, a waistcoat of his own choice (bottom button always left undone, bottom two buttons if you're feeling flash). Many Poppers plump for garish waistcoats in velvet or fur, sometimes with Union Jacks or Saltires, but because Cary hasn't a bean to his name, he's only got two waistcoats, one grey and stained, that his father used for weddings, and the other, slightly nicer, black with silver buttons, as worn by Eton's brighter boys, who get into Sixth Form Select; this waistcoat, with only the one ink stain, had been bequeathed to him by a leaver.

Cary doesn't have to look when he ties his bow tie, could tie it blindfold. He slips on his slightly nicer waistcoat, the one with the ink stain and the shiny buttons, and last of all comes the black tailcoat with the beautiful braid piping; though the tailcoat has a black button in the midriff, this is only ever for show. Cary mooches downstairs to the lobby. Some boys are ragging and a ball is hurled straight at his head. He catches the ball neatly with one hand, lobs it into the air, knees it, and then heads it into the dustbin.

The four boys gawk. 'Why aren't you on our football team, Cary?'

Cary laughs, doesn't miss a beat. 'Because then I'd have to play football.'

He is due in the College Chapel this morning, where he is supposed to police the juniors, but as far as he's concerned, the juniors could hold their own private rave and he couldn't care less. The Chapel is over 500 years old and is at the very core of the school – for it is in this Chapel that the boys must pray for the immortal soul of Eton's founder, Henry VI. The Chapel is not quite as big as Henry had hoped it would be – it was supposed to be nearly double the size and at least another 100 metres longer – but for all that, it is a fine-looking chapel, could put many Cathedrals to shame. The Chapel's twin, also built by Henry VI, is at King's College, Cambridge, which is bigger and almost identical in style, but for reasons which we will soon come to, is as a drab monk compared to a caparisoned archbishop.

Because Eton has always been prone to flooding from the Thames, the Chapel is on the first floor. Cary takes the 24 steps up to the ante-chapel at his usual three-at-a-time. The main entrance to the College Chapel is underneath the organ loft. To either side are line after line of oak pews, dark brown with age. The centre pews are reserved for the College choir, but the best seats in the house are at the back, running along the walls, not benches but individual seats, each with its own wooden wings that curve around your head. And it's from these seats that you have the very best vantage point of the vaulted ceiling; not that you can tell, but the ceiling is made of 1950s concrete, replacing the wooden fan vaulting that has been eaten out by deathwatch beetles.

As Cary walks in, Barty, the smallest boy in the school, holds out his fist. Cary gives him a wink and a gentle fist bump; it's nothing, but it's nice. As he walks to his seat, he is aware of a gradual stir, a whisper, and then the whispers turn into titters. He takes his seat and idly wonders why so many boys are smirking.

Cary sits back to enjoy the organ music, and muses on how politically incorrect it would be to say that the Nazis did Eton a huge favour in the Second World War – by dropping a bomb on the Upper School in 1940, which blew out almost all of the cheerless chapel windows. King's College, Cambridge, did not have the same luck – owing to a unique deal that Hitler struck with the British at the outset of World War II, whereby the Nazis agreed not to bomb either Oxford or Cambridge, in return for Britain not bombing two of Germany's oldest universities, Heidelberg and Göttingen. As a result, not a single Nazi bomb fell on either Oxford or Cambridge University, and so King's College Chapel, Cambridge, retains the dreary windows that were first installed there.

By contrast, Eton's bombed windows were replaced by the most magnificent modern stained glass, a Crucifixion above the altar by the pioneering Irish painter Evie Hone, and to the sides, four miracles and four parables by the great John Piper. These windows quite transform what would otherwise be a huge but rather mundane school chapel. It is no exaggeration to say that these nine windows are far and away the finest chapel windows of any school on earth. Because he's a cook, Cary's favourite window is, of course, the miracle of the feeding of the five thousand.

Cary's gaze wanders over the 15th-century wall paintings, very old, very worthy, once whitewashed away by the Puritans, now cleaned, but not so very interesting to look at. Amid the black wash of boys in front of him, Cary's eyes are drawn to a sharp splash of blue. It's a girl – the girl everyone's been talking about, the girl Viktor had been talking about. Lily. Cary looks at her more carefully. Could it be her?

And then she looks at him. And if ever there was a moment to change two people's lives, then this is it. These *coup de foudres* only happen once in a lifetime; but what is remarkable about this *coup de foudre* is that it hits both of them at the exact same moment, and he knows, and she knows, that they have both seen The One.

As for Lily, mildly minding her own business that morning, she'd been one of the first to arrive at the Chapel and had bagged a decent pew at the back. Just as the Chapel was filling out, she'd watched this boy come in. She liked the way he'd fist-bumped one of the juniors; it had clearly made the boy's day. He was a Popper, though instead of having a buttonhole, he'd tucked the flower behind his ear. And, unless he was an outstanding actor, he'd forgotten that he'd tucked the white rose behind his ear and had no idea why everyone was sniggering at him.

A dry hymn is followed by a forgettable lesson, and Lily finds that she is drawn to this Popper – and though she can't quite believe it, and although she only saw him for one second, it slowly dawns on her that she is looking at Cary. And as they stare at each other from the length of a cricket pitch, they have a conversation in dumb mime. She smooths back her hair, plucks a flower from behind her ear and smells it. Cary knows instantly what has happened, laughs. He also smooths his hair, takes the flower from behind his ear, for a moment offers it to her and then pops it in his buttonhole.

They have not said a single word. And they are already smitten.

CHAPTER 7

A few hours later, they meet for the first time – and, most fittingly, considering all else that is to come, they meet in The Project.

Cary is in the kitchen, making the evening stew. The kitchen is a large white cube, almost as high as it is long, with a wall of windows that should be letting in the sunshine but that have not been cleaned in years. The kitchen is cleanish, though the pots and pans are perhaps a little grubby. As for the clean-up after the morning breakfast, that has never been anything other than perfunctory; there's some oil on the floor from the bacon trays.

Cary has scrubbed up rather nicely, because he is aware that, on this day of days, he will be meeting the love of his life. He's even ironed his maroon athletics T-shirt and has selected one of the less ripped aprons from the laundry basket. He not only hopes that she'll come today, he knows it. It is written.

Renton and Fergie are helping to get things ready for the evening, when The Project opens its doors at 5pm and when Windsor's waifs and strays can have a hot meal and hunker down for the night. Some people find it odd that this Etonian enjoys being in The Project – but apart from a few exceptions, like Bruno, Cary prefers being in the company of the homeless. They tend to be more honest, more genuine, and always and without exception, they have much better stories to tell – though only if you have the time and the patience to listen.

He's just carrying the stew-pot to the hob when he senses a slight change of temperature in the room next door.

The door opens.

And in she comes.

In the last six hours, there are a lot of things he's thought about saying to this girl when they finally meet.

But in the end, and despite all the dry-runs, all he can do is stand and stare. And then he smiles, and because she knows it's going to be all right, she smiles too, and then they're both laughing at the sheer giddy excitement of it all.

'Lily,' he says.

'Cary.'

'I brought something for you.'

'What?' The smile never leaves her face.

'Let me just set this on the hob.' He takes two steps towards the range, and perhaps he shouldn't have been looking at Lily, but he'd probably have missed the grease on the floor anyway. His front foot shoots out in front of him. He shimmies, agile, almost rights himself, but the stew-pot gets the better of him and, as if in slow motion, the pot upends all over his front. Even as he's going down, he catches Lily's wide eyes.

'Ohh!'

Tepid stew floods the floor.

Cary is flat on his back, still holding onto the empty stew-pot. For a while, he just lies in the stew.

Lily comes into view, stands over him. 'Are you all right?'

'Not bad.' He gets to his knees, stands up. He's covered in carrots and onions and bits of meat. 'How was that for an introduction?'

'It was...' Lily ponders. 'Unique.'

'Been meaning to clean this floor for ages.'

'You get some fresh clothes,' she says. 'I'll start cleaning up.'

Cary finds jeans and a shirt in the slops basket and, after wiping off the worst of the stew, he returns to the kitchen. Lily is on her knees, scooping up stew with a dustpan. 'I don't think this floor has been cleaned since Christmas!' she says. 'I found a dead mouse in the corner!'

'You've done a great job!' He rummages under the sink for some floor cleaner. There is none. 'Do you think they even have a mop?''

'For emergencies only.'

'Does this count?'

A mop is eventually found – in the larder – and Fergie is dispatched to buy some floor cleaner.

But what Cary would remember of that afternoon was not the fall, and not the clean-up, but Lily helping him prepare the next batch of stew. They stood at the table amicably chopping carrots and parsnips. She leaned in to speak to him. Their shoulders touched.

'So why did your dad bring you to Eton?' he asked.

'He wanted his son to go to Eton – and when he didn't have a son, he sent me here instead.'

'Must be pretty tough on you though.'

'But I've met you.' She leaned over and plucked a piece of carrot from Cary's hair.

'That reminds me. I bought something for you.' From his rucksack, he produces a white rose that he'd bought from the Eton florists. 'May I?'

'Please.'

And though all is still, they are locked in a tornado's eye. With fluttering fingers, he sweeps her hair back and places the rose behind her ear. 'There.'

'Do you like it?'

'I would not have believed it, but you have become more beautiful.'

For Lily, it is that magical moment of relief that comes to all lovers when they reveal their cards for the first time, and when they realise that all their absurd fantasies are most entirely mutual.

'Thank you,' she says.

And then, because there is nothing else to be said, and because when you've met your match, there's no need for fencing and for games, and also because it's what they both want to do, and, well, it just feels like the most natural thing to do, they move towards each other and they hug, a hug that will see them through even when the whole world's against them. Cary doesn't know why, but he can feel tears stinging at his eyes.

They break off, look at each other, and Cary doesn't mind that she can see that he's been crying, because without a second thought, they do what their every instinct is telling them to do, and they kiss; firm, sweet, solid.

And draw back, and look each other in the eye, and because what's happened is so downright unbelievable, they just start chuckling.

He sighs, nestles into her neck, and inhales the apples in her freshly washed hair.

'I think and I hope that this is the start of something,' he says.

'I know it,' she says.

'You do?'

'My witchy ways.'

There's a light tap at the door, and after a lengthy pause, Fergie comes in. Our young lovers do not bother to separate.

'That's nice,' Fergie says. 'Two of my favourite people in all the world, and now you've finally found each other.'

'We have!' says Cary.

'Having a cup of tea with Renton on the bench outside if you fancy joining us.'

'Shall we?' he says.

'Let me enjoy this for just a little longer.'

A few minutes later, and after one more chaste kiss, Lily and Cary join Renton and Fergie on the bench in the street, where they sit thigh to thigh, the sun on their faces and warm tea in their hands. And as for those two old winos, who have not been loved in a long time, they are content to wallow in this love by proxy and to be washed over by wave upon wave of unabashed happiness.

In due course, the winos came to the matter at hand.

'So, young Cary,' said Fergie. 'Why were those chaps chasing you yesterday?'

'No telling tales?'

'We're in The Project, so it's Project Rules!' Renton said. 'You think we'd blab?'

'No, you wouldn't.' He turned to Lily. 'You know the rules?'

'I do – and I will adhere to them most strictly.' And now it was her turn, and she took his hand and kissed him on the wrist – and that was a sight to set the pulse racing. This beautiful girl was kissing his wrist! And then looking at him with adoration!

'I'll tell you,' Cary said. 'And I think you're going to like it.'

And out it all spilled as he told them of the drunken hijinks and the crazy chase. He did not mention his strange cigarette-smoking muse in the chestnut tree, but instead contented himself by saying that he'd wondered what James Bond would do.

'He'd escape!' Fergie said. 'And he'd get the girl!'

'And you've done both!'

'What a great story!' Fergie said, rubbing his hands, dreaming of his glory days. 'Makes me wish I was still in the game.'

'So what happened to Bruno and Viktor?' Lily said.

'The police gave them a grilling and let them go after a couple of hours,' Cary said. 'They're not going to be charged. But then they don't have to be.'

'And why not?'

'The Headman is more than capable of making both their lives a misery. He's seeing them in a day or two, making them sweat.'

'Lucky they won't squeal,' Renton said.

'They're my friends,' Cary said simply.

'Wish I had friends like that,' Fergie said.

'But you do!' Lily said. 'You've got Renton – you've got me, you've got Cary. What more do you want?'

'I'd like a lovely wife to hold my hand like you're holding Cary's now.'

And Renton, who'd learned a thing or two from all the tedious counselling sessions with his ex-wife, chimed in with his ha'pennyworth. 'Put it out to the universe – see if the universe delivers.'

A couple of Etonians were ambling up the street towards them, ready for their weekly Community Service at The Project, though unlike our two young lovers, they viewed their Community Service as more of a school skive.

'Here comes Fredster Campbell.' Renton hawked and, because there was a lady present, genteelly spat into his grimy handkerchief. 'Better take your hands off each other. Fredster's good company, but he doesn't know the first thing about Project Rules.'

Lily dropped her true love's hand, moved to the edge of the bench, and at the same time, Cary stood up to take the empty mugs.

'It's back to the pitface.'

Not a word needed to be said, but Cary and Lily knew that their great rippling secret must never be mentioned in Eton's hearing.

CHAPTER 8

Cary was abed, the house asleep, but though it was gone 1am, he was wide awake. He never needed more than four hours' sleep, which was how he managed to cram work and kitchen duties and all else into his days, but he had memories to revel in – seeing Lily in the Chapel; and the way she'd seen him in the Chapel; and the kitchen at The Project when she had kissed him goodbye – and said that he was both requested and required to meet her there the next day.

He heard a click, another click, and then out of the darkness spurted a flame. The gold lighter was cupped, the cigarette tip glowed red, and after a long draw and a cough, a contented puff of smoke eddied above the burry (Eton-speak for bureau).

'Mind if I light a candle?' Cary could just make him out. Fleming was dapper in bow tie and dark velvet smoking jacket. His waxed hair had an immaculate knife-sharp parting. 'So much more congenial than electricity.'

Fleming lit a white candle and pushed it into a glistering silver candlestick.

'That's better.'

Then, taking his time, he took a puff on his Morland and had a languid look around the room. There was not much of note; a tatty sofa, an even tattier armchair, and a lot of books lying in piles on the floor and the table. The walls were bare, apart from a film poster from The Italian Job, which had been left there by the previous incumbent.

'Still moving in?'

'No.'

'You like it spartan. Anyway – pretty girl.'

'She certainly is.'

'Bond was always good at getting the women – but, like me, he was never very good at keeping them.' Fleming smiled as his face disappeared in another puff of Balkan and Turkish. 'They either got dumped or they got dead.'

'If at all possible, I'd like to avoid the latter. Probably the former too, actually.'

'Oh... that first careless rapture of being young and in love, you lucky dog. Anyway, Cary – that's not why I'm here. I'm here because, this afternoon, you missed a very large trick.'

'I kissed her! What else were you expecting? I'm still a virgin!'

'I'm not talking about the girl. I'm talking about Fergie!'

'Ohh – I was a bit wrapped up with Lily.'

'As you probably know, Fergie is a reformed tabloid reporter. And when he described your antics in the grounds of Windsor Castle as being quite a good story, he didn't mean it was something with which to amuse your chums down in that foetid school pub.'

'Didn't he?'

'He meant that it might just possibly make quite a good article in one of Her Majesty's newspapers – something like, just possibly, *The Sun*, where they would bite your hand off for the story.'

Fleming stubbed out the barely-smoked cigarette and immediately started the rigmarole of lighting a fresh one.

'Do they pay?'

'They pay handsomely. Give Kim a call, another of my protégés, haven't heard from him in a while, he'll look after you. But you'd better not get caught, or you really will be facing the biggest high jump of your life! Call him any time after morning conference at 11.'

The glowing end of the fresh Morland weaved in the darkness as if Fleming was conducting his own orchestra.

'I'll do it,' Cary said. 'What do you think it might be worth? Hundred quid?'

Fleming's laugh was long and loud; the laugh of a middle-aged muck-raker who'd seen a lot and who'd heard it all.

'You still don't have any idea quite how big this story is – or how deep *The Sun* editor's pockets are. That rag is making over a million pounds a week. This story is not just about the world's most prestigious school, Eton College, it's about two of Prince William's actual schoolmates landing themselves in the ordure in the most astonishing fashion. Better yet, it's actually quite funny. It will be a tonic for the masses during their workaday week. Given the right treatment, a story like this could easily be worth four figures.'

'A thousand pounds?'

'And the rest!' Fleming grinned and continued to grin, even as he inhaled. 'I like your typewriter, by the way. Don't see them so often.'

'Thank you.'

'Once, when I was in my pomp, I had a golden typewriter.'

And with a puff of smoke, the master left the room, and Cary dreamed 007 dreams of beautiful women and men with murder in their hearts.

CHAPTER 9

Middle-class snoots tend to look down on Sun journalists, thinking that, because these febrile hacks write for the Great Unwashed, they themselves are fully paid-up members of the Unwashed. But anyone who knows anything about Fleet Street will tell you that tabloid reporters are invariably courteous and smartly dressed. Like any other tabloid, *The Sun* will have a few foot-in-the-door merchants who love to shout through letterboxes, but since people generally prefer honey to vinegar, most Sun reporters have a fair degree of charm. Sun reporters don't mind that a lot of people, including most particularly Prince Harry, think they're scum. In fact, they pride themselves on it. For they are not just the scum. They are the *Crème de la Scum.*

At *The Sun* in the 1990s, there was no-one who came any creamier than its resident toff, and that would have been me, Kim, Despoiler of Piano Mistresses. There were a number of advantages to being *The Sun*'s Old Etonian Reporter, not least that very few people could believe I actually worked for Britain's biggest daily tabloid. When you looked at me, and when I opened my mouth, you'd think I worked for something staid like *The Times* or *The Telegraph*. But to think of this (relatively) inoffensive fellow working for *The Sun* – inconceivable!

And then the next day, when you find yourself filleted like a kipper all over the front page, you just cannot believe that this mild-mannered chap has completely turned you over. 'But he seemed so nice,' you wail to anyone who will listen.

And of course I was nice – that is the essence of the tabloid reporter's craft. They ply you with drinks. They're cheery, engaged and, above all, they're interested, so very interested, in everything about you. And gradually, over the space of several drinks and several hours, you open up to your new best friend, and the next day are duly rewarded with your fifteen minutes of fame.

And it is this Sun staff reporter who is flashing his pass at the Fortress Wapping security guards and who parks up his battered Alfa Romeo in the car park.

I got a coffee and a bacon roll from the News International canteen and took a lift up to *The Sun* newsroom on the sixth floor. That newsroom no longer exists, and the space that it once occupied, 30 or 40 metres up, is now nothing but thin air, the whole building bulldozed to make way for chichi flats. As for *The Sun* newspaper, that is still just about holding on by its very fingertips, with a circulation that's now on the wrong side of one million. But in those days, in 1995, *The Sun* was selling over five million copies on a good day and thrummed with the thrill of being the cheekiest paper on the planet.

Above the double security doors at the entrance of *The Sun* newsroom, there was a sign – and though I had walked through those doors hundreds of times, it still gave me a buzz.

It was not a sign that would work for many other companies. It would not work outside a bank, or a school, or a shop, or a pub, or a bookies.

But somehow, at *The Sun*, it worked. The sign read: 'Walk tall – you're entering Sun Country' – and the staff did tend to walk just that little bit taller, the horizons limitless ahead of them as they were shielded in armour of Teflon. Tchah! Listen to me!

The Sun newsroom was, in my mind's eye at least, simply vast, over 30 metres by 80 metres, and right in the middle was the power, the back bench, where the top guns filtered and sifted through all the world's news. Giant copies of *The Sun*'s greatest/most infamous front pages – 'Gotcha!' 'It's The Sun Wot Won It!' – were dotted about the battleship-grey walls, and for the rest there were scores of grey desks, each with a computer and phone. The news desk and picture desk were near the entrance, with a pod of 20 news reporters' desks close at hand so that the reporters were within easy shouting distance of the four news editors. At the far end of the room, past the back bench and the worker-bee subs, were the sports-mad sports hacks and the oh-so-precious feature writers. One side of the newsroom was lined with offices, while on the other side was a corridor, which meant that the only natural light to filter into the newsroom was through the dingy skylights; unless you looked up, you had no idea if it was 10 in the morning or 10 at night.

I said a distracted good morning to the news desk and to the three secretaries; the news editor just shook his head.

One of the secretaries, Stella, smiled at me. 'Chin up.'

I skulked to my desk. I was like a man on an island beach who had heard reports of bad weather. I could sense the wind picking up and the waves turning to white caps as the sand stung my skin. There was one hell of a storm brewing.

I took another look at *The Mirror*'s Splash. Bain had done it again. He'd shafted me.

The Mirror was *The Sun*'s direct competitor, though much more left-wing, and the whole of *The Mirror*'s Splash was devoted to a story that, if Bain had been a gentleman, he'd have shared with me and the guys from the *Mail* and the *Express* and the *Star*. But no, Bain was not a gentleman, nor had he ever been a gentleman – Bain by name, and Bane by nature. I mean, I know we scum-sucking hacks may not appear to have many morals, but one thing we don't do is stiff our fellow scum-suckers! It's just not on! If you can't trust another hack then, well, really, it's the end of civilisation!

What had happened was this: The previous day, early doors, I had been sent off to Winchester, in Hampshire, there to doorstep the mother of the errant headmaster of Charterhouse public school. [To doorstep – both a noun and a verb. It involves a reporter and photographer waiting on a punter's doorstep until the punter either returns home or responds to the feverish knocking on the front door.]

Charterhouse is one of Britain's nobbier public schools, and since there's nothing tabloid readers love so much as reading about the misdemeanours of posh schoolboys and their toff teachers, this story was a beauty. The Charterhouse headmaster had been seeing a local prostitute, who was barely older than his pupils. Unfortunately for this 50-year-old married gent, he'd been recognised by his favourite call-girl, on account of having given a speech at her school the previous year. Cue: tabloid drama! Cue: salacious front pages rubbing the headmaster's nose in the ordure! Cue: a story that might run for the week, especially if the headmaster or his wife decided to start spilling their guts. (There's no fun at all for us humble hacks if a punter churlishly sticks to saying 'No comment!' How the hell are we supposed to make a story out of that – apart from perhaps writing that they'd 'furiously ducked' our perfectly fair and straightforward questions.)

Anyway, since the Charterhouse shagger was the story *du jour*, tabloid reporters and photographers had been dispatched all over Britain in quest of a new line. At *The Sun*, we had reporters outside his home in Surrey, his holiday home in Cornwall, his in-laws' home in Morningside, Edinburgh and, as for his mother's house in sunny Winchester, that had been left to *The Sun*'s number one reporter, and that we would be me, myself, Kim the human Labrador, with his shaggy coat and slobbering tongue, beloved by everyone, reviled by none.

I'd arrived at Mrs Bennett's doorstep at 7am, there to quiz her about her son's simply disgusting behaviour, but it seemed to me a little too early to be hammering on her front door. Besides – my photographer, Grubby, had yet to turn up. This was not a surprise.

I whiled away my time reading the papers, all of them,

and, since after an hour the front curtains still hadn't twitched open, I went off and bought a coffee from a local café. On these doorsteps, it's entirely pointless knocking the punters up too early, as what you're after is a proper sit-down chat; punters are unlikely to spill their guts if they've just got up and haven't even had breakfast.

Twenty minutes later, I arrived back at Mrs Bennett's doorstep with two cups of coffee – one for me, and one for Grubby to drink whensoever he deigned to show up.

A particularly unpleasant sight awaited me – Bain. Bain was not just there but was sauntering down Mrs Bennett's garden path, having obviously just knocked her up at 8.20 in the morning; what sort of idiot does that?

I left my car and, coffee in hand, dawdled over.

'Ah, morning, Kim,' he said. The oleaginous toad was chewing gum. 'Wondered when you'd turn up.'

'Turn up?' I said. 'I was here hours ago. You haven't just got her out of bed?'

'Course,' he said. 'What were you going to do? Wait till lunchtime?'

'So, what did you get?'

'Nothing,' he said, before adding a single fateful word. 'Much.'

'You bastard,' I said – because, since Bain was the most unscrupulous hound I'd ever met, I'd now have to go and knock up the good Mrs Bennett myself.

Bain, wearing a suit and a seedy flasher's mac, watched me go up the garden path. He still had the gum in his fat mouth but was now – so help me – picking at his teeth with a silver toothpick.

With a heavy heart, I knocked at the door. Footsteps coming down the stairs. The door was opened by an old white-haired woman in a blue dressing gown.

I went into my spiel. 'Oh, I'm so sorry to bother you, Mrs Bennett,' I said. 'It's Kim—'

'I told you to go away until I'd dressed and had my

breakfast!' she said, a tad crotchety given we'd never met, but then again, she had just been talking to Bain and that was enough to put anyone in a foul mood.

'Oh, I'm so very sorry,' I said. 'I'll come back when you're up and about.'

'And I still won't say anything.'

The door slammed in my face. People with more tender hearts might get affronted at having a door slammed in their face, but I've had so many doors slammed on me – literally hundreds – that I'm immune to it. (And, another perk of being a perky tabloid reporter, I'm also immune to being sworn at, which comes in especially useful during a marriage. But I digress…)

Bain was still waiting by the front gate, though he'd moved on from poking at his teeth to fingering the rim of his crusty nostril with thumb and forefinger – he was a real charmer, I can tell you.

'Told you,' he said.

'You didn't tell me anything of the sort,' I said.

'Makes my day seeing a door slammed in your face.'

'You must be very easy to please.'

Another reporter arrived, this time from *The Daily Mail*, and then another from the *Express*, and then an agency reporter from *South West News* and, pretty soon, the full mob was there, bunging up the street with our cars as we milled around the pavement. Eventually, even Grubby turned up. Now, just to attend to the small matter of his nickname: It was not some sort of reverse nickname like, say, Robin Hood's gigantic friend 'Little John'. No – Grubby was called Grubby because he really was damn grubby; permanently rumpled grey suit which looked like he slept in it, along with a grey/white shirt, some sort of stained tie attachment around his neck, scuffed black slip-ons, smudged glasses, and thick salt and pepper hair that had never ever seen a comb.

I gave Grubby his coffee.

'Ta.' He took a sip and spat it out. 'It's stone-cold.'

'Yeah, sorry about that,' I said. 'I bought it a couple of hours ago when you were due here.'

'I had another job to go to, Little Lord Fauntleroy,' he said, tipping the remainder of the coffee in the gutter.

'What story's that?'

'The same one you're on,' he said.

'I'll believe you,' I said. 'Thousands wouldn't.'

'Charming.'

By now, it was about 11am and, since the full pack was in attendance at Mrs Bennett's doorstep, we all of us agreed to play by 'Pack Rules'. That meant, if any of us were to come by a new line for the story – any fresh line whatsoever – they had to share it with the rest of the pack. Ditto with any pictures. This was obviously infuriating for the mad-masters back in their hell-hole offices, as they'd not be getting any tasty world exclusives, but for the hacks on the road, it meant we'd got our backs covered; we weren't going to be scooped any time soon.

'So we're agreed?' I said, having cast myself in my preferred role as the chairman of the pack. 'Pack rules?'

'Pack rules,' echoed the woman from *The Mail*.

'What about you, Bain?' I said.

'Yeah,' Bain said, still picking the rim of his nose. How much gunk did he have up there? 'Pack rules.'

'Excellente!' I said.

We agreed that one of our number, the smoothest, silkiest, most charming pack member, would once again go up to Mrs Bennett's doorstep, there to find out if, having breakfasted, she was in more of a mood to chat. On these sorts of pack jobs, you only want to send one reporter to knock on the door – if the whole pack goes up, the punter can feel overwhelmed.

Naturally enough, it was decided by general consensus that I should have the important job of making the approach to Mrs Bennett – firstly because I'm a charmer, and secondly because I'm almost entirely trustworthy.

Watched by the rest of the pack, I sauntered back up Mrs Bennett's front path and, as I went, I did not forget to smell the roses; heavenly – just heavenly. Why can't more reporters just be in the moment, and smell the flowers along the way? But no, they can't, they are forever chasing their tails, and forgetting to smell the flowers, as if this will somehow make for a better exclusive. I was distracted from my flower-sniffing by the sound of footsteps. Grubby was lumbering up the footpath.

'What are you doing, Grubby?' I said.

'I'm coming with you.'

'No, mate – it's better if I do this by myself.'

'Course I've got to come with you.'

'You must be joking!' I said. 'Have you seen yourself in the mirror! She'll run a mile if she sees you!'

'What about the pictures?'

'Look, Grubby,' I said, ever so patiently. 'I am fully aware that we need the pictures. But just let me do my silver tongue schtick, and then, when she's good and ready – and only when she's good and ready – I'll get you in.'

'I've got a silver tongue too,' he said brightly.

'Just go back to the car and leave this to me.'

'Oooh – get you, His Nibs.'

'Just let me do my thing!'

Grubby slouched back to the rest of the mob. I straightened my tie, shot my cuffs, and then, for old time's sake, checked my flies. I was still fully zippered.

I knocked on the door again. Bump-bump-bumpity-bump go the stairs. Mrs Bennett opened the door. She was still in her dressing gown.

I gave her my loveliest smile. 'Ah, Mrs Bennett, good morning again,' I said. 'I am here on behalf of the rest of the reporters, and just wondered if you had anything to say about—'

'I told you to wait until I'd had my breakfast,' she spat.

'Ah, indeed so, ma'am, terribly sorry.' I was momentarily taken aback as it was way past 11am; maybe she was one of these monk-like people who survive on one meal a day. 'What would be a more convenient time to have a chat?'

'I've told you!' she said. 'When I've had my breakfast!'

And slam goes the door again, no big deal there, and I mooch back to the rest of the hacks, and though I have been charm personified with the curmudgeonly Mrs Bennett, it's decided that the next person to make an approach – at, say, lunchtime – will be Bain. On these doorsteps, it sometimes works better if you change the batting order, though frankly, the thought of Bain having any more luck than me is laughable.

We were on a dinky little street in the heart of Winchester, St Swithun Street, and by very great good fortune, there was a pub just round the corner, the Wykeham Arms, and this meant that, while one or two of the pack kept guard at Mrs Bennett's doorstep, the rest of the reporters and photographers could get stuck in to what we do best – eating and drinking at our newspapers' expense. It was a lovely old pub in those days, pewter tankards hanging from the ceiling, lots of old school desks from Winchester College, and above the fireplace was inscribed the College motto, 'Manners Makyth Man', which I helpfully pointed out to Bain, but seeing as he was as thick as mince, he couldn't make head nor tail of it.

We caroused, we ate, we shouted and, very occasionally, we sauntered back to good Mrs Bennett's house to check that all was in order. When it was Bain's turn to go up the garden path to make his own grovelling foray, I certainly made sure I was there at the house to keep an eye on the double-dealer. She opened the door, by now fully dressed, and they had some sort of chat. Now she wasn't asking him in, but it was nevertheless quite a long chat. And he didn't get the old 'Door-Slam-In-The-Face' treatment. Was it possible that Bain had managed to beguile her with his own noxious patter? No, it was not possible. In fact, it was totally *im*possible.

'That was quite a long chat you had with Mrs Bennett,' I said as he wandered back to the pavement. 'What did she say?'

'Nothing,' he said. 'We were talking about roses.'

'Oh, yeah?' I said. 'What do you know about roses?'

'Quite a bit more than you, old cock,' he said, giving me a delightful little double slap on the cheek. 'I'm just off to the pub. You'll mind the shop for me?'

'Of course,' I said.

I mumped about on the doorstep. I didn't like it one little bit. Bain had been chatting to the woman for about four or five minutes, and there was a chance they might have been talking about roses, but much more of a chance that the hell-hound was lying through his teeth.

For the rest of the day, we continued to potter back and forth from the Wykeham Arms, and those without cars got monumentally pissed. By about 6pm, we decided that Boshoff, from *The Mail*, should make one final approach to Mrs Bennett. She had no more luck than me or Bain.

We all called up our respective news desks, and then, having confirmed that the rest of the pack were being stood down, we all took our leave of each other and, another fruitless doorstep done, went back home.

It was gone 10.30pm, and I was just wondering whether to treat myself to a nightcap, when my phone rang. It was Nigel, one of the night news editors.

'What's up?' I said.

'You're going to catch it,' he said.

'How so?'

'That Mrs Bennett, whose doorstep you've been watching all day, has given a full exclusive interview to T*he Daily Mirror*,' he said. 'Want to hear the Splash headline? "Head's Mum: My Shame".'

'What?' I said. 'What??'

'Bain's got every spit and cough.'

'He can't have!' I said. 'It was a pack job!'

'Pack job or not, he's got the exclusive.'

I was grinding my teeth in rage. How unlike me not to have guessed. But after all, how very like Bain.

'Just excuse me one moment, Nigel,' I said. 'Got to make a brief call. Be right back.'

I immediately called Bain. It sounded like he was in a very raucous pub.

'Hello?' he bellowed.

'Hey, Bain,' I said. 'You've stiffed us!'

'What? I can't hear you. Just let me get out of here.' The background noise diminished. 'What's up?' he said.

'What's up,' I said, 'is that we were on a pack job today and you've just thrown the rest of us under a bus!'

'Oh maaate, maaate,' he said and my stomach did a back-flip. [Small point of note – I realise that this may just be a very personal thing, but for me, there is no more irritating word *on earth* than that wheedling long drawn out "maaate". Whenever I now hear it, I have an almost Pavlovian reaction, such that I have to physically restrain myself from strangling the speaker on the spot.] 'Sorry about that, maaate!' he continued. 'I was going to let you know! Yeah – after we'd all been stood down, I was just driving back to London, when the desk asked me to try Mrs Bennett one last time, so I went back and she started singing like a canary. I was going to let you know, but, you know—'

'No, I don't know,' I said crisply.

'Well, you know, I got stuck in the pub, and time passed, and I forgot all about you.'

'Well, that's just great!' I said. 'Thanks a bunch!'

'Yeah, sorry, maaate,' he said. 'Look, I'll make it up to you, I really will.'

'Make it up to me?' I said. 'Do you have any idea of the bollocking I'm going to get tomorrow? Do you—'

'Sorry, maaate, you're cracking up, call you back.'

The phone went dead and, obviously, he never did call me back. I had one of those uneasy nights when you know that, come the next morning, you're in for one hell of a pasting – and though I can take a pasting better than anyone, it doesn't mean I much enjoy the process.

Which brings us then to where my story started, with me at

my desk in the newsroom, sipping my coffee and contentedly reading the papers.

'You useless piece of shit!'

He gave me such a start, I spilt my coffee all over my trousers. Spike, the gnarly deputy editor, had sneaked up on me via one of the newsroom's side doors.

I tried to jump to my feet but was shoved straight back into my chair.

'Good morning, Spike.'

'Don't you good morning me, you posh twat,' Spike said, now towering over me and poking me in the chest. 'What the hell are we paying you for? *The Mirror* is kicking you round the block! We send you on a doorstep, you don't file a word, and *The Mirror* gets the exclusive!'

I looked up at Spike, who, because he was 5' 4", preferred his victims seated. The man bristled with wild wolverine intensity, hair standing on end, fingers clenching, unclenching, as if there was nothing he'd have liked so much as to punch my lights out. He permanently looked as if he was on the verge of starting a fight or having a heart attack – or perhaps both.

'Sorry about that,' I said. 'We were on a pack job. Bain did us over.'

'You were on a pack job!' he said with astonishment. 'Since when have I ever, ever allowed pack jobs?'

'Seemed like the smart thing to do at the time,' I said, which might possibly have been true – at least, if Bain hadn't been part of the pack.

'So, it seemed like the smart thing to do, did it, you stinking toff?' Spike poked me in the chest again. '*The Mirror* is pissing all over us – with stories that you should be bringing in!'

Now – just on a small point of note, most of Spike's conversations were absolutely larded with swear-words, particularly the F-word, and the B-word, but since becoming an oh-so-ex Sun reporter, I have become such a benign soul that I am repelled by four-letter words, both written and oral, and they have thusly been excised out of Spike's conversations. If, however, you'd like a flavour of what Spike actually sounded like, you can salt his sentences with your own favourite swear-words. That last little outburst, for instance, would have contained at least five swear-words, possibly even seven.

I wheeled the chair back and Spike followed straight in, eyeballs bulging, breath stinking of the last piece of red meat he'd eaten.

'Bain did not behave like a gentleman,' I said, taking a prim change of tack. 'I trusted him!'

'You trusted him?' Poke to the chest. 'I can certainly trust you – to cock things up!'

'Do you have to poke me in the chest?'

'You don't like it?' Spike said. 'How do you like this?' Spike bent down, caught a leg of my chair and heaved. The chair careened backwards onto the floor. I cannoned into a wastepaper bin.

I got to my feet and, as elegantly as I could, brushed some of the fluff from my jacket sleeve. A glance over to the news desk revealed that the whole lot, news editors and secretaries, were goggling like meerkats.

'I thought Human Resources had warned you about your peculiar temper.'

'And I've warned you about leaning back in your chair!' Spike said. 'You could really do yourself an injury.'

'Shall I send you the cleaning bill – or put it on expenses?'

'No, what you will do, you Old Etonian toad, is get me some stories.' Spike made to poke me in the chest again, but this time, I was ready for it. Light on my feet, I skipped backwards.

'You're getting slow, Spike.'

'Get me some stories – or get sacked!' Spike raged off to the news desk. 'What have you bastards got for me today?'

I contented myself with flicking a V at Spike's back.

Bain's Splash was still laughing at me. I crumpled it up and tossed it in the bin.

Other news reporters drifted in, photographers wandered over.

'What the hell have you been doing?' said Grubby. 'Have you been in a fight?'

'Morning, Grubby,' I said, cracking open *The Daily Telegraph* – certainly no nasty scoops there. 'Who'd want to hit me?'

'The deputy editor, for starters,' Grubby said. 'You really got served by Bain.'

'Thanks, by the way, for being such a great help yesterday.'

'Now, what was it you said yesterday?' he mused, pawing at his blubbery lower lip. 'Ah yes – "Just let me do my thing". And I did let you do your thing, and now you've got egg on your face, and you want me to carry the blame.'

'Oh, right,' I said airily. 'It's got absolutely nothing whatsoever to do with you.'

'You're right,' he said. 'It's got absolutely nothing to do with me.'

'Of course,' I said, voice dripping with sarcasm. 'It's entirely my fault.'

'Good of you to finally acknowledge it – it's your fault.'

'Have you really got nothing better to do than annoy me?'

'I'll leave you to the important business of not bringing in any stories then,' he said, and mooched off in a haze of B.O. and fleas.

I sniffed, took a sip of coffee, and took a moment to compose myself before (once again) settling down to read the papers, scanning for follow-ups, for anything, anything at all, that might be spun into a story. When that failed, I started calling up my contacts, the people who'd given me stories in the past, just giving the tree another shake to see if any more fruit might yet fall to the ground. Nothing came of it. It would make reporters' lives a lot easier if, when they're ordered to bring in an exclusive, they could just make the call and the story plopped into their laps. (The more cunning reporters always have an exclusive or two on the back-burner for just such an eventuality; not me, though. I was one of those hand-to-mouth reporters who filed his exclusives the moment he got them.) But, for the most part, exclusives turn up in their own sweet time. They can be neither hustled nor cajoled.

I went to the vending machine outside the newsroom to get coffees for me and the three other news reporters. Well – what a great, great start to the day. Scooped by Bain. Knocked to the floor by Spike. Supremely vexed by the oafish Grubby…

Stella, the news desk secretary, came out into the passage. Like all of *The Sun*'s secretaries, she was very pretty – though it was also possible that their prettiness was linked to the fact that they were so very fastidious about never dating any of their Sun colleagues.

'There you are, Kim,' Stella said. 'Got a young lad wanting to speak to you.'

'Thanks for finding me.' I was intrigued. I didn't know many young lads. 'What's his name?'

'Wouldn't say. But I'll tell you one thing – he sounds just like you.'

'Better go and have a word, then,' I said. 'Like a coffee?'

'Thanks, but that stuff's muck,' she laughed. 'We've got our own coffee machine.'

'I know where to get my coffee in future, then.'

'For the use of the news desk and picture desk only – and their secretaries.' She held the newsroom door open.

I doled out the coffees and returned to my desk, where a red light pulsed on my phone. And with a click, the young lad was through, and was speaking to a real live Sun reporter.

'Hi, this is Kim,' I said, very soft, very pleasant, luring a timorous kitten down from its tree-top hideaway. 'How can I help?'

'Hi,' came the voice, and it was a type of voice I had not heard in a while, but which brought with it such a wash of memory. 'I think I might have a story for you.'

'Excellent!' I said. 'Can I call you back? Is there a number I can get you on?'

'No, I'm okay.'

'What's your story, then?'

And then the lad on the other end of the line did something very unusual. He just blurted out the story. A lot of tipsters who call *The Sun* start off trying to haggle over their fees before they've even revealed their wares. But, refreshingly, the boy dived straight in.

'It's a story about Eton,' he said.

'We are very much in the market for Eton stories.'

'It happened a few days ago.'

'On William's first day at school? I was there with the rest of the mob! What happened?'

'Two Etonians got drunk in Tap – and got caught in the private grounds of Windsor Castle.'

'That, my friend, is a very big story.' I started to relax. It was going to be fine. 'So, why did these boys break into the Windsor Castle grounds?'

'To see the Queen.'

I laughed out loud. 'That is good! And that has put the story on the front page! I presume they did not get to see the Queen.'

'No – the security guards picked them up within 15 minutes.'

'Have they been up before the Headman yet?' I said.

'They're seeing him this afternoon.'

'I hope they don't get the boot. This is a great story, and it's going to be worth a lot of money to you.'

'Oh – great.'

'I'm guessing that you're an Etonian, and so I'll just run you through a few bits of housekeeping, to make sure you don't get caught. That okay?'

'Yes.'

'First of all, you do not tell me what your real name is, and you do not discuss this with any person anywhere. You do not mention it to your best friend, or to your girlfriend, or to your relatives. You do not talk about it to anyone, ever. And that way, there's only one person who will know who you are and that'll be you, as even I'm not going to know your real name. Even if they put the thumbscrews on me, I still won't be able to name you.'

'Good.'

'Secondly – it goes without saying that *The Sun* would like this story exclusively. So don't go calling up any other papers with it. You might think you'd be paid more money, but for world exclusives, *The Sun* pays way more than all the rest put together. And, to be on the safe side, only deal with me.'

Ah, now here we should add a small point of interest. This: Of course it was going to be safer for the lad if he just dealt with me at *The Sun*; but we should not forget that I was very, very keen to keep this whale of a contact all to myself. Reporters only become star reporters by bringing in exclusives. So I was certainly not going to risk this boy being lured off to some other paper or, worse, being snapped up by one of my colleagues.

'Always use a public payphone, never the one in your house,' I continued. 'Don't call me at *The Sun* any more, I'll give you my pager number and my mobile number. Try the pager first. Call up any time, day or night, it's always on. Just leave me the number of the payphone you're at and, if I can, I'll call you back immediately. If I don't call back in five minutes, then you'll have to try later.

'But the main thing is, never ever put yourself at risk. If you think it's dodgy, if you think they might be able to trace the story back to you, then just keep it to yourself. There are going to be loads of stories coming out of Eton, so no need to break yourself.' I paused, wondering if there was anything I'd missed. 'Got a pen handy? I'll give you my numbers now.'

'I don't need a pen. I remember everything.'

'Amazing – wish I could do that.' I rattled off my pager number and mobile number.

'And last of all, for the moment at least, if the shit does hit the fan, then do please remember the dear school motto.'

'*Floreat Etona*? Eton lives? How's that going to help?'

'That's the official school motto – but the unofficial motto, which will serve you in much better stead, is this: Deny, Deny, Deny.'

'Deny?'

'One dark day, my friend, you may, through no fault of your own, come under suspicion, and you will be dragged into some private office, and they will try to trick a confession out of you. But I can promise you this. It will all be a bluff. Because I don't know who you are, and you won't – hopefully – have told anyone about your dealings with *The Sun*. So, should that dark day ever occur, just deny everything till they blow themselves out.'

'Got it.'

'For the moment, then, and if you haven't got anything more to tell me about the Windsor story, we'd better decide on what agent name you'd like to go by. And with you, I fancy colours.'

'Like in Reservoir Dogs?'

'Thought you'd be too young to have seen that,' I laughed. 'So, what do you fancy – Agent Blue, Agent White, Agent Green—'

'Agent Orange.'

'That kind of agent?' I said. 'Highly toxic and to be handled with extreme care?'

'It appealed.'

'Give us a call tomorrow when you know how the boys have been punished. And later in the week, give me a call, so that I can give you the immense amount of cash that will soon be coming your way.'

'Oh – one thing before I go,' he said.

'Fire away, Agent Orange.'

'I just wondered, on the off chance, whether Ian Fleming ever talked to you.'

I paused, utterly flummoxed; no-one, not ever, had mentioned Ian Fleming's name to me before. 'Now that is a question I never dreamed I would hear,' I said. 'But before I answer it, can I ask you a question. Does Ian Fleming talk to you?'

'He suggested I call you up.'

'Which, in turn, must mean that you are the proud owner of a certain special room in The Timbralls. Remarkable! So yes, Agent Orange, Fleming did speak to me. Can I give you a word of advice?'

'Please.'

'With Fleming in the wings, you will be doing things of which you would have thought yourself entirely incapable. You will achieve things you would not have dreamed possible – the most outrageous things, way beyond the ken of any ordinary Etonian. You will be riding the tiger. You will be in for the most exhilarating days of your life. But—'

'There had to be a but.'

'But once you are on this tiger, you will find it very difficult to get off. One day, however, you will have to steel yourself and you will have to get off that tiger. And when you do get off, there'll be one hell of a bump. Anyway…' I sighed, old memories of piano teachers and lost love, and doodled love hearts on my notepad. 'Enjoy it while you can.'

I leaned back in my chair and laughed. Who would have thought – believed – that my Eton education would be the absolute making of my career as a tabloid reporter? I'd bagged myself an Eton schoolboy who was efficient and plugged in and who was being nurtured by that old rogue Ian Fleming, which meant… which meant that it would probably work out just like Fleming's books. Things would work well for a while, and then they would end spectacularly badly and, somewhere along the way, someone would end up dead.

CHAPTER 10

Lily has decided that, for better or worse, she is going to immerse herself in the whole Eton experience. Not for her staying tucked away in her room, swotting away at text-books – even the very thought of it makes her want to yawn! No, of an evening, while her Arctic father is doing his house-rounds, and while her mother is playing her bridge, Lily will experience all that Eton has to offer. She will be going to the literary society, the political society, the film society and even the infernal crochet society – if such a society exists – just to get out of Farrer House, and to taste everything that Eton has to offer. She wants it all! And she's going to get it!

She can already play Fives, but, what the hell, she'll have a turn at squash and racquets and tennis, and maybe even rowing. And, in the afternoons, when she has no lessons, she will continue assiduously with her useful work for Eton's Community Services, and most particularly in helping out at The Project.

The previous day, when she'd returned to Farrer for lunch, there had been a formal-looking letter waiting for her on the hall table. Brown manila envelope, typed address on a stick-on label, perhaps one or two sheets of paper inside. A little voice told her to take the letter to her room, rather than open it in front of prying eyes.

She sits at her desk and flicks the envelope open with her Swiss Army knife that she'd been allowed to buy when she joined the Brownies. A handwritten letter – how lovely! She hardly ever gets handwritten notes and, as she looks at the signature, and as her heart bubbles with glee, she realises that in her hands is her first ever love letter, and that though they have shared nothing more than two chaste kisses, she is already wondering, dreaming, about what might be next on the menu.

Cary's letter is funny and poignant and wholly endearing and, at the end of it all, he wonders if she might have a very, very light lunch, nothing more than a mouthful, at Farrer on Tuesday so that later on he can prepare a proper lunch for her at The Project. She reads it once, twice, a third time – and within the next 12 hours, she will have read this letter many times over.

She jots off an effusive, positively joyous reply – when you have met your heart's desire, there is no need for coy game-playing – and puts on her running gear. She smiles. Lily has always considered herself quite a good runner. But that was until she saw Cary running. Was there anything that guy couldn't handle? And even that one very special thing – had he even tried it before? Probably – he was bound to be good at it, because Cary looked like he was a natural at everything he touched.

Letter in hand, Lily jogs down Judy's Passage, a high-walled walkway that connects Farrer to the hub of the school. The slap of footsteps behind her, and her gut gives a heave, because she doesn't even need to turn her head to know who's coming up behind her. How did he know she'd come out of the house for a run – was he actually looking out of the windows waiting for her?

'Off for a run?' Maxwell asks as he lumbers up next to her.

'More a little trot.'

'Mind if I chum you?'

'I'm going to be very slow,' Lily says, instantly cursing herself. Why didn't she just say she was going into the library?

'Great – had a massive weights session this morning.'

They run past Dr Gailey's house, and there is a security

guard and there is the young Prince himself in his muddy sports gear. Lily smiles at him and waves, and William smiles and waves back; sharp kid that he is, he realises instantly that he and Lily have a lot in common, for they are far and away the most exotic creatures in the school.

'You know the Prince?'

'Not until now,' Lily says. 'But I'm sure we'll become firm friends.'

Her nose twitches. She becomes aware that Maxwell smells absolutely vile. It's the layered smell of stale sweat that has built up on Maxwell's shirt after days and days of exercise and, now she's aware of the reek, it almost makes her want to gag. She breathes through her mouth.

They pass The Burning Bush and cross the road to the post box. Maxwell is watching, but Lily has turned the envelope so he will not see who it's addressed to.

'Writing a letter,' he says. 'How very old-fashioned.'

'I like it.'

Maxwell's twitching antennae divine that all is not as it seems. Jealous, unable to control himself, he just comes straight out with it. 'Who are you writing to?'

'Oh – just a thank you letter.'

'What did you get?'

Lily laughs blithely. 'I didn't know you were training to be a barrister.'

As the letter is popped into the post box, Maxwell catches a glimpse of the address. Doesn't see much, but might have seen the words 'Eton College', which could mean lots of things, could mean that she's writing a thank you letter to one of the beaks, but could also mean… A boy? No! How could she already be writing to a boy when she's not even been a week at the school? But then also perhaps possibly… Yes.

They cross back over the road and past that Victorian red-brick, The Timbralls – she blows the house a kiss – and then they're out onto Sixpenny, skirting all the schoolboy matches as they are watched by the beast with a thousand eyes. There is not a boy on the pitches who has not observed that the only girl in the school is going for a run with the burly rower.

'So, this is where Wellington won Waterloo,' says Maxwell. 'Imagine his guns up the road, Napoleon's Imperial Guard coming in from the golf course. And then suddenly they break, they're routed and all fleeing to Datchet.' Lily giggles despite herself.

Maxwell decides the time is ripe. 'I've been thinking a lot about that party where we met.'

Oh. God.

Lily ups the pace, starts to run quite hard. What she would so love to do now is run Maxwell into the ground so that he just gives up and leaves her be. He's breathing hard, but unfortunately can still speak.

'So, what would it take…' Maxwell gasps for breath. 'Is there any way…' Maxwell has turned the colour of a tomato. 'What I mean is… Do you believe in second chances?'

Lily would be better to ignore the question altogether. But for some reason – nerves, middle-class manners – she feels she has to reply. 'I suppose so.'

'What about me… Can I have a second chance?'

Lily doesn't answer. But on the other hand, she doesn't flatten him either. No, Lily, steely, ups the pace and ups the pace, grinding him down until she is all but sprinting, and Maxwell is labouring along with her, sounding now like a broken carthorse and, in a moment, she is free, she knows it, and Maxwell galumphs to a halt.

She is thirty, forty metres clear when she hears his plaintive cry, 'Please, give me a chance!' but Lily will not be giving Maxwell even a sniff of a chance and, as she runs next to the railway line that borders Mesopotamia, she vows to never again allow herself to be trapped with that odious boy – and that is odious in both smell and behaviour.

For Maxwell, stumping back to Farrer House, it's becoming a bit of an obsession. He finds Lily not just beautiful but utterly beguiling, and so he's been rebuffed again, and so he will just lean in harder. But was it really a rebuff? She didn't actually say she wouldn't give him a second chance. She didn't say anything at all, just ran off and left him for dust.

On the football pitches, the Eton beast notes that Maxwell is no longer with the new girl. Her father Arctic, refereeing one of the matches, has also registered what looked very much like a spat.

* * *

The next morning, the morning of Cary's first proper date with Lily, Eton's Headman, Giles Moffatt, is in danger of having an apoplectic fit. Though he is only in his forties, Mr Moffatt's bristling hair has turned quite white, as has his rather martinet moustache. You would have thought that Eton's Headman would act in the way of an affable Major-General, issuing orders, sailing on serenely, and would not get too bogged down with the small stuff. But Mr Moffatt can get very agitated about even the smallest things, can work himself into a rage at the sight of a boy's uncuffed shirt sleeves – 'You are an Eton pupil, and you are on display to the world!' – and, as if it isn't bad enough that those two boys wound up drunk in the grounds of Windsor Castle, the story has now ended up being plastered all over the front page of that simply vile rag, *The Sun*. And it was written, without a trace of shame, by an Old Etonian – '*The Sun*'s Very Own Old Etonian Toff' – the odious Kim, whom Mr Moffatt very slightly remembers teaching Latin nearly 17 years ago, one of the school dunces, and how absolutely typical that he has found his true level in life by washing up at *The Sun*.

Mr Moffatt's inordinately long-suffering wife, Nicki, is well used to the Headman's eruptions, but they don't normally start over breakfast.

'What is the matter now, dear?' she asks.

'Someone has sold an Eton story to *The Sun* newspaper!' His fist thunders onto the table. 'I would not have believed it!

Some boy has got so little loyalty for his own school that he has hawked a story to the tabloids!'

'May I see it?'

Mr Moffatt tosses the paper over. He would not normally sully himself with this excrescence of a newspaper, but he was alerted to the story when Kim – may he rot in hell! – cheerily called up he, himself, the Headman of Eton, and asked for a quote. Mr Moffatt did not speak to the wretch – he might have been unable to control his volcanic bile – but listened in to the conversation, and to Kim's castor oil questions and to his secretary Miss Robinson's bland 'no comments.'

So Mr Moffatt knew the story would probably be appearing in *The Sun*, but it never occurred to him that it would be plastered all over the front page – and, very slowly, he is being forced to digest a most unpalatable piece of gristle: that, for the duration of Prince William's five-year stay at Eton, every piece of school gossip, every expulsion, will end up in the pages of the biggest-selling English-language daily on the planet! His school, his pride, his joy, will become a worldwide laughing-stock!

Nicki Moffatt, reading *The Sun*'s story, forgets herself and unwisely titters.

'What's so funny?'

'It is a little bit funny, Giles,' she says. 'They were on their way to see the Queen – as you do when you get drunk at Eton!' She paws at her mouth to literally wipe the smile off her face, but this attempt to stifle her amusement transforms her giggle into a ripe laugh.

'It's made us look like idiots!'

'It's not that bad!'

There is a knock. The dining room door opens – and in strolls Mr McCreath. Mr McCreath may look like a wizened poacher, and may wear tweed suits, and may speak with a beguiling Scottish Borders burr, but these appearances are deceptive: a former police detective, he has been in charge of Eton's security for five years now and he has an uncanny super-power: he can exactly read an Etonian's mind.

'Good morning, Headmaster,' he says. 'Good morning, Mrs Moffatt.'

'Good morning, McCreath. Well, this a fine to-do!'

'They've gone to town on this one, sir.'

'Take a seat. Tea?'

'A thimbleful.'

Mr Moffatt pours. 'First thoughts?'

Mr McCreath is rarely ruffled and can never be hurried. He takes a thoughtful sip. 'It is a very serious problem you have here, sir – and it is not going to go away. I thought at first that it might have been someone from Windsor. But not anymore. It's almost certainly a boy, probably in the Sixth Form, and well-informed. He knew that the two miscreants were gated.'

'Why's he doing it?'

Mr McCreath is bald with thin tufts of grizzled grey hair above his ears. When he is thinking, he likes to curl this hair between thick farmer's fingers. 'Lot of reasons, sir.' Mr McCreath looks at Mrs Moffatt, who is hanging on his every word. What a pleasant face she has, rather pretty. 'The money is one of the reasons, and *The Sun* will be paying him a lot. But my hunch is that it's just the thrill of the chase. He's a loner and he's a romantic. He'll see himself as the Scarlet Pimpernel—'

'They seek him there, they seek him there,' Nicki chimes in.

'Quite. This story will be the talk of the school, and he'll love the notoriety. And that will be his downfall. He won't be able to keep it to himself. He's going to tell someone. And then that someone will tell someone else, and then we will upturn his room, his house and we will find the smoking gun and we will have him.'

'What are your plans?' In his mind's eye, Mr Moffatt sees himself as a Major-General receiving a report from one of his minions and, as such, he prefers a staccato style of questioning. Terse questions are more authoritative, more leaderly, more, dash it, military.

'*The Sun*'s mole has only just started. He will sell every

story he can lay his hands on. And, eventually, he's going to make a slip. They'll be paying him a lot of money. He'll get flash. He'll boast about it to a friend. He'll buy himself something he has no right to be buying. And, like *The Sun*, our pockets are also very deep and, for the right information, we are certainly not above paying our own sources. We will get him, have no doubt about it.'

'Keep me informed.'

'I will, Headmaster. I suspect this will turn out to be a formidable problem.' Mr McCreath gets to his feet. 'I will enjoy it.'

CHAPTER 11

Unaware of the forces that are being arrayed against him, Cary has skipped lunch and is shopping in Windsor. His parents, Anthony and Penny, give him a very modest school allowance which, if he buys nothing else, allows him to buy precisely three pints of beer a week.

But, having seen that morning's Sun Splash – 'Drunk Eton Boys Break Into Windsor Castle To See Queen' – Cary knows that, for the foreseeable future, his money woes are over. He has withdrawn his entire half's allowance from the bank and is intent on blowing most of it at the best fish shop in the county. Cary is not quite sure if Lily will like seafood as much as he does, but then again, she is his love, she is his soulmate, so of course she will love seafood as much as he does.

He buys a dozen Colchester oysters, a 1.5-kilo lobster, which is still alive and which he has only ever tasted once before, and he also buys a small tin of Sevruga caviar, which he has never tried, and which costs more than the rest of the food put together. Then: potatoes, some salad, several bags of oranges and, though he'd liked to have made the pudding himself, he won't have the time, so instead buys two dainty tarts, one chocolate, one strawberry, from a delicatessen he has been past many times and always been tempted by, but never before entered.

Fergie and Renton, who in so far as they have a position at The Project are the joint managers, have just finished their own late lunch of sausage sarnies, and are enjoying their tea on the pavement bench. They are tickled pink that Cary and Lily will be having their first date at The Project.

'Got it all nice for you, Cary,' says Fergie.

'Thank you, gents,' Cary says. 'I'll bet she's going to love it.'

He goes through the hall, with all its fold-up chairs and its square Formica tables, and into the kitchen, where he turns on the deep-fat fryer and puts a pot of water on the boil. He is a blur of activity, one moment peeling and slicing, and the next squeezing the oranges and, between all that, he's dicing cucumber and feta for a crisp Greek salad, but thinks better of the red onion, as more than likely, there will also be kissing and it would be a shame to mar it with onion breath.

This is how Lily finds her Cary when she comes into the kitchen. She stands in the doorway and watches with fascinated delight as he shucks oysters like he's been doing it all his life. She is wearing her very prettiest summer dress, with flowers of all colours, and some beige loafers; when you're as pretty as Lily, less is always more.

He looks up, catches her in the act, and beams. 'I'm not the oyster-shucker. I'm the oyster-shucker's son—'

'And you're only shucking oysters till the oyster-shucker comes!'

'Indeed I am!'

He puts down the knife, washes and then wipes his hands on his apron. He walks over to Lily and, like seasoned lovers, they slip naturally into each other's arms. They hold each other tight, and not a word needs to be said, because when they are like this, nothing else much matters, for all is right with the world. They look at each other and smile and still can't quite believe it, that they each of them are hugging this stranger they hardly know, but who gives every indication of being just as besotted as they are. And they kiss, chaste, and they kiss, less chaste, more pursued, and one more kiss, with perhaps a dash of ardour, a tiny tip, but when you've got the rest of your lives to spend with each other, then, in the matter of kisses, it's often more enjoyable to take the scenic route.

The alarm beeps and the lobster's 14 minutes are up and, after one last squeeze, Cary grabs some tongs and takes the lobster out of the roiling water.

'I hope you're hungry!' Cary slices the steaming lobster in half.

'I'm starved!' Lily comes over and, as Cary fries off the last of the blinis, she puts her arms around him. Now how good does that feel? She barely knows him, but what she does know is that it feels right. 'The boys were eating like horses and all I could do was poke my stew round the plate!'

'I hope I've made it worth your while!'

He leans round, kisses her – could he ever, ever have enough of her kisses? – and flips the blinis.

'Course you have,' Lily says. 'I'd go without lunch for just a single Cary kiss.'

Cary laughs gleefully, kisses her, and slides the blinis into a Tupperware box, before loading all his luncheon booty into a large wicker basket.

'A guy who boils lobsters, who makes his own blinis!'

'Didn't make the pudding – I've yet to learn the intricacies of being a *pâtissier*.'

'Where are we eating?'

'Follow me.'

He picks up the wicker basket and, taking Lily by the hand – is this really the first time they've held hands? – he leads her up the stairs, and up the next flight of stairs, past the bedrooms, and up the next flight too, past more and more bedrooms.

'Are we going to the attic?'

'Sort of.'

'How exciting!'

At the far end of the third floor, in the bathroom, an old wooden ladder has been stapled to the wall. Cary slings the basket over his shoulder and climbs the ladder. Up at the ceiling, he flips open the trapdoor and, a moment later, he's in the attic.

'Come on up!'

The attic is vast and dingy, lit only by a window at the end and a skylight. It stretches the length of The Project and is filled with all manner of clutter that has been dumped there over the years; suitcases left for safekeeping, an entire kitchen range, boxes and boxes of china, all sorts of machines, most of them dead, and enough chairs and beds and dressers to start a hotel.

'Where did all this stuff come from?' Lily wipes a cobweb off her cheek. 'There's tons of it!'

'It's a black hole. Once something goes in, it can never get out.'

'And we're having lunch here?'

'We could do.' Cary goes to the eaves and pushes open the skylight. A brilliant white rectangle of sunshine carves into the gloom. Cary steps onto a packing case and out to the roof. Lily follows.

The view is so unexpected, so extraordinary, that all Lily can do is goggle. Up above them looms Windsor Castle, below is the Thames winding its way to London, and spread all before them is Eton with its pinnacled chapel and its playing fields. The Project roof is M-shaped; two long gables side by side, separated by a long flat three-metre-wide strip. It is on this long strip that they are going to have lunch. That morning, Fergie and Renton dug out one of the nicer tables, round, cast-iron, from the attic, as well as two cane chairs and a wooden sun-lounger, complete with blue speckled cushions. They've even found, or perhaps liberated, a parasol, so that Lily and Cary will not have to fry in the afternoon heat. And since those two old gents adore both Cary and Lily, they've really gone the extra mile. There is a white linen tablecloth, silver cutlery that positively sparkles in the sunshine, white napkins and a jug of iced water.

'Oh, Cary!' Lily says. 'This is… this is…'

And because this whole experience is so utterly overwhelming, and because she has come from a school of fairly hard knocks, and because she has certainly never been doted on like this before, she starts to cry.

'It's beautiful,' she says, smiling through her tears.

Cary offers her a handkerchief. 'Those old boys have done me proud. I'll have to cook them up something extra special tonight.'

Arms slung round each other's waist, they walk the length of the gables to explore their new fiefdom. They are all but hidden from view, and the only people who can possibly espy them are the hawk-eyed guards on the battlements of Windsor Castle's Round Tower.

Lily watches as Cary deftly pours the fresh-squeezed orange juice and tops it up with San Pellegrino. They chink, they kiss and Cary raises his glass.

'To the first of our many meals together.'

'I do hope so.'

And they kiss again, softly at first, and then, just as Lily likes it, and just as it is so surely meant to be, her mouth blooms under his, and his arm eases around her back, and, thigh to thigh, they realise that, in the matter of lips and kisses, they are a perfect dovetail.

'Cary,' she says. 'I don't know you. I hardly know you at all. And yet it feels like I've come home.'

'Speaking for myself, these kisses, they are a ten.'

'You speak for me too.'

'Thank the Lord – imagine if I thought they were a ten, and you were only giving them a three.'

Cary brings out the oysters and, though Lily has never tried them before, she squeezes the lemon juice and eats with gusto. They try the caviar with cream and without, and decide that it's much over-rated and they might as well be eating lumpfish caviar. The hit of the day is the lobster. Cary pours over melted butter that's been infused with garlic. They smash the claws with a claw-hammer and eat the white meat with their fingers, the butter dripping down their chins. It gives Cary such joy to see Lily devouring the very last cindery scrap of the chips and to know that she has an appetite and that she's up for new tastes and new textures.

They have been talking of this and that, and delighting in plumbing the minutiae of each other's lives, and Lily has even learned why Cary has such an extraordinary super-white smile – his father is a dentist, and his mother a hygienist.

And, just in passing, Lily happens to mention the Headman's harangue in the School Hall.

'What did you make of the Headman's talk this morning?'

'I wasn't there.' Cary tops up her glass. 'They had me doing the roster in the Lower Chapel. What did he say?'

'He was very upset about the front page of today's Sun, and he especially wanted to know who had sold the story.'

'He just expected the tipster to own up, so he could then have the pleasure of expelling the boy.'

'Suppose it was worth a try. Perhaps the tipster is suffering from guilt pangs.'

'So, how did he know the mole was a boy? Could have been a member of staff. Could have been somebody from the Castle security – or the cops. Why does he think it's a boy?'

'Who knows?' she says and, as she says this, she looks at Cary, and it could be that she already knows him all too well, but she detects a whiff of a change in his demeanour, and a quiet instinctive hiss slithers through her head, and she knows for a certainty that Cary knows much more than he is telling. And where, oh where, has all this largesse, this caviar, these oysters, this lobster come from when, or so her sources have told her, Cary is on a full scholarship?

CHAPTER 12

Cary had finished cooking supper for Windsor's homeless, chicken stew this time, thick with vegetables, and with a couple of bottles of white wine thrown in for good measure, and as he mooched back to The Timbralls, he was on something of a high – he was in love and he was in funds, and he had a secret which he hugged tightly to himself. He'd almost blurted it out to Lily, told her that he was the Eton agent who'd sold the story to *The Sun*, but at the last moment, had held back. What had Kim explicitly instructed him? Don't tell a soul – and he supposed that probably meant he shouldn't tell Lily, but on the other hand, and since he'd have trusted her with his life, that also meant she could be entrusted with his career at Eton.

Cary breezed into the Timbralls lobby, trotted up to the top floor and was on his way to the toilets at the far end, when he walked past Bruno's room. He heard the oddest sound, a cross between a choke and a laugh. He knocked on the door.

He found Bruno and Viktor, both now gated and having to discover fresh ways of amusing themselves. Viktor had brought a dozen amyl nitrate poppers to the party.

They were both in full school uniform, tails and waistcoats, and Bruno had a tight noose round his neck. From chin to forehead, his entire face was bright red. The noose had been made from Bruno's dressing-gown cord. Viktor was happily playing the other end of the cord to keep it tight.

'Are you completely mad?' Cary said. 'What are you doing?'

'A popper for a Popper?' Viktor said. He was, or so he'd

led the boys to believe, the son of a rich Russian banker – one of the fabled Oligarchs who'd got criminally rich after the fall of the USSR. 'They are fantastic, Cary! They give you instant high. It is called spastic orgasm. It is not as good as real orgasm. But it is close.'

'Why the noose?'

Bruno eased the cord from around his throat. 'Auto-asphyxiation, Cary. Do you not know anything?'

Cary flopped onto the sofa. 'I know a lot of things but I didn't know you could get a thrill out of strangling yourself.'

'It is well known,' Viktor said. 'It cut the oxygen to your brain and it give you rush. Try it with a popper and it even more of a rush.'

'Anything else I should be trying?' Cary said. 'Shall I hit your knee a few times with a hammer? Maybe a little painful at first, but you'll love it when I stop.'

'That sounds very exciting!' Bruno said. 'Let us just try it!'

'I was joking, you idiot!' Cary said.

'I will try anything once—'

'Apart from sodomy and Cossack dancing,' Viktor said.

'Certainly not the Cossack dancing.'

Cary inspected one of the poppers, a two-inch gunmetal bottle with a rip-seal. 'Do I drink it?'

'That bad,' Viktor said. 'You sniff them. Want me to choke you a little? I would like that.'

'No, thank you.'

'You have no guts!'

'What's it do?'

'I can tell you precisely,' said Bruno. 'It increases the blood-flow to the heart. They were used to treat angina. But now, how ferry lucky for us,' (the one quirk of Bruno's perfect English was that he pronounced his 'Vs' with a soft 'F') 'is that the poppers haff come into the hands of students and sex club addicts.'

Cary sat on the edge of the sofa, pulled off the popper top, took a tentative sniff and then inhaled. It was like very strong solvent. Within moments, he had a euphoric head rush and, as quickly as it had come, it was gone, leaving him a little dizzy and tinged with gloom, as if he had forgotten something of the utmost import.

While Bruno retied the noose, Viktor looked on expectantly.

'What do you think? You like it, no?'

'I'm not sure,' Cary said. 'The rush was quite nice. But I'm feeling light-headed.'

'It is Newton's third rule of drugs – for every high, there must be an equal and opposite low,' Bruno said.

'This low doesn't seem like equal and opposite! The high only lasted a few seconds, and this feels like it's going to last for ages!'

'But what a high it was!' Bruno said, placing the noose round his neck again and turning to Viktor. 'Would it be more effective if I put the noose knot on my carotid artery?'

'We shall experiment.' Viktor grabbed another popper. 'In time, we will have found all necessary ingredients for perfect spastic orgasm.'

'A spastically perfect orgasm?'

'For me,' Viktor said, 'any orgasm perfect.'

Cary got up. 'I'll leave you two to experiment with your imperfect spasms.'

'Where are you going?'

'Clear my head with a run.'

Five minutes later, late afternoon glow in the sky, Cary was running hard over Agar's and Dutchman's. He hadn't been aiming to run there, but almost by default, he ended up at the athletics track. In those days, it was an old cinder track with a rickety pavilion – nothing flash about Eton athletics in the 1990s, but now it's all gone, cinders replaced with a proper track and a proper athletics centre, all state-of-the-art but with none of the history and none of the charm.

A small boy in white shorts and Eton's purple athletics shirt was running round the track. It was Barty Pleydell-Bouverie, not just the smallest boy in Eton but the smallest boy for three straight years in a row. He was 15, quite desperate to hit puberty, and eking out his ire on the running track.

'Looking good, Barty.'

Barty trotted to a stop and bent over to catch his breath, hands almost touching the ground. He looked up, smiled. 'You should see me when I look bad.'

'Fancy some Fartlek training?'

'With you?' Though they were both runners, they were long-distance loners; they'd never run together. 'Yes!'

They trotted round the track in companionable silence. Cary was the first to spot their housemaster, Mr Ormerod, sitting on plumped-up pillows in the pavilion. Of an afternoon, Mr Ormerod would often flee the boredom of the house matches to seek the solace of the pavilion. They waved at him.

'My dad did this cool race last year,' Barty said, by way of making conversation. 'You'd be brilliant.'

'What is it?'

'It's called Tough Guy. It's muddy. And it's tough.'

'How tough?'

'Miles and miles of mud. And there's an assault course.' Barty beamed. He'd got a lovely toothy grin, deliriously happy to be running alongside Cary. 'Please let's do it. It'll be fun!'

'Ready for the sprint?'

'Hit me.'

They ran flat out, Barty's little legs pistoning. For an instant, he was ahead, but Cary cruised alongside. He didn't run past Barty, he chummed him.

'And 300 metres easy,' Cary said. 'Tell me about the assault course.'

'It's got tunnels filled with mud!' Barty said. 'And wires to give you electric shocks! But the best bit, my dad said, was jumping off a five-metre plank into a freezing pond. He got an ice cream headache! Will you do it?'

'I'll think about it.'

Sprint again, jog again, dream of Lily again.

'Will you do it?'

'How are we going to get there?'

'Ormerod will take us. My dad will take us. Who cares how we get there?'

Another sprint, Mr Ormerod contentedly watching from the pavilion.

'Will you do it?'

'Can I think about it?'

'You're normally so positive!'

And so they loped along and so Cary mulled it over. Mud and electric shocks and dank, dark tunnels and, always, and as ever, Lily's kisses. 'When is it?'

'January!' piped Barty. 'Sometimes, it's so cold the pond freezes over. You change in a barn – and there's not a shower in sight. Will you do it?'

'And sprint.'

But it would make quite a change from running round the track – round and round, and round and round; might be a step up.

Barty was gasping. 'Please?'

Cary still wasn't sure. Painful, pointless and ultimately futile… He noticed Ormerod waving a wine bottle in the air.

'Cary!' Ormerod called. 'You couldn't give me a hand with this Sancerre!'

'Of course, sir.' Cary jogged over, took the bottle and pulled the cork in one. 'Everything shipshape?'

'And Bristol fashion, my dear boy – how beautifully you run, a gazelle on the savannah, or perhaps Desert Orchid in the Cheltenham Gold Cup.'

On the table beside him, Mr Ormerod had set a small wicker hamper. It contained, as it usually did, a bottle of Châteauneuf-du-Pape, four handsome rummers, some Emmenthal cheese and a small rustic salami. Since graduating from Homerton, Cambridge – gosh, how he'd loved those formal dinners! – Mr Ormerod had worked in a number of schools before finding his correct station at Eton College. He suited its history and its quaint traditions very nicely.

'I've been finding the corks on these old bottles more and more problematical, Cary.' Mr Ormerod said.

'Try one of those gas pump corkscrews?' Cary asked.

'Yes, I've heard of those new-fangled things, but on the other hand, I do so love my Laguiole.' He picked up the corkscrew, with its curved ebony handle, and gave it an affectionate kiss. 'Care for a glass of Sancerre or does your training preclude alcohol?' he said, before calling out to Barty, who was still lurking by the track. 'Barty! Come and have a drink!'

Mr Ormerod poured three glasses. Barty, utterly tongue-tied – he was having a glass of wine with the housemaster and the house captain! – took a shy sip.

'See this corkscrew?' Mr Ormerod said, wagging it at Barty. 'It belonged to my grandfather when he served with the Royal Lancashires in the First World War. I like to think of him in the trenches with his mess-mates, opening bottles of claret with it – this! This very corkscrew! Made to the same design that dear Jean-Pierre Calmels first conjured in Laguiole in 1829.' He sighed and dabbed at his eyes with his silk handkerchief. 'It was the last present his wife – my grandmama Dolly – ever gave him.'

'Oh?' said Cary. He stood on the pavilion step, dropping his left heel to stretch his Achilles. 'What happened – if you don't mind my asking?'

Mr Ormerod swirled the rummer and took the smallest of sips, lips smacking with pleasure. 'I adore the ritual of pouring the wine as much as I do the drinking,' he said. 'So, my Grandfather Rodney, he was only 23 at the start of the war, newly married, his whole life ahead of him – what dreams he had! He was an English teacher – like me. He taught at Blackpool Grammar. How I would have loved to have met him.' He broke off to cut himself a slice from the Chorizo Iberico. 'Want some?'

'No, thank you.'

'So, the war starts, and his friends are signing up, and his pupils are signing up, and there is Rodney wanging on about Restoration tragedies, of all things, when he knows what he ought to be doing is killing Germans, so the dear fellow signs up and, just before he goes off to the front, his young wife gives him this beautiful corkscrew. It was on him when he was blown up at Passchendaele – July 31st, 1917 – blown up so completely that this, my beautiful Laguiole, was one of the few things that was left of him. It still has a splinter of shrapnel in the handle! In due course, it was returned to my grandmama and, six months later, she gave birth to my father, Rodney.' He paused and ever so delicately cut the rind off the salami. 'They gave him a posthumous Military Cross – and I have that too, but what I treasure above all else is this corkscrew. Even if I live to be a hundred, I will not uncork a bottle with anything else – though I may need more friends like you to wield it!'

'What a sad story.'

'It is sad, yes – but life-affirming too. Rodney knew he was probably going to die in the trenches. So, he seized every moment. Every night, every single night, he was partying like there was no tomorrow – because one day, he knew, there would be no tomorrow.' Mr Ormerod looked up and smiled. 'And here is our good friend, Mr Barne!' He waved vigorously at the man who was beetling up the track towards them. 'Barne, my dear fellow,' he called. 'May I tempt you to a glass?'

Mr Barne nodded to Barty and gave Cary a pat on the back as he shuffled into the pavilion to sit next to Mr Ormerod. 'Cheers, m'dears!'

Mr Barne was, like Mr Ormerod, one of that special breed of beaks who might not fit quite so well at any other school, but who were a perfect fit for Eton. Wiry to Mr Ormerod's plump, small to Mr Ormerod's tall, and Edinburgh Morningside to Mr Ormerod's Midlands, Mr Barne's greying hair was Brylcreemed to military perfection, not a single rogue hair in that thick thatch and, as for his trim moustache, that alone took up a full 15 minutes of his morning ablutions. He taught History and Cary was one of his especial favourites. Such hopes, such dreams, he had for the boy – and quietly, ever so delicately, he had been trying to instil in Cary the idea that there could be no higher calling in life than to read History at Cambridge University. But whenever the matter came up, Cary, that brilliant, infuriating boy, would so uncivilly insist on sitting upon the fence, blast him!

'How are you, boys?' he asked, fingers automatically straying to the snuffbox in his waistcoat pocket. 'What are we in training for now?'

Cary gave his most winning smile. He hadn't been quite sure when he'd trotted over to the pavilion. Now he was certain.

'Barty's had an idea, sir,' Cary said.

He stood on the steps, twirling his wine glass, Michelangelo's David made flesh, and the two middle-aged men goggled; they were in heaven.

'I'm sure it will be a good one, then.' Mr Ormerod laughed – because he knew, he just knew, that he was about to be tapped up.

Cary had this incredible knack for getting people to do exactly what he wanted. You could come out with all sorts of reasons why his ideas were outlandish, impossible, but in the end, he always talked you round and, in the end, you did what he wanted. Because you liked him – and, very occasionally, because it was a good idea. God knows where it would all eventually take him, but Mr Ormerod was agog to find out.

'It's in January, sir… and we were rather hoping you'd drive us there, give us moral support.'

'So what is it – amaze me!' Though it was September, Mr Ormerod was feeling a little flushed. He eased at his starched stick-ups with a dainty fingertip.

'It's a race, sir. A race which Barty and I would like to take part in – along with anyone else in the house who wants to come.'

'I think Cary could win it!' Barty piped.

'A race in January?' Mr Ormerod mused. 'Some sort of steeplechase?'

'It's called Tough Guy, sir.'

'Tough Guy?' Mr Ormerod shivved a sliver of salami and passed it to Mr Barne. 'Does this sound like your sort of thing, Barne? Are you a Tough Guy?'

'A tough guy?' squawked Mr Barne. 'Dear me, no! I am a cerebral guy. A passionate guy.'

He took a pinch of snuff, Copenhagen Long Cut, and placed it into his anatomical snuff box, the long thin triangular indent on the back of the hand between wrist and cocked thumb. He sniffed and let out a volcanic sneeze, before squinting at the sky through watery eyes and letting off another almighty sneeze.

'Do you have to buy the strongest snuff in existence?' Mr Ormerod said. 'You'll do yourself a mischief.'

Mr Barne dabbed at his nose, before continuing as if absolutely nothing had happened, 'I am an endearing guy. An affable, congenial guy. I am a modest, upright gentleman of a guy. But a tough guy – absolutely not.'

'And nor have you ever been – thank the Lord!' The two men delightedly chinked their glasses together. 'Cheers!'

'Will you drive us there – it's in Staffordshire?'

'Drive you there?' Mr Ormerod said. 'We'll make an outing of it. Why, by the way, do they call it Tough Guy?'

'Isn't it obvious, my dear Ormerod?' Mr Barne said. 'The race is a complete breeze. All you have to do is turn up to this, this Staffordshire bog, and they give you a medal. On a plate!'

'Quite right, sir,' Cary said. 'It should, in fact, be called Easy Guy.'

'And will there be much mud?' inquired Mr Ormerod.

'It's all mud.'

'Oh, goody.' Mr Barne probed into his snuffbox again as Mr Ormerod clapped his hands to his ears. 'You'll have to start beasting yourselves on the assault course.'

CHAPTER 13

What a kerfuffle it was, getting Agent Orange's money – though to be fair to the lad, Agent Orange was going to have much, much more of a kerfuffle spending it.

The Sun's news editor, Robert, correctly suspecting that my source was an Eton schoolboy, had been all for stumping up a measly £2,000.

'Two grand?' I laughed in disbelief. 'For an exclusive Splash! You have got to be joking! This guy, I don't know who he is, but I'm pretty sure he's on Eton's security team and he's going to want top dollar. He's not going to risk his job for two grand!'

Stella was listening intently as she busied herself with the diary. She knew perfectly well that my Eton mole was a schoolboy. I gave her a cheery wink.

'Do you think he might go for six grand?' Robert said.

'Of course he will, but what I do know is that Eton is going to provide a very rich seam of stories over the next five years, and what I don't want is for this guy to go off to somewhere like the Screws, just because he thinks he can get more money.'

'Yes,' Robert said. 'Quite.'

It would be bad enough losing an Eton source to *The Mirror*, but to lose him to *The Sun*'s sister paper, *The News of the World*, would be unconscionable. And anyway… it had been an okay Splash, maybe a little bit of stretching about the business of the boys wanting to see the Queen, but a good story, which had got Robert out of a hole on a newsless Wednesday. Besides: *The Sun* was making more than a million a week, most of which was being poured into those thundering cash-drains Sky TV and *The Times*, so why not spread the love?

'Ten grand?'

I thought about going harder, but ten grand would be fine for Agent Orange's first outing.

'Thank you – that will do the trick nicely.'

A very special yellow form was filled out, then signed and counter-signed by the news editor, the managing editor and the editor himself. I took the form to the News International bank on the ground floor and, if the Internal Revenue inspectors could have seen what happened next, they would have had a complete seizure. The form was passed through the security tray and, after a short phone call, I received three inch-high bricks of used £20 notes, all made out to one Agent Orange and not a penny of tax to be paid on any of it. Trickier to do that today, but in 1995, *The Sun*'s most secret tipsters were all paid in hard cash. (This all changed a few years later, when tipsters' payments had to go through the books – and in consequence, all of News International's most secret, secret sources, all of those high-ranking police officers, all of those Ministry of Defence mandarins, found themselves caught up in Operation Elveden, and a fair few ended up in jail. Sometimes, it would seem, the old ways really are the best.)

I was meeting Agent Orange in the Truva restaurant, just outside Waterloo. Probably all gone now, but in those days, the Truva was a jolly Turkish restaurant, with white plastic tablecloths, and pictures of Truva (Troy), Istanbul and the springs at Pammukkale. I'd arrived 20 minutes early, taken my favourite seat, right in the far corner, with a commanding view of the whole restaurant, and Agent Orange strolled in ten minutes later. We inspected each other as we shook hands. God knows what he made of me, just another drone in a pinstripe suit, but as for Agent Orange, he was tall and lean, with a dazzling smile and the most amazing blue eyes; absolute cat-nip for girls, without a doubt.

A waistcoated waiter brought over apple teas, Turkish coffees and plates of baklava.

'I've never tried Turkish before,' he said, taking a sip of the apple tea, and taking in the pictures. 'Ian Fleming sends his best.'

I laughed and stirred brown sugar into the gloop. 'Does he now, the old rogue?' I said. 'Well send him my love when you next see him!'

'Haven't seen him for a little while.' He bit into the baklava, pastry flakes pittering onto the table.

'Fleming doesn't do chit-chat. You'll only see him when he has something to say.'

'I rather guessed that.'

'I've brought you some money. How much do you think I've got?'

He patted his mouth with a paper napkin, wondering if he was being tested. Of course he was being tested. 'Maybe a thousand? That'd be nice.'

'It would.'

He watched as I opened my briefcase. 'Three grand,' I said, putting a thick brown envelope on the table. I brought out another envelope, placed it on top of the first. 'Six grand.' I smiled. 'Is there more?'

'I didn't think there was. But now you've asked, I know there is.'

'You're good.' I placed the third brown envelope on top of the two others. 'Ten grand in used twenties. That's your lot.'

'Ten thousand pounds!' He opened one of the envelopes, gave the money a riffle. 'Thank you!'

'Plenty more where that came from.'

'And there's going to be plenty more stories for you to write about! May I take the money? It all looks a bit dodgy sitting there on the table.'

'Like I've just bought a kilo of coke.' My pager bleeped.

As ever, and as always, it was the news desk. The more you're enjoying yourself, the greater the likelihood that the news desk will wreck the party. 'Do you know, Agent Orange, that we make a lot of cash payments like this – and that some of my more unscrupulous colleagues keep a large chunk of the money for themselves. The cheeky bastards only give you half or even a quarter of the sum they've actually drawn out from the bank!'

'But you wouldn't do that.' He zipped the envelopes into his bag.

'Certainly not!' I said. 'I may have some rat-like cunning, but I wouldn't dream of stiffing a contact. Besides – you know what sometimes happens? After a short while, contacts get fed up and call the news desk to complain about the derisory amounts of cash they've been receiving... and then... the news editor realises these most secret sources are only being paid half their due, all is revealed and another epic Fleet Street career has gone up in smoke!'

'What advice have you got for me?'

'Yes,' I said. 'I've got to go in three minutes. The number one rule is that you've got to be very, very careful how you spend this money. If they get wind of you suddenly buying yourself fancy new clothes, then they will absolutely turn your room over, under the drawers, into the mattress, beneath the floorboards. If you hide anything in your room, they will find it.'

'Got it – no conspicuous consumption.'

'Good for the soul. These stories are a much bigger deal now that Prince William's there. And that means they'll be much more embarrassing.'

'All the more for me.'

'Correct!' I dug into my jacket pocket. 'This is the very latest Motorola pager, all paid up for the next year. Hide it somewhere it will never be found, keep it on silent, check it occasionally. I'll only page you if it's important.'

'Is there any particular kind of story you're looking for?'

'Give us all the gossip you've got.' We stood up and I planted a £20 note on the table. 'Though, rather bizarrely, the only stories we can't run are anything at all concerning our young Prince.'

'Goodbye, Kim.'

'I think this is the beginning of a beautiful friendship,' I said, before presciently adding, 'and remember now! Don't get caught!'

CHAPTER 14

Over the next 24 hours, Cary will ignore two of the strictures that have just been laid down for him in the Truva.

At best – at very best – he thought *The Sun* might have swung to a couple of thousand. But ten grand! He won't even risk having his rucksack on his back, but instead holds it tight in his hand.

Rather than meekly returning to Eton, he catches the Tube to central London to buy some presents. Cary has never been jewellery shopping before, but he certainly knows of a place that will be only too pleased to relieve him of his money, and that is New Bond Street. And again, though he doesn't know many jewellers, he has heard of a place called Cartier. Though he is just wearing jeans and a hoodie, he walks straight in.

'How may I help you, sir?' says a woman in her early twenties, a senior sales representative, according to her name-tag, who is called Fiona. Fiona has an immaculately coiffed brown bob, makeup just so, the sort of woman who wouldn't even have given Cary a second glance, except that he is now standing in front of Cartier's showcase of rings. He looks like he's ready to buy.

She quickly sizes him up – dressed shambolically. Certainly doesn't look like he's got the cash. Doesn't look like he should be anywhere near New Bond Street.

But on the other hand… he might just be rich. It's so difficult to tell these days! She has no idea whether she's dealing with a hobo or the son of a billionaire.

Cary smiles, warm and genuine. 'I'm so sorry for my dishevelled appearance, Fiona,' he says. 'I didn't know I'd be coming here today. But I've had something of a windfall and I wanted to buy a ring for my girlfriend.'

Fiona warms to this oddly endearing boy. 'You've come to the right place, then.' She slides from behind her counter and unlocks the case. 'What sort of ring are you looking for?'

Cary inspects the rings; the gaudy diamonds, the sapphires, the rubies. 'I think that one, please, Fiona.'

'The Cartier Tank – gorgeous.' Fiona takes the ring out of the case and passes it to Cary. 'Eighteen-carat gold, with a square-cut citrine. Understated. Beautiful.'

Cary tosses the ring in his hand. 'I'm not sure about the size.' He looks at Fiona's hands. 'She's got lovely fingers – like yours. Would you try?'

'Of course.' The tank ring slips intimately onto the ring finger of her right hand.

Cary admires the ring. 'Perfect,' he says. 'How much?'

'One thousand, eight hundred and fifty pounds.'

'Discount for cash?'

'Ahh, well.' Fiona falters. It's not the sort of question she's ever been asked before in Cartier.

'My grandmother does not believe in banks,' he says. 'One of the problems of being caught up in the war in Germany. So, instead of writing me a cheque, she gives me cash.'

Being one of Cartier's senior sales representatives, Fiona is allowed a certain amount of latitude when it comes to the clientele, particularly the nicer ones. 'For cash?' she says. 'I suppose we could go to ten per cent off?'

'Call it sixteen hundred and you've got a deal.'

'Well...' Fiona has never given a fifteen per cent discount in her life! 'All right, then.'

'Thank you, Fiona, you're very kind.'

While Fiona gives the ring a polish and tucks it into Cartier's iconic red box, Cary discreetly tries to pull out £1,600 from one of the wads, cursing himself for not doing it earlier.

Fiona not only sees the brown envelope but glimpses the two others in the rucksack. It has already crossed her mind that the grandmother story is moonshine and that this silver-tongued charmer might just as easily have pinched the money.

'And who shall I make the receipt out to?'

'Lord Ormerod, please. Of Glencore.'

'Glencore? I've never heard of that.'

'Just a little place we have in the country.'

'Lovely.' Cary counts out the money on the desktop and is handed the receipt and the ring box.

'Thank you, Fiona.'

With a wave, he is gone, and Fiona has to take a seat because she's still not quite sure what has just happened, but there lurks the suspicion that she has just been on the receiving end of a heist. Lord Ormerod of Glencore, indeed! She counts the notes again, examines them closely, and has the horrid suspicion that Lord Ormerod has passed off a wad of forgeries.

Cary just has time to trickle into the kitchen department at Peter Jones on Sloane Square, where he haggles for five minutes before catching the train back to Eton. He sits directly behind the driver in the first seat of the first carriage, and ponders where he will find a hidey-hole in The Timbralls for his money and his new Motorola pager, a place that must be close to hand but also utterly secret.

* * *

Done with the tedium of evenings in Farrer House, Lily is off to the movies to see, of all films, South Pacific. McArdle, the master in charge, has loved this musical since he first saw it as a small child with his mother; he can't get enough of the film and, like all of the best teachers, he's out to infect his pupils with his own peccadillo. It is now an Eton tradition that, every September at the start of the school year, Mr McArdle screens South Pacific.

By chance – perhaps – a funny little chap from the house, Fredster Campbell, is heading in the same direction. He's a year younger than Lily, which is fortunate, because – or so she fancifully thinks – that means he will have no designs on becoming her boyfriend. These infernal boys are just everywhere, clamouring for attention, chatting her up, staring soulfully into her eyes; when could they just please leave her be? Apart from one very special Etonian, and Cary can do with her as he pleases. In fact, not that the kissing and the hugging aren't blissful, but she hopes that, sooner rather than later, she might get to do with Cary exactly as **she** pleases.

But for the moment, Fredster is fine, a pup bouncing along beside her, thrilled to be talking to the only teenage girl in six square miles.

'Do you know what the film's about?' Fredster yaps.

'A guy and a woman falling in love,' Lily says.

'Bet they split up halfway through. That's what happens in every single love story I've ever seen. It makes me sick!'

'But they'll get back together by the end.'

'And that makes me even more sick! Why can't the story end with them splitting up? That's what happens with most relationships.'

Lily happens to look up. She knows it's him immediately – from his height, from his walk, from the pheromones that make her blush.

'Such a cynical head on such young shoulders,' she says to Fredster.

They walk over the Parade Ground, where thousands upon thousands of Eton Rifles have marched and saluted, and arrive at the world's most lavish school theatre, the Farrer Theatre, with 400 creamy leather seats, a cinema, and stage enough for an all-singing, all-dancing musical.

Cary holds the door open for Bruno and, catching sight of Lily, keeps it open. They haven't seen each other that day and this chance meeting provokes an almost Pavlovian response. They are hungry for their lover's kisses.

But they are wisely wary about being seen to be in love at Eton, so this evening, there is unlikely to be any illicit kissing.

'Welcome,' he says.

'Thank you.' Lily catches his complicit eye and they share a secret smile.

Cary catches a trace of her musky perfume, severely more potent than that poxed popper of amyl nitrate.

Since becoming an Etonienne, Lily takes much more care with her clothes and her appearance – and that's not just for Cary. She knows that the very moment she walks into the theatre, she will undergo the most minute scrutiny from every boy in the room. She is so used to it now that she carries herself like a queen, displaying an attitude of the most lofty indifference. Be damned to all these slobbering teenagers!

She follows Fredster into the theatre, and the pulse of conversation tremors for a second, as the cinema-goers swallow the uneasy fact that they're being joined by a girl.

Fredster leads the way up to a pair of seats near the back row. 'This all right for you?'

'Champion.'

The boys in front of Lily are lumpen 14-year-olds, so see nothing wrong in turning round to gawk at her.

Fredster sees them off. 'Haven't you seen a girl before?'

'Not a girl at Eton, no.'

'Where's your manners?'

'It's all right, Fredster,' Lily says. 'A cat may look at a queen.'

'Miaow!'

Another miaow, and another miaow, and after a minute of Chinese Whispers, the whole theatre is alive with the cats' miaows.

McArdle, about to watch his favourite film for the 74th time, pats his Parsons terrier on the head and yells, 'Simmer down – your cats are scaring my dog!'

'Toe-rags!' hisses Fredster.

Lily laughs and forgets for a moment that she is the object

of such singular attention. She watches as Cary comes in with, presumably, his friend Bruno. And as she watches Cary, Fredster watches her.

McArdle has managed to cast his spell over Lily. She loves South Pacific every bit as much as McArdle did when he first saw the film with his mum – so many great songs, though as she artlessly tells Fredster, her favourite is when the girls are singing about washing that man right out of their hair.

When the lights go up, she looks for a last glimpse of her Cary, but he has already disappeared.

They're among the last to leave.

'It's brilliant!' bubbles Fredster. 'It's my new favourite film! Thank you, sir!'

McArdle beams. 'Glad you liked it, Fredster.'

'Thank you, Mr McArdle,' Lily says. 'I'm going to buy the music.'

'The live show is even better.'

Lily leaves Fredster, to head into the world's most underused toilet, Eton College's Ladies Powder Room.

The Powder Room smells heavenly, gardenia at a guess, with floor and walls of white marble and four handsome cubicles.

She notices that one of the doors is locked. The heavy oak door swings open. Cary is standing there with a red rose between his teeth.

'Ahh,' she says, gliding into his arms. 'I wondered where you'd got to.'

Cary tucks the rose behind her ear and kisses her. 'I wondered if you'd find your way in here.'

'I followed your scent like a bloodhound.'

They kiss and they kiss and, with each kiss, they become ever more ardent, hands roaming downwards to pluck at zippers and tease through tense cotton. They break apart, and stand and stare.

'Don't take this the wrong way, Cary, darling.'

'I won't.'

'But your kisses are leaving me rather unsatisfied.'

'They're more a prelude.'

'A wonderful prelude.'

'Never had a prelude like them.'

'But I think I'm about ready to start on the main course.'

Lily kisses him again, adjusts her dress, primps her hair and, refreshed and renewed, she leaves the Ladies Powder Room to find Fredster still waiting for her.

'Good to go?' he asks.

'Very much so.'

'You've acquired a red rose since I last saw you.'

'So I have,' she says, smiling as her hand brushes her ear.

* * *

As Mr McArdle locks up, Cary discreetly leaves the Farrer Theatre to find Bruno sitting on the steps, tippling on cherry brandy.

'Like some?' He offers the bottle to Cary.

'Thank you.' Cary takes a swig, coughs; it's got quite a kick.

'So she found you?' Bruno eases himself up. 'I have just seen her leave. She looked like she had been kissing an angel. Tell me, Cary, this ladies' powder room, what is it like?'

'Classy. You'd like it. Freshly laundered hand-towels. Padded loo seats. A scent rack filled with all the classic perfumes. Every conceivable kind of makeup; lipsticks, mascaras, blushers. Taps made of solid gold. A shower with a large variety of citrus unguents. And should the ladies care to relax, there are two armchairs, a La-Z- Boy and a television. A small fridge with two bottles of Champagne. Some cashews and a large box of Milk Tray—'

'I will move in tomorrow.'

They mooch over the yard, past stony dead classrooms. 'Do you know, Cary, I sometimes wish I was gay.'

'Oh yes?'

'At this school, you could have many, many lovers, you could have one for every day of the week! But if you are heterosexual, there is only one girl and she has been taken in the first week by my friend Cary!'

'If it's any consolation, I don't think she'd go for you, even if she were single.'

'I would be lucky to make her top three hundred!' Bruno laughed as he stared up at the star-bright night. 'Let me show you how to stargaze.' He promptly lay down in the middle of Common Lane. He was lying in the middle of the road.

'How does this improve your stargazing?'

'It is so simple, Cary.' Bruno took another tot of cherry brandy and belched. 'Here I am, staring at the infinity of the cosmos. At the same time, I am lying in the middle of the road. I could be run over at any second!'

'And?' Far from joining Bruno on the road, Cary edged to the pavement.

'Do you not understand? On the one hand, infinity – on the other, the infinity of death!'

'You might be onto something. Stare out over the ocean – while standing on the edge of a precipice!'

'Or listen to a lecture by the headmaster while sitting on the edge of the School Hall balcony!'

'You'd jump off out of sheer boredom!'

Some car headlights crept down Common Lane, McArdle heading homewards. He was puttering along at twenty or so in an old red Volvo, headlights neatly dipped. The car was getting quite close. In his tailcoat, Bruno blended perfectly into the tarmac.

Cary had assumed that, at the very last moment, Bruno would jump out of the way. His friend did nothing. The Volvo got closer and closer. All Bruno did was turn his head to laugh at McArdle, his face and his teeth bright white in the headlights.

McArdle banged on the brakes. The car came to a dead stop and stalled, a front tyre no more than a yard from Bruno's head.

Bruno, still laughing, bounded up and ran off back down Common Lane. Cary followed in the shadows. From behind, McArdle was shrieking his rage.

'You hooligan! I could have killed you!'

Bruno ducked down past the Fives courts. In two minutes, they were on Sixpenny and strolling back to The Timbralls, Bruno cock-a-hoop, unable to stop laughing.

'How did you like that for a... a game of chicken?'

Cary had yet to see the joke. 'You nearly killed McArdle, never mind yourself.'

'That must be the best natural high I've ever had!'

'Next time you want to lose one of your nine lives, include me out.'

They let themselves into The Timbralls through Ormerod's private quarters. They were just signing themselves in when one of the kitchen maids, Minty, bustled down the stairs.

'Oh, Cary, there you are, thank God!' Minty was wearing her most formal clothes; black skirt, white shirt, white pinny. She had been helping out with one of Ormerod's little supper parties. Slicks of long dark hair were wet on her cheek. She was flushed and flustered. 'What's up?' Cary asked.

'He's got a foul bunch over tonight, and... and... anyway, the chocolate sodding soufflé has been burnt to cinders.'

'Cinder soufflé, now that I must try,' Bruno said.

Minty's look was withering. 'I was hoping to find something in the boys' kitchen.'

'Leave it to me.' Cary gave her a soft stroke.

She gave Cary an impulsive hug and, tidying her hair, trotted up the stairs.

Cary went through to the house kitchen. There wasn't much of anything, as Mrs Parker liked her food delivered fresh daily. He found a bunch of old bananas on the turn.

Bruno had loafed in to watch. 'You are not cooking those? They are nearly black!'

'Taste even better.' He found a pot of strawberry jam and some double cream. 'Don't wait up.'

Cary passed the dining room as he took the food up to Ormerod's private kitchen. He could hear a parade-ground voice that could carve through brickwork. Either its owner loved the sound of his own voice or he just didn't know when to shut up.

He found Jazz in the kitchen, fussing with the burnt soufflé tin. Minty was straining at an expensive bottle of dessert wine with Mr Ormerod's precious Laguiole corkscrew.

'Hello, Jazz,' Cary said. 'You look like you could do with a drink.'

'You offering?'

'I am.' He took the wine bottle from Minty, gave the Laguiole a couple of turns and pulled the cork. 'Château d'Yquem! Very fancy! Take a seat, ladies – let's see what you make of it!'

'Should we?' Jazz said.

'Perks of cooking for this rabble.'

Jazz and Minty gingerly sat at the table, still not quite believing that things might yet turn out fine. Cary went to the drinks cabinet, ignoring the plain glasses to take out three cut-crystal goblets. He gave them a polish and poured the wine.

'Cheers!'

'Cheers, Cary.' The girls took a dubious sip.

'This is quite nice,' Minty said. 'I like it.'

'Won't Mr Ormerod notice we've had half the bottle?'

'Just sit back. Do you want some cheese?'

'Maybe in a little bit.' Minty sipped some more Château d'Yquem before wiping the sweat from her forehead and heaving a loud sigh of relief.

Cary had already slung his tailcoat and waistcoat over the back of a chair and was sporting a white apron. He placed the largest frying pan on the hob and threw in a pack of butter and the entire pot of jam 'How many we cooking for?'

'He's got eight guests – and one arsehole,' Minty said.

'That'd be the gent with the delightful voice I can hear now. Haven't we got some music to drown him out?' Cary switched on Ormerod's radio, listened in disgust for a moment, and promptly retuned it to Capital. It was one of the hits of the year, Shaggy's Boombastic. 'Much better.'

The girls sipped and watched in wonderment as this whirring blur peeled ten bananas, sliced them down the middle, and laid them out in the simmering jam. He even flipped the bananas in time to the music. In under ten minutes, the bananas were cooked, slightly charred and with the jam turning to caramel. Minty made to get up but Cary waved her back.

'We haven't even got the plates yet.'

'I'll get them.' He turned the heat down and, after a brief wipe of his hands, went through to the dining room. He was intrigued to get a glimpse of the monologue man with the stentorian voice.

He glided into the room and, after giving a nod to Ormerod, gathered the plates like a pro – another skill he had learned from Mrs Parker. The monologue continued. So far, Cary had only been able to see the back of his blunt bullet head.

'Everything all right, Cary?' Ormerod gave Cary's shoulder an affectionate pat.

'Just helping the girls out.'

'You're a dear boy.'

Cary left with four plates up his left arm and two in his right hand. He scraped the leftovers into the kitchen bin and put the plates into the dishwasher. The girls were rapidly cheering up. They didn't demur when he poured them more wine.

Back in the dining room, Cary was clearing the last of the plates when he all but dropped a carrot into a woman's lap. He'd just caught sight of the man with the blunt bullet head, the man who'd spent the last 15 minutes jawing on about National Service. It was Lily's father, the stiff Geography beak!

Cary cautiously studied the man and, by a process of elimination, identified Lily's mother: she was the only guest who was not bothering to conceal her complete boredom. She stared at the pictures of Eton behind her husband's head and wished she were a million miles away.

When Cary served the fried bananas, Arctic was the only guest not to say thank you. He just moved a little to the side, as if his plate had been delivered by an invisible elf.

Cary poured the dessert wine. He was amused at the coos of admiration – 'What a delicious pudding!' 'Some more cream, please.'

Lily's mother, Tor, finally derailed her husband. Cary was pouring her a glass of wine when she turned to him. 'What do you think, young man? Should we be bringing back National Service?'

All eyes turned to the new waiter, who seemed to have taken over from the maids. Arctic stuttered to a halt.

'Good point, Tor,' Ormerod said. 'What do you think, Cary?'

'Send all the school-leavers off to the army for a year or two?' Cary toyed with the bottle of wine. 'Be like a cheap version of boarding school, weaning the children away from their parents. But why not teach them something useful? What about two years of catering – or two years of painting and decorating?'

'Brilliant!' said Mr Barne.

Mr Barne was naturally a standing fixture at Mr Ormerod's supper parties – and he thought Arctic was a moronic oaf. His fingers strayed towards his waistcoat pocket and the allure of his mother-of-pearl snuffbox, but given that ladies were present, he desisted.

'Teach the school-leavers to cook or paint or change a plug. Got to be better than learning to march and polish a pair of boots.'

Arctic sent a foul look at Cary. The boy was slightly familiar, though he couldn't place him. 'It's not about teaching them to march or polish shoes – it's about teaching them discipline.'

'I fear,' Ormerod said delicately as he spooned up the last

of the banana, 'that National Service has never been very popular in Britain.'

'That was fifty years ago. Today's teenagers are crying out for order. For rules.' Arctic topped his wine glass up from the decanter in front of him, not bothering to offer any to his neighbours.

'Are you, Cary?' Ormerod asked.

'After five years at Eton, sir, I'll have had a bellyful of rules,' Cary said.

'Hear, hear!' Tor said. She had taken a bit of a fancy to this young man, who was so deftly dealing with her husband.

'And you would have them all turned into caterers?' Arctic sneered.

'Learning to cook is a wonderful skill – a skill to last a lifetime.' Cary picked up the port decanter from the mahogany sideboard and set it next to Ormerod. 'Personally, I'd like to see them teaching cookery at Eton.'

'So you know all about it, do you?'

'He does know all about it!' crowed Barne. 'He's been learning to cook at Eton since he was 13 years old!'

'What – baked beans on toast for his mess-mates?'

Ormerod gave a gentle laugh. 'You've been hoist with your own petard, my dear chap. Cary has been cooking the boys' breakfasts – all the boys' breakfasts – for over three years now. Three times a week, he cooks supper for Windsor's homeless.'

'That would be at The Project,' cooed Tor. 'You must know my daughter, Lily.'

Cary was polishing a pair of huge brandy balloons. 'Lily?' he said, ever so casually. 'I've seen her, but I don't know her.'

'She's been working there during the summer holidays. You must say hello.'

'I'll do that.'

Cary cleared the plates and left the grown-ups to their port. In the kitchen, he set the two brandy balloons in front of the girls and poured them each a large tot of Adelphi Armagnac.

'Cary!' Minty said. 'You're trying to get us drunk!'

'And what would be so wrong with that?'

'Absolutely nothing!' Jazz said. She swirled the Armagnac, sniffed and sipped and dreamed.

* * *

Arctic was annoyed for a number of reasons when he walked back to Farrer House with Tor – the uppermost of which was that insufferably arrogant boy, Cary. Now, there was a boy who really could do with a two-year spell in the army. And the way Barne and that nincompoop Ormerod had hung on his every word, and as for Tor, she wouldn't shut up about him.

'So charming,' she prattled. 'Delightful boy.'

It'd make a cat vomit!

Arctic was off to his bedroom when he saw the light under Lily's door.

He knocked and went in. She was curled up in bed, reading.

'Had a good evening?' he asked.

'Very,' Lily said. 'Went to the film club to see South Pacific. It was wonderful.'

'The musical?'

'You'd hate it.'

'What are you reading?'

'Nicholas Nickleby.' She flashed up her Jilly Cooper, which had now been disguised with a Charles Dickens book cover.

'That's the stuff. We met a boy at The Timbralls tonight. I gather he works at The Project.'

'Oh – and who's that?' Her knees drew up a little tighter.

'Boy called Cary. Do you know him?'

'A little.'

'Very bumptious.'

'How did you meet him?'

'We were having supper with that prissy Ormerod and this Cary boy just came in, bold as brass, and commandeered the entire party. First, he's taking away the plates, then he cooks our dessert—'

'This is just now?' She held her book in front of her face to hide her laughter. Only Cary could go straight from kissing her in the Ladies Powder Room to cooking his tutor's pudding.

'Yes! And next thing, he's being asked to sit down at the table, and is drinking port, cool as you please, and is chatting to your mother, God help us, about bridge!'

Lily laughed. 'Certainly knew how to get into her good books.'

'I did not take him to at all – one of the most conceited boys I have ever met.'

'And you normally try to see the best in everyone.'

The irony swirled clean over Arctic's head. 'I would be giving that boy a very wide berth, if I were you.'

'I'll bear that in mind.'

Tor breezed in, a little tiddly after Cary had kept topping up her port glass. 'Hello, dear, we met the most lovely boy – '

'Daddy's just been telling me about him.'

'You'll like him, I know you will.'

'And how do you know that?'

'If I'd met him at your age, I'd have been all over him like a rash!'

'For God's sake, woman!' Arctic stomped out of the room. As if that Cary boy wasn't bad enough, Tor was now trying to foist him on their own daughter!

CHAPTER 15

Minty and Jazz had gone back home, very merry, each of them giving Cary a lingering kiss on the cheek, which would have made their jealous boyfriends seethe. Cary switched on the dishwasher and finished off the last of Minty's Armagnac.

So, he'd met Lily's parents and locked horns with her bull-headed father. It might have been easier, simpler, if he'd just sucked it up like a good little Eton schoolboy. He sighed. He never did easy and he absolutely never did simple.

Cary turned off the lights and went downstairs to the boys' library, which had been named after the Timbralls' most famous student, one Ian Fleming. There was a TV and a few armchairs and over a thousand books, including, of course, every one of Fleming's novels. Lines and lines of bookshelves on the walls, as well as two seven-foot racks perpendicular to the wall. The further rack created a little snug in the far corner, where you could hide yourself from the rest of the house. It had an armchair and an Anglepoise lamp. Cary had spent many hours tucked away reading there.

Cary was not reading tonight. He was searching the bookshelves for a very particular kind of book. He wanted something that was both thick and unreadable.

On one of the top shelves, close to the door, he found exactly what he was looking for: the complete collection of Walter Scott's novels, untouched since the day they'd first arrived in the Timbralls library, thick with decades of dust.

Cary pondered a question that few had ever pondered before. Of Scott's collection of unreadable reads, which was the most unreadable? He plumped for a book he'd never heard of, The Fortunes of Nigel. He took the book to his favourite armchair and set to with a pair of kitchen scissors. He was snipping out a hideaway for his new pager.

'Hidden in plain sight. Couldn't have done better myself.'

'Glad you approve.'

Fleming was flicking through his own books. 'Wonder how many Bond books I'd have written if it hadn't been for my most untimely death.'

'You didn't need to write any more,' Cary said. 'He's the most famous spy in history. He's the most famous literary character that's ever been created.'

'I'll take that.' Fleming laughed. 'Walter Scott can keep his rotten black monument in Edinburgh.' He pulled up an armchair and lit a cigar, puff-puffing until it glowed. 'Kim did you proud, didn't he?'

'I'll say.'

'Must have gone out on quite a limb to get you that much. Going to become quite a big cash cow for you. What are you going to spend it on?'

'I don't know.'

'You should get yourself a car.'

'A car? I can't even drive!'

'I'm aware of that, you ninny!' Fleming said. 'Get some lessons and get your test. We need wheels.'

'Wheels!' Cary said. 'I'll do it.'

'Good. Very glad, by the way, that it's going so well with Lily. I don't bandy this word around often, but I believe you've met your soulmate.'

'I know I have!'

Fleming hitched up his dinner jacket trousers and leaned forward conspiratorially. 'Kim would not have approved of you doing something as risky as buying that ring. But then he has never been in love like you have.'

'No? I heard some story about Kim and a piano mistress.'

'Typical Kim affair.' Fleming threw his head back and laughed. 'He falls in love with the most gorgeous women – and, one way or another, somehow, some way, it always ends spectacularly badly.'

'Just like Bond.'

'Yes.' Fleming eyed the ash on his cigar. 'You are going to be different. At least, I hope you are.'

* * *

Maxwell, poor reviled Maxwell, only wants to love and be loved and, though there might be plenty of potential girlfriends out there for him, he has set his heart on Lily. The more he is rebuffed, the more he wants her.

Over and over again in his mind, he replays the memory of that kiss at the party. So he'd been too eager, too ardent. Was that so bad?

But Maxwell has enough nous to play it cool. No more trotting after her while she's off on a run; no more chatting to her on the way to the next div.

She doesn't appear to have any friends at all in Farrer – except for that oily wretch, Fredster Campbell. Maxwell has seen them chatting. They even went to the cinema together.

It occurs to Maxwell that Campbell may know things. Useful things. He collars the boy after lunch. Campbell is in a tracksuit, racket in hand.

'Off squashing, Fredster?' Maxwell is all affability.

'I am.'

'Good man!' Maxwell says. 'Great game, ought to be in the Olympics.'

'It is in the Olympics.'

'Good – excellent. Fancy a game, one of these days? Like to see the young talent coming through.'

'OK.' Fredster is perplexed. In the past two years, Maxwell has barely said two words to him.

'Tied up with rowing most of the time, but a game of squash will do me good. A week today, say 5 o'clock?'

'OK.'

'I'll see you then – and bring your A-game.'

'I'm going to need my A-game? I thought you were a rower.'

* * *

Both Cary and Lily were of a mind. They were more than ready for the main course. They were ravenous for it.

They had not been able to meet at The Project for a couple of days, but had consoled themselves with daily letters, which had left the furnace fires so stoked that they would have melted marble. Cary had also given Lily the number of his new pager, said he'd been given it by someone in the trade. Lily called it.

'Hello – what is your message?'

Lily was momentarily surprised. It hadn't occurred to her that she'd be speaking to a human being. 'I've never done this before,' she said. 'How does it work?'

'You give me your message, I type it in and then I send it.'

'Oh – right. I thought you might have some voice recognition system.'

'That's ten years off – another machine to do me out of a job. What would you like to say?'

'Um… This is my first time. I'm not sure I'll be very good at it—'

'Is this the message that you want to send?'

'It is.'

'All right – I'm not sure I'll be very good at it. Any more?'

'But I'm going to keep practising. And I look forward to doing a lot more of it in the future. With you.'

'That it?'

'Love, Lily.'

'Very nice. Lucky I don't have a dirty mind.'

'It is,' Lily said. 'Goodbye.'

Cary read the message that night, after he'd retrieved his pager from The Fortunes of Nigel. It was a shame he couldn't reply. He'd just have to do it the old-fashioned way and send a letter.

The next day, that day of days, the day when Lily and Cary were to finally allow themselves a taste of The Main Course, they both took meticulous care over their appearance. Not that either of them needed to do anything much at all, because both Lily and Cary just glowed with love and a healthy dose of incipient lust. Such huge butterflies fluttered in their stomachs that they could barely eat lunch.

Cary was the first to arrive at The Project, and was cooking steak and kidney pie for fifty. He had two helpers, Joe and Matty, a pair of on-off drug addicts in their mid-20s, who wanted to learn to cook. They dreamed of one day becoming sous-chefs in a local hotel or restaurant, or anywhere at all that would pay them a daily wage.

Cary diced an onion at slow speed and gave the knife to Joe. 'Fingertips back, otherwise you'll slice them off – and I've got the scars to prove it!'

Matty was set to work making five kilos of pastry. Cary browned off portions of meat. The radio was on, mugs of tea poured and, over and above it all, Cary had this crazy sense of anticipation, with this one single thought that seemed to pop into his head every minute: she's coming; I'm going to see her; and if I'm lucky and if I don't mess it up, I'm going to take her clothes off. If.

Lily was more than just coming. She had arrived 30 minutes ago, peeping into the kitchen to see Cary with his trainees. She had now put on three loads of washing and had folded 40 pillowcases and 40 duvet covers – and, like Cary, the same busy-bee thought drifted constantly through her head. She was enjoying the wait – what did they call it? she mused. Yes, Delayed Gratification, the foundation stone of the entire Protestant religion. Lily was indeed the girl at the dinner table who liked to leave her favourite morsels for last.

Finally, pillowcases and duvet covers folded, bedroom windows opened, and gratification delayed for a decorous amount of time, she went into the kitchen. The meat was simmering on the stove. Cary was with the lads, peeling carrots and potatoes.

He smiled and put down his knife. She leaned over to kiss him.

'Hello,' she said.

Cary got up. 'Be back in a while,' he said.

Matty and Joe smiled knowingly. The irony of Cary's position was, for the moment, rather lost on him. Not a single person who stayed at The Project would have dreamed of gossiping about these two young lovers. The Project folk may have had their woes, but they knew how to keep a secret. Cary, on the other hand, was intent on going to *The Sun* with every single piece of Eton gossip that came his way.

Cary and Lily had not even made it up two flights of stairs before they broke off to kiss each other. Cary stood on the landing, Lily on the step above. Nose to nose and lip to lip, they were the perfect height for each other.

They climbed the ladder and then they were in the attic, kissing and pawing at each other. Lily helped him off with his shirt.

'In here or outside?' he asked.

'Shall we try the sun-lounger?'

'I'd love to love on the lounger.'

They climbed through the skylight and, fortunately for them, it was another Indian summer and they drank in the last dregs of the sunshine. And now that the moment had arrived, and they realised there was everything to be gained from slowing down, they lay on the sun-lounger, Lily on top, and in between kisses, they chatted. She pulled off her hair band and, when they kissed, her long hair curtained them from the world.

'I've brought you a very small present,' she said.

'What a coincidence,' Cary said. 'I have brought you a very small present, too.'

'What if we've brought each the other the same thing?'

'Then we will be destined to spend the rest of our lives with each other.' They turned easily on the sun-lounger and now it was Cary on top. 'What have you got me?'

From her skirt pocket, she pulled out a slim box. It was wrapped in red paper, the size of a large matchbox.

Cary gave it a shake. 'It's quite light. I wonder what it could be.'

'I hope you approve.'

Cary tore open the paper – kissed her. 'I very much approve.' It was a box of ten condoms.

'It's not a bit forward?'

'Not a bit.'

'I was hoping – and I know they're yours now, and you can use them how you like – but I was hoping that you might use them all with me.'

'I would love to.' He kissed her. 'And I love you too.'

She hugged him. 'I think I've been in love with you since the day we first kissed.'

'For me, I think it happened when we saw each other in the Chapel. Would you like your present?'

'Please. Though if you'd like to try one of those condoms, then that would be present enough for me.'

'I'll give you this first. Something for you to wear when we make love.'

'Making love with Cary,' she giggled. 'How delicious that sounds. I'm going to be making love with Cary. Cary is going to make love to me.'

From his pocket, Cary produced a small cube of a box that was wrapped in silver paper. A whisper in the wind – 'Careful'.

But it was too late now; Lily already had the box in her hands, was shaking it, admiring it and, in a moment, the paper had been ripped off and the box revealed.

'Cartier, no less,' she said.

'You know your stuff. I wouldn't have recognised it.'

'My grandmother had one, turned purple with age. But this – this looks very new indeed.'

And Cary suddenly saw the elephant trap that yawned in front of him. He knew his Lily and he knew precisely what would happen next.

'It's a ring!' Lily said. 'The most beautiful ring I've ever seen!' She slipped it onto her right ring finger. She held her hand up, admired the sparkling citrine.

'I love it!' she said. 'And it will indeed be the only thing I'm wearing when we make love.'

And then, of course, the cogs started to whirr, and the smile started to falter and Cary was quite powerless to do anything about it.

'Where did you get it?'

'I bought it from Cartier.'

'Cary, dear, will you tell me where you got the money from?'

'I think you know.'

'Oh dear.' She sat on the edge of the sun-lounger and started to cry.

Cary was beside himself – shock and disbelief, and not a little astonishment at how quickly everything had unravelled, this thunderbolt out of a clear blue sky. He put his arm round her waist, and Lily sat miserably, crying.

'I'm sorry,' he said.

She dried her eyes with the heel of her hand. 'I can't wear it now, you know.' She took the ring off, put it back in the box and returned it to him.

'I must be a complete idiot,' Cary said. 'I thought you'd love it.'

'I do love it, Cary, but I don't like the way you got hold of it.'

'You're right.' Cary hefted the Cartier box in his hand.

'How much did they give you?' Lily's eyes were puffy and red.

'Ten grand.'

'Ten thousand pounds – that's an enormous sum!'

'Certainly a lot more than I'd expected.'

Lily got up and gave a resigned laugh. 'I really thought I was going to lose my cherry today.'

Cary looked up, wiped a tear from his eye. 'Me too.'

'You too?' she said, momentarily taken aback. 'I'd always thought…'

'No – first time.'

She sniffed, fingers locking, unlocking, tears dripping onto her knees. 'I don't even mind much that you're selling stories to *The Sun*. But I do mind how you're spending this money. Ten thousand pounds – and you spend a whole chunk of it on some useless bauble for me! What were you planning – taking us off to the smartest hotels in London, whisking me away to Paris for the weekend? But I don't want luxury. Or jewellery. Or lobster, or oysters, or Sevruga caviar, which might as well be couscous. All I've ever wanted was you. I guess you didn't realise that I'm not that kind of girl.'

Cary gave a wry smile through a mist of tears. 'I guess, if I'd thought about it for more than five seconds, I would have realised you were never that kind of girl. I saw all this money and I've never seen so much money in all my life. It went to my head. All I could think was to buy you something nice.'

'I'm sorry, Cary.' She stood by the skylight, and all he wanted to do was get down on his knees and beg for forgiveness. 'You know, when we first kissed, and when this thunderbolt first hit me, I really thought that miracles could happen – that the first person I ever fell in love with was my perfect match. More fool me.'

She slipped through the skylight and she was gone, and that amazing Indian summer was gone with her. Cary lay back on the sun-lounger, staring sightlessly up at Windsor Castle, and he continued to lie there when it started to rain. The rain came in hard and cold, blending with his tears and drenching him from head to toe.

CHAPTER 16

Fleming didn't come to him that night. But Cary didn't want to talk, anyway, least of all have his tail pulled by the maestro. Would James Bond cry if he was dumped by a girl? Never! Fleming wouldn't get it – he'd just laugh and tell him to move on.

But Cary wasn't even considering moving on.

Instead of going for his normal six-mile run at dawn, he headed off to the Eton Rifles' assault course to beast himself on walls and monkey bars, and crawl through mud and scrape through tunnels. It suited him mightily that he was surrounded by misty drizzle.

Back in the warmth of the Timbralls kitchens, he found Mrs Parker and Mrs Webber inspecting a large box on the floor.

'That looks interesting,' Cary said. 'What is it?'

'Letter here says that it's come courtesy of the Eton caterers at Bekynton – and in all the time I've worked here, they've never sent us so much as a sausage.' She inspected the letter. 'Shipped down from Peter Jones in London – who'd want to waste their time shopping there?'

'How exciting!' Cary said, mind for a moment taken off his own misery. 'Let's open it!'

The ladies sat while Cary slashed the box top with a knife. He squatted, lifted the contents out and placed it next to the range.

'It's a Gaggia!' Mrs Parker stroked the smooth chrome curves. 'Just like the one I had—'

'When you were on honeymoon in Florence,' Mrs Webber recited. She retrieved a bag of coffee beans from the bottom of the box. 'Kopi Luwak, whatever that is, all the way from Bali.' She tossed the bag to Cary. 'You'll know what to do, won't you, Cary?'

Cary flicked through the Gaggia's instructions. 'Three double espressos coming right up.' He plugged the Gaggia in and filled the water reservoir. He smelt the new coffee beans. 'Musty. Got a bit of farmyard about them.'

'Funny kind of bean.'

Cary preferred to grind his beans by hand with a pestle and mortar. He felt more connected. It was a bigger hit to the nose. He ground and inhaled and thought of Lily – and how she'd love to be trying this new type of coffee. Mrs Parker and Mrs Webber, he was not so sure.

'What have you done to your hands, Cary?'

'Oh,' he said, inspecting his palms. They were nicked and grazed. He'd barely noticed. 'It's the ropes from the assault course.'

'Need a bandage?'

'I'll be fine.'

Cary had spent the past week closely observing how the professional baristas made their coffees. He poured the coffee grounds into the filter holder, tamped it down and, after only the tiniest of fiddles, clicked it into the Gaggia. He took a warm cup from the oven and, as Mrs Parker and Mrs Webber waited for their first sip of black nectar, Cary read up about the coffee they'd soon be drinking.

'I've heard of this – but I've never tasted it.' He brought the three double espressos over to the kitchen table. 'It's called civet coffee. It's the world's most expensive coffee.'

'Really?' Mrs Parker tapped out a spoonful of brown sugar, stirred and inhaled. 'It is a bit musty, isn't it? Sort of earthy.'

Mrs Webber took a tentative sip. 'Nutty? Bit of caramel? It does smell odd, though. What's it got to do with civets?'

'I believe it's been through a civet cat.'

'What do you mean "through"?'

'The civet cats eat the beans and the coffee farmers go round collecting the droppings.'

Mrs Parker spat her coffee straight out over the table. 'This coffee is made from civet poo?' she screamed. 'Disgusting! I never thought I'd say this, Cary, but take that shit out of my kitchen!'

Cary tried the coffee. It was a little odd. 'Interesting, but not for everyone,' he said, taking another sip. It was like the beans had been fermented. 'I'll make you a couple of double espressos with the old Illy coffee,' he added soothingly.

Mrs Parker eyed him. 'You knew exactly what you were serving us.'

'How could I possibly know?'

'You only told us after we'd tried it!'

'There, there, Mrs Parker,' Cary chided. 'A little bit of civet shit never did anyone any harm.'

Mrs Webber giggled. 'You've got a nerve, Cary. If it had been anyone else, she'd have thrown you out of the kitchen.'

'And here we are, Mrs Parker, a double espresso just like the one you had on your Florentine honeymoon, and made from your favourite Illy coffee beans.'

Feathers still very much ruffled, she added sugar and stirred. 'Spiking my coffee, you're the limit, Cary.'

'I'll try it on Ormerod. He's not as squeamish as you ladies.'

'Mr Ormerod!' squawked Mrs Parker. 'Give him half a chance and he'd be eating road-kill!'

* * *

Having had her heart broken by her one true love, Lily had not had a good night of it. Had she been too harsh on him? Was it a deal-breaker? Why not just tell him she didn't want the ring – and then continue with those adorable kisses, as well as all the other delights that had been promised?

Like every human who has ever walked, and who has

called time on a relationship, she was riddled with regret. After breakfast, she walked the short way up Judy's Passage. The Prince was going the other way to the Lower Chapel.

'Hi, kid,' she said.

'Hi, Lily.' It amused her to have forged this secret link.

Lily would normally have gone to the Chapel, as she liked the music. But today, the seniors were all crammed into the School Hall, where they were due to be harangued by Mr Moffatt.

Standing owl-like on the school steps, just next to The Burning Bush, was Mr McCreath. He was like Ian Fleming's greatest villain, the Child Snatcher from Chitty Chitty Bang Bang. He could size the boys up in seconds. He could smell out the mischief-makers and the miscreants – save one. He hadn't yet been able to sniff out *The Sun*'s Eton mole.

One boy immediately came to his attention. He was a jangly 15-year-old, furtive, trying to blend in but not succeeding. A troublemaker – and perhaps that morning in the very act of making trouble. Mr McCreath didn't yet know the boy's name, but that was of no account. He would not forget him.

Eton's School Hall and the library just next to it were built at the dawn of the 20th Century, a memorial to the 129 Etonians who'd lost their lives in the Boer Wars. Two boys' houses were knocked down and, in their stead, were built the hall and library, two imposing neo-classical buildings, made from Portland stone and decorated with swags and stone fruit. Inside the barrel-vaulted hall, there was room enough for about 500 boys, with a balcony at the back, and an organ at the far end.

The hall was full, the boys were chattering. Mr Moffatt strode onto the stage towards the simple lectern. He was in full bristling fig. The Eton uniform does not admit of much variation, either for the masters or for the pupils, so Mr Moffatt was wearing the standard black suit, black gown and white bow tie, though he liked to express his arch individuality by wearing black loafers with *red* tassels.

Mr Moffatt had decided to adopt a tactic he had seen in a recent series on The Dark Charisma of Adolf Hitler. At the Nuremberg rallies, he'd learned, Hitler had a peculiar way of getting his audience's attention. Mr Moffatt tried to do the same thing with these 500-odd recalcitrant Etonians. He didn't say a word.

He fiddled with his notes. He took a sip of water. He stepped back from the lectern, stepped forward again, fiddled some more with his notes and, as he twitched, the tension grew. He glared at the boys and glared at Lily, who was sitting directly in front of him; he'd been very much against allowing her into the school, but there were past precedents, and so he'd had to accede to Arctic's demands. It would have been more helpful if Lily hadn't been quite so pretty. She had trouble written all over her, just see if she didn't. And then, doubtless, it would end up all over the front pages of Her Majesty's Most Repellent Press.

Mr Moffatt began very softly – so that, or so he hoped, the boys would be hanging on his every word. 'I'm not happy,' he said. He looked at Lily, but annoyingly, she was looking away to the wings. 'I'm not at all happy…'

Some of the boys had started to titter. Somebody was stealing his thunder.

A boy ambled onto the stage – wearing tails and top hat, and, from the look of things, no trousers. Mr Moffatt did not recognise the boy, who was carrying one of those boom box things. The boy wandered over to the front of the stage and gave Moffatt a nod.

'What aren't you happy about, Chief?'

'What are you doing? I will see you on the Bill this afternoon.'

'Who's Bill?'

The boy put down the boom box and stood jauntily in front of him – hands on hips. Mr Moffatt observed for the first time that this boy was wearing high heels and fishnet tights. The horrid suspicion that he had been set up. A glance at the audience; the boys' attention had been effortlessly grabbed by this, this interloper. Even that girl Lily was enthralled, agog to see what happened next.

'Get off the stage this minute!'

'Keep your hair on Mr Mo-Fo!' The boy – whom Mr Moffatt suddenly realised was not a boy at all but was actually a full-grown woman – leered at the audience and was rewarded with a great howl of laughter.

'I said, get off!'

He wondered whether to manhandle this grotesque woman off the stage but decided that would not be seemly behaviour for the Headman of Eton College. If only one of Prince William's personal security guards could come on stage and, and, arrest her, manhandle her, just do for her!

'You're a bit of a crochety one, aren't you, Mr Mo-Fo? Who's rattled your cage, Pops?'

She unbuttoned her tailcoat to reveal that, underneath, she was wearing nothing but a black leather basque. She placed her top hat on the lectern and uncoiled her hair to let down a raven black mane; she was very pretty. From her tailcoat pocket, she produced a microphone.

'Hello, boys,' she purred, and was met with wolf-whistles and cacophonous applause. 'And a girl, I see!' She smiled at Lily. 'What's it like being the only girl in the school, dear? Me? I'd cut through these boys like a bullet!'

Some of the wolf-whistlers were standing up, and the rowdies up on the balcony were stamping their feet. Arctic, sitting stern at the back, was as outraged as the Headman.

Mr Moffatt stood adither by his lectern. Should he stay, should he go? But leaving would mean a huge loss of face – he would have conceded the battlefield to this, this preening monster. Heave her off the stage?

The slattern primped her hair; she was loving every moment. 'My name's Amanda. I'm here to sing a song for a very special man – a man who, over the years, we have all come to know and love. I understand that, to you, he's just the Headman. But to me, he'll always be... My Master.'

She stooped and, as she pressed the play button on her boom box, she blew Lily a kiss.

Lily was amazed, enthralled, and wondering how much more bizarre this show would get – and as it happened, it was going to get a whole lot more bizarre. Amanda was singing Lily's favourite song from South Pacific – 'I'm going to wash that man right out of my hair'.

While Mr Moffatt looked on – perhaps it would have been better to have quit the stage, after all, but he couldn't leave now – Amanda strutted about, dry-washing her hair and flirting with the boys. She drank in the cheers and the wolf-whistles.

Lily wondered if the song was mere coincidence; of course, it couldn't be. But was it a sign to wash Cary right out of her hair? She wondered if she shouldn't be giving Cary a second chance; up until the Cartier ring, he'd been pretty much perfect. She glanced to the side. A very tense Fredster Campbell also happened to be sitting in the front row. He gave her a shy smile and, over the hubbub, she caught him mouthing – 'For you.'

Amanda finished her song, gave the boys a handsome bow and, after placing her top hat jauntily on her head, she jumped off the stage. She bent down and gently pinched Lily's cheek.

'Good luck, darling.'

And with that, she was gone, sashaying down the main aisle and out of the hall.

Mr Moffatt snapped out of his trance. 'Stop that woman! Stop her!'

Arctic shouldered his way through the cheering boys in the back row. He snatched at Amanda's tailcoat but missed her. He followed her out of the hall – not running but walking as briskly as his status permitted. He was in time to watch Amanda trip lightly down the School Hall steps before climbing into the taxi that awaited her at The Burning Bush. As the car peeled away, she turned and blew him a kiss.

Mr Moffatt was white with rage. 'I don't know who hired that woman,' he said. 'But I will find out and, when I do, I will make things exceedingly unpleasant for the culprit.'

By the next afternoon, Mr Moffatt had started to simmer down a little – especially as the culprit had indeed been discovered; Mr McCreath had played him just beautifully.

Mr Moffatt was inclined to expel the boy. But he would make up his mind after he'd heard what the wretch had to say for himself.

CHAPTER 17

An English lesson with the affable Mr McArdle, who had mellowed much with age. He was back to teaching Romeo and Juliet again. He had taught this play to hundreds and hundreds of Etonians. Perhaps they ought just to film his complete set of Romeo and Juliet classes, with the same questions being asked over and over again – and that way, McArdle would still be able to teach Romeo and Juliet long after he was dead.

Mr McArdle could sense but could not quite place the ticklish vibe of those harum-scarum 15-year-olds. One of them, Fredster Campbell, was markedly less bumptious.

The knock at the door explained why. It was that nice lad, Cary. Some of the Poppers, when they were out on this peculiar errand, behaved with the most appalling manners, storming into the classrooms and bellowing at the teachers. Cary was different.

'I'm so sorry to bother you, sir,' Cary said. 'Is Campbell here?'

'He is.'

'I'm afraid the Headman would like to see him at noon – if that's all right.'

'Of course.'

'Thank you very much.'

Cary quietly closed the door behind him. The classroom was awash with whispers as the boys realised that Mr Moffatt had indeed found his culprit.

Ten minutes later, Fredster Campbell raised his hand. 'May I leave?'

McArdle placed a hand on the boy's shoulder. 'Good luck.'

Fredster left the room – and he was not at all sure whether he'd ever be coming back. When he'd hired Amanda, it had seemed like the most hilarious prank in history; now, not quite so hilarious. At least Lily had enjoyed it.

He was surprised to find Cary waiting for him. 'Hello?'

'Got nothing on.' Cary stood up. 'Thought I'd chum you over.'

'Oh – right, fine.'

'How did they know it was you?'

'They didn't, the bastards,' Fredster said. 'They had some video footage of a boy walking with Amanda. McCreath just knew it was me.'

'Tough,' Cary said. 'He's pretty angry. What are you going to say?'

'That I thought it would be a funny prank?'

'You'll be out for that.' They were walking up Common Lane. Cary recognised the spot. It was just where Bruno had been stargazing in the middle of the road. 'Say you were being bullied. Say the bullies had been terrorising you for over a year; this was the only way to make them stop.'

'Good line.'

'Where did you pick up Amanda?'

'From Pink's, that strip-joint in Windsor. Paid her a hundred quid.'

'Don't say that, either – say you just came across her in Windsor. Paid her twenty.'

'Got it.'

'And since you did 'fess up, you might as well get all due credit for it. Tell the Headman you felt honour-bound to own up. You never know – he might even swallow it.'

'Thank you, Cary.'

'Though you'd have saved yourself a whole world of trouble if you hadn't owned up in the first place.'

The pair walked up the age-old staircase. It reeked of sweat and polish. Two other boys were also waiting outside the Headman's study.

'I'll be leaving you here,' Cary said. 'Great show, by the way. The best thing I've ever seen at Eton.'

'Thanks!'

As Fredster Campbell stewed on his misdeeds, Cary took a brisk walk to Windsor. He now had all the information he needed and, after paging Kim, barely had to wait a minute in that secluded phone box before the phone rang. The conversation was brief.

Cary sauntered back to Eton for a light lunch in The Timbralls. He was sanguine, almost cheerful, about the upcoming interview he had arranged for 4pm. It would be the most ticklish interview of his life – and though he knew exactly what he wanted, needed, to say, he also realised there were all manner of ways in which he might yet again manage to botch it.

CHAPTER 18

Lily was the last to join the meeting – and since it was to be a vaguely formal meeting, it was being held in Renton and Fergie's office. It was a good-sized room with high windows that stretched up to the high ceiling, though they could have done with a clean. The windows were grimy, the grey carpet was grubby, and piles of paper and piles of books lay haphazardly on the tables and on the filing cabinets. On the table by the window, there was a coffee machine that hadn't worked in five years and a dead cactus. There was a very large safe, which was used, in the main, to keep Fergie's lunchtime sandwiches out of harm's way. On the walls were cheap prints and old newspaper cuttings. Outside was a patio with a walnut tree and a privet hedge gone wild, but the patio door had been locked some years before, and no-one had ever found the key. Dead centre of the room was a round table with a white Formica top; this was where Renton and Fergie sat with Cary.

Cary stood up when Lily came into the room – went over to her, touched her elbow. 'Thanks for coming.'

'Hello,' she said. Lily was not at all sure what the meeting was about or where it was going – or even if she wanted to be there. But she'd received a letter from Cary, and it had promised much.

'Got a pot of tea on the go,' Fergie said. 'You'll have a cup?'

'Please.'

'And Cary's even bought some Bourbon biscuits,' Renton said. 'Must be a bigger deal than I thought it'd be.'

Tea was served and Lily found herself joining in the talk about the weather, which had been particularly fine for the time of year, perhaps even an Indian summer, though it did seem as if autumn was about to properly set in.

Cary was fiddling with his mug. Lily realised with a pang that he was nervous.

'Sooo...' he said. 'I'll bet you're all wondering why I asked you here.'

'No – not at all, Cary,' Fergie said. 'Always good to chat.'

'Just one thing – is The Project a registered charity?'

'Is it a charity?' Renton said testily. 'You think Eton College is going to send its pupils to help out at some random doss-house? Of course it's a registered charity! I can even show you the certificate if I could ever lay my hands on it.'

'Of course – sorry.'

'And?'

'First, I'd like to apologise. Lily – I'm sorry.'

'What are you apologising for?' Renton said. 'I never apologise.'

'And look where it's got you,' Fergie said. 'Let the boy talk.'

'Second – I'd like to make a donation.'

'All very formal, Cary.'

Cary flopped three brown envelopes on the table. 'It's £7,842. In cash.'

Renton and Fergie stared at the money before turning to each other.

'£7,482?' Fergie said. 'That's an unusual sum of money.'

'I had some incidental expenses. And then I saw the light.'

'Not that we're overly picky about where we get our donations from, but do you mind my asking where you got this money?' Renton said. 'Haven't been holding up the local bookie, by any chance?'

Fergie had taken the notes out of the envelopes and gave them a riffle. 'Judging from the band on these twenties, which reads "News International", I would guess that Cary got this money from *The Sun* newspaper.'

'Hadn't noticed that,' Cary laughed. 'It is from *The Sun*. You'll be able to use it?'

'I'll say,' Fergie said. He threw a wodge of loose twenties across the table. 'It's all been pretty hand-to-mouth. The bedrooms are bare. The common room, the kitchen – this office – they've all seen better days—'

'What he's saying is that The Project hasn't had anything spent on it in years,' Renton said. 'It could do with some TLC.'

For Lily, speechless, this was turning out to be the most remarkable interview of her life. She hadn't expected much. And she certainly hadn't expected anything like this. 'TLC,' she said. 'Tender. Loving. Care.'

She took Cary's hand.

'Happy?' Cary said.

'I am,' she said. 'Have you called *The Sun* about Amanda?'

'I was speaking to *The Sun*'s resident toff only three hours ago.'

'Good,' Lily said. She brought his hand to her lips and kissed his knuckles. 'If you don't sell the stories, somebody else will—'

'And they'll just piss the money down the drain.' Renton coughed up some phlegm and discreetly wiped it into his handkerchief.

Fergie beamed at the pair of them. 'I'm so glad. It would have been very awkward here if you weren't on speaking terms.'

Cary couldn't stop smiling. Renton couldn't take his eyes off the money. 'What were your incidental expenses, if you don't mind my asking?'

'I bought Lily a ring,' Cary said. 'And I bought the two very nice cooks in my house a new coffee machine. There were some teething problems. Some other matters that had to be attended to.'

'These the cooks that taught you your kitchen skills?' Fergie said.

'Mrs Parker and Mrs Webber.'

'Mrs Parker and Mrs Webber.' Fergie pondered. 'They sound nice.'

The room subsided into contented silence, each with their own thoughts and dreams. Of those two grizzled men, Renton was wondering just where to start with all the money and Fergie was conjuring images of that alluring duo, Mrs Parker and Mrs Webber. Cary realised that, somehow, he'd plucked this relationship, only very slightly charred, out of the fire. And as for Lily, it was as if she'd been adrift on the high seas, not a ship, not a person to be seen, when suddenly and quite unexpectedly, she had found herself floating into safe harbour.

'Will you gentlemen excuse us?' Cary said.

'Off you go, my chickadees,' Fergie said.

Hand in hand, our young lovers left the office.

Fergie scratched his bald head. 'What are we going to do with all this money?'

'Get some bedside lamps for the rooms?'

'That'd be nice.'

'Have a go at cleaning up the patio?'

'That'd be nice, too.'

'Though we have lost the key and we can't get out on the patio.' Renton coughed up more phlegm into his handkerchief and, now that Lily had gone, curiously inspected the contents.

'So many things we could spend it on.' They were both overwhelmed with apathy. The prospect of having to go out and spend all this money seemed insurmountable.

'Why don't we put it in the safe – and we'll spend it when we think of something to spend it on.'

'Good idea!' Fergie said. 'Let's make a fresh pot of tea!'

Just outside the office, Cary and Lily were kissing, the air spangled with the promise of urgent lovemaking. Up the stairs, they could barely walk three steps before breaking off to kiss each other again. With his hand cupped easily about Lily's waist, Cary led the way to the bathroom and up the wooden ladder.

'Inside or out?' Cary asked.

Lily surveyed the scene. 'It's a little different from last time.' Next to the sidelight was a double bed with plumped white pillows and a crisp white duvet. On a side-table was an ivory candle and a posy of wild flowers. Lily turned back a corner of the duvet. 'So, you were expecting me?'

'Not expecting – hoping.'

'I like it.'

'It was quite a job getting it up here. The bed was here already but the mattress is new. I had to pull while Fergie shoved. He nearly dragged me through the hatch!'

Lily stretched up to take off her blue V-neck. She sat on the side of the bed and patted beside her. 'Come join me.'

Cary knelt on the floor between her knees and kissed her.

'Let's wipe last week,' she said. 'Start all over again.'

'I've got you a present.'

'That's nice. I've got you a present, too. Would you like to open it?' She handed him a box wrapped in red paper.

Cary gave it a shake. 'Is this what I hope it's going to be?' He tore the paper off a large box of mixed condoms. He kissed her. 'My best present ever. Thank you.'

Lily started to tug at Cary's T-shirt, pulling it over his head. 'I'd like to start now – unless you're busy.'

'No – not at all. Though, actually...' He reached under the bed. 'Here's your present.'

'I love presents!' With one hand stroking Cary's chest, she ripped off the brown wrapping paper with her teeth. 'Ohhh,' she said. 'I hope it wasn't too expensive?'

'Bought it for a quid from Oxfam.'

Lily flicked through the pages of the Kama Sutra, pausing to admire one of the raunchier pictures. 'You know, Cary, there are two kinds of people in this world – those who start at page one of the Kama Sutra and who diligently work their way through—'

'And there are those who throw the Kama Sutra on the floor and go for whatever page opens up.'

'So which kind of a guy are you?'

'Never really thought about it before – never had the need.'

Button by button, Cary released Lily from her cream shirt. She was wearing a white bra. As Cary stretched to stroke it, the Kama Sutra fell to the floor.

Lily picked it up, admired the picture. 'Girl on top. I'll be in charge – which bodes very well for the future.' She stood up, unclipping her skirt. She writhed seductively as Cary tugged the skirt down her legs. 'Your turn.'

Cary kicked off his trainers, hopping as he took off his socks. 'From my research, I understand that socks on can be a passion-killer.' Lily sat on the bed and, in her turn, eased off his trousers. He toppled onto her. They kissed and they explored and, in time, pants and bra joined the other discarded clothes on the floor.

'About those condoms?' Cary said.

'Not yet,' Lily said.

'No?'

'I don't like the taste of rubber.'

'But we've got minty ones.' Cary flicked through the contents of the box. 'Bubblegum—'

'Might make me want to chew.'

'Banana—'

'Appropriate.'

And so, after a lengthy amount of taxiing around the airport, taking in the sights, dawdling past the control tower, and the hangars, not to mention the three fire engines, Lily decided that gratification had been delayed long enough. A number of condoms were scattered on the floor.

'Didn't much like the taste of any of them,' she said.

Though they have been on the bed for over an hour, Cary is unable to take his eyes off her. 'What about cherry?'

'Is it time for that main course we talked about in the Farrer Theatre?' She wriggled up.

'I love you, by the way – very much,' he said. 'My bounty is as boundless as the sea, my love as deep, the more I give to thee—'

'The more I have, for both are infinite. Studying Romeo and Juliet, are we?'

He laughed. 'Indeed I am.'

'Now, a little less conversation? If you could let me concentrate for just one moment...'

After teetering for so long along the edge of this bubbling waterfall, Lily allowed herself to be swept into the abyss and, seeing her fall, Cary plunged after her. By the time they were both truly spent, there were a number of condoms on the floor, some flavoured, some not, and the pictorial Kama Sutra had become rather dented. And though there are ways and ways of losing your virginity, this way would have to be right at the top: two virgins who are a match and who are besotted with each other.

They lay in each other's arms on top of the duvet. The skylight was open a few inches and a deliciously cold breeze played over their skin.

'Thank you,' Cary said.

Lily stroked his arm. 'I wonder what it'll be like when we don't use a condom.'

'When we're trying for a baby?'

'I can't wait!' She gave him a hug. 'Not that I haven't been sated by the main course, but is there room for pudding?'

'Wouldn't be a proper meal without afters.'

'Where shall we go for honey now?' Lily dropped the scuffed Kama Sutra on the floor. 'The Magic Mountain?'

Cary inspected the full-colour picture and smiled his approval. 'And I'll get to see your face—'

'Unlike last time—'

'Though you do have the most beautiful back.'

'Never been complimented on my back before – but then I suppose nobody's ever quite seen it like you have.'

'That's enough playing with your food – come here.'

CHAPTER 19

While Lily and Cary savoured their beautifully fragrant puddings, I was in Windsor, interviewing that flagrantly beautiful woman, Amanda. I was enjoying the interview much more than I'd expected – and though my twitching antennae did occasionally get things wrong, I thought she was enjoying it too.

Tracking Amanda down had been relatively simple. Sun reporters may hope for the best when they're hunting somebody down – but they always expect the worst. I'd thought it might take a day or two to find her, but no, I'd popped into Pink's and there she was, tinkling on the piano. The club wasn't busy. The boss was delighted that one of his stars was going to be in *The Sun*.

Interviews being such fraught situations, where a single misplaced word can send a skittish interviewee running for the hills, it's of primary importance to get the pictures in the bag. Words can be spun and stretched and cobbled together, but photos – at least in the days before digital fudging – had to be genuine.

When Grubby eventually shambled into Pink's, Amanda went backstage to put on the black basque and tailcoat she'd worn in the School Hall. It was chilly and she wore a long brown overcoat. We walked down to the river. Amanda larked with her top hat and cooed seductively to the camera, very Marilyn Monroe.

I had wanted to take her back to Eton to pose on the School

Hall steps, but Grubby was twitching to return to Wapping to develop the film. The picture was earmarked for the next day's front page and we were already cutting it fine. Amanda gave Grubby a hug and left a lingering lipstick kiss on his cheek. She took my arm and we set off for The Boatman.

'Is this interview worth anything?' she said.

'It depends,' I said. 'How much would you like?'

'Thousand pounds – would that be too much?'

I was charmed. Most people get greedy when they have a Sun story, but Amanda was a beguiling mix, a bawdy innocent.

'Should be able to get you two thousand, if you like.'

'I just might, Mr Kim from *The Sun*!'

It was all so jolly as we walked along the river to The Boatman, Amanda turning heads every step of the way and absolutely loving it. The pub, one of the oldest in Windsor, was just as timeless as I remembered. We took a table by the river.

Amanda wanted a glass of Champagne and, being the well-trained reporter that I am, I bought the whole bottle. I poured two glasses of Taittinger – and, naturally, my phone rang.

It was Robert, the news editor. 'When are you filing?'

'I'll file the first take in ten minutes.'

'Quicker.'

I knocked off the glass of Champagne and pulled out my shorthand notebook – still, even today, the fastest way of turning an interview into an article.

I took her through every detail of her Eton show, from how she'd been picked up to the boys' thunderous reaction.

'How did the Headman take it?'

'He was livid! It was priceless!'

I broke off to call up the News International copy-takers, reading out Amanda's quotes direct from my notepad. She was 24, a music student by day and a pole-dancer by night.

I ordered another bottle of Champagne – hell, I'd leave the car and come down by train the next day to pick it up.

The interview continued, Amanda leaning over the table to touch my arm, her knee occasionally touching mine, occasionally resting against my thigh.

'You're very thorough, Kim,' she said as I returned to the table after phoning over my fifth take.

'The mad-masters are insatiable,' I said. 'I've given them over 2,000 words and, in five minutes, they'll be on the phone again, wanting to know the measurement of your inside leg.'

She giggled. 'I wouldn't normally let a guy measure my inside leg on first acquaintance, but seeing as you're my first Sun reporter, I'll make an exception.'

I nodded sagely. 'I am particularly thorough when it comes to inside legs. Busts are another speciality.'

My phone rang again.

'Good stuff,' Robert said. 'What are her measurements?'

I laughed – 'That's just what I said you'd ask.'

'If you knew I was going to ask it, why didn't you include it in the copy?'

'Because I had to give you something to ask me. Hang on – I'll just find out.' Amanda jotted the numbers down. 'She's 5'10" and her measurements are 36-24-36.'

'The perfect hourglass – lucky you.'

'You always told me you make your own luck.'

'Take her out for dinner and keep your phone on.'

'For you, Robert, my phone is always on.'

Having listened to only half the conversation, Amanda was curious. 'What did he say?'

'Apparently, your figure is the perfect hourglass – and I'm to take you out to dinner.'

'Was that an order?'

'It was – *The Sun*'s news editor has expressly ordered me to take you out for dinner. Where shall we go?'

Amanda trapped my leg between her knees. 'I've never been ordered to go on a date before.'

'Fancy a stroll over to Eton? Somewhere like The Cockpit?'

'Why Eton?'

'I have to lay an old ghost.' I got up. 'I've just got a bag to pick up from my car. Back in a moment.'

The pair of us, now thoroughly at ease, walked over Windsor Bridge to Eton. It was late afternoon, the last shafts of sun shimmering on the river. We stopped in the middle of the bridge.

I turned to her, stroked the hair from her forehead. 'Do you know I've never kissed anyone in a tailcoat before.'

'I thought you said you went to Eton.'

'I'm a very late developer.'

* * *

Maxwell usually loved hard exercise, but not this time. The sweat was getting into his eyes and he hardly had a moment to catch his breath – and this pimpled waster was playing him like a fiddle.

They'd had four games of squash and Maxwell had won precisely eight points.

'Very good fun, thank you.'

Maxwell glared at the grinning Fredster Campbell, who looked like he could do with a good punch in the mouth. 'So, why weren't you expelled for your School Hall stunt?'

'I was being bullied.' Fredster took a swig from his water bottle. 'They made me do it.'

'But there are no bullies in Farrer House.' Maxwell eyed the water bottle, wished he'd brought his own.

'I didn't name any names – not even yours.'

'And Moffatt swallowed it?'

'I'm still here, ain't I?' Fredster swished the water in his mouth and spat it back into the bottle. 'Like another game?'

'No, I do not.'

'Maybe a game of Fives later in the week?'

'I'll have to check my diary.'

Fredster was pulling on his tracksuit top. 'You know who's good at Fives? Lily!' He zipped up his racket. 'She's class.'

'Lily plays Fives?'

'She used to play here with her friends during the holidays.' Fredster held open the glass door for Maxwell. 'I reckon she's the best player in the house.'

'Really?'

'She beat me.'

'She never mentioned that.'

They walked past the Fives courts.

'Maybe she's one of those weird people, who doesn't like to brag! Who'da thunk it?'

Maxwell mulled over how best to use this interesting nugget of information. 'Is there anything else she's good at?'

'She's a good runner – as I think you know. And I believe she can swim. Arctic had her in that pool before she was even in nursery.'

Visions of Lily in a skin-tight swimsuit or, better, a bikini; Lily diving into the pool; Lily getting out of the pool; Lily under the shower, washing that shampoo right out of her hair.

'We should get her playing for the house. Certainly the Fives team, if she's as good as you say she is—'

'Don't take my word for it. Give her a game. If your Fives is anything like your squash, she'll cream you.' Fredster took a swipe at a dandelion. 'Why don't you start up a house Fives ladder, singles rather than the usual doubles? Might be a nice way for Lily to get to know the boys in Farrer.'

'Get to know the boys in Farrer?' Maxwell repeated. 'That would be a nice thing to do.'

CHAPTER 20

The Sun newspaper was fast becoming the bane of Mr Moffatt's life. Not content with wrecking his School Hall speech, that woman – that woman! – was now on the front page of *The Sun*, grinning like a jackanapes beneath the most vexsome headline: 'Eton Your Heart Out, Headmaster!'

Mrs Moffatt was giving the story her full attention. 'She's very pretty,' she said. 'I wish I'd been there.'

'It was an utterly revolting spectacle!'

'You used to quite like South Pacific.'

'Not when it is harmful to school discipline.' He scowled at his wife's paper again. 'It's not news! A woman disrupts a school assembly and they stick it on the front page!'

'It's quite fun. I'm reading every word of it!'

'Pah! How can these idiots call this news?'

'I'm not 100 per cent certain, darling, but I suppose these idiots know a thing or two about what sells newspapers.' She carefully licked her finger and turned to pages 4 and 5, where there were yet more beguiling photos of Amanda. 'They've got a picture of you too, darling. Looks like an old file picture. If I were you, I'd send them something a little more flattering.'

'I will do no such thing!'

'Have some more coffee.'

Mr Moffatt had thought about having the damnable Amanda prosecuted for criminal trespass, but that would have kept the story rumbling on for weeks, months – might even turn her into a star!

The Headman of Eton had much power pulsing through his

fingertips. On any day of the week, he could issue his orders, and could then utter the three most powerful words on earth, words, which for centuries, have been used by British naval captains – Make It So.

But there is, as Mr Moffatt is rapidly coming to learn, another side to this coin. For, anyone who has the power to say 'Make It So' must, in their turn, learn to 'Suck It Up'. The President of America – sometimes, even he has to suck it up; suck it up from the donors and from the senators and from the lobby groups. The Dotcom billionaires, who can summon up a private jet at the snap of their fingers, they also have to suck it up from their children's teachers and from their spouses and from their in-laws. And as for the Headman of Eton College, it seems the fates have decided that, for every time he utters the words 'Make It So', he must Suck It Up tenfold. What really sticks in Mr Moffatt's craw is that, long after he's Sucked It Up, he's left with this acrid after-taste that lingers late into the night.

And he was really having to Suck It Up with *The Sun*. He fulminated on this Kim lowlife. What sort of warped human being would sell his own school down the river? Would run stories to embarrass or shame his old masters? Would—

A knock at the door. Miss Robinson, his efficient secretary, stood in the doorway, her A4 notebook in hand, ready at a moment's notice to take down any of Mr Moffatt's 'Make-It-So' musings. Alongside her, flat cap in hand, stood Mr McCreath, though looking unusually flushed for this time of day.

'Good morning, Headmaster. I'm sorry to interrupt your breakfast.'

'What is it, Miss Robinson?'

'There is a reporter waiting to see you.'

'Has he made an appointment?'

'No, he did not,' Miss Robinson said primly. 'He turned up at your office five minutes ago and asked if he could have a word.'

Mr Moffatt played with his coffee cup, flicking the handle back and forth. 'Would this reporter happen to be an Old Etonian shyster?'

'I don't know if he's a shyster, Headmaster, but he does have an air that is peculiar to Old Etonians. I told him to make an appointment. He said he'd wait.'

'Where is he now?'

'In my office, reading a great pile of newspapers.'

'You left him in your office! He'll be nosing through your filing cabinets, snooping through your in-tray!'

'Will you see him?'

'No, I will not see him! Not today, not tomorrow, not ever! He's a disgrace to Eton and his sole motive in being here is to embarrass us!'

'He seemed very nice when I chatted to him – brought you a bottle of malt whisky – your favourite, as it happens, an 18-year-old Macallan.'

'You didn't accept it?' Mr Moffatt's fingernails bit deep into the palms of his hands. 'I'd rather drink arsenic! Get him out of the school and tell him that, if he ever sets foot at Eton again, I'll have security on him.'

'He didn't look like the sort of person who could be bluffed like that.'

Why? Why?? What had he done in his life to be tormented like this?

Mr Moffatt swallowed. It was both a physical action and a mental one. 'Tell him, please, that I will not be available today.'

Mr Moffatt did not notice what happened next, though the moment was not lost on his perceptive wife. As Miss Robinson left the room, she tucked her greying hair behind her ear, before darting a fond glance at Mr McCreath.

Mr McCreath leaned over Nicki's shoulder to look at *The Sun*. 'Our mole is getting very efficient.'

Mr Moffatt stood glumly by the window and looked out over the cloisters. 'What I would give to have that mole in front of me now and to be expelling him from the school.'

Mr McCreath joined him. 'For myself, I always prefer the chase.'

They watched a man in a blue pinstripe suit saunter out

of the cloisters. Mr McCreath retreated behind the curtains, but the Headman, not so quick, was caught in the act. 'Good morning, Headmaster!' came a cry from the far side of the cloisters. 'I hope you like the malt!'

Mr Moffatt remained at the window for some time. 'He is not only against us. He is also extremely impudent.'

Mr McCreath had been turning this tanglesome problem over in his head. 'We understand boys – but we do not understand newspapers. They are not our world.'

'They're running rings round us.'

'I have a suggestion to make.'

'Oh, yes?'

Mr McCreath outlined his outlandish idea.

The Headman was, naturally, horrified.

But after a while, he realised Mr McCreath might be onto something. It was counterintuitive. It might just work.

'We've got nothing to lose, Headmaster.' Mr McCreath chuckled. 'We might even make some money out of it.'

'Any money will have to go to the school charity.'

'Of course, Headmaster, that goes without saying.'

'We'll do it after the first drugs bust.'

'I'll round up the usual reprobates for some not-so-random urine tests.'

'Good,' said the Headman, before unfortunately adding the fateful words, 'Make It So.'

* * *

Cary was in Lower School with its row upon row of black desks and black benches, and black pillars that stretch the length of this long room, and where every inch of black woodwork had been chiselled and scratched with over 500 years of schoolboy carving. Most Etonians couldn't have cared less for lessons in this room, but for the romantics like Cary, Lower School had a rare charm – it was the oldest classroom in the world that was still in use and, jostling next to him on the long black benches, were the shades of Wellington, and Shelley, and Captain Hook, and Bertie Wooster – and, of course, Ian Fleming.

Cary was in a History lesson taught by that Not-So-Tough Guy Mr Barne – and, unlike any other boy in the school, Cary was allowed to do whatever he pleased. Cary was one of those irritating people who had an eidetic memory. He scanned the page of a book and it stayed in his memory for good. That was why Cary would soon be taking not three but five A-levels; and this was why he could go to Oxford or Cambridge or Harvard or Heidelberg, to study any subject that took his fancy. And it was all so effortless. He was brilliant – but he still didn't know what he wanted to be brilliant at. The law, politics, banking, even accounting; Cary could have shone in any of these careers, but so far, he had yet to come across anything that made him hungry.

His parents, Anthony and Penny, pushed so very hard for their brilliant son to do something brilliant, and his teachers, nudging, jostling, were doing their level best to put polish on this extraordinary gemstone that had come into their possession. How far would he go, they wondered, what could he do? Because, with Cary, it was more a case of what couldn't he do. He was a teacher's dream, the full unbelievable package.

With all these limitless possibilities, Cary should have been having a fine time deciding what he wanted to do next. He excelled at History and English and Economics and Geography, and surely it would have been easy enough to plump for the subject he liked best.

And there was Cary's problem. He enjoyed History and English well enough and had browsed through 'most every book in the School Library. But he had yet to find a subject that made him want to bet the farm and to say those three golden words: 'I'm all in.'

He was all in with Lily. Definitely.

And he knew that what he enjoyed most in life – apart from Lily – was cooking with Mrs Parker and Mrs Webber and making the lives of Windsor's down-and-outs just a little easier. He would have actually made a superb social worker – though many people, teachers, parents, would have considered that a failure. Not that being a social worker isn't wholly admirable, but for Penny and Anthony, it would have been a waste of Cary's talents. They wanted acclaim! And glory! And being a social worker – fulfilling though it might well have been for Cary – certainly wouldn't fulfil any of his parents' dreams and aspirations.

During this History div, then, Cary was sitting at a bench close to the front and was surrounded by books – twelve books in all, and all of them open. The beaks had, at first, found this habit most discombobulating, for while they talked, Cary would nose through piles and piles of books, leafing through indexes, truffle-hunting for gems. A few beaks, before they knew any better, would try to catch Cary out, and would question him about whatever they'd been talking about – only to have the boy turn the tables on them, not only précising the entire lesson in three succinct sentences, but then skewering the beak with some devilish question. After a year or two, the beaks knew to leave Cary be. He'd read his books and ask his questions – and never, not once, take a single note.

Mr Barne the Scotsman was talking about the 1707 Act of Union when, for better or perhaps for worse, Scotland cleaved itself to a greater power, and the English finally acquired a cleaver that was mighty enough to build an Empire. Apart from Cary, there were ten other boys in the div, studiously scratching away onto their A4 paper. Bruno was doodling rope knots on his notepad and dreaming of poppers and fresh ways to get high. Viktor was scribbling at his homework for the next lesson. Cary, meanwhile, was riffling through a book of Scottish history, glancing at the index and dipping in for more morsels. He raised his hand.

Mr Barne was only too happy to take the question; there would follow five minutes of parry and riposte, and he would almost certainly be bested. But there would be no dishonour in that. 'Cary?'

'As a Scotsman, do you think the Act of Union was the best thing ever to happen to Scotland?'

What a ticklish question for this proud Scot. 'It was certainly the best thing that ever happened to England – and, for us Scots, well, I suppose so. Without the Union, neither England nor Scotland would have ever gained such stature on the global stage.'

'So, since we're one country, why do we have so many different laws?'

'Aye, we do that, we do that.' Barne patted his waistcoat and plucked out his snuffbox. He sniffed a pinch of his new German snuff, Schmalzler, and let out a sneeze to rattle the windowpanes.

Bruno looked up. 'May I try, sir?'

'By all means, Bruno.'

The snuffbox was passed along the desks and all the boys gave it a try – and promptly regretted it, sneezing and caterwauling; Viktor was so affected that tears started streaming from his eyes.

'Aye, boys, snuff's for the big boys.' Mr Barne returned the snuffbox to his waistcoat pocket. 'But to return to your question, Cary – in Scotland, the land of John Logie Baird, and of David Hume—'

'Who is Hume, sir?' Bruno asked.

'Only one of the greatest philosophers ever to have walked this earth—'

'Is he up there with Plato?'

'David Hume has had more impact on Western civilisation than Plato and Socrates put together.'

'Then how is it, sir, that I have not heard of him?'

'Because of the impoverishment of your education. Now—'

'And to think of the school fees.'

'Bruno, dear, are you aware of the word "horticulture" and what it means?'

'I am, sir.'

'Allow me to use the word "horticulture" for you in a

sentence.' Mr Barne made a great show of taking another pinch of snuff. 'Ready, boys? I think you'll like it! In the words of the great Dorothy Parker, "You can lead a whore tae culture but you can't make her think".'

The boys guffawed and, to Mr Barne's delight, Cary lifted his nose from his books and laughed along.

'In similar vein, Bruno, you can stick boys in Eton, you can force-feed 'em culture, but even with the best will in the world, you still won't be able to instil any reason.' Mr Barne licked his finger and chalked up his hit by dabbing a one in the air. 'To continue – Scotland is the land of the great, the legendary philosopher David Hume, and the land of John Logie Baird – who invented the television, Bruno, just in case you're wondering – and of Sean Connery, an actor of note, Bruno, who you may have seen in the talking pictures. But above all else, Scotland is the land of civilisation and, in this civilised realm, we have many laws that help to make the world a better place. For instance, if you are in Scotland, anywhere in Scotland, and you happen to be caught short, then you can just knock on anyone's front door and they are obliged to let you use their toilet.'

Viktor sniggered. 'Imagine if you'd had curry!'

'Quite,' Barne said. 'And the Scottish jury system is so much superior to that of the Sassenachs. In England, it's either black or white for a jury; they can only find a defendant guilty or not guilty. But the Scots have a delightful area of grey, whereby a jury can find the case "Not Proven".' He flicked a scratch of snuff off his waistcoat. 'Which, I daresay, is the same as a guilty verdict, but without the condign punishment.'

Mr Barne was about to expound further on the many merits of the Scottish legal system, when he saw something that he had never seen before. Cary had, as usual, been ferreting through a history book. He took his Eton Fixtures book out of his tailcoat and scribbled a note inside the back of the green cover. Mr Barne was so intrigued that he leaned over to look. It was a list of Useful Stuff.

CHAPTER 21

Lily had been to a most uninformative meeting of the Eton political society, where the former Prime Minister Ted Heath had given a talk about… something. Lily had not even the foggiest idea. And, as she walked back from Upper School with Fredster Campbell, she marvelled at how such a senior politician could be such an awful orator.

'You're lucky to still be here.' Lily cuffed Fredster on the shoulder.

Fredster got a delicious tingle from the blow. It was the first time she'd ever touched him. 'I'm on my final warning. It's gone on my written record.'

'And will this record stay with you for the rest of your life, or will it eventually be wiped clean?'

The Prince was walking in the opposite direction. He held up his hand, and grinned when Lily gave him a high-five.

'You'll be getting an invite for tea at Windsor Castle, if you don't look out,' Fredster commented.

Lily was so happy she could have skipped the length of Judy's Passage. She was in love – and she was in love with one of the good guys. She was still revelling in her Kama Sutra memories. Some of those things… she didn't know whether to laugh or blush, and so she did both. Not that there was anything whatsoever to compare it to, but for a first time, she reckoned it was probably a perfect ten.

Back at Farrer, the Dame, Miranda, offered her a toddy before she went to bed.

'Never had a toddy before,' Lily said as she followed Miranda into her hothouse-hot suite of rooms.

'You'll like it.' Miranda had not only clocked that Lily was happy but – unlike Lily's blunt instrument of a father – she had also divined the reason why. Lily was obviously in love and, to look at her, had acted on her impulses. Miranda could not have been happier. She'd known Lily since she was a girl, had seen her Arctic father hammer and hammer this square peg into a round hole, but for all his hammering, Lily had resolutely refused to be knocked into any sort of shape.

Since Arctic liked to keep his rooms at slightly below zero – 'never did the Eskimos any harm!' – it was such a delight for Lily to kick off her shoes and snuggle down into an overstuffed armchair.

Miranda made the toddy and Lily delved into the heap of travel brochures on the coffee table. They were about all manner of exotic countries all over the world, some of which she'd never even heard of.

'Where are the Comoros?' she called.

Miranda came through with the lemon and honey toddies and topped them up with a slug of whisky. 'They're a group of islands near Madagascar. The capital is called Moroni. For some quite unaccountable reason, it always reminds me of your father.'

Lily almost choked on her toddy. 'When are you going there?'

'Over Christmas. I'll try and knock off Madagascar while I'm about it.'

'Would it be awful if I said that I would love to join you?'

'Of course not – I hate spending Christmas in Britain with nieces and nephews and grumpy sisters and grumpier brothers-in-law! Five years ago, I had another foul Christmas in London, and vowed never to spend Christmas in Britain again!'

The whisky started to do its wonderful work, and Lily said things she would never have dreamed of saying to her parents. 'I always long for Christmas to end,' she said. 'I know I shouldn't be saying this, and I know how lucky I'm supposed to feel, but it's become this ritual where, every year, we all have to do exactly the same thing. We have breakfast, we go to church, my uncle and aunt come over on the dot of 12.30, and then, over the sherry – concentrated orange juice for me – we unwrap our presents, and I say thank you to my parents for their joint gift, which is, in fact, just a present from Mummy because Daddy can't be bothered to get me anything.'

'I never get any presents at Christmas – it's very liberating!'

'I'll get you a present. And, after we've listened to the Queen's Speech, with Daddy standing up, and after we've eaten our dry turkey, we have a long walk down to the river, and my aunt asks me what I want to do with my life. Then we come back to play Trivial Pursuit for two hours – and I shouldn't say this, but I suspect that Daddy has looked at all the questions beforehand.'

'Why don't you do something different this year?'

'Maybe...'

'Maybe some charity work?' The thought hangs idling in the air, though Miranda is far too canny to push it. 'I see they've started up a house Fives ladder – singles.'

'Have they?''

'Just gone up. And do you know what I'd like more than anything? I'd like to see you at the top of that ladder. A girl at the top! You could beat any of them; I've seen you play, so I know you could!'

'You think so?'

'I know so! It'd be a nice way to get to know the boys in the house.' Miranda reached over for the bottle and turned her toddy into a large whisky. 'But from the look of you, Lily, you're not interested in meeting anyone new.'

Lily blushed. 'How did you know?'

'Maxwell will be gutted.' She leaned forward to massage her bare toes. 'Too bad.'

* * *

Journalists develop acute antennae for things that don't smell right. My antennae were twitching in alarm at this peculiar telephone call.

I'd been at my desk, tip-tapping away at not so very much, when Stella put a call through.

'Some gent wanting to speak to you,' she said.

'Anything else?'

'He wouldn't say.'

And, with a click, the mystery caller is through. 'This is Kim.'

'Think I might have a story for you.' It was a middle-aged man, with a soft Scottish Borders brogue.

'You've come to the right place,' I said. 'Do you have a name, by the way? Can I call you back?'

'No.'

'Okay – so what's your story?'

'It's an Eton story.'

And that was when I started to prickle. Not anything I could put my finger on, but I could sense the distinctive flash of an amber alert. 'Fire away.'

'Six boys have been caught in random drugs tests.'

'Bound to happen,' I said.

'I suppose it was.'

'Do you know anything more?'

'The drugs included cocaine, magic mushrooms and marijuana.'

I tapped my pen on my notepad. 'May I ask how you know this? Are you a master at the school?'

'I cannot say.'

I proceeded with the utmost caution. 'Don't call up any other papers,' I said. 'If anything comes of it, there will be a lot of money in it for you. Is there any name you'd like to go by?'

'You can call me… Call me Mickey Mouse.'

'Okay, Mickey – give me a call if you learn any more.' I rattled off my contact numbers. 'I look forward to paying you in person.'

The story was confirmed by the School Office, though as usual, the Headman had no further comment to make. It made another Splash – 'Eton Drugs Bust' – and, a while later, I was driving down to Slough with £4,000 worth of used £20 notes in my briefcase. I didn't really know why I'd picked Slough for this meet-up, but some prickling instinct told me to keep this man well away from Agent Orange.

I arrived at the Three Tuns half an hour early. It was a coaching inn, nearly two centuries old, with a fire and murky brasses, and – or at least in those days before it was given a chintzy refurb – it had a deal of charm. I drank black coffee and surveyed the near-empty pub. Apart from the pub landlady, the only other person there was a middle-aged man in the corner. The man was wearing tweed. He nursed a pint as he wrote into a notebook.

After a couple of minutes, I walked over to him. 'This might seem a little strange, but are you Mickey Mouse?'

'I am.'

'I'm Kim.'

'I thought you might be.'

'I'll just get my coffee. Another pint?'

'Please.'

What a strange man! Sitting in the corner there, knowing perfectly well who I was, and yet not introducing himself. It was like… it was like he was on a fishing expedition.

I brought over my coffee and a pint of Directors. 'So – nice to finally meet you.'

'Always good to put a face to a name.'

'Got some money for you.' I opened my briefcase and handed over a brown envelope. '£4,000, if that's all right.'

'That will do very well.'

'You're obviously very well connected. What do you do at Eton College, if you don't mind my asking?'

'No, I don't mind you asking.'

'And?'

'And I'm not going to tell you.'

I bought more time by adding two lumps of sugar to my coffee. I slowly stirred. I couldn't make the guy out. Definitely not one of the teachers. A local shopkeeper, perhaps, but even that didn't really fit; to have that sort of detail about the drugs bust story – he knew the exact drugs – meant that he had to be part of the College community. Maybe one of the support staff, a janitor or groundsman, maybe from the bursar's office.

Maybe not.

'Got you a pager, if you want it,' I said. 'So I can contact you.'

The Motorola pager was inspected. 'Aye.'

'If you need to call me, it's best to use a public payphone.'

'Pagers and payphones, so that's how it's done.' The Motorola was tucked into a coat pocket. 'Daresay you're coming to Slough quite often these days. The Three Tuns is a nice pub.'

'It is.'

'How many Eton insiders do you have now?'

'Some and some.' I drained my coffee and decided not to have another. 'I can't really fathom you out, Mr Mouse. Why did you sell this story?'

'Why do you think?' He drank his pint, eyes never leaving mine.

'People have lots of motives for giving stories to *The Sun*. Sometimes it's for money, sometimes it's for revenge. And sometimes the motive is completely off the wall. Like with you.'

'I have my reasons. Does it make any difference to you? I thought all you were interested in was the story.'

'I'm also interested in building a relationship with my sources. It helps if we're friends.'

'Why's that?'

'Because then it makes for a more convivial time when we meet up, and instead of having just coffee, we have lunch, and when I'm haggling on your behalf with my mad-masters, I will haggle just that little bit harder.'

'I see.'

I stood up. 'Thank you. I look forward to hearing from you.'

'You will.'

I left the pub and stood outside in the bracing rain, face turned to the sky, mouth open. What a fantastically mucky meeting. But then… just as Mr Mouse had said, so long as the stories were good, then what matter his motives?

CHAPTER 22

Cary and Lily had soon established their own blissful routine. Three or four times a week, they both went to The Project. After a couple of hours' work – Cary in the kitchen, Lily in the laundry – and after gratification had been delayed a sensible but not ludicrous amount of time, they would flit to the attic. The family pack of condoms was spent within the week.

Cary had passed on a couple of tips to *The Sun* – a story about a little light arson in a boy's room, and another about a beak who'd been caught kerb-crawling; not Splashes, but solid page leads.

He was also learning to drive. He knew the theory of driving. Putting it into practice was not so easy. There were so many things to do – steer, and change gears, and dib-dab with both feet, and all at the same time. His driving instructor, Teddy, would pick him up from The Timbralls after lunch and they'd hack around the back streets of Windsor.

Cary would drive and Teddy would talk, fulminating about Europe and the grey Prime Minister, John Major.

Teddy had stopped off at a garage to buy some Werther's Originals and to top up his Mini Metro. Cary waited patiently in the front seat.

'Bit poky, isn't it?'

Fleming was in the back seat, primly placing Teddy's tartan rug over his knees. 'Bond wouldn't be seen dead in a car like this.'

'I'll see if I can get something a little more roomy when I pass my test.'

'That is some way off.'

'Teddy said I should book my test for next month.'

'You can book as many tests as you like, Cary, but that doesn't mean you'll pass them. But look on the bright side – failure is good for you.'

'It builds character.'

'So it does, Cary. The thing about failure is that it always tastes like shit. But after you've had a good lot of it, then you are able to swallow it down more quickly. If you're not used to the foul taste of failure, then it can take weeks, months, to swallow – and there are some people who are so terrified of that shitty taste, they won't even throw their cap in the ring. They are risk-averse. They are the wet blankets – and though they won't ever fail, they will never achieve anything of note.'

'Excellent,' Cary said. 'I'll be eating so much shit that I might even get a taste for it.'

'Now – interesting that our man at *The Sun* knew about that drugs bust before you did.'

'I suppose Kim's got another Eton mole.'

'Though he'd never say.' Fleming sniffed the hem of the rug. 'How nice. It smells of grass. He's been having a picnic.'

Cary perked up. 'I'd love to take Lily on a picnic.'

'If that's what you call it.'

'We might eat some food, too!'

'Enough of this frippery. I fear, Cary, that you have an ordeal ahead of you; several ordeals, and tonight's will be one of the worst.'

'Is it a big fail?'

'You will see it as such.'

'Oh. How do you know these things?'

'I have...' Fleming's voice dwindled to a whisper of nothing and, in another moment, he was gone. Teddy was coming out of the garage, unwrapping a Werther's and popping it into his mouth.

The rest of the driving lesson and the rest of the day were smothered with a fire-blanket, stifling the oxygen, snuffing the joy. The afternoon was spent waiting for this random thunderbolt to strike, with no idea where it would come from or who it would hit.

And when it did come, and even though he'd expected it,

it was just as devastating. It might not have been a fail. But it certainly tasted like one.

Supper is chicken curry with chapatis and mango chutney. Cary tries the lime pickle but doesn't much like it. Boys hollering, boys scuffling, boys snaffling an extra chapati. Cary drinks two glasses of water and eats a strawberry yoghurt. He hardly says a word. This horrid presentiment that something is wrong, but not being able to put his finger on it.

He goes to his room and tries to read but nothing sticks. He starts to write a letter to Lily and fills it with memories and fanciful dreams. He takes off his trainers and puts on some slippers. He's still wearing the same jeans and sweatshirt he wore for the driving lesson. It's dark by now. He draws the curtains.

The alarm bell rings for a second. The Timbralls boys return to the dining room for the evening prayers. Cary is one of the last boys to troop in. He takes a seat at the top table, by the window at the far end of the room.

Mr Ormerod stands at the lectern near the door. He makes a joke about the boys' performance in the house Field Game competition.

One of the junior boys plays Beethoven's Moonlight Sonata on the piano. Cary has heard this piece so often that he is inured to it. It is wallpaper music. He neither likes it nor dislikes it.

Mr Ormerod opens up his Bible and starts to read. It is one of Mr Ormerod's favourite texts, from Ecclesiastes, an old man who's heard it all and who has seen everything. Mr Ormerod relishes the words from his King James Bible – 'To every thing there is a season.'

Cary doesn't hear it at first, thinks it's nothing. But the whisper gets louder. He sits up, pays attention.

'Where's Bruno?'

Cary scans the room, realises Bruno isn't there. Realises he hasn't seen Bruno since tea.

Fleming is whispering directly in his ear. 'Go now – now!'

Cary gets up, eases behind two boys' chairs, and walks straight down the middle of the room. Every eye is on him.

Mr Ormerod stops. 'Everything all right, Cary?'

'Excuse me, sir.'

Cary leaves the room. After a pause, Mr Ormerod continues. His words echo after Cary as he takes the stairs three at a time—

'A time to be born.

Cary hurtles round the corner and up the next flight.

'And a time to die.'

Cary thunders down the corridor. Bruno's room is the last on the right, bigger than the others, gloomier than the others.

Cary knocks on the door. He tries to go straight in, but something's blocking the door. He pushes hard, harder, until there's enough of a gap to squeeze through.

A thin light seeps in through the windows. He flicks on the lights, steels himself.

Bruno is kneeling on the floor. He's still in his sports gear from the afternoon match. His head is suspended a foot from the floor. It is quite purple and his dry tongue lolls out of his mouth. Biting into his neck is a noose made from his dressing-gown cord. The other end of the cord has been tied to the hook on the door.

Cary heaves Bruno up by the shoulders and flicks the dressing gown cord off the hook. He eases Bruno down to the ground and starts working at the cord round his neck. The slip-knot is so tight, he can barely work his fingers under the cord.

He kneels in the pool of urine and works at the slip-knot with his teeth, Bruno's neck clammy on his lips.

The knot eases a little. Cary yanks with his fingers and tugs the noose over Bruno's head.

Footsteps on the corridor.

'Help!' he yells. 'Help!'

Viktor darts his head into the room. 'What has happened?'

'Call an ambulance.'

'Is he dead?'

'Just call 999.'

Cary knows exactly what to do. His father taught him when he was eight. He's practised it every year since. He opens Bruno's mouth, checks for blockages and gives 30 brisk chest compressions. He gets the correct tempo from the Bee Gees' song 'Staying Alive'; he used to think it was funny. He can all but hear his father telling him to make the compressions solid – 'hard enough to break his ribs'.

Blows two full breaths through Bruno's lifeless lips, and nothing is happening, there's no response at all and, though he could go on all night, his hopes begin to wither.

More chest compressions, more full breaths. Boys clustering in the passage outside. Viktor comes in to help with the compressions, and then Mr Ormerod is fluttering into the room, so shocked that he looks like he'll faint to the floor. He sits on the bed and watches without saying a word.

The sound of sirens coming up the road. Footsteps thundering down the corridor. Two paramedics burst into the room, one with a large backpack.

'He's been hanged?' A paramedic unzips his bag and pulls out a defibrillator.

'He has.' Cary moves to give the paramedics room but remains kneeling on the floor in the pool of urine.

The paramedic cuts up the front of Bruno's shirt with heavy-duty scissors, slaps two sticky pads on either side of Bruno's chest. He presses the green button. For a fraction of a second, 3,000 volts arc through Bruno's chest. Nothing.

'Again,' Cary says.

Another thump. And – nothing. All is still, and now they're not staring at a boy any more, they're staring at a corpse.

'It's a no-go,' the paramedic says. 'I'm sorry.'

Cary helps lift Bruno onto the stretcher, covers him with a grey blanket, straps him in tight. He insists on carrying his friend out of the house, taking the front end of the stretcher. Every door along the corridor is open, boys soundlessly gawking as Cary trudges past with the stretcher. More boys on the lower corridors, and a gaggle of boys in the lobby, still and silent as the body is carried out of the house.

Cary slots the stretcher into the ambulance. He gives Bruno's forehead a kiss goodbye. The ambulance leaves without sirens. Cary returns to the house. Mr Ormerod is waiting in the lobby. They go through the Fleming Library to his office. Mr Ormerod gets Cary some water and asks desultory questions, and then two detectives arrive. They go through the story over and over again; they keep asking how Cary had known something was wrong.

'I don't know,' Cary says. 'I hadn't seen him all evening.'

'Had he tried this form of auto-asphyxiation before?'

'Not that I know of.'

It's gone 10pm by the time the detectives leave. Cary goes back to his room. All is just as he had left it; Lily's letter awaiting his sign-off, everything the same, and yet everything entirely different, and his best friend's dead, hanged in a moment of dumb idiocy.

Cary sits at his burry and weeps. What a waste, what a ridiculous way to go – trying for a quick high and strangled on your own dressing-gown cord. He pulls back the curtains and gazes out at the star-bright night. He thinks of Bruno, and how his friend once lay in the middle of the road and stared up at these same stars and mused on infinity. And now Bruno has become a part of it.

Cary had expected Fleming to come and Fleming came on the dot of midnight. He wore a dark suit and a dark tie and he brought along a bottle of Rémy Martin.

'I'm sorry,' he said.

He went over to Cary's burry. Bruno's cut-crystal schooner stood in solitary state by the lamp and, while all else was broken, the beautiful tracery on the glass remained the same, the boy still chasing the girl, and the girl still chasing the boy through their field of vines. Fleming filled the glass and gave it to Cary.

'To Bruno,' he said.

'To Bruno.' Cary downed it, the cognac burning the back of his throat, and he almost had a mind to throw the glass against the wall, but then, no, he'd keep it, and every time he drank from it, he would send up a prayer for his friend. 'How did you know it was going to happen?'

'I have a sense of when someone is coming to join me. I had been expecting Bruno for some weeks.'

'Oh.' Cary proffered his glass for a fill-up. So, Bruno's death was already in the stars – whether he'd hanged himself or whether he'd been run over by McArdle's car.

'I had a lot of friends die on me,' Fleming said. 'It tastes just like failure. It tastes like shit.' He sighed and rubbed his cheek. 'But, like failure, death can be empowering.'

'It can?'

'Every time a friend dies, it is a great call to arms, reminding us that we've not got long. We could be dead tomorrow and, if not dead, we might be injured, disabled, destined to spend the rest of our lives in a wheelchair. The death of a friend is a wake-up call.'

'Get it while it's hot?'

'I used to believe that I was living my life for my dead friends, my dead relatives – even my dead father. Everything I did, my books, my spies, my villains, Bond, Blofeld, Scaramanga, they were all, in their own way, a tribute to the people who'd passed on. And what you now do with your life, Cary – it won't just be for you, it will also be for Bruno.' He topped up Cary's glass. 'I know a little of that, boy, and I can tell you that his spirit will be by your side – and he will revel in every one of your grand adventures. Now – let me tell you about the Wizard of Oz...'

Cary dozed a little and, when he woke, Fleming was gone. He licked his lips and could still taste the cognac.

So, he could wait till tomorrow afternoon but that wasn't getting it while it was hot – that would be getting it when it was stone-cold stale. Wait till tomorrow to see Lily – pathetic! He wanted to see her and he wanted to talk to her, and he'd just get right on and do it. Fleming would approve. Bruno would definitely approve.

He pulled on his hoodie, some hand-me-down he'd found at The Project. He tip-toed down the passage past Bruno's room. Blue and white police tape had been stuck across the door.

He pushed down the emergency bar and the fire door swung soundlessly open. Cary left the door slightly ajar so he could get back in, and trotted down the fire escape. All his hours on the Eton assault course had given him muscles and agility. He sprung up onto the bins, jumped onto the wall and dropped into New Schools Yard, out of the house and out on the prowl. It would have been a mistake to take the direct route to Lily's house, as the whole area around Prince William's house was riddled with CCTV cameras. He looped round over Sixpenny and past the Fives courts, and the air was cool and crisp. His friend was dead, and he was still wiping the tears from his eyes as he jogged to see his lover.

He jumped over the wall into the Farrer House garden. A few lights were still on, boys scribing away at their extra work, hoping for good grades, hoping for good exam results, hoping for a good university, and a good job and a good salary and a good wife and good children, and then, before they knew it, a good funeral and they'd made it safe into the ground, and there wouldn't be getting anything anymore while it was hot because they'd be stone-cold dead.

Lily had said that her room was on the corner on the top floor. Her curtains were drawn, window slightly open.

Cary sized the house up. He could have done with some rope. The only way up was the drainpipe. It was cast-iron, built to last. The brickwork was slick and wet; could have been better, but it was what it was. In no time at all, he was up past the second floor. He had the good grace to realise that what he was doing was just about as stupid as Bruno's self-strangulation. One slip and he'd be joining Bruno in the morgue – and, with that very thought, his foot did slip and he thumped hard into the wall. There was a light on nearby. Cary stayed quite still. When nothing more happened, he continued to climb up the drainpipe and hauled himself onto the roof. For a while, he sat there with his feet dangling over the edge, and he knew that Bruno was with him, and that Bruno was loving it, because there they were, with the stars up above and a big fall beneath them.

He walked along the roof and stood directly above Lily's room. If he were to fall through the roof, he'd land on her bed. He wondered what to do next. He wondered if this was even a good idea.

CHAPTER 23

Lily has been having the most numbing nightmares. She has been in that halfway house between the living and the dead, and she has had a sense of fleeting spirits, though she does not know why. She is left with a gloomy sense of foreboding.

At first, the singing is part of the dream. Cary is with her. Cary is comforting her. He's holding her hand and he's singing that great anthem from what is now her new favourite film, South Pacific – 'Some Enchanted Evening'.

That hovering moment as dream blurs and blends with reality, and she is dragged back to life and is staring at the ceiling – and listening to Cary singing. It has to be Cary. Who else could it be?

She can't work it out. Is he in the room?

No – he's not in the room. But he's close.

She gets up, opens the window. 'Is that you, Cary?'

'It's fortune's fool.'

She looks up, sees his face silhouetted against the Milky Way.

'Cary!'

She has a whole stream of questions to ask – like what he's doing on the roof, and why he's on the roof, and how, indeed, he's even managed to climb onto the roof. They can wait.

'Come in.'

'I was hoping you'd say that. Open the window wide, I'll swing down.' He has another thought. 'You'd better be ready to grab me!'

Lily opens the window. Cary slips over the roof-edge and

hangs onto the drain. It's a little awkward. He flicks back with his legs and, as they swing forward, he lets go of the drain. The momentum almost carries him into the room but it's not nearly the stylish move you see in the movies. His legs are in Lily's room but he's falling backwards, paddling at empty air with his hands. He's all but fallen out of the window when Lily snatches at his belt, holding tight with both hands, feet braced against the wall.

Cary leans up and grabs the edge of the window. He pulls himself into Lily's room and into her arms.

'You're a life-saver,' he says, and bursts into tears.

She's kissing him and holding him as tight as she can. 'What's happened?'

'Bruno.' He holds her tight, tighter, tears dripping down his nose and onto her shoulder. 'He's dead.'

'What – how?'

And out the whole horrid story tumbles, and telling the story out loud only seems to make it more horrific and more senseless.

Lily hears him out until there's nothing left. There isn't anything left to say. Over and over again, you can think about the loss, the waste, the stupidity, but after you've said it twice, three times, you're just repeating yourself. She kisses his tears.

'I'm sorry.'

She kisses his cheek, his lips turn and the kisses are ever more urgent. Trousers are ripped off, nighties are discarded and, in a matter of moments, they are doing just exactly what every tingling sense is telling them to do. They are making the most explosive, impulsive love. No languorous love-making tonight, no dallying through the dented pages of the Kama Sutra; it is hard and hungry as they both give free rein to their instincts.

Cary is both laughing and crying, mind just completely discombobulated, but while all else is in flux, he knows he has his lodestar: Lily.

'I've had a change of plan,' he says. 'As of tonight, I'm going to be living each day as if it were my last.'

'Good.'

'And, of course, I've got plans and dreams, and you feature in every one of them, but from now on, I will carry Bruno everywhere with me.' His finger traces up her hip and over her belly. 'And he's only got one thing to tell me.'

'What's that?'

'When did you last watch the Wizard of Oz?'

'Last Christmas – maybe.' She snuggles into Cary. 'Are you ready for more?'

'I am.'

'I quite like this freestyle approach to love-making.'

'Who needs the Kama Sutra! We can just make it up as we go along.'

'How very radical! So, tell me about the wisdom of the Wizard of Oz.'

'There's a great piece of life-affirming philosophy in it,' Cary says. 'It's not from Dorothy; nor the Scarecrow; nor the Tin Man; nor even the Cowardly Lion.'

'It couldn't be Toto?'

'Not even Toto! It's the Wicked Witch of the West, with her green face, and her shrieking laugh and her scratchy pearls of worldly wisdom.'

'This I have got to hear.'

'At the end, the witch lifts up this large hourglass. She turns it over and the blood-red sand starts to trickle out. And she's got something pretty important to say.' He drags his nails languorously up her back. 'She cackles at Dorothy – and this is what she says: "Do you see that? That's how much longer you've got to be alive. And it isn't long, my pretty – it isn't long!"'

'It isn't long,' Lily repeats. 'I love it.'

She pulls out another condom. 'I gather that some lovers don't like these interludes for condom emplacement—'

He sniffs and cuffs a tear and laughs. 'Where did you hear that?'

'I've been reading Cosmo for improving tips.'

'You don't need any improvement whatsoever! You could not be improved! You are unimprovable!' He tears the condom wrapper with his teeth.

'Very well – but what I was going to say was that I quite enjoy the interlude. I enjoy watching the emplacement of the condom—'

'But the main reason you like it is because it's yet another opportunity to delay your gratification.'

'I blame my Calvinistic upbringing.' She places his hand just so. 'And now I am ready to be gratified.' She kisses him as they fuse into each other's wide eyes. 'Gratify me.'

By chance, Miranda, the Dame, is padding past Lily's door, and can hear the unmistakable sound of Lily being loved. Miranda does not know who her favourite girl is with, and nor does she much care; she's happy that Lily has found love. She hopes it's someone nice. But then how could he be anything else? If he's good enough for Lily, he's bound to be nice.

Three hours later, and after not one wink of sleep, Cary slips on his clothes. Lily puts on nightie, dressing gown and slippers. She opens the door and beckons for Cary. She leads the way down the corridor, past Miranda's room and past her slumbering parents, and down the three flights of stairs. She unlocks the front door. A brief hug and a kiss on the porch and Cary is gone, loping off into the mist. Lily locks the front door behind her and returns to her room. The family pack of condoms is returned to its hideaway, and Lamby and Babs take up their rightful positions on the pillow. In under a minute, her light is switched off and all is as it once was, though now, far from having night terrors, Lily is replete as she picks over bedroom memories.

At the far end of Farrer House, there is one other Eton pupil who is also awake. He is very hurt and very annoyed – and all the love and yearning he once had for Lily have, in an instant, been turned to hate.

Farrer House is a curved crescent shape, so the boys at one end have a view of the boys at the other end.

Maxwell heard Cary going up the drainpipe. He heard the thump when Cary slipped and cussed and crashed into the wall, and he knew, without a doubt, that it was a boy climbing onto the roof. He turned off his light and waited by the window to see what would transpire. It was a very still night. He could hear the sound of singing. The next moment, Lily opened her window, and this thing, this guy, this boy in black, swung down from the roof and into her arms.

Maxwell does not know the identity of Lily's secret lover. But that can wait. All he knows is that he hates her now more than he has ever hated before, and this hatred is twinned with fury and with guile, and he may have to bide his time, but he's got a lot of that. If he waits patiently enough, he will see a chance to do her down and he will take it.

CHAPTER 24

For his office, Mr McCreath had commandeered a room in Lupton's Tower and his window overlooked the School Yard, from where he could see the boys coming and going and forever dreaming of new ways of making mischief. The School Yard was Eton's hub, dripping with over 500 years of history, the Chapel to the left and Lower School to the right. Dead ahead was Upper School, which took the full hit from the Nazi bomb that punched out the chapel windows and, right in the middle of the School Yard, was the mottled green statue of Eton's founder, Henry VI.

Mr McCreath's office was breathtakingly bare, just a desk and two wooden chairs, though he had allowed himself the luxury of a single picture on the wall. It was a picture of the man whom he considered to be the greatest of Eton's headmasters, Dr John Keate, an irascible man who was only 5ft tall, and who, it was said, could never be put out of humour – because his ill-humour was permanent. He loved to cane the boys and, on June 30, 1832, memorably flogged 80 boys in a single day; towards the end of The Great Flogging, the flogger flagged, but rallied when the boys began to cheer. When the doughty Dr Keate retired two years later, he said his only regret was that he hadn't flogged a whole lot more.

Mr McCreath stood by the window, stirring a cup of coffee that had been brought to him by the – how could Mr McCreath possibly do her justice? – simply delectable Headman's secretary, Miss Robinson. He was surprised at himself. He'd thought that the fires of his once raging libido had been snuffed out long ago, but now, here he was, a man in his fifties, discovering that his libido was more than just smouldering, 'twas ablaze. But how to proceed? Obviously, with all due caution, especially bearing in mind that Miss Robinson was a very highly respected colleague. But ohhh! What a beauty! And demure, and efficient, and eminently respectable; the only wonder was that she hadn't been snapped up long ago.

Being unused to the ways of women, and being completely unable to divine that sometimes a cup of coffee can be more than just a cup of coffee, he had no idea if his ardour was reciprocated. Ask her out for coffee? Too tame. Ask her out for dinner? He recoiled in horror at the very thought. No respectable spinster would dream of going out for dinner on a first date. Take her out to the pictures? There was that very good Scottish film, Braveheart, showing at the Screen Cinema in Windsor… Thoughts of hand-holding in the dark and lips perfectly puckered for a kiss…

Mr McCreath's delightful musings were interrupted – rudely interrupted – by the Headman bursting into his office without so much as a knock on the door.

'Good afternoon, Headmaster.' Mr McCreath eyed Mr Moffatt over his coffee cup. The Headman's bow tie was askew. 'What has occurred?'

'I will tell you just exactly what has occurred!' Mr Moffatt paced Mr McCreath's office, fingers clenched. 'News of this boy hanging himself in The Timbralls is already in the public domain! I've just had that repellent man from *The Sun* call up, asking me for a comment!'

'And what did you say?'

'I will not sully myself by speaking to that bottom-feeder!'

'I'm sure Miss Robinson handled him appropriately.'

'How can the story have got out so quickly?'

'Boys don't often hang themselves at Eton, Headmaster.' Mr McCreath had taken up his station back at the window. He was watching three boys, whom he'd caught smoking round the back of the swimming pool. They were on their knees, picking moss from between the flints – and they'd be moss-picking for the next three hours. Good for the flints and good for the soul. Since Mr McCreath had taken over as Eton's head of security, the School Yard had never been so spotless. 'It would have been the talk of the school by breakfast time.'

'Is it possible this wretched mole is in The Timbralls?'

'That is a possibility, Headmaster.'

But by the next day, when Mr McCreath was reading *The Sun*, he realised it was more than possible that Eton's mole could have been in The Timbralls. What was striking about the story was the sheer level of detail – including the fact that the boy hadn't hanged himself on purpose, but had been getting high on self-strangulation. It also mentioned that he was still in his sports gear after playing the Field Game.

Mr McCreath pondered whether this peculiar detail would have been widely known around Eton; possibly, possibly not. He recalled that the hanged boy, Bruno, had been caught drunk in the grounds of Windsor Castle – a story that had also made the front page of *The Sun* newspaper.

He went to his filing cabinet and pulled out the house photos from the previous summer. He found the photo of Ormerod's house, out in the Timbralls garden, the nippers sitting cross-legged at the front, the librarians sitting behind them with Mr Ormerod and, behind them, were standing two rows of mischief-makers. Mr McCreath took off his glasses and pored over the picture, as if, from his very attitude, the rogue schoolboy might give himself away, but for the moment, Mr McCreath drew a blank. Perhaps it was because his mind was only half on the job. What if, instead of taking Miss Robinson to see Braveheart, he took her for a walk to Windsor Great Park, and then afterwards, natural as could be, they could stop for a cup of tea somewhere and, over the scones and the tea-cups, he could lean over and kiss her...

* * *

Bruno's death was the catalyst. Lily had got her lover and she'd got her education – and now she wanted the whole lot, everything that Eton had to offer.

She decided to join the house Fives ladder, which had been up and running for several weeks. After lunch, and as the boys were streaming out of the Farrer dining room, she diffidently buttonholed Maxwell. For some reason, which she had not yet been able to divine, but for which she was immensely grateful, Maxwell had been keeping himself to himself for the past three weeks.

'Maxwell,' she said. 'Could I have a word?'

'Yes?'

'I hear there's a house Fives ladder. I wondered if I could join it.'

'If you must.'

'How very charmingly you put it, Maxwell – well, I think I must.'

Lily had no idea what had rattled this peculiar's boy cage, but he seemed to have the hump. He might even have the hump with her, though the machinations of Maxwell's tiny brain were hard to comprehend.

'Put your name on the bottom of the ladder – work your way up. Assuming you won't be too tired.'

She gave Maxwell a sharp look. 'Whatever do you mean by that?'

'I'm just saying, it's important to get a good night's sleep.'

Maxwell stalked out of the dining room. He couldn't know. Could he? Was it possible? They'd tried so hard to keep it secret. But one of the enduring problems of the Eton goldfish bowl was that secrets rarely remained secret for very long.

CHAPTER 25

The nights are closing in and the air is thick with autumn leaves. It is still dark as Cary trots out to Eton's assault course where, in the space of a month, he has become remarkably proficient with the ropes and the monkey bars and the pits and the tunnels. Barty Pleydell-Bouverie trots alongside him – having unwittingly earned Cary and The Project some £4,000 by coming back from half-term with his head shaved as smooth as a billiard ball. Barty had promptly been sent back home and told not to return to Eton until he'd got a wig. The story had made a page lead in *The Sun*, and then, thanks to Barty's unusual surname, he had been tracked down to his home in North Berwick, where he had happily posed for pictures on the beach.

Barty had taken to joining Cary on his morning runs. He could keep up when they were running over the fields, but the obstacles were hard going. Barty was fervently waiting for that fabled Growth Spurt. For the moment, he was having to make do with spindly legs and stripling muscles. So, while Cary scrambled with ease up the cargo nets, Barty toiled as if trapped in a spider's web. Cary was waiting for him on top of his favourite obstacle, The Table. It was a table built for a giant, with four immense legs and a platform that was a full 15 metres high. On one side was a scramble net to get up and, on the other, was a thick climbing rope for sliding down.

Cary watched Barty crawl underneath barbed wire and into a pit of mud. It'd be at least another three minutes before he made it to the top of The Table. The sun was just peeping up over the frosted skyline, the night's candles were burnt out, and jocund day stood tiptoe on the misty treetops. Cary was the King of Eton and all that it contained.

Ian Fleming came over to join him, leaning against the railings, drinking in the view.

'Just beautiful,' Fleming said. He took another puff on his cigarette and flicked it over the side, watching the glowing end spiral down into the dew. 'Bruno would have loved it up here.'

'He would – though assault courses were never really his thing.'

'I suppose not.' Fleming eyed Cary meditatively, like a stockman sizing up a bullock at the market. 'Bad do, what happened to Bruno. How are you getting on?'

'Bearing up.'

'I'm sorry.' Fleming tapped out another Morlands from his silver case, lit the cigarette and blissfully inhaled. 'Most boys, I can tell how it's going to turn out for them. You've got me stumped, Cary.'

'I'll take that as a compliment.'

'I sense great things ahead of you. But I have no inkling where you will find this greatness.'

'I'm pretty flummoxed, too.'

Barty, covered in mud, was floundering up the cargo net. His hair was now an inch long so, thankfully, he no longer had to wear his ridiculous wig.

Fleming inspected the boy. 'He really is quite small, isn't he?'

'Though he be but little, he is fierce.'

'Think I'll have him in my room in a couple of years.' Fleming dabbed at the dew and licked his finger. 'So, you're off to London for your latest payment from Kim. Where's he taking you?'

'I don't know. Probably some café near Waterloo.'

'Shall I tell you what that rat is doing? He is taking his

new girlfriend, Amanda, out for very expensive dinners to the Ritz and to the Cipriani and to the Gay Hussar – and he is then running these dinners through on his expenses, claiming to his mad deputy editor that he has, in fact, been dining with his number one Eton mole. So, why don't you ask him to take you somewhere decent for a change?'

'I've never been to a restaurant in London before.'

Fleming looked over at Barty, who was having some trouble pulling himself onto the top of The Table. 'Christ, it's high up here - almost gives me vertigo.'

'I'd better give Barty a hand.'

'I would recommend you ask Kim to take you to Quo Vadis in Soho.' Fleming flicked his third cigarette over the side. 'And when you're there, do be sure to visit the flat upstairs.'

'I'll do that.' Cary grabbed Barty by his muddy collar and hauled him up.

The boy smiled, teeth bright white against the black mud that covered his face. Cary shook out the rope, tested that it was taut, and let himself over the edge of The Table. After a brief chat with Barty, he made a controlled slide down the rope.

* * *

As usual, I had arrived early – and, as usual, I was dressed in a blue suit, blue shirt and dark tie. Cary had also made an effort. He was wearing a seersucker jacket, very popular in the 80s, and now right back on trend.

It was Sunday lunchtime. Quo Vadis was cool and deliciously dark, with thick white linen tablecloths, silverware that gleamed, old prints of London and enough flowers to fill a hothouse.

Now, the first ten minutes of that Quo Vadis lunch are a bit hazy. We chatted a bit about Eton. Cary passed on some gossip which, if suitably stretched, might make a page lead. I ordered a bottle of Pol Roger Champagne. I poured two glasses.

I ordered for the both of us – a dozen oysters, I think, to be followed by roast suckling pig.

Everything was in order. I took a sip of Churchill's favourite fizz; it was excellent. I was wondering if I could spin the lunch out to two hours, perhaps even three.

'So, how are you spending all your Sun loot?' I asked.

'I'm not,' Cary said.

'No fancy clothes, no flashy holidays?' I said.

'I'm doing exactly what you told me, Kim,' he said. 'I'm being ever so discreet.'

'But it's safe, though?' I said. 'You're not going to lose it?'

'Safe as can be.' He picked up his glass, twirling the stem between long fingers. 'It's actually in a safe.'

'The least I know about it, the better,' I said, clicking open my briefcase and taking out four thick envelopes. 'Twelve grand.'

'Thank you.'

And that was when it all started to get rather exciting.

I was just pushing the envelopes across the table to Cary. A burly man stepped over, grabbed me by the collar and hoisted me to my feet.

'Gotcha!'

I gave a start. And then I saw who it was. I patted down my collar and resumed my seat.

'Bain,' I said. 'Dear me, have they really started letting the likes of you in here?'

Bain. Bain of the Charterhouse headmaster scoop. Bain of the 'Maaate, maaate' pleadings. Bain, who was far and away the most unscrupulous hound I'd ever met – and that's saying something. He was a little younger than me, with short-cropped dark hair and pouched eyes in a pasty face. Most striking of all, however, was his gold eye-tooth. It glittered in the candlelight. Bain pulled over a chair and poured Champagne into the nearest empty glass, a large water tumbler. He knocked it off in two large gulps and helped himself to more.

I tried to hide my twitching anxiety. 'I see the deportment lessons are going well.'

Bain roared with laughter, leaning over to pinch my cheek before lolling back to survey the room. 'Lovely little restaurant,' he said. 'Heard of it, but never been in.'

'Though it's always lovely to see you, what are you doing here?'

'Spotted you near Oxford Street – all very cloak and dagger, and I thought to myself, there goes a man who's paying off one of his contacts.' He poked at the envelopes on the table. 'And I was right! Looks like over ten grand to me.'

'I've absolutely no idea what you're talking about,' I said.

'This lad your drug-dealer, then? Even your cocaine habit isn't this big!' He leaned over the table and extended his hand to Cary. 'I'm Bain, by the way – taught Kim everything he knows. And you are?'

'I'm Frank – Kim's nephew, though I'm flattered you think I'm one of his contacts.'

Bain laughed. 'So, tell me, Frank – if that is your name – why is your Uncle Kim giving you such large sums of money?'

Cary lied easily. 'Not that it's any business at all of yours, Bain, but my great-grandmother died in the spring. She insisted that all her great-grandchildren should each be given £10,000, or ten grand, as you say, and what's more, it was to be paid in cash, the better to diddle the tax-man.' He raised his glass. 'To great-granny.'

I sipped. 'She was a game old bird.'

'How highly implausible,' Bain cackled. 'And what was the name of your dear old great-granny?'

'I thought Watt was the name of the engine driver,' Cary said.

'You're good, you're really good!' Bain grabbed hold of my leg and squeezed tight round the knee-cap. 'Got an answer for everything, hasn't he, the young scamp?'

'Wouldn't you be better off with a Big Mac?' I asked.

Bain was enjoying himself. 'I've got a better question – why, oh why, did you pick Quo Vadis for the handover?'

'It's very simple,' Cary said. 'When they were first married, my great-grandparents used to live in the flat upstairs. She always used to say it was the happiest time of her life.'

'Plausible,' Bain said. 'But unlikely. So, if they really did live in the flat upstairs, you'll know all about its very famous occupant. Who lived there?'

Cary smiled pleasantly and drank Champagne. 'I didn't know we were playing twenty questions.'

'Humour me.'

'Of course he knows Karl Marx lived upstairs,' I said.

'Spoilsport!' Bain said. 'I liked seeing him squirm. So, my lad, what are you going to spend all this lovely money on?'

'I was going to take my girlfriend to Goa for the winter.'

Bain leaned over to pat the back of Cary's hand. 'Ever thought about a career in journalism?'

'Not if it means working with the likes of you.'

'Sauce!'

A cheery waiter brought over the dozen oysters. As soon as they were on the table, Bain scooped one up, squeezed a lemon and poured the oyster into his mouth. 'Down the little red lane it goes!'

'Now, if you don't mind, Bain,' I said. 'You have entertained us long enough.'

'Am I intruding?'

'No more than usual.'

Bain made to grab one of the brown envelopes on the table. I slapped his hand away.

'All right!' Bain said. 'I know when I'm not wanted!' He got to his feet. 'Always a pleasure, Kim, never a chore.'

'I so wish I could say the same.'

Bain stared intently at Cary for a few seconds. 'And, as for you, young man, I never forget a face – and I greatly look forward to seeing you on the Fourth of June.'

'What happens on the Fourth of June?' Cary asked innocently.

'That's Eton's Parents' Day – as you very well know!'

He ruffled my hair and, whistling the Eton Boating Song, he mooched out of the restaurant.

I let out a very long exhale. 'Sorry about that.' I scribbled an imaginary bill in the air to a passing waiter, poured out the last of the Champagne and, when the bill came, immediately paid in cash. 'We'd better go. It'd be just like Bain to be waiting outside for us. We'll use the emergency exit.'

Cary tucked the four envelopes into his rucksack and followed me outside. I led the way through Soho's alleys to a little Italian restaurant. I ordered pizzas and beers and, when the beers came, I was so rattled that I downed my glass in one.

'So, who is Bain?' Cary said.

'Bain by name and bane by nature.' I poured a glass of the best Italian wine in the house, Barolo. 'He is, truly, one of the banes of my life.'

'But who is he?'

'He's my opposite number at *The Daily Mirror* – went to Harrow, don't you know. He'd give that disgusting gold eye-tooth to have an Eton contact like you.' I gulped the Barolo. 'And, if he can't have you as a contact, then the next best thing would be to burn you.'

'He wouldn't do that!'

'He most certainly would.'

We had eaten some pizza and drunk most of the wine when, chatting about this and that, I passed on a bit of Eton gossip that I'd heard – 'I hear there's a new girl at the school.'

Cary was eating. A piece of pizza went down the wrong way. He choked, coughed, choked again, before finally coughing it up.

'Are you all right?' I poured some water. Cary drank it.

'I'm fine.' Cary coughed again.

'The girl at the school?'

'She's a housemaster's daughter.'

'Do you know her?'

'She's very pretty.'

'If you hear anything at all about her, I'd love to know – the only girl at Eton! Surrounded by hundreds of hungry boys! Let me know if she gets into any scrapes – drunkenness, duelling Etonians, pregnancy, all that sort of thing.' I examined the empty wine bottle, wondered whether to buy another. 'Now that would be a great story!'

'No more wine for me,' Cary said. 'How did you find out about this girl, if you don't mind my asking?'

'Other sources,' I said. 'He's the oddest contact I've ever had. Can't make him out.'

'Oh, yes?'

'I've no idea why he's doing it. You – you're in it for the money, for the hijinks, for the adventure. But him, when I see him, downing his pints of Old Peculiar, I hear alarm bells.'

'What does he know of me?'

'Nothing. You are classified Most Secret.'

'Except Bain now knows what I look like.'

I pulled at my lip. 'It's not ideal.'

* * *

Bruno's memorial service was being held in the College Chapel. All of Bruno's year were in the Chapel, as well as all of his house and an assortment of friends.

Maxwell, of course, was there, because he was in Bruno's year; he'd never known Bruno that well, but the little he had known of him, he had disliked intensely. Bruno had been a loafer, an idler, a slack-bob boozer and, as to the bizarre way he'd died, Maxwell hadn't been in the least surprised.

But, as Maxwell stared at all the boys and all the masters who'd gathered to say farewell to Bruno, there was one small thing he couldn't understand: what was Lily doing at the memorial service?

Lily was wearing black, blending in beautifully with the

tailcoats. She was sitting on the other side of the Chapel from Maxwell. He studied her carefully. While the Headman droned on, she wiped away a tear.

Maxwell wondered about her connection with Bruno. She wasn't in the same house, or the same year; she shared no tutors with Bruno, nor belonged to any of the same clubs. Maybe they'd never met, and Lily had just come along to get a taste of a memorial service. Maybe. And then maybe... Maybe Lily had known Bruno. Maybe they were old friends. And maybe, and more interestingly, Bruno had been friends with her mystery lover.

It was like a punch to the gut. Lily had a boyfriend – and it should have been him. Lily was sleeping with somebody else – and it should have been him. Lily was giving her kisses to some other Etonian – and it should have been him. And, if it hadn't been for this other lover who'd turned her head, it would have been him.

Her lover was in the Chapel now, he was sure of it. He watched Lily for any secret sign that she might make; a conspiratorial smile, perhaps, or a kiss that was blown across the Chapel. But Lily was circumspect, serene. She did not look at any of the boys, nor smile at them. She studied her hymn book and occasionally wiped her eyes.

The boys in Bruno's house were all in a gaggle right underneath the organ. Their housemaster, Ormerod, sat behind them; he was openly crying, how utterly pathetic.

Maxwell wondered if Lily's lover might be in Ormerod's house; that would explain how she came to be at the memorial service. But who could it be? A boy in his year, or someone from the year below?

Maxwell's gaze was drawn to a grizzled old man. Unlike everyone else, he was wearing tweeds. He was sitting directly opposite the boys in Ormerod's house. The man had no interest whatsoever in the service. He appeared only interested in Ormerod's boys.

Maxwell eventually placed him. He was McCreath, the

head of security – though why he should be at Bruno's memorial service was anyone's guess.

Another hymn, another turgid reading from the Bible. Finally, the dirge service came to an end, Bach blared from the organ and the boys filed out. Maxwell was watching for it – and he was rewarded.

Lily made a small slip. When she left the Chapel, walking out underneath the organ, she looked over at Ormerod's boys and gave a nod. Of course, it could have meant nothing. More than likely, it meant everything.

Maxwell sidled out of the Chapel and down the stairs, following her discreetly. In his black tails and black trousers, he was perfectly camouflaged for skulking in the shadows. He turned his collar up to hide his white shirt.

He didn't know why he was stalking her, but something told him she wouldn't be heading straight back to Farrer.

Maxwell lost sight of her, but shouldered his way through the crush by the School Office. He saw her cross the road. She walked past the School Hall, past The Burning Bush, and now should innocently be strolling down Judy's Passage.

But she didn't stroll down Judy's Passage. She walked down Common Lane, which was a much more circuitous route to Farrer – if, indeed, she was even going to Farrer. Maxwell crossed to the other side of the road and followed from a leisurely distance.

He couldn't quite believe that Lily, his Lily, was actually about to meet her secret lover. No – she was taking the air, was enjoying Eton at night, but then Maxwell suddenly realised she was in earnest: she really was about to see her lover! If Maxwell had a mind, he could catch them in the act.

Instead of taking a left turn back to Farrer, she continued on down Common Lane, past more school buildings, and then out into the wilds of Eton; certainly no place for a girl at night.

Lily walked up the lane to Eton's astronomical observatory, a square block topped with a white dome. She seemed to know exactly where she was going. Maxwell could just make her out in the darkness, a shade more black than the surrounding shadows. Then he picked it up. It was the sound of her lover singing.

Maxwell heard it and he wondered how to punish her. He could just call in the school security, let them catch the lovers *in flagrante*. He could do that. But he also wanted to find out the lover's identity. He wondered if he could do both. He sprinted back into Eton town centre.

* * *

Lily followed Cary into the observatory. He shut the door behind them and locked it and they fell into each other's arms. They held each other tight for one minute, two minutes, with not a word said.

They kissed and they kissed some more, and had a hug to end all hugs.

'I wondered if you'd come,' Cary said.

'I nearly didn't,' she said. 'I couldn't see anything behind me, but I had a sense of a stalker.'

'Did you now?' Cary said.

'It was probably nothing.'

'If I've learned anything at all this half, it's to listen to your instincts—'

'Can you guess what my instincts are telling me to do?' She sinuously wrapped her leg around his thighs.

'Our instincts are as one.' He lifted her skirt, kissed her. 'Tell me about your stalker.'

He took her by the hand and led her through to the observatory proper. It was cold and it was black as pitch. He lit a candle and, in an instant, the observatory came to life, a cannon-sized telescope with a brace of smaller telescopes to the side.

Lily went over to the telescope, took a squint. 'Now, who would stalk me?' she said.

And in an instant, she had the answer. 'It's Maxwell.'

She took a seat behind the telescope, spinning the main pivot wheel as the telescope tracked upwards.

'Maxwell the rower?' Cary said.

'Yes. I met him at a party in the summer and, to my eternal shame – not to mention regret – I kissed him.'

Cary kissed behind her ear. 'Must have thought he was in with a chance.'

'Not then – and certainly not after I'd met you.' Lily twiddled another wheel. 'I've never seen the moon look so big!'

It was while she was looking at the moon's craters, and while Cary was unstrapping her bra, that she knew for certain that it was Maxwell. 'I think he might have seen you when you climbed into my room.'

'He did?'

'He's been very cool since then.'

Cary had already laid a rug out on the floor. He opened a bottle of fresh apple juice and poured two glasses. 'Anything else?'

'He alluded to me not getting enough sleep. It was bizarre. Didn't think much of it at the time.'

Cary sat on the rug and pulled Lily down next to him. 'These instincts of yours,' he said.

'These instincts?'

'I think we should listen to them.'

* * *

The porters in the School Office were sipping coffee and watching EastEnders when a call came through. It was somebody who claimed to have spotted two people breaking into Eton's observatory. There was no further dialogue. As per the standing instructions, the head porter, Mr Alterman, called it through to Mr McCreath, who had retired to his ice-cold office, where he was tippling on his one indulgence, a bottle of Laphroaig from Islay; to some, the smoked peat whisky was too acrid, but to Mr McCreath, it was nectar.

Since he had nothing better to do, he crossed the School Yard to quiz Mr Alterman.

'And what did the caller sound like?' Mr McCreath asked.

'Irish accent, deep voice – probably a prankster.'

'Or somebody trying to disguise their voice. Did they say anything more?'

'Just slammed the phone down.'

Mr McCreath stroked his beard, pushing his chin up towards his nose. Why would anyone want to break into the observatory?

'I'll have a look,' he said, and pottered off down Common Lane to investigate.

* * *

Cary and Lily had indeed followed their instincts: they were making love. For them, the positions of the Kama Sutra were for when they were in the warmth of The Project, and when they had a bed and time to experiment. But sometimes, as that night, they were just hungry for love, and all those fancy tantric positions from the Far East were forgotten for something more basic, more primitive, and often more satisfying: girl on top.

It was so dark that all each of them could see was the grey glow of their lover's face. Lily was so cold that she put on Cary's tailcoat and smothered him tight. They cocooned themselves in the blanket.

'Well, this is new,' she laughed.

'Like it enough to repeat it?'

'Undoubtedly!' She kissed him. 'The whole world is now our bedroom – we can make love anywhere and everywhere!'

'We will be like beasts in the field!'

Now was not the time for stringing out their ardour. They instinctively moved up a gear.

Lily whispered in his ear. 'Do you hear that?'

'It sounds like a key in the door.'

Everything stopped; a smoothly running engine that suddenly seizes up. They watched and they listened.

* * *

Mr McCreath had never been into the observatory before. He put the key in the keyhole and tried to unlock the door, but found he had the wrong key; he tried another and another and, on the fifth attempt, the lock clicked and the door swung open. He flicked on his torch and stepped inside – and then, because he was an old hand, he locked the door behind him.

He could smell it immediately. It was very out of place in an observatory. It was the smell of roses. He walked into the main room, letting his torch play over the walls and the telescopes. He spotted something pink on the floor – scratched it up and sniffed. Fresh wax from a rose-scented candle. A plain candle might just be a japester; this pink candle could only have been brought for a lover.

Mr McCreath checked out the rest of the observatory. There was a small storeroom where the lovers might be hiding, though he had a sense the birds had already flown.

He was about to leave when he noticed some small splashes on the floor. He dabbed and licked his finger. He wasn't certain, but it was probably apple juice.

Walking back to the office, he mulled the problem over. At a guess, he'd say they were young lovers. They'd been drinking apple juice and they'd needed somewhere snug for their evening tryst. Almost certainly connected to Eton in some way – how else could they have got the key?

So: probably an Etonian with some connection to the astronomical society.

And, as to the identity of this Etonian's lover – well, it could be one of the maids, or the cooks, but in these matters, he preferred the rigorous application of Ockham's Razor, whose principles were first laid down by the great William of Ockham: slice away at all the fanciful ideas and stick with the most simple theory until the facts indicate otherwise.

So, what was the need to go searching for miscreant girls in Windsor or Slough when the simplest explanation – by far! – was that she was already in the school. That she was, in fact, the only girl in Eton: the very comely girl who was the daughter of a housemaster and whom he'd just seen at the memorial service – and who, not two weeks ago, had more than likely been having sex in the School Hall, right after the Headman's assembly.

* * *

Just as people do after a near miss, Cary and Lily were laughing. If they hadn't followed their instincts, Mr McCreath would have caught them rolling around on the floor of the observatory – but as it was, they'd left the observatory five minutes before he arrived there and had been watching him from the long grass fifty yards away.

Lily leaned down and kissed Carey. 'So, what brought him to the observatory?'

'Your stalker tipped him off.'

'Very bad manners. We're going to have to be more careful.'

'Even more careful.' Cary rolled up the blanket and slung his arm around Lily's waist. 'Let's be getting you back.'

'How much longer till you pass your driving test?'

'Quite soon – I hope. If only there were some way I could get hold of a great wodge of cash, and then I could buy us a car—'

'Yes?'

'Couldn't I just keep a small slice of *The Sun*'s money? I'm not looking for anything flash.'

'You can't.' Lily snuggled in next to him, loving the feel of his hand on her hip. Their bodies were the perfect shape for walking alongside each other.

'It would be the tiniest slice imaginable.'

'You can't,' Lily said again. 'It would feel like blood money. If you spend a single penny of it on yourself, then I just know this… this whole precarious edifice will come tumbling down.'

She stopped. They turned and they kissed and then they continued to walk.

'And that's why I love you,' he said. 'Though what would be so terribly wrong with this precarious edifice tumbling down, anyway?'

'Good point.' They broke off for another kiss. The more they kissed, the more they wanted to kiss.

'As far as I'm concerned,' Cary said, 'so long as I've got you, then the whole world can tumble and fall.'

Lily was still glowing when she trotted upstairs to her bedroom. She dropped her dress onto the floor and had a shower.

Arctic could hear her singing, but did not have the wit to realise that this was the first time he'd ever heard his daughter singing in the shower. Later on, when she was at her desk writing her diary, he went into her room and wished her good night. There was something unsettling about the whole experience, which he would only be able to put his finger on much, much later. He would remember the way she snapped the diary shut, and how he'd hovered at the door. And he'd remember, also, the black dress that was hanging on the back of the door. It was the dress Lily had worn at that unruly boy's memorial service. Arctic had glanced at the dress, but – at least at that stage – had thought nothing of it.

'Oh – you've got a bit of red wax on your dress,' he'd said.

'Must have been the votive candle I lit for poor Bruno.'

'Did you know him?'

'A little.'

'He was in that Ormerod's house, wasn't he? Bunch of ne'er-do-wells, if ever there were.'

'If you say so.'

Arctic looked at his daughter and, for the first time, realised she could not care less what he was saying. He could have said that the moon was made of smoked gouda, or – more ludicrously – that Eton was about to go fully co-ed, and she'd have still said exactly the same thing: 'If you say so.'

He was leaving the room when he noticed that, along with the red wax, there was also a grass stain on the hem of her black dress. He might have asked her about it, but there didn't seem much point, as there was only one thing she wanted and that was to be left alone.

Teenage daughters! How did these girls become so utterly unfathomable? If he had a peep at her diary, he might be better able to understand what made her tick.

So: as Mr McCreath stands by his office window, waiting for that magical moment when the Headman's secretary, Miss Robinson, will give him a shy wave while she walks across the School Yard, and as Cary retires to his room for another night of mourning his friend, and as Lily re-opens her diary to continue to write of all that has happened that day and all of her dreams that are yet to come, a wretched beast disentangles itself from a yew hedge, and emerges into the streetlights of Common Lane. It is Maxwell.

He'd watched Mr McCreath walk out to the observatory, and then – disappointingly – had watched Mr McCreath walk back again, empty-handed. He didn't know why, but he continued to wait, and a full 30 minutes later had been rewarded by the sight of Lily walking along with... with Cary! Cary the runner! Cary with his hand on her hip and Cary, who was stopping every 20 yards to kiss her!

Maxwell did not feel anger or rage – or any of that white-heat emotion that calls for an instant outlet. No, he might have felt that an hour earlier, when he'd first followed Lily to the observatory, but now he knew the identity of her lover, all he felt was a deadly cold calm. He'd get him and he'd get him good, and when he got this Cary, this tosser, he'd deliver such a knock-out blow that the boy would literally never be able to get up again.

CHAPTER 26

Cary had had his last Michaelmas half at Eton, and New Schools Yard was filled up with Maseratis, new Volvos and highly polished Audis, as parents flooded in to Eton to take their darlings back home for Christmas.

Cary was getting the train. He'd started getting the train home to Yorkshire a couple of years earlier because the drive back to Hawes, in the Dales, had been up there with the quite electric pain of his one and only root canal treatment, given to him by his own father.

So, instead of getting into the padded leather luxury of some brand-new car, Cary ambled out of The Timbralls with just a small rucksack on his back.

Barty was getting into the front seat of his father's black Bentley.

'Give you a lift?' the father asked, somebody big in banking, a knight of the realm even, or so Cary had heard.

'Thank you, sir, but I'm just walking to the station.'

'In the rain?'

'I love the rain.'

'Come on, Cary – get in. Barty's told me all about you.'

Barty hopped into the back and Cary eased into the front seat. It was the flashiest car he'd ever been in. Leather seats that warmed up; a dashboard with walnut inlay; a padded steering wheel.

'Like a Coke or a bun or anything?' the dad asked. He was bald with tufty hair slicked back over his ears, and had reached that resplendent age in life where he couldn't care a fig what people thought of him. 'Got a long drive ahead, so we've got a lot of provisions.'

Cary took two Cokes from the mini-fridge and passed a can to Barty, who sat in the back in dumb awe. His father and Cary were in the same car, with him, and were chatting to each other.

'I hear you've taken Barty under your wing,' said Barty's father.

'He doesn't need to be under any wing, sir—'

'Call me Archie.'

'He's more than capable of taking care of himself.'

Unlike most parents, Sir Archie did not quiz Cary with humdrum questions about careers or university, but instead talked about Tough Guy and about a race he'd once run in the Sahara Desert.

'I'll never forget the heat,' he said. 'On the hottest days, it was 54 degrees. Most people don't have a clue what that means. It means drinking 11 litres of water – and sweating so much that you never once need to stop for a pee.' Sir Archie did not even seem to notice that they'd been stuck in traffic for 30 minutes.

Of his own accord, Cary mentioned that he had no idea what he wanted to do with his life.

At Slough station, Sir Archie produced a sleek silver card-case. His thick creamy card was simple and expensive. 'Keep in touch.'

'Thank you.' Cary gave Barty a wave.

Cary cashed in his travel voucher to Northallerton and pondered that great teenage imponderable: why did he always prefer his friends' parents to his own?

There was a difficult matter to broach with them.

He'd decided not to spend Christmas with his parents.

Instead…

Cary wondered just how this was going to sound. They'd go absolutely mad!

Instead… He plans to spend his Christmas elsewhere; he thinks, he hopes, that it will be the best Christmas of his life.

* * *

'What?'

'What did you say?'

Cary tried again. 'I'm going to spend Christmas cooking for the homeless in Windsor.'

'But… but you can't!' wailed his mother, Penny. She was sitting in the back seat of their immaculate, middle-aged Rover. 'Great Aunt Pat and Great Uncle Richard are coming round on Christmas Day! James and Rosie are coming with their new baby! And we're seeing the Grants on Boxing Day! You love the Grants!'

Cary's father, Anthony, wearing jacket and tie as if he were picking Cary up from Eton rather than Northallerton Station, was also unhappy. 'Poor show, Cary, poor show.'

'I'm sorry.' Cary wished he'd caught the bus home from Northallerton. 'I'd have let you know sooner, but they only decided to have a Christmas dinner a couple of days ago.'

'What is this place? What is this thing?' Anthony was so distracted that he pulled out in front of a bus without indicating.

Penny – dressed as if she was off to church – leaned forward to touch her only child on the shoulder. 'Who are these people? Do they mean so much to you? Do they mean more to you than your own family?'

Cary patted the hand that remained on his shoulder. 'Of course they don't, Mum,' Cary said. 'But I'm the only cook they've got.'

Penny started to cry. She thought back to the day she gave birth to Cary, that small pink miracle lying on her chest, probably the happiest she'd ever been and, out of nowhere, she'd thought of her favourite film, It's a Wonderful Life, with the great Cary Grant, and that's why she'd insisted they call their boy Cary – seventeen years, gone in the blink of an eye, and now he was all grown up and moving on.

Anthony expressed his annoyance by vigorously pulling at his wispy hair. 'It all sounds most odd.'

'Cary – you're only 17,' sniffed his mother. 'You've got plenty of time for all these, these things. It's my favourite day of the year – and now you won't be there! Where will you spend the night?'

'They've got plenty of beds at The Project,' Cary said. 'I'll only be gone a few days, back in time for the New Year.'

'It sounds like a whole lot of nonsense to me,' Anthony harrumphed.

'You could come and help out, if you like. You might like it.'

His father gave the expected reply. 'You have got to be joking.'

Cary started to smile and had to stare out of the window into the rain. He was recalling just exactly how the idea of a Christmas party had come about.

He'd been giving Fergie and Renton another brick of Sun money – this time, courtesy of some boys who had caught a number of sewer rats in catch-'em-alive-o cages, and had then released them during a Latin exam. Boys squealing, beaks leaping, rats scurrying and the three culprits howling with laughter.

Renton had stared moodily at the mound of money that was sitting on the table. 'What are we going to do with all this?'

'We'll think of something,' Fergie said. 'Why don't we have another cup of tea?'

'For every thousand we spend, you're bringing in ten!' Renton said.

'Oh, I am so very sorry,' Cary said. 'How thoughtless of me.'

'Don't worry, Renton.' Fergie dunked his Digestive. 'We'll find something to spend it on.'

'It's more than fifty thousand quid! In readies!'

'Good lad!' Fergie nudged Cary's elbow.

'I've never seen so much money in my entire life!'

Lily had come into the office with a shopping bag from Poundland. 'Got some decorations to brighten the place up,' she said, giving Cary a kiss. 'Make it feel a bit more Christmassy.'

'I've got it!' Fergie said. 'I've got a great idea! We could have a… A Christmas Party! On Christmas Day! With turkey and crackers and, and trimmings!'

'It's hassle enough running this place without having a Christmas party!' Renton tugged at his *'plumage'*, as he called it, the voluminous thatch of white chest hair that poked from the top of his shirt.

'Oh, puss,' Lily said. She pulled out some purple tinsel and draped it over the old curmudgeon's shoulders before giving him a kiss on the cheek. 'I think it's a lovely idea.'

'And it would help put a small dent in this horrible pile of money that's cluttering up your safe,' Cary said.

'But… but who…?'

'I'll do it,' Cary said.

'But how can you do it? You won't even be here.'

'I'll order the food and drink this afternoon – and I'll pick it up when I come back on December 23rd. Cook it all up on Christmas morning.'

'Come on, Renton,' Fergie cackled. 'Cary's organising it and it's going to be brilliant.'

'And I'll help,' Lily said – and Cary squeezed her hand, and suddenly, and most unexpectedly, it looked like it was going to be the best Christmas ever.

But until then… Cary had to contend with a week with his parents. They were pestering him for details of just where he intended to go to university and what he intended to read. Cary duly answered all their questions, but he was on autopilot, because what he was really considering was that most revolting of all prospects: least worst options. There was the possibility of Politics, Philosophy and Economics at Oxford;

or History at Cambridge; or law at Harvard; or English at Queen's, Belfast; or could it be Brown, or Princeton, or should it be Archaeology, or Economics, or... Should it be none of the above? No more exams, no more sweatshop essays, and two fingers to the treadmill.

It was all so wearisome, and his parents' hectoring was wearisome, though actually there was something of more immediate concern. He'd never cooked Christmas dinner for a hundred before and it might be middling tough.

CHAPTER 27

Being the son of both a dentist and a hygienist, Cary had his teeth checked not once, not twice, but three times a year, and these check-ups always coincided with the first day of the school holidays. First morning he was back from Eton, in fact, first thing on that first morning, and before Anthony had seen any of his regular patients, Cary had to take his seat in the chair-o'-pain.

In matters of dentistry, his father, Anthony, was an Old School driller. He believed, just as his father and his grandfather before him had believed, and his great-grandfather also, that a stitch in time saved nine: cavities, no matter how small, had to be drilled and filled. Some dentists preferred to leave cavities be, see how they developed, but not Anthony, because as he had learned through bitter experience, if you didn't fill a cavity, then it would only ever get bigger.

Cary's mother, Penny, in pristine white uniform, was sterilising her husband's various instruments; Anthony, ponderously flicking his lower lip, familiarised himself with Cary's notes; and as for Cary, he was sitting, docile as a sacrificial lamb, in the chair-o'-pain. He was looking up at the ceiling and was listening to the peculiar sound of his father's rumbling stomach; none of them had had breakfast.

There were so many things he could have told his parents. He could have told them he'd got a girlfriend, a housemaster's daughter, no less. Or he could have told them he'd raised over £50,000 for a local Windsor charity, The Project. Or perhaps tell them about Ian Fleming; or about Bruno hanging himself; or about climbing onto the Farrer House roof. Or…

'I've passed my driving test.'

'Mmmm.' His father, spectacles on the end of his nose, licked his fingertip and turned another page of the notes.

'What did you say, Cary?' Penny looked up.

'I've passed my driving test.'

'Did you hear that, darling?' she said. 'Cary's passed his driving test.'

'Really?' Anthony looked up. 'Shouldn't you be spending your time revising for your A-levels, rather than learning to drive?'

'Can't I do both?'

'You can learn to drive any time.' His father sniffed before returning Cary's notes to the filing cabinet. 'You only get one shot at these exams.'

'I know you're on a full scholarship, Cary, darling, but we have had to spend quite a lot on your school fees—'

'Haven't had a foreign holiday since our honeymoon.' His father humphed over and sat on his bony leather dentist's stool – the same stool that had belonged to his father, and to his grandfather, and to his great-grandfather also.

'Any chance of you putting me on the insurance for the Rover?'

'And open wide, please.' The light, bright as a searchlight, was turned onto Cary's face.

'Can I be insured to drive the Rover?'

'Hmmm,' his father said. 'I don't think so.'

'Any reason why not?'

'All in the fullness of time, Cary, all in the fullness of time. And a little wider, please.'

Cary subsided back into the dentist's chair, mother hovering by the spit-basin, father probing at gums, tongue and teeth.

'A little bit of over-brushing on your eye-teeth, I've warned you about that,' Anthony said, little mirror clinking against Cary's teeth. He began to hum a tune to himself, that great Yorkshire anthem: 'On Ikley More Bar T'at'.

Cary knew all about the song. He had heard it many times over – knew all about the swain who was being chided for going out on Ilkley Moor without a hat (bar t'at). The lad is told that he'll likely die of exposure on the moor and then his body would be eaten by worms, and the worms in their turn would be eaten by the ducks, and the wheel would come full circle when the ducks were eaten by the Ilkley townsfolk.

For Cary, it felt like his father had rammed a sharp knitting needle into the base of his neck.

It was his father's drilling song.

'Another cavity, I'm afraid,' his father said on cue. 'Or at least the beginnings of one. The drill, please, Penny.'

Cary moved his head to the side. 'What's the beginning of a cavity?'

'Exactly what I said, Cary.' His father riffled through the drill bits. 'You've got a cavity. Needs filling.'

'And I'm just getting it straight – no local?'

'You know the drill – pardon the pun.' Anthony snapped on thin rubber gloves. 'You've had worse. That root canal treatment you had four years ago.'

Cary did know the drill. His father believed that children's dental cavities were best filled without anaesthetic, so that children would learn through practical pain to make a better job of brushing their teeth.

Anthony gave the drill a quick whirl.

It was all so horribly familiar; his father's face up close, bald head shining like a mirror, his mother's concerned face looming behind and, above it all, the soundtrack of the drill; his father seemed to enjoy the noise.

'I think I'll have those wisdom teeth out next year.' Anthony started to hum his Ilkley Moor tune again.

Cary shut his eyes and thought about all the things he'd rather be doing. He'd rather be with Lily – of course. And he'd rather be in the Timbralls kitchen; or in The Project; or out on the assault course; and actually… there was nowhere in the world he would less rather be.

Cary moved his head to the side, his father's fingers slipping out of his mouth.

'Excuse me,' Cary said.

'Not a problem.' Anthony eased back. 'Get yourself settled.'

Cary undid the plastic bib around his neck. 'I think I'll leave it for now, if that's okay.'

Anthony sat back in his dentist's chair, drill drooping in his lap. 'What are you doing, Cary?' he said. 'You've got a cavity. I have to fill it.'

Cary got out of the chair, stood up, now towering over his parents. 'No – I have the beginnings of a cavity,' he said. 'I think I'll leave it for the moment.'

His father gawked, his mother squawked – 'But Cary!'

Cary walked to the door and gave his parents a smile of beautiful pure white brilliance. 'I'd like to thank you both for looking after my teeth all these years.'

'You're not leaving, Cary!' his mother said.

'You come back here, Cary!' his father said, but their boy had gone.

He had left the room and, a moment later, Cary's dumbfounded parents were listening to the sound of the front door being slammed with majestic finality.

* * *

All was quiet in the accounts department at News International; the bosses were away having lunches and extra-curricular canoodles, and only one person had been left to hold the fort, a witless trainee called Caspian, who would be eating *Al Desko*. He had been away ten minutes to pick up a pasta salad from the canteen. When he returned, the phone was ringing.

'Accounts?'

'Oh, I'm sorry to bother you.' It was a soft voice, reminded Caspian of his grandfather. 'I'm just checking up on a wee payment that was due to me.'

'How can I help?'

'It's for an Eton story I gave *The Sun* two weeks ago.'

Caspian tapped at his keyboard. 'Cash payment?'

'It was.'

Caspian called up a list of *The Sun*'s most secret contacts. 'Ah yes – the Eton stories. You have been busy! Which one are you – Agent Orange or Mickey Mouse?'

'I am Agent Orange.'

'Hang on a mo – let's just check now.' Caspian scratched at his neck and scrolled through the list of payments – unaware that he had been joined by Roy, News International's head of accounts.

Roy had just returned from lunch in The Old Rose. He'd been with News International for over two decades, dealing with taxmen, dealing with journalists; he'd seen every trick in the book.

'Now, let me see – Agent Orange—'

Roy's ears pricked up. He sidled up behind Caspian, looked at the screen.

'What's going on?' Roy asked.

'Excuse me, caller,' Caspian said blithely. 'Just putting you on hold.' He turned to Roy. 'One of *The Sun*'s Eton tipsters calling up about a payment.'

Roy was alarmed. 'Let me speak to them.'

He snatched the phone from Caspian. 'Who is this?'

'Agent Orange – who are you?'

'I'm Roy Davis, News International's head of accounts. So, Agent Orange, when did you receive your last cash payment?'

'Och – Kim gave it to me a week or two ago.'

'For how much?'

'A few thousand – in used twenties.'

'Exactly how much?'

'What is this – the Grand Inquisition?'

'Not at all – I'm just trying to establish that you are who you say you are.'

'If that's your attitude, I'll take my stories to *The Mirror*!'

The phone crashed down. Roy stared witheringly at his new trainee, before retreating to his office to make a rather delicate phone call.

I was spending my day off trying to pick a tasteful Christmas present for, well, the girl who was almost a girlfriend. I hadn't yet had the 'exclusivity' conversation with Amanda, but seeing that she made her money from, amongst other things, pole-dancing, that might have proved awkward.

A pager message came through: 'Call Roy Davis, News International chief accountant, ASAP.'

I made the call. What could it be? I'd never spoken to the chief accountant before in my life. Had my dodgy expenses come back to haunt me?

More unnervingly still, it was Roy Davis who was contrite.

'We've had a security breach. I'm very sorry.'

'Oh?'

'It's to do with your contact, Agent Orange.'

'Oh?'

'Somebody has been masquerading as Agent Orange to find out details of his payments.'

'What?'

'And he does now know that your contact is called Agent Orange.'

I'd been holding my breath. I exhaled. 'Could have been a lot worse.'

'I'm sorry.'

'What did this person sound like?'

'Middle-aged man, Scottish Borders accent, if I had to guess.'

'Thank you.'

I wondered who could have made the call. It could, of course, have just been coincidence about the Scottish accent, but it probably wasn't.

CHAPTER 28

Both Mrs Parker and Mrs Webber were very sniffy when they entered the kitchens. By rights, and by tradition, they should have been at The Boatman in Windsor, and should have been unwinding with white wine, and laughing at the old stories, the best stories, and, later perhaps, would be reminiscing about drinking Double Espressos on Florentine honeymoons.

But Cary – Cary! – the boy who had wheedled his way into their hearts had called them up, and had begged them to help him out, and so, instead of spending their Christmas Eve getting quietly pickled, they were having to go to this, this, well, let's be frank, this doss-house for the homeless, to help Cary with his prep-work.

Cary was late. He was still picking up all the food – and there was a lot of food to be picked up.

'So, this is it?' Mrs Parker wiped the edge of the oven with her hand and inspected a greasy black fingertip. 'This place is filthy!'

'Er – yes.' Renton and Fergie had never met two such terrifying characters in their entire lives.

'Would you like a cup of tea?' Fergie tried to smile. Some teeth were missing. It was a smile that could best be described as interesting. 'I've just made a pot.'

'Listen to me, Fergie, or whatever your name is,' Mrs Parker said. 'This place is a health hazard!'

Mrs Webber opened one of the drawers and inspected

a grimy ladle. 'If this was a restaurant kitchen, you'd be shut down!'

'And the fridge!' Mrs Parker had indeed found the fridge, with its limp vegetables and bits of old cheese and stinking chicken. 'This stuff could kill you!'

'You don't have to be so mean,' Renton said, fighting a hopeless rearguard action.

They'd rather been looking forward to meeting Mrs Parker and Mrs Webber – had even showered that morning and put on their least moth-eaten jackets. Cary had said they were the sweetest ladies he knew. Well, maybe they were sweet with Cary, but they didn't seem at all sweet now, in fact rather bitter.

'Why hasn't Cary cleaned the place up?'

'He's the cook,' Renton said. 'Matty and Joe are supposed to do the cleaning.'

'They're very good at cleaning the pots and pans.' Fergie wrung his hands. This was going horribly! 'And they load up the dishwashers with all the plates. I don't think they realised they had to clean the oven.'

'Or the fridge? Or the sink?' Mrs Parker ran a finger along a shelf, blew at the dust. 'Pardon my French, but this place is a shit-hole.'

'I'm very sorry.'

'What is this place?' Mrs Parker stood square in the middle of the kitchen, hands on hips.

'It's a shit-hole, Mrs Parker.'

'We haven't had a case of food poisoning since the summer!' Renton said.

'That was during the holidays when Cary was away—'

Mrs Parker was working herself into the most towering rage. Had she ever in her life come across two such imbecilic men? 'It's a shit-hole!' she said. 'And what do we do with shit-holes?'

Fergie inspected a piece of flaky skin that he'd pulled off his scalp. 'We clean them up?'

'Get that man into Mensa! Yes, we are going to clean this

kitchen up until it is so spotless that you could eat your dinner off the floor.'

'Why would you want to eat your dinner off the floor?'

'Shut up and get me some Jeyes!'

'What's that?'

'God help me, it's cleaning fluid!'

'I don't think we have any.'

'Well, Mr Brain of Britain, why don't you go down to the shops and buy some!'

'Yes, Mrs Parker.' Fergie bobbed as if taking leave of the Queen. 'I'll go right away.'

'And you!' Mrs Parker pointed a gnarled finger at Renton.

'Yes, Mrs Parker?'

'You are going to clear all the shelves, and you are going to wash every single pot, pan and spoon in this filth-hole!'

'But a lot of it's already clean.'

'What did you say?'

Renton cowered. 'I'll start the washing right away.'

* * *

Cary wheeled one of Sainsbury's biggest trolleys through the winding Windsor streets and back to The Project. He'd bought a lot of veg and a lot of condiments; the booze and the turkeys had – thankfully – been delivered that morning.

He manhandled the trolley up the step and pushed it through into a very silent and very tense kitchen.

Fergie was on his knees, attacking the grey lino with a scrubbing brush. He gave Cary a shy Gollum-like smile. Mrs Parker glared and he got back to work. Renton was engrossed at the sink. He appeared to be cleaning every pot and pan in the kitchen.

'Call that clean?' Mrs Parker said.

'It's clean enough!'

'It may be clean enough for you, Renton, but for me, it's still filthy.'

'What did your last slave die of?'

'What did you say?' Mrs Parker instinctively snatched up a saucepan, as if there was nothing she'd like more than to crown Renton over the head.

'Me? Nothing.' Renton looked over his shoulder and was exceedingly glad to see Cary was back. He might lighten the mood a little; he certainly couldn't make things any worse.

'Cary!' he said. 'Need a hand there?'

Cary sized up the situation in an instant. 'You all look like you could do with a drink.'

Fergie looked up, a wee timorous mousie poking its nose out of a hole. 'Can I have a cup of tea, please?'

'Of course you can.'

'I'll need something a little stronger,' Renton said.

'Only when you've finished these pots,' Mrs Parker barked. 'And I mean properly finished!'

Now that Renton had been routed, Mrs Parker accepted Cary's kiss.

'How do you put up with these two?' she said.

This was no time for half measures. If this Christmas was going to work in any way at all, Cary knew he was going to have to do a lot of the heavy lifting.

'Let's open some Prosecco!'

Now that alcohol had been added to the mix, the atmosphere started to thaw – like an iceberg in the Arctic Ocean, unseen to the human eye, but slowly, imperceptibly melting. Cary poured drinks and made tea, turned on the radio and chattered away about his week in the Dales. He was relieved in the extreme when Lily arrived. She looked just her usual gorgeous self, snug in a red coat and a white beanie. They hadn't seen each other in a week.

Cary jumped straight off the top of the step-ladder and boomed onto the floor.

'Lily!' he said. 'Now – let's get you in the right position.'

'What's the right position?'

'Just here.' He pointed to a spot in the middle of the kitchen.

Lily observed the bunch of mistletoe that had just been hung from the ceiling.

'The perfect position.'

She stood demurely in front of Cary and they had one chaste kiss, but one kiss can never be enough if you've had a week away from the love of your life, so they kissed again, and again, as arms started to enfold –

'Ahemmm!'

Cary broke away. 'Ah, yes! Mrs Parker! I have been forgetting my manners! Mrs Parker – may I introduce Lily.'

'Very pleased to meet you.' Mrs Parker shook Lily's hand; she had already realised she must be more cordial with Lily than she had been with those two wizened reprobates.

'And this is dear Mrs Webber,' Cary said.

'How lovely to finally meet you,' Mrs Webber said, and though Lily was going in for a handshake, Mrs Webber turned it into a hug and a kiss on the cheek. 'Cary said you were special – and he hasn't exaggerated.'

Now that both Cary and Lily were in the kitchen, Mrs Parker eased up from her relentless harrying. They all sat round the table, with knives and glasses of Prosecco (tea for Fergie), all slicing and dicing and peeling. Cary ensured that no glass ever ran dry, and that Fergie's mug of tea never turned tepid. Renton was as meek as a chastened schoolboy and, when he was reprimanded for his sloppy peeling, he instantly replied, 'Yes, Mrs Parker.' Fergie and Mrs Webber appeared to be getting on slightly more cordially and, as for Cary and Lily, they were knee to knee and chopping carrots, blissed out on love.

The six of them finished the prep-work in 90 minutes, and Cary and Lily were twitching to excuse themselves. All that sitting at the table playing footsie had been like the most ardent foreplay.

They left the kitchen and headed up to their eyrie in the attic, but desire overcame them in the upstairs bathroom, so they merely locked the door and made do with the sturdy basin.

Downstairs, now that the kitchen was spick and span and

now that all the prep-work had been completed, Renton and Fergie sat at the table with Mrs Parker and Mrs Webber. Without their ringmaster, nobody had the first idea what to say next.

Renton and Mrs Parker took the plunge at the exact same moment – 'We've got a Christmas tree,' and 'We've got to go.'

'After you,' Renton said.

'No, after you.'

'Ah, well – now that we've chopped carrots together, Mrs Parker, I wondered what you like to be called?'

'I like to be called Mrs Parker.'

'Of course, Mrs Parker – of course.' It was like blundering through a minefield of Victorian etiquette, never knowing when he'd set off the next boobytrap. For no reason at all, he happened to glance up at the mistletoe.

Mrs Parker was onto him like a terrier. 'Renton! Did you just look at that mistletoe?'

'Is there anything wrong with looking at mistletoe, Mrs Parker?'

'There certainly is, if it's going to put depraved ideas into your seedy little mind.'

'Yes, Mrs Parker.'

'Kindly try and behave like a gentleman – if you know what that is.'

'I used to.'

Mrs Parker bumpered the last of her Prosecco. 'Why have you two let this place go? It could be quite nice, but you've turned it into a dump!'

Fergie was biting the inside of his cheek so hard that it hurt. He poured himself some stone-cold tea. Not that he'd had high hopes about the afternoon – not that he'd thought anything would ever actually *happen.* But he'd been looking forward to it, and now all he was looking forward to was these horrid women leaving.

'It's not a dump,' Fergie said.

'What did you say?'

'It's not a dump. We like it here – and we're providing a useful service.'

'You don't know what you're talking about! You haven't got a clue! Now, you listen to me – this place is the pits! It's the very bottom of the pit! I've never worked in such a dump before!'

'Excuse me.' Fergie got up from the table and left the room. He didn't even try to hide the tears that poured down his cheeks.

CHAPTER 29

Coming from good Presbyterian stock, Mr McCreath may not have actually believed in God, but he most certainly did believe in going to church on Christmas Day – and it was on that day of days that Mr McCreath would experience his first and only miracle.

Since he lived in a small flat down by the river in Windsor, he made his Christmas obeisances in that fine old chapel, St George's. He arrived in plenty of time and took a seat in his favourite pew, on the right-hand side at the back. The chapel, glorious Medieval Gothic, was even older than the College Chapel at Eton.

Mr McCreath had a commanding view of the whole chapel and all who entered it. And, on this day of days, he was wearing his best tweed suit and his father's old deerstalker. He had spent some time over his grooming. His beard was trim and sleek, and his hair, such as it was, was neatly trimmed.

He liked the orderliness of the Christmas service. He liked to sing the same carols and listen to the same readings, and he enjoyed the unchallenging Christmas message. And though the Dean of Windsor might have dismissed Mr McCreath as a 'Chreaster' – a lightweight Christian who only went to Church at Christmas and Easter – Mr McCreath had his own stout Protestant values and did not feel the need to parade them every week at communal service.

All was proceeding as it should, and the chapel was

filling out nicely, when Mr McCreath was thrown into the most utter confusion by the arrival of Miss Robinson. He spotted her the moment she came in – well, how could he not have spotted this quite delectable creature? She was wearing a tasteful grey coat, cinched at the waist, and because it was Christmas, she had a jaunty red hat, trilby-style, with a sprig of holly in the hat-band. Mr McCreath, usually so acute to all these delicate nuances, wasn't sure if she'd seen him. She might have glanced in his direction. He couldn't be sure. But if she had seen him, she certainly hadn't wanted to sit anywhere near him, and had taken herself to a pew on the other side of the church.

Mr McCreath now had no ears for the carols and, as for the Christmas message, the Dean of Windsor might as well have been reading from the Eton College Rule Book, for all the impact it had on Mr McCreath.

His big dilemma was whether to go up for Communion or not. Usually, he couldn't be doing with Communion, but if Miss Robinson was going up for her Christmas bread and wine, then Mr McCreath resolved to follow her. He would kneel next to her, his mind seemingly on Holy Thoughts, and then he would glance and turn to her and say, 'Why, Miss Robinson – how very lovely to see you!'

And Miss Robinson, having taken her sip of Christ's blood, would smile and say, 'Why, Mr McCreath! Happy Christmas!' And then, on impulse, she would lean over to kiss him on the cheek, but at the exact same moment, Mr McCreath would be turning towards her to say something of great interest, and her lips, those succulent red lips, would in fact collide with his mouth and…

Miss Robinson did not go up to take Communion but instead stayed resolutely in her pew, hands demurely in her lap as she mildly observed the Communion-goers.

No matter! Mr McCreath would merely exit the chapel as soon as the Christmas service was over, and would then loiter outside, there to pounce on Miss Robinson when she, in her turn, left St George's – 'Why, Miss Robinson! I thought it was you! Happy Christmas!' And then he would extend his hand, which she would ignore completely and would instead move in immediately to kiss him on the cheek, but at the critical point, she'd move to the wrong cheek, and those red, red lips would end up impacting on…

Mr McCreath furtively skulked outside the chapel, tensely watching the Dean repeat his Christmas platitudes to the exiting church-goers. But the spate of people streaming out of St George's had started to dwindle, and he just couldn't understand it, because surely Miss Robinson should have come out by now – and, in a moment of stunning clarity, he realised she had left the chapel by the rear exit. He barged back into the chapel, going against the flow, and saw immediately that Miss Robinson had gone. He almost broke into an unseemly trot as he headed down the aisle towards that damnable rear exit, and left the church again to find… absolutely nothing. Howl! He'd missed her! He scanned left and right, he looked everywhere and, for a moment, felt like sprinting off in one direction or another like some witless chicken. But it was hopeless, hopeless; this bird had well and truly flown, possibly never to return. Mr McCreath did not believe in destiny. But he had a lingering sense that, on this one, with Miss Robinson, the fates were against him.

Hands thrust deep into his pockets, head down, heart closed to the world, Mr McCreath stumped to the nearest pub, any pub, to drown his sorrows and foreswear having anything to do with women ever, ever again. What was he thinking! With Miss Robinson? It was inconceivable – inconceivable! – that she didn't already have a boyfriend, a paramour, a lover, some horny-handed beast with a prime head of hair and lips that were kissable…

He went into the Horse and Groom and ordered a pint of Theakstons and, because it was Christmas, and because he'd blown it with Miss Robinson, a whisky chaser.

He sat on his bar-stool, glaring at his pint. What on earth

could she possibly see in him? He was one up from the local rat-catcher, whereas Miss Robinson – could he ever dare call her Louise? – whereas Miss Robinson was world-class, not just beautiful, but ladylike, sensible…

'Why, Mr McCreath – is that you tucked away in the corner there?'

Like a man on his last legs in a parched desert, a man who'd seen so many mirages that he had come to believe all was shimmering fantasy, Mr McCreath lifted up his doleful eyes – to see Miss Robinson standing next to him at the bar.

'Why – why, Miss Robinson!' he said, brain suddenly convulsing.

'Happy Christmas,' she said, and then, easy as anything, she leaned over and kissed him on the cheek.

'Can… can I…'

In Mr McCreath's head, there rang the jarring sound of crashed gears.

* * *

Cary had been up since 4am on Christmas morning, putting the four huge turkeys into the ovens, boiling up the milk for the bread sauce, and finally laying the dining tables in the hall.

Breakfast had consisted of a bit of bread and butter on the hoof, but Cary was in flow and he was loving it.

Lily arrived mid-morning, having had a perfunctory breakfast with her parents. She and Cary were so happy that they just stood in the kitchen, hugging and kissing and stating their love. Fergie and Renton came in for some tea, but those two gentlemen were only moderately happy, because there were matters that had yet to be resolved: Mrs Parker and Mrs Webber.

Strong words had been bandied about on Christmas Eve, and these had been neither forgiven nor forgotten. The memories stung.

They heard a clatter next door; battle was about to

commence. Fergie brushed at his waistcoat. For that day and that day only, he was wearing his Christmas best; mustardy cords and a green waistcoat with a beautiful jacket that had once been bought in another lifetime, before he'd drunk it all away. Renton had also scrubbed up rather nicely, quite the dandy with a red polka-dot bow tie.

Mrs Parker and Mrs Webber entered the kitchen. They had also made an effort, Mrs Parker in a matronly blue dress and Mrs Webber in racy scarlet. More importantly, Mrs Parker had brought a peace offering.

'Baked some cakes for you,' she said briskly, and put a large wicker basket on the table. From the basket, she produced three large Tupperware boxes, each with at least 20 cupcakes.

'Dear Mrs Parker,' Renton said. 'How kind of you.'

'I'll put the kettle on!' Fergie said.

They all sampled the cupcakes with their tea. Both Renton and Fergie were in agreement that they were the best cupcakes they'd ever eaten.

'You must have been up all night making them,' Renton said.

'Knocked them out this morning,' Mrs Parker said.

'Thank you,' Renton said. 'They will be much appreciated.'

Joining this now mildly tepid band were Minty and Jazz, not best pleased with their boyfriends, who had signally failed to deliver any decent Christmas presents.

'Know where I think they got them?' Minty took a sip of Harvey's Bristol Cream and decided she liked it. 'From the petrol station last night!'

'He got me a box of chocolates and a torch!' Jazz said. 'He hadn't even bothered to wrap them!'

'I know what you should give him for Christmas!'

'What's that, Mrs Parker?'

'The elbow!'

Windsor's waifs and strays had begun to arrive at The Project. They couldn't believe that their drinks and dinner were being served by those two irresistible goddesses; Minty and Jazz were in their formal Eton kit, black skirts and white blouses, simple yet extraordinarily effective, and, had they been single, they could have happily had their pick of any number of the Windsor scallywags. Not that the girls were ready to dump their dopey boyfriends just yet, but if – if – they had been single, then their two kitchen help-mates, Matty and Joe, looked like a reasonable bet; funny and considerate, and, above all else, absolutely worshipping the ground they walked on.

The Christmas dinner was nothing short of a triumph; Cary carving and ladling, Lily and Mrs Parker doling out the veg and all the trimmings, and Fergie and Renton up to their elbows in soap-suds, though, after 15 minutes, Renton was tapped on the shoulder and told to find something else to occupy him, such as a beer bottle, because he looked tired and Mrs Webber was very good at dish-washing. It was to be the happiest Christmas Fergie could ever remember – standing there at the twin sinks next to Mrs Webber, chatting about nothing of note, but gradually connecting. They discovered that, amazingly, they had both made that great Catholic pilgrimage to Santiago de Compostela.

Without any effort and without even noticing what is happening, their sun-starved tendrils twist and entwine.

The Christmas dinner finally drew to an end in the late afternoon. Then there were presents to be opened.

Since Cary – still – didn't have a bean to his name, he had made most of his presents at Eton's Drawing Schools. For Mrs Parker and Mrs Webber, and for Renton and Fergie, and for the two girls, he had turned some pottery tea mugs. They were surprisingly well executed, quite dainty with a beautiful glaze, and were accepted with universal delight.

A mere mug was not remotely going to cut it, however, for the love of his life. Instead, he'd gone along to the School of Mechanics, where he had found a lump of walnut gathering dust in the storeroom. He turned it into a chunky bangle and, after it had been sanded and waxed, it could have held its own against any of those expensive baubles from Cartier. More importantly: Lily loved it.

In her turn, Lily had bought him a Parker pen and some paper. It seemed that all the presents had been given and received – until Fergie gave Cary a light nudge.

'We got something for you, Cary. It's outside.'

Fergie and Renton led the way out of The Project and the rest of the little party followed. Outside was a very old brown Mini. A red bow had been stuck on the bonnet.

Fergie gave Cary a key fob. 'Happy Christmas.'

Cary was delighted. 'You've bought that Mini for me? Thank you!' He hugged Renton and Fergie.

'It's insured, everything. Just a small way of showing how much we appreciate what you've done for us.'

'I love it!' Cary said.

Lily was holding tight onto his arm. 'It's amazing!'

'Do you think there's enough room on the back seat?'

'Cheeky!'

It was chilly. The rest of the party soon went inside, but Lily and Cary lingered next to his Mini.

'We'll be off on excursions!' Cary said.

'Let's go to the seaside!' They were hugging each other. Cary was about to suggest that they go upstairs to the attic, when he caught sight of a man ambling along the pavement.

For a moment, he could feel Fleming next to him, urgently plucking at his sleeve, hurrying him inside. But it was too late for that.

'Have a care,' Fleming whispered.

Cary had had three glasses of Prosecco and several turkey sandwiches. His guard was down. It took a moment to appreciate the danger.

Cary disengaged from Lily and smiled at the man. 'Happy Christmas, Mr McCreath.'

Mr McCreath, flush from whisky or, perhaps, honey-scented love, stopped to chat. 'And a very happy Christmas to you too, Cary – and it's Lily, isn't it? Though I don't think we've been formally introduced.'

Cary suddenly recalled an odd pager message he'd received

from Kim. Somebody had called up News International's accounts, masquerading as *The Sun*'s Eton agent. The man had given very little away about himself – though his voice had a noticeable Scottish burr.

Coincidence?

Mr McCreath clicked his fingers. 'And what have you been up to here? It looks like you've been cooking.'

'Just been helping out with the Christmas dinner.'

'What an admirable thing to do over Christmas,' Mr McCreath said, turning to Lily. 'And have been helping out too, my dear?'

'A little bit,' Lily said, and because she'd had nothing to drink, she was much more fly than Cary. 'I'm just going inside to get my coat.'

'It is a bit cold, isn't it?' Cary said and was about to follow her inside, and, later, could have kicked himself for not doing so, but Mr McCreath had started talking again, and was pointing up at the clear night sky.

'It's a very clear night tonight, isn't it – you can see the Milky Way in all its glory. Are you a stargazer?'

'Not really, no.'

'You don't, perhaps, visit Eton's observatory? With your girlfriend?'

'No, I don't think so.'

'I'd keep it that way, then.' Mr McCreath's unblinking eyes were dead set on Cary. He nodded to himself and sniffed. 'Do you know that winter is my favourite season of the year? Most people, they seem to love spring or summer, but for myself, I have always preferred winter, when the nights are drawing in, and when you can treat yourself to a hot toddy, aye, and when the leaves have fallen from the trees.' He took a step towards Cary. 'Now, you might think this fanciful, young man, but when I see these gaunt trees, with their leafless branches standing stark against the skyline, I sometimes think they've been dosed with some chemical—'

Cary felt like he'd been given a sharp kick to the shin. He winced, stooping to rub his ankle.

'With some chemical,' Mr McCreath continued. 'Something like Agent Orange.' His eyes had never left Cary, but for some peculiar reason, the boy was bent over and kneading at his leg.

'Sorry,' Cary said. 'Cramp.'

'Happy Christmas.'

Cary and Fleming watched the Scotsman as he wandered away.

'Thanks for the kick,' Cary said.

'You're definitely one of the suspects,' Fleming said. 'But he's not quite sure.'

CHAPTER 30

Maxwell had not had such a good time of things. For Maxwell, there had been no Christmas kisses underneath the mistletoe, there had been no presents that had been made with love, and there had been no girl, no anything, to cuddle and to joke with and to do all those things he so longed to do – and which he now knew that his Lily was doing with that Cary upstart.

But the one thing Maxwell did possess was patience. He could bide his time. He could wait. And, when he saw his opportunity, he would strike.

With Lily, Maxwell had not yet come across any means of doing her down, but with Cary, there were several possibilities, not least that cock-eyed scheme to take a bunch of Etonians to the Tough Guy race… And now that Maxwell thought of it, if he managed to do down Cary, then by the same token, he'd also be hurting Lily, and that was all to the good.

He didn't actually know if he wanted to kill Cary. He hadn't really thought it through. Maxwell mulled over this abstruse point after he returned late to Farrer. Setting the trap had been easy-peasy and would doubtless be blamed on the hooligan townies.

But would it be too awful if Cary killed himself? Maxwell's vacant moon-face cracked open with a big stupid grin. Well… if Cary ended up in the hospital, that would be great, but, frankly, if he ended up in the morgue, that would be even better. Why, Lily would suddenly be single, and very possibly in need of a shoulder to cry on…

* * *

The Tough Guy race was due to take place in late January, when the organisers would be praying for snow on the ground and ice that was thick enough to skate on; they prided themselves on having created the world's most unpleasant assault course.

Cary had got together a team of a dozen boys to take part in this piece of advanced lunacy, and they were all greatly looking forward to charging through the killing fields, not to mention swimming the freezing swamps and crawling through the slime in the Vietcong tunnels. The team usually met up at the weekends for a spell over the Eton assault course, but it was only little Barty who had the stomach for accompanying Cary over the course at 6am. For most boys, this sort of early morning exercise would have been a punishment. Barty loved it.

That morning, Cary was unsettled by a conversation he'd just had with Fleming. He'd pulled back the curtains to reveal another very cold, very wet day. Fleming had been watching him.

'You push yourself hard, Cary.' Fleming dusted at a drip of ash that had fallen onto his silk dressing gown. 'Maybe give yourself the morning off?'

'Barty's up. He'll already be waiting for me on the Slab.'

Fleming sighed and tipped his cigarette into an old coffee mug. 'I knew you'd say that.'

'Why did you suggest it, then?'

'I had to try.'

Barty was indeed waiting on the Slab, a terrier pup desperate for his first walk of the day. He high-fived Cary and they set off out into the darkness. It was so dark that Cary could hardly see where he was putting his feet. They ran hard over the fields and, without even a pause, threw themselves at the assault course.

Cary would remember a lot of things about that morning.

He'd remember the beautiful sting of the cold rain on his skin, and opening his mouth and letting the raindrops fizz onto his tongue.

He'd remember sitting on one of the walls and leaning down to help Barty up, and the realisation that he couldn't care less about winning the Tough Guy race, only that he was going to run it with Barty and, if Barty needed to take his time through the Vietcong tunnels, then Cary would hang back to help him.

He'd remember following Barty through the mud pits, and laughing as he unsnagged the boy from a piece of barbed wire.

And Cary would remember climbing up the cargo net to the top of The Table. He was noticeably faster than the first time he'd been up it three months ago – stronger, and more agile, and even though the rope was wet and slippery, he was up the net like a monkey. He waited at the top of The Table, drinking in the view. He hauled Barty up, and then, same as always, same as he'd been doing for the previous three months, he took a firm hold of the climbing rope, cracked it a couple of times to check it was taut, and let himself over the edge. The next bit, he couldn't remember so well.

He started to slide down the rope – and then it snapped, broken off clean in his hands. A horrible feeling of falling, arms windmilling backwards, and then the quite stunning shock of hitting the ground. The audible sound of breaking bones. An arc of pain washed over him as he stared upwards, Barty's horrified face peeping out from the top of The Table.

And then lying there on the ground, lashed by the rain, and touching his leg, and not understanding what he was feeling before dully realising he was touching a piece of shattered thigh bone that had lanced through his skin.

Barty shinned down the cargo net and stood over Cary, his mouth a perfect circle of astonishment. Cary blearily looked up at him.

'Run and get an ambulance. Knock up any house you can find.'

'Shall I move you?'

Cary tried to smile. 'I don't think you could, Barty. Off you go.'

He watched Barty race off into the rain. The shock and the adrenalin were gradually wearing off and he could feel this hellish pain in his leg and in his back – please don't say he'd broken his back – and it was like he was glued to the ground and the mud was leaching the heat from his body. He was shivering uncontrollably; though, after a while, he didn't know how long, he was starting to enjoy the mud; it was like he was covered with a warm quilt. So very tired, he could have happily fallen asleep, might have been quite nice to sleep there in the mud at the bottom of The Table.

He was just drifting off when he felt a hard slap on the face – and then a second slap, harder. He opened his eyes. It was Fleming, kneeling in the mud.

'Wake up, boy, you can't leave me now.'

'What?'

'Go to sleep here and you'll join Bruno. You'll never see Lily again.'

'What?'

'Do you want to see Lily again?'

'Yes.'

'Stay awake, then. Sleep and you die.'

Cary groaned. The thought of sleep had never seemed so enticing.

'You've got to stay alive for Lily.' Fleming was beside himself, wiping the mud off Cary's face with his silk handkerchief. 'Think of all the things you have yet to do with each other.'

Cary smiled. 'I'd like to marry her. I'd like to have children with her.'

'That's good,' Fleming said. 'So please try and avoid dying on me. It was bad enough with Bruno.'

'You knew this was going to happen, didn't you?'

'I had a sense of it. Tell me more about Lily.'

'This'll be quite a story for *The Sun*, won't it?'

'It will.'

* * *

Barty sprinted down the road to Dorney, not really sure where he was heading. A house loomed out of the rain, curtains drawn and all asleep inside. Barty started ringing the bell and hammering at the door.

'Help!' he shouted. 'Help, help!'

A dog barked and an upstairs light came on. Barty could see someone shambling down the stairs. Maddeningly, they put the door on the latch-chain before opening it. It was an old man. An Alsatian barked as it slavered to get its nose round the door.

'Who is it?'

'I'm a boy from the College,' Barty said. 'There's been an accident. My friend's hurt on the assault course. Can you call an ambulance? Please.'

The old man turned the information over in his mind. 'Are you alone?'

'Yes, I'm alone – please, please can you call an ambulance?'

The man grudgingly slipped the chain and opened the door. He had to hold the dog back. 'Biscuit! Calm down!'

He dragged the dog off to the sitting room and slammed the door. The dog whined and started barking. The man went back into the sitting room.

'Shut up, Biscuit!'

'Please, sir!'

The old man returned to the front door. The dog continued to bark. 'You're covered in mud.'

'Yes, I'm sorry, but can you please call an ambulance?'

'What are you doing out at this time of morning?'

'Look, we were going for a run – please, please call an ambulance!'

A woman's head appeared at the top of the stairs. 'Who is it, Gerry?'

'It's a lad who claims he needs an ambulance.'

The woman belted up her pink dressing gown as she came down the stairs. She inspected Barty.

'You're all muddy!' she said.

'My friend's hurt!' Barty was so frustrated that he all but stamped his feet. 'Call an ambulance! Please!'

Gerry looked at his wife. 'Do you want to make the call or shall I?'

'I'll make the call!' Barty said. 'Just let me use your phone!'

'You're not going up the stairs like that!' the woman said.

'I'll make the call,' Gerry said. 'Where is your friend?'

'On the Eton assault course. He fell off The Table.'

'What do you mean, he fell off The Table?'

'The Table!' Barty said. 'It's one of the obstacles on the assault course! Cary fell off it!'

Gerry stumped up the stairs to use his bedside phone. His wife glowered at Barty as the mud dripped onto her white carpet.

'Can I borrow a blanket, please?' Barty said.

'Why do you want a blanket?'

'My friend has had a big fall and is lying in a pool of mud. I think he's going to die.'

The woman inspected Barty slowly – still not sure it wasn't all some elaborate wind-up. Biscuit continued to bark.

'Give me a moment, I'll get my coat,' she said. 'Wait on the porch, so you don't drip mud on my carpet.'

One step at a time, she retreated up the stairs. Barty wondered if he should just grab a rug and head back out into the rain.

Several minutes later, the woman came back down the stairs, step by slow step, one hand tight on the bannisters. She was wearing some old trousers and a jumper. She went to the kitchen to find her coat, before plumping down onto a chair to put on her Wellingtons. She came out of the kitchen and gave herself a leisurely pat-down.

'Gerry! Have you got the car keys?'

Gerry's head appeared at the top of the stairs. 'Where did you say this boy is?' he called.

'He's on the Eton College Assault Course – at the bottom of an obstacle called The Table.'

Gerry mumbled into a phone.

'Gerry – have you seen the car keys?'

'They're where you last left them!'

The woman patted herself down again and shambled back to the kitchen. 'Found them! Right – let's go and see this friend of yours.' She dug out a torch and a blanket from the cupboard by the stairs and led the way out to an old Volvo estate. 'I'm not having you in my car like that. You'll have to go in the boot.'

'I'll go anywhere!' Barty climbed into the stinking dog cage and the woman slammed the boot shut. He crouched on an old bit of carpet that was matted with dog hair.

'The assault course, the assault course,' the woman sang to herself as she poked away at the dashboard with the car key. 'Where is the assault course?'

'Close to the athletics track.'

'Where's that?' She started the car, gunned the engine.

'I'll guide you,' Barty said.

'You'll have to speak up, I can't hear you!'

'I'll guide you!'

It was difficult for Barty to direct the woman from inside the dog cage, as he couldn't see anything. The woman slowly headed back towards Eton, driving straight past the entrance to the athletics ground. 'It's there!' Barty said. 'You've missed it!'

The old Volvo grumbled into reverse and she nudged it towards the track. Grunting with the effort, she got out of the car and opened the boot.

'Thank you,' Barty said, deciding to take charge. 'I'll take the blanket to my friend – you stay here. I'm heading towards that thing that looks like a big table—'

The woman squinted into the grey rain. 'It looks like a big table?'

'Yes, just over there!' Barty pointed. 'Wait in the car for the ambulance – keep your lights on.' He grabbed the torch and the old blanket and then, on a whim, snatched up the bit of dog carpet.

He ran across the assault course, hugging the rug and the carpet tight to his chest. Cary was just where he'd left him, underneath The Table. For one wild second, Barty thought he could hear the sound of conversation.

He knelt in the mud, put his hand on Cary's forehead. Cold and clammy. Cary's eyes flickered open.

'Hi,' he whispered. 'We having fun yet?'

'Been having the time of my life with a dotty old woman and a mad Alsatian.' Barty threw the piece of dog carpet onto the mud and, as gently as he could, rolled Cary on top. Cary groaned as his thigh bone jagged upwards.

'I'll try and keep you warm,' Barty said.

He planted the torch in the ground so that it lit up The Table, and then lay on the carpet next to Cary. He pulled the rug on top of them. Barty didn't rightly know what to do next, but it seemed best to try to keep Cary's spirits up.

'This is cosy,' Barty said. 'Never snuggled up to a Popper before.'

'Hope you don't get a taste for it.' Cary started to laugh but it hurt his ribs. 'Did you see what happened to that rope?'

'It had been cut,' Barty said. 'Just a few strands left to keep it in place. Snapped as soon as you put your weight on it. Still – it could have been worse.'

'It could?'

'Could have been me who was first down the rope!'

Cary smiled. With the rug and with Barty next to him, he was warming up a little. 'How long before the paramedics get here?'

'Pretty soon, I hope – that is, if Gerry ever managed to make the call.'

'I'll take him round a bottle of whisky,'

'Maybe two – they weren't happy about all the mud I dripped on their floor.'

Barty saw flashing blue lights winking in the rain. A pair of headlights nosed across the assault course.

'They're here,' he said.

'Thanks,' Cary whispered. 'You've done good.'

Barty eased himself out from underneath the blanket and waved to the ambulance. It pulled up ten metres short, headlights full on Cary. A paramedic jumped out.

'How is he?'

'Broken his leg, maybe more,' Barty said. 'He's very cold.'

The paramedic pulled back the blanket, whistling as he saw the thigh bone. 'Let's get you to hospital.'

A second paramedic brought over a stretcher. They hefted Cary straight up on the piece of old dog carpet and eased him onto the stretcher.

'Can I come too?' Barty said.

'Course you can, son,' the paramedic said, tousling Barty's hair, and now that Barty was done, and now that he no longer had to try and save his friend's life, he burst into tears.

CHAPTER 31

Lily waited by the Slab in Farrer for Fredster Campbell, blissfully unaware of the effect her white shorts and coltish legs were having on Eton's schoolboys. Boys came down the stairs, looked at her and looked again, and then five minutes later, found an excuse to go back up the stairs so they could reappraise the legs that swung so gracefully on the Slab.

Fredster Campbell was late because he had been having his weekly shave. His skin was smooth and his tracksuit was pristine and he reeked of Armani aftershave. You might have thought he was on a date, but all he was doing was playing Lily at Fives. Since she'd started at the bottom of the Fives ladder, Lily had been methodically working her way up. She hadn't yet challenged Fredster, who was at the top, but they'd played a couple of games.

'I've had an idea.' Fredster held the Farrer door open for Lily.

'Why do I always get this feeling of dread when I hear you've had an idea?'

'Because you fear being put in the shade by my brilliance.'

'What's your idea?'

'Why don't we play Fives on the original Fives court?'

'Next to the chapel buttresses?' Lily mulled it over.

Eton Fives originated after boys started hitting a cork ball against the side of the College Chapel. At first, they'd used their bare hands, but it had been easier on the fingers to wear padded gloves. Since those early days, Eton now had dozens of Fives courts, all of them exact replicas of the original court by the side of the Chapel. They had roofs and no moss, but they had none of the history, nor a patch of the magic of Eton's original Fives court.

'That, Fredster, is a very good idea indeed!'

'Knew you'd like it.'

They headed off up Judy's Passage.

'Do we ask permission?' Lily said.

'No!' Fredster said. 'Never! In situations like this, Lily, you must remember the inspirational words of Rear Admiral Grace Hopper, as taught to me by my uncle Toby. She said that, if you have a good idea, you must act on it immediately – because it's much easier to apologise than it is to ask for permission.'

'So we just go onto the court and start playing?'

'Yes!' Fredster did a puppyish jig, playful, just a little flirty. 'And when the porters come out and tell us we shouldn't be playing there—'

'We just say we're very sorry!'

Fredster would quite like to kiss her. At that moment, laughing, long limbs striding next to him, she was the most beautiful girl he had ever seen.

They walked past the School Office and into the School Yard and – unaware they were being watched by Mr McCreath from his office window – they immediately started to knock up against the side of the Chapel. The sides of the Fives court were formed by two huge buttresses and, unique to Eton Fives, a chunk of stone balustrade, four feet high by two feet wide, which jutted out into the court.

They padded the ball back and forth, nice and easy, no tricksy shots, no flailing for the ball, but when the game began in earnest, Lily started sending it wide. She was a left-hander, which was an advantage, and had an uncanny ability to send the ball landing right in the corner by the stone balustrade, or Pepperpot, where Fredster found it all but unplayable.

Again and again, she repeated the same deadly shot and she kept racking up the points.

'I thought it was a fluke the first time you did that,' Fredster said.

'I've been practising.'

She demolished him in the first game, 12 points to four. Fredster opened a can of Coke and offered it to her. She took a swig and gave him back the can. He liked it that her lips had just kissed the same can. She was so out of his league. What would it be like to kiss her?

They were chatting about running. Lily was thinking of taking part in the school steeplechase.

'At least there'll be a new winner this year.' Fredster offered her the Coke. She shook her head.

'How do you mean?'

'The Champion is out.'

'The Champion – you mean Cary?'

'He's in Intensive Care in Windsor.'

'What?' Lily had seen Cary only the previous afternoon; had been gratifyingly reconnecting with Cary less than 24 hours ago. 'What's happened?'

'He's lucky to be alive!' Fredster was thrilled to have the scoop. 'The police have been called and everything. Some people say they're treating it as attempted murder!'

'Ohhh.' The news is a sharp slap to the face. 'I'm so sorry. I've got to go. Appointment with my tutor.'

Without another word, Lily ran back to Farrer, not even bothering to check for traffic as she sprinted across the road. She didn't know what to do. But she knew she had to see him.

Fredster sat on the College Chapel steps and finished the rest of his Coke, wondering what had just happened, and not having the wit to work it out. But Mr McCreath, still watching from his office, knew exactly what had happened. Lily had just heard the news that her boyfriend was laid up in hospital.

* * *

Lily dashed upstairs to her room and pulled on a tracksuit. She could call a cab but that would take ages going round the long loop to Windsor. She'd borrow her mother's bike.

Arctic happened to be going out to watch a House football match. He caught Lily in the bike-shed.

'Where are you off to, then?' he asked, unlocking his fusty old bike and placing his gown into the wicker basket.

'Just off out,' Lily said.

'Have you asked your mother's permission to use her bike?'

'Why ever wouldn't I?' Lily fiddled with the combination lock; she knew the lock number was her mother's birthday, May 27, but it wasn't working.

'So, if you asked your mother's permission, why didn't she give you the combination to her lock?'

Just in time, Lily remembered that Tor had perversely reversed her birthday digits on the lock.

'She did.' Lily snapped the lock open and wheeled the bike out of the shed.

'Where's your helmet?' Arctic asked but Lily had already disappeared, and Arctic was left with the disagreeable realisation that his daughter had started to lie to him.

Lily pedalled hard down the Eton High Street, narrowly avoiding a couple of sightseers on Windsor Bridge. She followed the signs to the hospital, locking up the bike and tearing into Intensive Care. A nurse told her she'd just missed the hospital's visiting hours. She pretended to leave, but when the nurse disappeared onto a ward, she doubled back. She found Cary's room. She couldn't quite believe she'd made it so quickly – only 30 minutes ago, she'd been playing Fives.

Now that she'd found Cary's room, she paused, drew breath. How bad was he? Would it be that bad? The moment of truth.

Lily opened the door.

She could hardly recognise Cary. His eyes were shut and

his head swaddled in bandages. Pink tubes hedgehogged out of his arm. His entire leg was in a cast from groin to ankle. A middle-aged couple were sitting on either side of the bed.

'Hello?' Lily said.

The man, peppery, tweedy, scowled at her. 'It's not the time for visitors.'

'How is he?' Lily walked over to the bed and stood over Cary.

'You shouldn't be here,' the man said.

'I just want to know how he is.' She looked at Cary more closely. He was quite white.

'He needs to rest.'

'Just tell me how he is!'

For the first time, the woman turned to Lily. 'He's stable and no longer critical,' she said. 'Now, can you leave us?'

'I'm sorry – you must be Cary's parents,' Lily said before coming out with the most brazen lie. 'He's told me so much about you.'

'And who are you?' the man asked.

'I'm... I'm his friend,' Lily said.

'He's never mentioned you before,' his mother said.

'Now, listen to me, young lady, we've had a very long journey down here, and we'd really rather prefer it if you left us alone with our son.'

Lily knew she was beaten. She kissed her fingertips and gently touched Cary's lips.

'Don't do that!' the man said. 'Please leave.'

'Of course.' Lily was leaving the room when Cary stirred. His eyes fluttered open.

'Stay,' he whispered.

'He's awake!' Cary's mother said, leaning over to listen to her boy. 'What did you say?'

Cary looked straight at Lily. 'She stays,' he said.

Cary's father harumphed. There was no chair for Lily, so she perched on the very edge of the bed.

'Mind out!' Cary's mother said.

'Sorry.' Lily squatted next to the head of the bed.

The mother grudgingly moved her seat to give Lily a little space. For the first time, Cary smiled.

'Thanks for coming,' he said, voice barely above a whisper.

'What happened?' Lily took his hand and kissed his knuckles.

'Had a bit of a fall,' Cary said.

'More than a bit!' the father squawked.

'A big bit, then.'

Cary held Lily's hand and his eyes shut and, for the first time since he'd been in hospital, he felt safe and fell fast asleep.

'I'm Penny,' the woman said. 'And this is Anthony.'

'Hello,' Lily said.

'I didn't catch your name,' Penny prompted.

'No, you didn't.'

'And how do you know Cary?'

Lily stood up. Now that she knew Cary was safe, she wanted to be with her real friends.

'Goodbye.'

As she left the hospital, she felt a leaden weight lift from her shoulders. Cary was safe – Cary was going to be fine. No wonder he'd never, not even once, mentioned his parents! They had more starch than an Eton collar; Arctic would have felt right at home with them.

She popped into The Project. Fergie and Renton were aghast at the news. They gave her hugs and sympathy and, over a pot of tea, they discussed what Cary would want them to do.

'He'd want us to make the call!' Renton said.

'Are you sure?' Fergie said.

'He'd make the call! It's at least five grand going begging!'

'We still don't know what to spend it on.'

'Listen to you!' Renton noisily dunked his Digestive. 'Would you prefer a safe that's empty of cash?'

'All right, then, make the call.'

'I will make that call!'

It was all but dark when Lily parked her bike up in the Farrer cycle-shed. Her father was waiting for her, reading *The Daily Telegraph* with half an eye on the front door.

When Lily walked into Farrer, he pounced.
'Lily,' he called. 'Will you come in here?'
Lily walked into Arctic's office. It was freezing, cold as charity, her breath turning to dragon puffs.
'Where have you been?'
'A couple of errands.'
Arctic folded up his paper with great deliberation. 'I understand from your mother that you did not, in fact, obtain her permission to use her bicycle.'
'Didn't I?' Lily said airily. 'I'm sorry.'
This was not nearly good enough for Arctic, who had been fulminating on this matter for over an hour. 'You should not borrow things without permission!'
'You're right – I'm sorry.' Lily almost smiled at her father, exhilarated to have suddenly discovered such an impenetrably strong position. All power to the great Rear Admiral Grace Hopper! Lily would never ask for permission to do anything ever again! She'd just do as she pleased – and when people complained, and when her father moaned, she'd just say she was sorry, very sorry.
'And you went out without helmet or lights.'
'Yes, I did,' Lily said. 'And I'm sorry about that too.'
'Don't be cheeky, Lily.'
'I'm sorry?'
'If you were one of my boys, I'd have you out moss-picking.'
'Yes, but I'm not one of your boys.' Lily sashayed to the door. 'And I'm sorry about that too.'

* * *

The story of Cary's fall on the Eton assault course had legs. *The Sun* had the initial scoop, but the story was quickly picked up by the rest of the pack. A Detective Inspector from Windsor was interviewed. He said the police were treating the case as attempted murder.
The Mirror's resident Old Harrovian, Bain, was picking

his teeth. He'd had a bacon roll for breakfast and scraps of bacon were stuck in the nicotine-stained gaps between his molars. He poked them out with a silver toothpick – just as he did after every meal. The larger bits were inspected and re-ingested, the smaller bits flicked onto the grey carpet of the *Mirror* newsroom in Canary Wharf.

Bain was smarting. *The Sun*'s mad-masters did not have a complete monopoly on kicking recalcitrant news reporters around the newsroom and, yesterday, it had been Bain's turn to be given a roasting for missing the story on the Etonian's assault course accident. This morning, he would be given a second roasting, noisier, more sweary, for missing the follow-up: the boy who'd had the fall was in the same house, The Timbralls, as that other boy who'd hanged himself. There was talk of a Timbralls curse; there'd even been speculation that the house was still stalked by the ghost of an old boy, one Ian Fleming.

Bain was going through all the day's papers, starting off with *The Mirror*, and then moving on to *The Sun* and *The Mail*. He was puzzled by The Sun's coverage of the Eton boy's fall. Having broken the story two days ago, he'd expected them to be heading the charge – but no, they barely gave it a mention.

But *The Daily Mail* had done a proper number on the story, a two-page spread.

Bain turned the page. The piece of bacon on his fingertip remained unflicked. *The Mail* had got an actual picture of the idiot Etonian who'd had the fall. Bain did a double-take, squinted at the picture again, and began to chuckle.

'Nice to meet you, Cary.' He caressed the picture. 'Haven't you been a naughty boy!'

* * *

Cary had been told that he'd be staying in hospital for some time. It wasn't great – but it could have been one hell of a sight worse. He'd got books, he'd got Lily and, best of the lot, now that he was no longer about to die, his parents had driven back home to the Dales.

He was expecting Lily later in the afternoon and, for the moment, he was contenting himself by writing her a love letter. He knew she adored his letters – because he adored receiving her letters and, in all matters of import, their feelings were always entirely mutual. She'd tucked her first letter under his pillow and he'd found it just as he was going to sleep. He could not read it too often.

Not that his relationship with Lily was entirely based on making love, but love-making was an important part of the mix; he wondered what it would be like with this huge cast on his leg. Would they – could they – in the hospital?

Cary's reverie was broken by a brassy rat-a-tat-tat on the door. A pudgy man in a blue suit walked in.

And Cary flinched.

'Cary!' Bain said. 'I thought it was you! How are you?'

Cary attempted a recovery. 'Do I know you?'

'Now, now, now, Cary – where are your manners?' Bain plumped himself down on the chair next to the bed and pulled out a pack of bubble gum. 'Want some?'

Cary shook his head.

'How did I know you weren't the sort of chap to chew gum?' Bain unwrapped a couple of pink bricks, popped them into his mouth, and gave a contented stretch, legs straight, hands behind his head. He seemed in no hurry whatsoever. 'Do you think somebody was really trying to kill you?'

'Who are you?'

'Shall I tell you something, Cary?' Bain grinned as he chewed, gold tooth glinting. 'You can't blag a blagger. And I've been blagging since before you were born!'

'What are you talking about?'

'I'll tell you exactly what I'm talking about! I'll make it so simple that even a child of five could understand it; so simple that you, with your brilliant Eton brain, will be able to understand it in a matter of moments.'

'You don't half talk a lot.'

'Feisty!' Bain said. 'I love it! I told you last time you should be a reporter – you're a natural!'

He pressed the gum to his teeth and blew a bubble. 'Not allowed to do that in the newsroom. But with you, Cary, I can do as I please.'

'What are you doing here?'

'What am I doing here?' Bain blew another bubble and stared out of the window. 'I'm getting an exclusive interview for *The Daily Mirror*!'

'Are you, now?'

'And if I don't get it, then as soon as I leave this fine hospital, I will be hightailing it to Eton College to have a chat with that most affable headmaster, Mr Moffatt, to whom, in short order, I will reveal the name of the callow Etonian who has been flogging stories to *The Sun*.' He grinned, pickled eyes lost in crinkled skin, and picked the rim of his nose with his signet-ringed pinkie. 'How do you like them apples?'

A nurse knocked on the door and wheeled in Cary's lunch. She looked at Bain, sprawled in his chair in his stained suit.

'Is this man bothering you?'

'Bothering him?' Bain said. 'We're old friends, aren't we, Cary? Just having a nice catch-up.'

'Is that right, Cary?'

Cary shut his eyes. He wanted to think it through but there wasn't time. 'He can stay.'

'Really?' said the nurse.

'Yes.'

'Of course I can stay,' Bain said. 'How could he possibly turn out one of his oldest and dearest chums?'

The nurse looked askance at Bain and, in silence, placed a tray of stew and apple tart on the bed table. 'I'll leave you to catch up.' She glowered at Bain before she left.

'Beef stew with dumplings!' Bain said. 'Mind if I have a bite?'

'I've suddenly lost my appetite.'

'Good-o!' Bain stuck the bubblegum on the side of the plate and forked up a mouthful. 'Not quite up there with the oysters we were having in Karl Marx's favourite restaurant, is it, now!' He laughed. 'It tastes like shit!'

'God, you're a reptile.'

'Thank you!' Bain cackled with laughter. 'Now, first things first – let's get your picture. We want you looking moody and soulful.' He produced a compact Olympus Twin camera from his pocket and fired off three frames. 'Next – my favourite part, the interview! I could use my good old-fashioned Teeline shorthand, but for little weasels like you, Cary, I prefer to use my trusty tape-recorder.'

Cary groaned. He had a hammering headache. 'How long is this going to take?'

Bain unwrapped more bubblegum. 'We're in no hurry at all!' He switched on the mini-recorder and placed it on the table next to Cary. 'This will take as long as it takes. That, my old cockeroony, is the sheer unadulterated joy of blackmail!' He strode over to the window, opened it, and inhaled. 'Doesn't it smell sweet? And here's one more thing to think about! Just imagine how happy your little keeper Kim will be when he reads my exclusive in tomorrow's Mirror! He'll fairly be choking on his Coco Pops!'

CHAPTER 32

Cary had been moved onto one of the general wards. He was leafing through university brochures, still pondering what to do when Eton life stopped and when the rest of his life started. Go to university – or go travelling? Or even… get a job?

And, much more pertinent, where did Lily fit in? How were things going to work out when he'd left school and she still had another year on the hamster-wheel?

Lily's next visit did not begin well. She sat next to him on the bed and kissed him. She leaned against one of the tubes in his arm. He yelped. She apologised and, the next moment, as Cary yelled, 'Mind out!', she knocked over a jug of water, and the crash in the silent ward was like a bomb. A nurse clucked round, cleaning up the glass and the water, Lily standing next to the bed trying to be helpful, Cary not doing anything much but smiling and trying to be cheery.

The nurse took away the mop and the broken glass.

'Sorry,' Lily said.

'Shall we start again?' Cary said. 'Pretend you've just got here.'

Lily turned on her heel, walked out of the ward and then walked straight back in again.

'Darling Cary.' She kissed him. 'When am I going to be allowed to get my hands on you?'

'Just as soon as I can get out of here.'

'I'll sit on the chair rather than the bed.'

'That's very thoughtful of you.'

'I'd be unable to resist you and I might knock some of your tubes.'

'I'd offer you something to drink – but for some reason, they've taken my jug away.'

They laughed. It was all fine – everything was going to be fine. They were in love, they'd found their soulmate, and nothing else much mattered.

Lily picked up one of the university brochures lying on the bed. They were from all over the world.

'Any of these universities taken your fancy yet?' she asked.

'It'd be a start if I knew what I wanted to study.'

'All these options, all these careers ahead of you – and meanwhile, I'm going to be stuck here for another year at Eton.'

'And I'll be visiting you every week.'

Lily toyed with one of the apples in the fruit bowl. 'Don't fob me off,' she said. 'When you leave school, you'll be travelling the world. You won't set foot within a million miles of Eton.'

'Of course I'll be coming back.'

'Trekking across the country to be with me? You might even be in America.'

'So, I won't go to America, then.' Cary took her hand and kissed it. 'You are the one.'

'I'm the one for the moment – but who knows how we'll feel in a year's time when we're no longer seeing each other every day, when, when… you'll have dozens of girls mooning after you.'

'Please don't say we're having a fall-out – are we?'

'No.' Lily took a bite from the apple and offered it to Cary. He shook his head. 'We're just talking about what happens, say, in September, when I'm still stuck here studying for my exams, and you will be footloose, fancy free, and no teenage girl will be able to resist you.'

'I daresay you won't be short of male attention, either.'

'Cary!' she said. 'So, what does happen to us when you leave?'

'I don't know.' Cary shrugged. 'It's a long way off, isn't it – six months away. Anything could happen by then.'

'Would you like to go to university with me? You take a year off. We could start as freshers together?'

Cary didn't immediately reply. It wasn't that he didn't want to go to university with Lily. But he wasn't even sure he wanted to go to university. Lily saw his hesitation, and prickled.

'So, you don't want to go to university with me?' Lily took another bite from the apple, decided she didn't like it and threw it in the bin. 'One thing I do know is that, when the summer's over, we're finished.'

'How can you say that?' Cary said. 'I don't know anything much – but what I do know is that, come what may, I want you in my life.'

'How's it going to work out?'

'I don't know. Why do we have to have it all planned out? We've got each other – we love each other. We'll sort it out.'

Lily was crying. She'd been stewing on this for some time. Was this love or was it puppy-love – and either way, how could it ever last past the summer? They could give it a try, but… it was hopeless. There'd be other head-turners, other loves, and this Eton affair would become nothing more than a memory.

'We'll sort it out?' she echoed. 'Cary, we're just a couple of kids – we don't know the first thing.'

'I know I love you.'

'And when we split up, which we will, I know it will be utterly devastating—'

'Hold on!' Cary said. 'Where has this all come from?'

'Sometimes I feel it'd be better just to have a clean break.'

'But this is all months away,' Cary said. 'Who knows what might happen!'

'And instead of just breaking your leg, you might be actually dead in a ditch – how can you say that everything's going to be fine, it'll all work itself out, when it quite obviously won't work itself out, and one moment you're sliding down some stupid rope, and the next you're in hospital. You think you're so smart, Cary, and you think you've got it all covered, but if your broken leg has taught me anything at all, it's that you certainly don't have everything covered.'

'So I'm not allowed to think that something wonderful will happen?'

'You can think all you want, Cary, but a fat lot of good it will do you.'

'Where's all this coming from?' Cary said. 'Why can't we just enjoy the next six months together, and then in July, we'll see how we feel?'

'You'll be gone and I'll be stuck here – and how do you think I'll feel about that?' She wiped her cheeks, but the tears wouldn't stop.

'It'll be fine,' Cary said a little too breezily.

'Don't say that!' Lily said. 'How can you possibly say that? You have no idea if things will be fine or if they'll be disastrous.'

'I wish I could say something to calm you down.'

'I don't need calming down!' Lily said. 'What I need to know is what's going to happen to us at the end of the summer.'

'And that, I can't tell you,' Cary said. 'I can tell you that I love you. I can tell you that I have hopes and dreams. I can tell you that I hope you'll always be in my life. But what happens in the summer, and how it all turns out – well, I'm hoping for the best. But I don't know.'

'Hopes and dreams!' Lily said. 'What use are they?' She stood up, wiping the tears from her cheek. 'Bye.'

* * *

As lovers are wont to do, Lily was soon weighed down with regret, but she couldn't go back to the hospital because it was out of visitors' hours, and now that Cary was on a ward, she certainly couldn't reconnect with him in the only way that lovers are meant to reconnect.

Doleful, she made her way back to Farrer. She wished she knew how things would turn out for her and Cary. What she couldn't bear was to be one of those teenage lovers who tried to carry on dating when one or other had moved to pastures new, and gradually the calls and the visits diminished and then eventually, after a few months, the relationship just withered and dropped dead. It wasn't like they were married with children. Perhaps the best thing might be just to let Cary fly free – and if, in a few years' time, and after he'd 'sown his university oats' (God, she hated that expression), then they might find themselves back together again, though most probably they wouldn't, and even if they did, they'd both have evolved and… and…

She shuddered at the revolting thought of Cary with another love.

All these things Lily was mulling over as Maxwell accosted her in the High Street. He'd been rowing and, as usual, his T-shirt reeked of stale sweat; she smelt him before she saw him.

'Hello, Lily,' he said. 'Haven't really seen you this half. What have you been up to?'

'Nothing much,' came the standard reply.

'You look a little out of sorts, if you don't mind my saying so.'

'No, I don't mind.' She paused. She thought. She realised she found Maxwell wholly offensive. 'Though what I do mind is your B.O. You stink, Maxwell.'

'I'm so sorry for sweating while I'm out on the river. How very thoughtless of me.'

'That's not fresh, it's weeks of sweat. You just never bother to wear a clean shirt.'

'Who's rattled your cage?' Maxwell said before adding, in a moment of clarity, 'You've just come back from seeing Cary. How is he?'

'What do you know about Cary?'

'Only what everyone else knows.'

Lily was horrified. She would have liked to terminate the

conversation, but could not resist picking at the scab. 'And what's that?'

'That your boyfriend nearly managed to kill himself on the assault course, more fool him!'

It was like a physical slap to the face – and Lily responded in kind, literally slapping Maxwell round the face, hard enough to make it sting. Maxwell stepped back, dabbed at his cheek.

'You're a little bitch, aren't you?' Maxwell stalked off.

It was unfortunate that they were right next to the School Library; a lot of people were watching them. News of the slap soon reached Arctic's ears and, for Lily, it was the perfect cap to a perfectly shitty day; her father requested to see her in his study.

She had been in her room, reading but unable to read. She'd tried to write up her diary, but what was there to write when all she wanted was to be with Cary, larking around with Cary, making love with Cary – and why should Cary have any idea how things were going to turn out after he left Eton? If only she had just a little of his bullish optimism – but then, it was she who was going to be stuck in the Eton goldfish bowl while Cary was long gone. Come the autumn, he'd think of her for a while, he'd write and he'd visit, but how could it ever last, two teenagers in a heady school romance? Once Cary had left, the spell would be broken. Besides – Cary was a catch. He was gorgeous and funny and considerate – and… and… He was the total package. It wouldn't be long before girls started tipping their hats at him, simpering, and flirting and, though Cary might be able to resist them for a while, eventually they'd wear him down, and Cary might do the decent thing and break up with Lily, but there was a chance, a tiny chance, that he might dally with two-timing… this buzz of thoughts swirled unending through her head, only to be broken by Arctic knocking on her bedroom door.

Without actually setting foot into her room, he poked his bullet head in through the doorway. 'Ah, Lily – can I have a brief word in my office?'

'What about?'

'I'd rather talk about it downstairs.'

'I'll pop down shortly.'

Arctic scowled. She'd pop down shortly? 'No boy would dream of talking to me like that.'

Lily snapped her diary shut. She'd had a spat with her boyfriend after lunch, and then she'd had that foul confrontation with Maxwell in the afternoon, and now she could see no problem whatsoever in going for the full Trifecta with her father.

'But I'm not one of your boys,' she said. 'I don't know why I have to keep reminding you.'

'What's this all about?' Arctic said. He took a tentative step into the room. 'What's happened to my girl? You're so different – you used to be so happy and conscientious.'

Lily bristled as she looked at her father. 'I do find it amazing that you thought bringing me to Eton wouldn't change me. I've left all my friends. I don't see any other girls from one day to the next. And the only thing I do see is hundreds and hundreds of carbon-copy boys, who treat me like a complete freak – so yes, maybe I have changed a little since the summer.'

Arctic stood awkwardly in the doorway. 'I hear you've been having boyfriend problems.'

'Who told you that?'

'If you are going to start slapping boys in the middle of the school, then word soon gets around.'

'That Maxwell prat! I wouldn't touch him!'

'Look, Lily – I know you once had a dalliance with Maxwell—'

'Could you please leave my room now?'

'Not until I've had my say.'

'I think you'd better listen to me carefully.' Lily stood up, cradling her fist, marshalling her thoughts. 'I'm asking you politely to leave my room. I have had an extremely tiring day, and if you stay here for even a few seconds longer, then I will start to say things you will not want to hear.'

Fatefully, Arctic paused. Never in his life had anyone spoken to him like that before. Not his wife, not his rowing coach, and certainly not his stripling pupils.

'How dare you talk to me like that.'

'Get out of my room.' Everything that had happened to her that day coalesced into one luminescent ball of rage. 'I want you out now.'

Far from leaving, Arctic stalked right into the middle of the room and stood in the centre of the rug, hands on his hips. 'I think you forget yourself, Lily – this is my house. I am quite literally the master of this house and I can go into any room I see fit. You also forget that I am not just your father but your tutor—'

'Why are you still here? Leave my room!'

'You had sex with him,' Arctic said. 'And now he's broken up with you.'

'You are a complete moron!' In her rage, Lily hurled an open ink pot at her father and hit him square in the stomach. Black ink exploded onto his shirt and face, dripping down onto his grey suit trousers.

'How, how, how? What is this?'

'Get out!' Lily shouted – so loud that her mother, Tor, could hear; Miranda could hear; most of the boys in the house could hear. 'Get out, get out, get out! Why are you still in here! I'm sick of the sight of you!'

Retaining what little authority he still had left, Artic brushed himself down. 'Disobedient wretch,' he said – and finally, way too late, he left Lily's room. 'You'll hear more of this tomorrow.'

'You make me sick!'

As soon as Arctic had left Lily's room, she kicked the door shut behind him.

Miranda happened to be coming out of her suite. 'Everything all right there?' she asked.

'No, not at all,' Arctic said, suddenly aware how ridiculous he looked, spattered in black ink. 'To ignore her behaviour would be to condone it.' Miranda just stared at him as Arctic continued. 'I am afraid Lily must be punished for what she has done.'

'Yes?'

'It is the correct thing to do, Miranda. If I ignore it, just carry on tomorrow as if nothing's happened, then Lily will believe she can lose her temper with impunity. I will not tolerate it!'

Miranda delicately toed the carpet with her slipper. 'She's your daughter, she's in this strange new school.'

'What of that? You think that because Lily is my daughter, the school rules don't apply to her?' He was enjoying having this conversation in the passage with Miranda; Lily would be hearing every word of it. 'Quite the contrary! In this house, I cannot show any favouritism! If she breaks the rules, she must be punished.'

'I'd cut her some slack, if I were you.'

'I will have her on the Bill tomorrow, see if I don't.'

'You'll have your own daughter put on the Bill!' Miranda was horrified. 'Are you completely mad?'

'Not mad – just making an example of her. And in future, she will learn that it is a very bad idea indeed to go against her father's wishes.'

Miranda could see she was only adding fuel to the fire. 'I will tell you what is a very bad idea,' Miranda said, slowly shaking her head, 'and that is to have a family dispute settled by the headmaster.'

'She must be disciplined. I have decided it. She will be up before the Headman tomorrow afternoon.'

'God help us!'

CHAPTER 33

Mr McCreath had been forewarned by the delectable and eminently chaste Miss Robinson of Lily's 12:30pm interview with the Headman, Mr Moffatt. Like the rest of the staff, Mr McCreath thought it an extraordinarily bad idea, but Arctic had been adamant that his daughter be punished just like any other Etonian.

He wondered whether to tell Cary. Possibly not.

There was one small matter he wished to pick Cary's brain about. He stopped off at a Windsor greengrocer to pick up an appropriate bag of grapes. He'd already checked the hospital's visiting times and sauntered past the reception and onto the ward. He found Cary with a pile of open history books on his bed.

Cary looked up. 'Mr McCreath, sir,' he said. 'Good afternoon.'

'Good afternoon, young man. How are you?'

'On the mend – glad I'm not in a morgue.'

'I've brought these grapes for you.'

'That's very kind of you – tempt you to one?'

'No, thank you.' Mr McCreath sat down and made a leisurely survey of the ward and its occupants. The room was light and airy, four beds down one side, four down the other. It was only half-full and the other patients, middle-aged men, broken in mind and limb, were asleep. 'Tell me about the *Mirror* interview.'

'Ahhh… yes.' Cary had expected to be quizzed about the *Mirror* interview, but after hearing nothing for four days, had hoped the school had moved on.

'School rules explicitly state that boys are not allowed to talk to The Press – as I'm sure you know, Cary. So, what happened?'

'He got me when I was still half out of it,' Cary said. 'I'm very sorry.'

Mr McCreath stroked his beard, weighing up this wily boy's words. 'I thought as much,' he said. 'There was no matter of payment?' He watched carefully for any reaction.

'God, no!' Cary said. 'This guy Bain came in, told me an interview might add some publicity to the police investigation. He started asking questions. I answered them.' Cary decided a small lie might be appropriate. 'He was very charming.'

'I see, I see,' Mr McCreath said, before decisively rubbing his hands together. 'The good news is that this is precisely the sort of story we have been waiting for.'

'It is?'

'We have been looking to send a warning shot across the bows of the tabloid press for some time – this Mirror interview is perfect.' Mr McCreath leaned back, crossing his ankle over his knee. 'We would like to report this story to the PCC, the Press Complaints Commission, which regulates the British press. What this man Bain did is completely outrageous! Coming into a hospital and interviewing an Eton schoolboy while he's still high on Tramadol! It's an open-and-shut case. *The Mirror* will have to print a formal apology. This reporter Bain will hopefully be sacked. And we will be showing the rest of the tabloids, and *The Sun* in particular, that we are out to get them. What do you say?'

Cary was horrified. If Bain was reprimanded by the PCC, and if he was perhaps sacked, he'd be absolutely certain to drag Cary down with him… 'Can I think about it?'

'No need to think about it, Cary – just sign this letter of complaint. We'll take care of the rest.'

'Very good,' Cary said. 'But I'd still like to think about it.'

'Toch, Cary! There's nothing to think about. The slippery

sod bamboozled you! Sign this and you would be doing the school an immense favour.'

'I don't know.'

'And other matters, matters perhaps closer to the heart – matters relating to various extra-curricular activities that may be occurring at The Project – these may be...' Mr McCreath paused, searching for the right word. 'They may be overlooked.'

'Thank you, Mr McCreath, I quite understand.'

'So you'll sign?' Mr McCreath produced a four-page document from his breast pocket. 'We've finally got the bastards.'

'As I say, I'd like to think about it.'

'What's there to think about?'

'I'd be making an enemy – several enemies. There isn't much upside for me.'

'Apart from us turning a blind eye to Lily.'

* * *

Arctic was one of those pig-headed men who prided himself on being stubborn; who, once he had made a decision, believed it was set in stone. He had never knowingly made a U-turn. If he was in a hole, he'd keep on digging. This steely resolve did very occasionally pay off, particularly when it came to rowing a single scull; most of the time, however, it did not.

Various beaks had tried to dissuade Arctic from putting his daughter on the Bill. Ormerod, the wet blanket, had taken him by the elbow – by the elbow! – and had told him he'd be a laughing-stock. People – beaks, dames, boys – were already saying he was so incapable of dealing with his teenage daughter that he had to send her to the Headman for discipline. And, apparently, all she'd wanted was to be left alone. And had she really thrown a pot of ink at him?

But Arctic's mind was made up. Since there had been so very few girls at the school before Lily, the rules on disciplining masters' daughters were opaque. So she would be dealt with just like any other unruly Etonian. Her name went down in the Bill book, along with the nature of her misdemeanour – intemperate behaviour towards her tutor.

Once Lily had been put on the Bill, the full majesty of Eton's disciplinary machine was thrown into action and, at noon, while she was in an English div, a diffident Popper knocked on the door, and begged the beak's pardon but was Lily in the div, and would she possibly be available to see the Headman at 12.30?

She most certainly would.

She had dressed like a Queen, in lush black from top to toe, and – thanks to Miranda's coaching that morning – she had her plan of campaign; not so much a line of defence as an all-out attack. At 12.25, when she took her leave of the div, the boys banged her out of the room, thundering their desk-tops up and down; and when boys walked past her on Common Lane, they capped her, lifting their fingers as they would to one of the beaks; and when Mr Barne spotted her as he came out of the library, he patted her on the shoulder – 'Good luck, Lily.'

There was one boy who joined Lily on the Bill. He was quite a short boy with short-cropped hair that was pillar-box red. He was running on the spot, arms pumping up and down, knees up high, and his tailcoat, which was far too big for him, flapped about his back like the wings of a gigantic raven. He stopped when he saw Lily and gave her a huge toothy grin.

'Are you Barty?' she asked.

'I am,' he said, amazed and delighted to be talking to the only girl in the school. 'How do you know my name, Lily?'

'I know all about you,' Lily said. 'You're a friend of Cary.'

'You know Cary!' Barty said. 'We love Cary!'

'Some people are saying you saved his life.'

'I don't know about that,' Barty said. 'If I could find the bastard who did it, I'd... I'd...'

'Knee him in the balls?'

'Definitely!'

'So, presumably, the Headman wants to quiz you about your new hair colour?'

'Is it me?'

'It's a lot better than when you were bald!'

'You know about that too?'

'Cary told me—'

Miss Robinson emerged from the Headman's study. It was difficult to say what was different about her today; could have been her hair, could have been her skin, but she definitely looked like her tail was up.

'Hello, Miss Robinson,' Barty said. 'Nice to see you again.'

'Hello, Barty,' she said, not overly accustomed to chatting to boys on the Bill.

'Do you like my hair?'

'It makes you look like a punk rocker, Barty.'

'That's exactly what I was hoping for – thank you, Miss Robinson.'

'The Headman will see you now.'

'I'll pop right in, then.'

When Miss Robinson had disappeared back into her burrow, Barty pulled out a small tape-recorder, switched it on, and tucked it into his tailcoat pocket.

'Something to listen to when I'm a pensioner,' he said. He pulled out a pencil from his inside pocket, snapped it, and then gave himself four stinging slaps on the cheek. 'I'm coming!' he said jauntily and walked into the Headman's study.

Lily coolly stared out of the window, idly wondering if this was the end of her Eton career. Well, bring it on! She might go to the local Sixth Form College… or… she might travel the world with Cary. Anything would be better than staying in Farrer for another year.

Barty was all smiles when he left Mr Moffatt's office. He had to buy some brown hair dye and pick some more moss. He held his hand up and Lily high-fived him.

'Mr Moffatt will see you now,' he said. 'Have fun.'

Lily walked into the Headman's office. She didn't bother to close the door behind her. It was a lot warmer than her father's office – and a lot cosier. He even had a coal fire, and was standing in front of it, gently warming his bum; the position looked a little forced, as if Mr Moffatt had spent some time deciding where best to be standing when Lily entered the room.

'Hello, Lily,' he said, hands behind his back. He was surprised by the girl. She didn't look even remotely nervous – far from it! She looked poised. 'I understand your father is very angry – angry enough to put you on the Bill. I've never heard of this happening before. Can you tell me what it's all about?'

Lily smiled. She wouldn't have thought it, but she was enjoying herself. 'I'm afraid I can't,' she said. 'I'm sorry, Headmaster.'

'And why not?' Mr Moffatt was finding this all most unsettling; Etonians never normally looked quite so assured when they were about to be punished.

'I must apologise,' Lily said. 'On behalf of my father. This is a family matter and that's just where it should have stayed. I'm sorry you've been dragged into it.'

'But I have now been dragged into it, and you are now on the Bill. I'd very much like to hear your side of the story.'

'That's as may be,' Lily said. She smiled at that line. Miranda had given it to her. They'd spent an hour rehearsing this conversation – and this dullard Mr Moffatt was trotting out every line, just as they'd predicted it. 'But as I say, this is a family matter – and if I were to be discussing what occurred last night with anyone at all, then I think...' She paused, looked out of the window. 'I think it would be with Social Services.'

'Social Services?' Mr Moffatt said. 'Surely there's no need for that.'

'On the contrary, Headmaster.' Lily produced a small leaflet from her jacket pocket. 'This has all their contact details, and if I'm not completely and entirely exonerated, then I will be calling them up the very moment I leave this office.'

'But, but…' Mr Moffatt was unmasted and unmanned; why had he ever, ever allowed a girl, this girl, into the school?

'Furthermore, I would like a formal apology for the humiliation of being put on the Bill and, lastly, I would like a lock and key for my bedroom door – I'm the only girl in the school and I need my privacy.'

'But you threw an ink pot at your father!'

'I'm afraid that's absolutely none of your business, Headmaster – but it will most certainly turn into your business if I call in Slough Social Services.' She took another look out of the window. Two squirrels were scampering up the trunk of an old beech tree – a male chasing a female, but perhaps, quite possibly, a female chasing a male. She smiled, thought of Cary.

'Lily, Lily, there's no need for that!' Mr Moffatt squawked. 'I asked for you to come and see me to try and repair your fractured relationship with your father—'

'What utter rubbish!' Lily said. 'I've been put on the Bill and you thought I'd just roll over and take my punishment! Well, I'm not having it! So – do I get my apology, or do I call in Social Services?'

Mr Moffatt writhed. Having to eat humble pie – in his own study! And he, the very Headman of Eton! The fire was suddenly far too hot for him and he shifted greasily to the cool of the window.

'Lily,' he said. 'I'm sorry that—'

'Apology accepted,' Lily replied promptly. 'The only other matter is that I want a lock on my bedroom door, so I no longer have to suffer the intrusions of people I do not wish to see. It is outrageous!'

'I'll…' The Headman wrung his hands before completely throwing in the towel. 'I'll see to it.'

'Thank you,' Lily said. 'I think that's all.'

It was a conversation the like of which Mr Moffatt had

never experienced before. He was so confused that, as Lily left the room, he ended up saying to her retreating figure, 'Thanks for coming in.'

He could have kicked himself! He, the Headman of Eton College, and he'd just been kicked around like the cat by a 16-year-old schoolgirl!

Lily found Barty waiting for her outside the Headman's study. The tyke had been listening to every word.

'You smashed it!' He waggled his tape-recorder. 'I got every word of it!'

But it was what happened two days later that would define not just Lily's Eton career but perhaps even her life. Well, who knows how it might have turned out for her; maybe she was always meant to be with Cary, but after that interview, it was as if the points had switched on the train tracks, and Lily's life was suddenly thundering towards a new destination.

Back at Farrer House, Arctic was soon informed of the Bill debacle. The only way he could deal with it was to pretend it had not occurred.

'Good morning, Lily,' he said to her the next day, and was met with a cool reply of 'Good morning' as if she, also, did not want to ever refer to the matter again. A locksmith was called in and, when Lily arrived back from her morning divs, she found a new lock on her bedroom door. There was only one key. She turned the key in the lock and the bolt clicked home with a satisfying snap.

Barty was soon playing the recording of Lily's conversation to his classmates. Copies were made of the tape. Within just 24 hours, there was hardly a boy in the school who had not listened to the Headman's Rout.

For this, there were two consequences. The first came in the morning assembly, when Mr Moffatt was about to address the senior boys. Lily had been waylaid by Fredster and had been one of the last pupils to enter the School Hall. Mr Moffatt was already standing at the lectern on the stage, and the hall itself was alive to a rumbling hum. Lily came in through the central doors and was walking up the aisle with Fredster. Boys looked, boys twitched – she was well used to that by now – but the mumbled chatter was sliced with a knife and, like some great giant rousing itself from its slumbers, every boy in the hall stood up.

'What's going on?' Lily whispered to Fredster.

'It's a courtesy,' he said. 'When a woman enters the room.'

'Are they doing this for me?' Lily said.

'You're going to see quite a lot of it.'

And so she did. For the remainder of her career at Eton, every time Lily entered or left a room, whether it was a classroom, or the School Hall, or the Chapel, every boy would stand up for her and, of course, it was a delicious courtesy to the only girl in the school, now much more than a girl but a comrade. But it was also a subtle two fingers to Eton's establishment, and so led to the second consequence of Lily's scrap with the Headman; one way or another, he was going to find a way to do her down.

CHAPTER 34

Cary had not seen Lily for three days though he had heard her. Barty had visited him in hospital and had played him the tape, laughing louder and louder every time he replayed it.

'She's lovely!' Barty said. 'I mean, I know she's the only girl in the school, but she could be a really snotty girl – but she's not at all. Do you know her well?'

'Quite well,' Cary said.

'If I were a bit older and a bit taller, I'd want a girlfriend just like her.' Barty helped himself to one of the last of Cary's grapes.

'At least you know what you're looking for – that's a start.'

'She will be my girlfriend template for all time.' Barty flicked up a grape with his thumb and leaned back to catch it in his mouth. 'Do you think she's got a boyfriend?'

'Probably.'

'Course she has – girl like that would have been snapped up long ago!' He flicked up another grape but was distracted by the door opening. The grape bounced off his nose and onto the floor. 'And here she is!'

'And here she is,' Cary repeated, and this grin trickled onto his face, and Lily was smiling at him too and, while Barty goggled from the floor as he retrieved the grape, Lily leaned over the bed and kissed Cary.

Barty said. 'I should have guessed!'

Lily kissed Cary again and, sitting delicately next to him on the bed, and without jolting any of the tubes in his arm, she turned to Barty. 'Guessed what, Barty?'

'Guessed that you were dating each other!' Barty said. 'If anybody truly deserved each other, it's you two!'

'Thanks very much indeed, Barty; we'll invite you to the wedding.'

'I'd love to come – I'll be a page, or an usher, or a ring-bearer, and I can sing quite well – I'm hoping to get into the College Chapel choir when my balls drop– so I could sing for you too, Ave Maria's my favourite, though maybe you'd like something a little more modern—'

'Barty, dearest.'

'Yes, Lily?'

'I haven't seen my… my fiancé, for three days now.'

'Right, right!' Barty slapped his hand to his forehead. 'I'm gone, I'm out of here!' he said, backing out of the ward. 'Get well soon, Cary, and let's get running!'

The door swung shut and the middle-aged men dozed on the ward and Lily snuggled in to the love of her life and all was right with the world.

'Hello,' she said, and kissed him again.

'Hello,' Cary said.

'I'm sorry,' she said.

'And I'm very sorry too.'

'Know what I realised these past couple of days?'

'Apart from how to best the Headman in his own study?'

'What I realised, Cary, was this,' Lily said, and because his lips were just a few inches away from hers, she had to kiss him again. 'None of us have any idea what will be happening in six months' time – we might get some horrid disease, or get run over by a bus—'

'Or have an almighty fall.'

'Yes, you could also have a big fall and break your leg and end up in hospital for a couple of weeks, and there are any number of horrific things that might happen to us – but we might as well be optimists. Who knows what will happen when you leave school? But over the last three days, I have been of the opinion that…' She broke off.

Even though Cary was laid up in a hospital bed, and with a wisp of stubble on his chin, and hadn't had a proper bath in days, he was looking quite handsome. She had to kiss him again, long and lazily.

'Of the opinion that?'

'Of the opinion that things are going to work out just fine for us.'

'Especially now that you're my fiancée,' he said.

'Precisely.'

They kissed some more, hands beginning to roam as they reacquainted themselves with each other's curves. Cary looked over at his three ward-mates – all dead to the world, dreaming the dusty dreams of middle-aged men.

'Time to make up?'

'Here?' Lily kissed him.

'Those old boys would love it!'

'Aren't there doctors and nurses popping in to the ward?'

'I have a sudden urge to go to the toilet. You couldn't wheel me there?'

'Shall I bring a blanket?'

'And a pillow.'

Lines and tubes were quickly disconnected and Lily, much stronger than she looked, hefted Cary to the side of the bed and slipped him into the wheelchair. She tucked a pillow and blanket over his lap and, watched by one of the middle-aged dreamers, she wheeled him out. The corridor was empty. She pushed Cary into the disabled toilet and locked the door behind her.

'Cosy,' she said. 'Well lit. Intimate.' She kissed him. 'Beautiful white walls that are uncluttered by pictures. The sexy astringent smell of Domestos. Cary, you spoil me!'

'A disabled toilet in a hospital – and you. I would not be anywhere else.'

Lily smiled, and languorously pulled her dress over the top of her head. She tossed the blanket and pillow onto the floor.

'The wheelchair to start, don't you think?'

'Perfect,' he said. 'Are you going to lock the wheels or shall we scud around the toilet together.'

'Wheels locked,' she said, bending to click the locks home. 'Otherwise, we might do you an injury—'

'It'd be worth it.'

'We wouldn't want to do you any permanent damage.' She stood in front of Cary, luxuriating in her nakedness. 'How do you turn me on? Let me count the ways.'

Cary reached for her. 'I've never said this before – but I think it's appropriate: please be gentle with me.'

'Gentle enough?'

'Gentle perfection.'

And so Lily and Cary made up in the only way on God's earth that lovers were ever meant to make up – for mealy-mouthed apologies are all well and good, but it is only the physical connection that can wipe a lover's slate clean.

'I'm quite close,' Cary said.

'Only quite close, Cary, darling – I've been and gone!'

'You wouldn't have any condoms with you?'

'I haven't,' Lily said brightly. 'I knew I'd be kissing you today, but it hadn't occurred to me we'd be coming to—'

'Coming in?'

'Coming in the disabled toilets.'

'Just have to be careful, won't I?'

'Let me make the bed.' The floor was just a little grubby. She made a little nest with pillow and blanket by the window and helped Cary out of the wheelchair and, not that there was any residual anger or hurt, but the slate was more than wiped clean, it was made brand new.

Somebody rattled the door-handle from the outside, but they didn't say a word and, just a few minutes later, and because they were teenagers, and because they could, Lily was stroking Cary's shoulder.

'Are you ready to be careful with me again?'

'I'm getting a taste for *au naturel*. Where did you prefer?'

'I think the wheelchair. Let's get you back in it.'

Returning Cary to the wheelchair was more difficult. Lily dropped Cary on the floor. Cary winced as one of the IV tubes in his arm jagged on the radiator.

'Sorry,' Lily said. 'Are you all right?'

'It's nothing,' Cary said, though his arm hurt like hell. It was more than just a light stab.

'It should be me who's being more careful with you.'

'Forget the arm – come here.'

Later, sated and happy, Lily wheeled Cary back to the ward. One of the middle-aged buffers was now wide awake. He smiled and silently clapped his hands. 'Wish my wife did that when she came to visit.'

Cary laughed as Lily helped him back into the bed. 'I'm sure she did once.'

'Never in a hospital.'

* * *

That night, as the middle-aged men snored and farted with spousal impunity, Cary couldn't sleep but couldn't stay awake; he was delirious, sweating, arm aching, whole body shivering.

A cold hand pressed on his forehead. It was Fleming. At least, Cary thought it was Fleming standing over him in the moonlight. 'You don't look so good, Cary.'

'I'm… bearing up.'

'Really? Glass of water?'

'Please.'

With great delicacy, Fleming held the glass to Cary's lips and helped him drink. 'More?'

Cary gave a glassy nod.

A week afterwards, when Cary looked back on that decisive conversation, he could never be quite sure whether it had happened – or whether he'd dreamed it. As they often did, they talked about Lily.

'Now, that girl,' Fleming said. 'She's a keeper. You are both fortunate – and unfortunate. There are some people who go their whole lives without ever dating a keeper. But—'

'But what?' Cary whispered through chapped lips. He felt like he was burning up. 'What's so unfortunate about dating a keeper?'

'It's obvious, Cary – when you're dating a keeper, you've got to keep them! So, you will never experience the joys of sowing your wild Eton oats.'

'Keep your oats – I don't want 'em.'

'Well said!' Fleming laughed, pulling out his cigarette case 'Think they'll mind if I light up? The other thing is that, if – and I'm sure you won't, but if you let go of a keeper, then you'll always regret it. You can search the whole world, and you will never find anyone to touch them!'

'She's a keeper,' Cary repeated.

Fleming took a third puff of his cigarette and, as usual, stubbed it out and started going through the elaborate process of lighting up another.

'I'm glad you appreciate that. Half the battle's won,' he said, before adding conversationally, 'Do you know, with these cigarettes, Cary, the first puff is nectar? The second is good – and the third is merely okay, and that is why I stub my cigarettes out after just three puffs, though I am minded, actually, to start stubbing them out after just two puffs! How very decadent!'

'I did wonder,' Cary said.

'So, since Lily is a keeper, you might as well keep her, especially considering all that is to come.'

Cary was starting to see stars as Fleming's face shimmered in and out of focus. 'How do I keep her?'

'You're a bright boy, Cary – you'll work it out. The clue lies in a certain History lesson you had with Mr Barne in the Lower School – you even made a note of it.' He stubbed out the cigarette, looked at his cigarette case, and then studied Cary. 'Do I have time for another? I think not. Before I go, let me give you one more thing to ponder. It's an old Arabic proverb. I find it most empowering – as does Bond. Trust in God – but tie up your camel.'

'That's elliptical.'

Fleming stepped over, face right up close to Cary's. 'It's all very well being the optimist and hoping that things will work out for the best in this best of all possible worlds. That's trusting in God. But you still have to take all due precautions.'

'Like tie up my camel?' Cary's sparrow heart was fluttering fast and weak.

The glass dropped and shattered on the floor, and the three middle-aged men woke from their twitching dreams to see that their young ward-mate was fading fast. Alarms were pressed, nurses were called – horrified at Cary's pasty face and the purple patches spreading up his arm and asking of each other, 'Just what has happened to him this afternoon, what has he been doing with himself?' and then it was straight into surgery, and back into Intensive Care, and though Cary was saved, that was the end of his Easter half, and he was not out of hospital till midway through the Easter holidays – not much wiser about his academic future, but much, much more clear about his future with Lily, and he sent off the requisite letters and took all due precautions, so he would be able to keep this keeper. He tied up his camel.

CHAPTER 35

Mr Moffatt was up at 5am, bestriding the fields of Eton, truly master, headmaster, of all that he surveyed, when he stepped in some dog poo. The soles of both black loafers were coated in the foul excrement. He cussed and fulminated about how he would like to spifflicate the miscreant dog-owner. What was so particularly irksome was that the disgusting faeces adhered not just to the leather soles of his loafers but also to the red tassels.

So: while Nicki Moffatt read *The Daily Telegraph* on the other side of the breakfast table, Mr Moffatt attacked the loafers with polish and brushes. He had first wiped off the excess excrement with a damp cloth, and he was now bringing the loafers back to their usual gleaming sheen. But cleaning the tassels was more problematic.

He had cleaned the dog muck off the red tassels, but when he had held them to his nose, they smelt disgusting. He succeeded in masking the smell with Domestos, but the bleach turned the tassels from brilliant pillar-box red to limp pink and, at least to Mr Moffatt's discerning mind, they looked a little bit queeny…

He delved once again into his shoe box and, with an old toothbrush, applied red polish to the pink tassels, and briskly rubbed them with an old cloth. He did this between thumb and forefinger and, after the earlier annoyance of stepping in the dog shit, it was soothing, enjoyable even, except that Nicki, damn her, interrupted his tasselled meditations by snorting with laughter and remarking, 'You look like an old Moroccan beggar looking for Baksheesh!'

'Whatever do you mean?' Mr Moffatt was affronted. He was the Headman of Eton College – and though he was indeed polishing his pink loafer tassels, he was in his full headmasterly regalia; suit, tie, the rest, so how could he possibly look like some wretched Moroccan panhandler?

'It's the way you're rubbing your fingers together.' Nicki laughed, rubbing her own thumb and forefinger together. 'Baksheesh! Baksheesh!'

'What an utterly preposterous notion!'

Seeing her husband on the run, Nicki turned the knife. 'I'll never see you in the same way again!'

'You're as bad as the schoolboys.'

He held his loafer up to the light. It was extremely vexing because the red tassels were now dotted with pink splodges – and what on earth was the bloody point of wearing red tassels on your loafers unless they were completely pristine? Well – there was nothing for it. He'd just have to put on some more red polish, and he would have to rub it in, and he would continue to do that until the tassels were as red as when they first came out of the box – and that was how Mr McCreath found him when he walked into the Headman's breakfast room some 20 minutes later.

'Good morning, Headmaster – Mrs Moffatt.'

'Good morning, Mr McCreath.' Mr Moffatt took one more scan of the loafers – not perfect, still a bit of pink, but it'd have to do.

He was not one of those OCD types who lined up the baked bean cans in the kitchen cupboard and, besides which, it was, well, slightly indecorous for the Headman of Eton College to be seen by mere minions polishing his tassels. He slipped on his loafers, bending down to ease them over his heel; they were just a little bit snug. Were his feet getting bigger, or could the shoes actually be getting smaller? Perhaps it was his socks; they were the grey cashmere socks Nicki had bought him for Christmas, very thoughtful of her, but Mr Moffatt was, in fact, of a mind that he preferred the cotton-mix socks from Marks and Spencer, which were cheaper, and which didn't make his feet sweat so much.

'Headmaster?'

'Oh, yes, Mr McCreath – good morning to you.' He put down his polishing cloth and gestured expansively towards the coffee pot. 'Take a pew. Will you have some coffee?'

'Thank you, Headmaster, but Miss Robinson has already attended to my needs.' Mr McCreath pulled up a chair at the end of the long dining table, where he sat like a prim spinster, knees together, feet tucked under the chair, hands cupped in his lap.

'Oh, has she?' Mr Moffatt said, suddenly hit by the unmistakable whiff of a staff romance. He gave a knowing look to his wife, but her nose was still buried in the newspaper. 'Now, how is our complaint proceeding against *The Daily Mirror*?'

'It is not proceeding.'

'And why, pray, is that?'

'The boy, Cary, is refusing to cooperate.'

'Why ever not? Does he not know that we, this school, want to teach the tabloid press a lesson?'

'I have explained this to him. He says he doesn't want to get involved.'

'Why ever not? What does he think he's playing at?'

Mr Moffatt pushed his chair back from the breakfast table and crossed his ankle over his knee, eyes flickering briefly over his loafers and his cashmered ankle – the tassels were fine; you had to look very hard indeed to see even a trace of pink.

'I can't say. He just won't sign.'

'Won't he, now? And what leverage do we have on this boy?'

'Some and some, sir. I believe he is currently dating Lily—'

'He's dating Lily – the only girl in the school? Why was I not informed?'

'It has only just come to my attention, Headmaster.'

'We can certainly turn the screws on there.'

'I believe they met at The Project.'

'What's that?'

Nicki looked up from her newspaper. 'It's a homeless hostel in Windsor – part of Eton Action.'

'Quite so, Mrs Moffatt,' Mr McCreath said. 'This boy, Cary, does a lot of the cooking there, while Lily helps with the laundry—'

'I'll bet that's not the only thing they're doing there!'

'I daresay it's a possibility, Headmaster.'

'More like a probability!'

'Certainly, if he's anything like you were, darling.' Nicki Moffatt poured herself more coffee.

'If Cary is refusing to help us with our action against *The Mirror*, then he needs to be taught a lesson. We will start with The Project.'

'They'll just start having sex outside,' Nicki said, stirring the milk into her coffee before waspishly adding, 'Like you used to do.'

'Thank you, Nicki.' Mr Moffatt flexed a plastic smile at his wife. 'You're being most helpful.'

He did so wish that, when he was dealing with staff, she might show a little more respect – not for himself, of course, the humble Mr Moffatt, but out of respect for the majesty of the rank that had been conferred upon him.

* * *

On this day of days, Cary was out of his wheelchair and off his crutches and back in Fleming's old bedroom. He was also back running again, though very slowly, and back strapped into his school uniform, and even the starched white collar brought back pleasant memories.

But what he had been waiting for, and what Lily had been waiting for, was their grand reunion in The Project.

The Project was not as he remembered it. It looked tidier. The walls had been painted. There was a jug of daffodils in the hall. And, as he walked through to the kitchen, he heard a shout of laughter, Mrs Parker's laughter no less; it seemed that, while he had been in hospital, much had changed at The Project.

When he walked into the kitchen, it was like coming home – and that was exactly what it said on the banner that had been hung over the ovens – 'Welcome Home Cary!' And they were all there – Fergie and Renton, both sitting at the kitchen table, and on the other side of the table were Mrs Parker and Mrs Webber, and Minty and Jazz were there too, Joe and Matt slavishly hanging on their every word, marvelling at these two goddesses who had, for the second time, graced The Project with their presence. It would seem that Renton had made a large batch of pastry, and had folded it so that it looked like a baby, which he was handily holding in the crook of his arm. This pastry baby was one of the funniest things Mrs Parker had ever seen, and she was simultaneously chuckling and mopping at the tears on her cheeks. Renton was thrilled.

And there, of course, sitting in state at the end of the table, and laughing nearly as much as Mrs Parker, was Lily. She looked more than just happy, she was in bliss; she was blooming.

The moment Cary came in, they were all out of their chairs, and there were kisses from the ladies, and handshakes from the men, though be damned to formality, and Cary hugged the lot of them. Fergie was at first a little shy, but then getting into it, and Mrs Webber was so happy to see her protégé that she was now wiping the tears from her cheeks, just like Mrs Parker.

The table groaned with food – for Cary's arrival, they had laid on what was nothing less than a banquet; three huge cakes, chocolate and coffee, and, because it was Fergie's favourite, a Victoria sponge. And there were sandwiches, scores of sandwiches; cucumber, salmon and potted meat, all of them with their crusts neatly trimmed by Fergie, just exactly as Mrs Webber liked them. And there must have been at least 100 fairy cakes, not to mention tarts and eclairs and cream buns and doughnuts, and Bakewell slices and a loaf of banana bread. Not that Cary and his friends would be able to even make a dent in all this food, but it was they who would take the first cut before Windsor's waifs were allowed to have their fill.

Cary sat at the head of the table, holding hands with Lily, knees tight together, and Mrs Parker, quite garrulous for once, was telling how she and Mrs Webber had stepped into the breach once Cary had been put out of action.

'It's different from cooking for the Eton boys,' she said. 'They're much more appreciative—'

'And they're much more polite!' chimed Mrs Webber.

Cary helped himself to a cucumber sandwich and Lily squeezed his knee and let her fingers gradually wander up his thigh.

'And we've opened up that office door!' Fergie said proudly. 'Mrs Webber found a locksmith, and he opened that door in a jiffy and, because we're a charity, he wouldn't take any money at all, even though we were offering him some of your twenties...' He trailed off, not sure if he'd said more than he ought, before continuing, 'And, in the morning it's a little suntrap, and we like to sit out there and have our tea.' At the thought of that, he sighed contentedly and poured himself another cup.

Renton was going round the table, offering slices of the coffee cake which he himself had made that morning. Mrs Parker took a slightly dubious bite, and was pleasantly surprised.

'Why, Renton, this is very good – very good indeed. Did you really make it yourself, or did you buy it?'

'Yes, I did make it myself,' Renton said. 'My mother, believe it or not, was the cook at the local grammar school—'

'You're having me on!'

'I am not having you on, Mrs Parker – for over 20 years, she was the school cook at Ealing Grammar, as was, before it became Ellen Wilkinson School for Girls. I used to help her make the cakes.'

Mrs Parker was impressed – and she wasn't easily impressed. 'Well, it's the best coffee cake I've ever tasted!' she said handsomely.

'Thank you, Mrs Parker,' Renton said. 'That means a lot to me.'

Minty and Jazz, meanwhile, were as two Duchesses sitting in state before two awestruck groundlings. Matty and Joe were hanging on their every word, star-struck and tongue-tied, not quite believing they were in the same room as these… these two *angels.*

Cary was thinking all manner of things, not least that a speech might be appropriate, to thank his friends for all their many kindnesses. It was funny, but he couldn't imagine enjoying the company of his own family nearly as much – and he certainly couldn't ever imagine such a feast being thrown in his honour. He tinged his teacup and was just getting to his feet when the kitchen door swung open. Mr Moffatt walked in.

Cary quickly recovered. 'Good afternoon, sir,' he said. 'Cup of tea? Cucumber sandwich?'

Mr Moffatt looked – or so he thought – resplendent in his full headmasterly rig, but to the rest, he looked a tad overdressed.

'No, thank you,' Mr Moffatt replied. 'This is not a social call.'

'It isn't?' Cary said.

'It is not. May I have a private word?'

'You may.' Cary smiled to his table-mates. 'Excuse me one moment,' he said before picking up his teacup and following Mr Moffatt out to the hall.

Mr Moffatt had run through this interview several times. He was well prepared; he was looking forward to it. 'I understand that you are not going to help the school in its formal complaint against *The Daily Mirror*?'

'I'm very sorry,' Cary said. 'It's not for me.'

'That is what I thought you'd say.' Mr Moffatt sniffed and started to walk around the hall, fingers running lightly across the tabletops. 'You enjoy working in this hostel, don't you?'

'I do.'

'And quite the feast they've laid on today.'

Cary took a languid sip of tea; Mr Moffatt found it quite inexpressibly annoying.

'An amazing spread,' Cary said. 'Though most of it will be eaten by the local homeless.'

'And your girlfriend – she likes it here too?'

Cary drank more tea. He couldn't yet see where this conversation was going. 'She loves it here.'

'Well – Lily will then be as disappointed as you are to learn that I have decided to sever Eton's links with The Project.'

'I see.'

'I see – sir,' Mr Moffatt corrected.

'And may I ask, sir, why you're cutting Eton's ties with The Project?'

Mr Moffatt, shoulders back, hands clasped behind him, strutted round the hall. 'Because it is my wish,' he said. 'Is there anything more you'd like to know?'

'Not at all, sir. Tell you the truth, though, The Project doesn't need people like me any more – it's standing on its own two feet.' Cary knocked back the last of the tea. 'Will you tell them or shall I?'

'It is my decision,' Mr Moffatt said. 'I will inform them.'

'Very good, sir.'

Cary courteously held the door to the kitchen open and Mr Moffatt blithely returned to the feast. He paused for a respectful silence, but there was none. One of the old men was pouring tea, and one of the old women was helping herself to more sandwiches.

'Ah,' he said. 'I have decided—'

One of the women, stout and obstreperous, nudged the man next to her. 'I've decided to have another slice of your coffee cake, Renton – can you cut me a slice?'

'Oh, yes!' said the second woman. 'Can I have a slice too?'

'Now, when you made this cake, did you use instant or real coffee?'

Mr Moffatt tried again. 'I have decided—' only to be interrupted by the taller man, bald, who was wandering around with a teapot gibbering to each of the women, 'Can I offer you a top-up?'

Mr Moffatt bounced on his toes. 'I have decided—'

Mrs Parker finally took notice of the peculiar man standing behind her and nudged Mrs Webber on the elbow. 'Do you see he's got red tassels on his loafers?'

'I've never seen a man wear red tassels before.'

Mrs Parker raised a hand, the awkward schoolgirl at the back of the class. 'Excuse me for asking, but why have you got red tassels on your shoes?'

This was not a question Mr Moffatt had ever been asked before. He wore red tassels both because they were stylish and because they set him apart from the rest of the Eton herd; he did not feel the need to justify his tassels to these cretins sitting around a table in a homeless kitchen.

'I have decided—'

'I might buy some red tassels for my granddaughter,' Mrs Webber said chattily. 'They'd go very nicely with her white sandals. Do you mind my asking if you bought them separately or were the red tassels already attached to your loafers?'

'Of course he bought them separately!' Mrs Parker rounded on Mrs Webber. 'No shop would dream of selling black loafers with red tassels—'

The more wizened of the men, the frightful Renton, now took a squint at the loafers. 'They're not really red tassels, are they, though? I'd describe them as more pinky.'

Mrs Parker pushed her glasses up her nose to make a proper examination of the tassels. 'You're right, Renton – they're pink! And a very unusual pink at that? Do you know what – I think he dyed them himself! That's not a colour you're going to find in the shops.'

'When I was a kid, we used to have a man who wore red tassels!' said the other ridiculous man. 'He stuck them on the side of his black cowboy boots. He didn't half look a prat.' He stared happily into his teacup. 'But it was very useful for us kids. He was the local nonce – and we all knew we had to look out for the man with the red tassels! Happy days!'

'Stop talking about my tassels!' Mr Moffatt exploded.

'Touchy!' said Mrs Parker. 'If you didn't want us to talk about them, why are you wearing them?'

'She's got a good point,' said the more wizened man. 'Imagine if you came in here wearing a red Superman cape – are we just supposed to ignore it, as if it's some unsightly boil on the end of your hooter? No, mate—'

'I am not your mate!'

'Whatever – you only stuck those red tassels on your shoes so they'd be noticed and, now that we've noticed them, you can hardly expect us not to want to talk about them—'

'Maybe we're not being suitably…' Mrs Parker paused, coffee cake in mid-air, as she strived for the right word. 'Reverential,' she said triumphantly.

'Quite so, Mrs Parker,' said the more foul of the two men. 'Please watch and learn.' He now stood up, airily walked past Mr Moffatt, and then pretended to catch sight of his shoes. 'What beautiful tassels!' he said. 'And such a brilliant shade of red, not remotely pink! They. Are. Exquisite!' He fell to his knees, hands cupped in front of him. 'May I kiss them?'

'Get away from me!' Mr Moffatt shrieked. 'I am cutting Eton College's ties with The Project! With immediate effect!'

The more stupid of the men raised his hand. 'Excuse me for asking, but who are you?'

'He's the man in the red tassels!' cackled the woman with the cake.

'I am the Headman of Eton College! And these two pupils you have here now will not be returning to The Project.'

'By order of the Red Tassel!' That was Renton, and now the whole party dissolved into a great howl of laughter, though Lily and Cary did their best to stifle their giggles.

Mr Moffatt glowered and, turning on his well-tasselled heel, quit the kitchen.

CHAPTER 36

After Cary and Lily had been banned from The Project, the old Mini came into its own. As the Headman's wife, Nicki Moffatt, had so presciently predicted, Cary and Lily were now making love in the woods and fields of Berkshire. Sometimes, they'd walk to any Eton spinney and, whatever the weather, would make love on a blanket.

Other times, more daring, they'd explore Berkshire. Cary usually left the Mini parked up in a quiet Windsor back street. He and Lily would walk separately down to Windsor and then, timed to the minute, would meet up in a discreet alleyway next to one of the hotels. Behind the kitchen bins, they would transform themselves into a couple of teenage hippies, with sunglasses and long blonde wigs and cheap hand-me-downs they'd bought from Oxfam.

Perhaps these two foolhardy lovers really did have a death wish; perhaps, all along, they wanted to be caught.

One Saturday afternoon in early summer, they hit upon driving to the beach. Lily wanted to swim in the sea with her boyfriend, and then to lie on a towel on the pebbles, holding his hand. They could have found a leafy knoll by a riverbank, and could have swum in the freshwater, but Lily was adamant: she wanted to swim in the sea and to bask in the sun and to lick the salt off Cary's skin.

It was a risk, but then, if you're not taking risks, you're just slowly coasting into the buffers, and so, because his lover willed it, Cary of course decided to drive her to the sea. He studied the maps. The nearest beach, so far as he could tell, was Weston Hard in Woolston, close to Southampton. The round trip would take at least three hours; there would almost certainly have to be an interlude for love-making on the way down, and then there would be the swim and the ice creams and, without doubt, there would be more love-making on the way back. They were really looking at getting back to Eton by 7pm, just before Saturday roll-call, or Absence. It was going to be tight. And yet… quite unimaginably thrilling. While all the rest of Eton were rowing and chasing cricket balls, they would be out of bounds, way out of bounds, and driving to the sea to make love; so many school rules were being broken, and so many different ways to get expelled, and that only added to the delirious excitement of it all.

They had not seen each other in three days, and so their first essential stop was just a few miles out of Eton. Cary bumped the brown Mini down a farm track and, before the engine had even stopped ticking over, they were feverishly kissing and fumbling. Cary was already shirtless by the time they scrabbled up to the top of a haystack and sated themselves amongst the roof rafters.

'We connect so perfectly,' Lily said, pulling her yellow summer dress back on, and brushing the hay off Cary's trousers. 'Take me to my beach.'

'Yes, ma'am.'

As Lily sang along to the Spice Girls' hit, 'Wannabe', Cary bumped the Mini down the pot-holed track and continued to head for the sea. They could smell it before they saw it. Lily squealed and, not even bothering to shut the Mini doors, they ran over the tufty marram grass, and stripped on the shingle. Then, watched by an incredulous dog-walker, they charged into the sea. The water was at its bracing best and, without even having to say a word, they swam out to sea, keeping pace with each other with a sweet, easy breaststroke. A hundred metres out, they stopped and trod water, watching the dog as it charged over the beach, and watching the dog-walker as he lit a cigarette, and it was all so deliriously exciting. They were like a couple of old lags who, after a long stretch, had finally made a successful jail-break.

'Shall we swim to the horizon?' Cary said.

'Yes.' Lily smiled. It was not that the water was any warmer, but it was tingly cold now, actually quite pleasant. 'And we'll keep on swimming to the horizon until one of us says it's time to turn back.'

'Let's do it.'

'And I'll tell you one thing, Cary, my darling, my one and only love, it won't be me.'

'Let me tell you something, darling Lily, love of my life – it will almost certainly be me!'

And they continued to swim out to sea and, when Cary flipped onto his back, the dog-walker was nothing but a pin-prick on Weston Hard. The move onto his back sent a fantastic twinge up his newly healed leg, and it could have been cramp, or it could have been just that he hadn't exercised like this in a long time, but he suddenly realised he was absolutely shattered.

'I'm done,' he said. 'And I'm cramping!'

'Cary!' Lily said, swimming over to him. 'How thoughtless of me – I'm so stupid!'

'No, I'm fine, just a twinge in the leg,' and they now started the long haul back to the beach, and Cary was going more and more slowly, until he had to concede defeat. 'Just need a bit of a break,' he said. 'I'm a little sore.'

'Let me tow you back,' Lily said. 'I was the one who dragged you out here. I'll drag you back.'

'Really? It won't tire you out?'

'I've spent five years waiting for this moment,' Lily said.

'Maybe for a little bit?'

Cary floated limply in the water, Lily cupped her hand under his chin and, ever so gently, he could feel Lily's powerful kicks beneath him, and could sense that he was being dragged through the sea. It was pleasant to be on his back, and to feel the sun on his cheeks and to watch the clouds scud across the sky, and to have totally surrendered himself to this beautiful girl who was so strong and competent and who was taking him home. He realised that now was the moment, and that there would never be a better moment.

'Lily,' he said. 'Will you marry me?'

Her head was only a foot away from his. 'I was wondering what you were thinking.'

'I was thinking that I want to marry you. But do you want to marry me?'

'Why not?' she laughed. 'When shall we do it? Are we going to wait till you've left school? I wonder what the Headman would make of that: "Hello, sir, great to be in my last year at Eton – I believe you've already met my husband, Cary?"'

Cary sighed contentedly. 'I don't know when we're going to get married, but just so long as you do want to marry me, then that's fine for the moment.'

'Do you think they'd let us marry in the Chapel?'

'Without doubt – once you'd got your parents' permission, seeing as you're only 16 years old. I'm sure your dad will be completely overjoyed when he learns that you're getting hitched.'

'I'll tell him he's not losing a daughter but gaining a son.' Lily was laughing so much that she swallowed a mouthful of sea water, coughing and spitting before she eventually regained her composure.

'My folks will go absolutely mad,' Cary said. 'A teenage wife isn't really what they have planned for me!'

'Why will marrying me stop you from doing what you want to do?' Lily said. 'Will it choke your ambition?'

'Not at all,' Cary said. 'With you as my wife, I'll go higher and I'll go further.'

'Correct answer,' Lily said and, though she was getting a little cold, she liked the erotic feel of Cary's back on her stomach. 'And the kids?'

‘Kids won’t cramp us,’ Cary said. ‘They’ll be the best bit of the whole ride.’

Cary leaned on Lily as she helped him out of the sea, and they stumbled through the surf. The scar on Cary’s leg was livid red against his ivory-white skin. They towelled each other down on the pebbles before pulling their clothes back on. It was gone 5pm; hard to believe they’d only been away from Eton for three hours. The Mini was exactly as they’d left it, doors still wide open. They hugged and hopped in and, within minutes, the heater was going full blast and the Mini was warm and they were both smiling at each other, and not a word needed to be said, because they both knew they had done something momentous. And, really, there was only one possible way to celebrate. They were both ravenous for each other. They drove off the beach to find somewhere more secluded.

Lily was still as distractingly beautiful as ever, and she was also distractingly undoing his fly buttons; and it could have been the swimming, or his upright position in the Mini, but Cary’s leg was cramping up; and then, lastly, there was the way Lily’s tongue was teasing at his earlobe, so erotic, and he had to turn to kiss her, just a brief peck on the lips, and that was all it took because, a moment later, they’d veered off the road and were shooting down a grassy embankment. Cary could do nothing but steer. They crashed through a wooden fence, smashed rails, splinters flying, and the car bumped and juddered through a muddy field before it stalled and, seatbelts straining, they came to a complete dead stop.

‘Are you all right?’ Cary asked.

‘Yes,’ Lily said. ‘You okay?’

Cary didn’t feel like he was in any pain, though it would be a while before the adrenalin wore off. ‘I think I’m good.’

Lily kissed him. ‘That was close!’

Cary tried to start the car up – they might even have been able to drive straight back to Eton, no harm done – but the Mini was dead. They were in the middle of nowhere, and they were not just out of bounds, they were a long, long way out of bounds, and getting back to Eton in 90 minutes, though not impossible, was not going to be easy.

'We've got a little walk ahead of us,' Cary said. They left the car and trudged through the mud, holding hands and loving life. 'Better see the farmer to tell him the good news.'

They vaulted a gate in the corner of the field and, at the edge of the next field, they spied a farmhouse.

The farmer was in his shirtsleeves, buttons straining against his belly, and was not at all happy at being disturbed during his tea.

'You've smashed my fence and you've left your car in my field?' He scratched at his thick thatch of blond hair.

'I'm very sorry,' Cary said. 'I'd like to pay for the damage to your fence and for all the hassle.'

'I'll bet you do.' The farmer glowered, hands on his hips.

'I do,' Cary said. He tugged his wallet from his back pocket. 'Would £500 cover it?' He produced a thick wedge of £20 notes.

The farmer gawked. 'Five hundred pounds, lad? You don't have to pay that much.'

'No honestly – take it,' Cary said. 'It's the least I can do.'

'Well... well,' the farmer said. 'That's handsome of you. Thank you. Like to come in for a cup of tea? You must be a bit shaken up.'

Cary looked at Lily. She smiled and nodded.

'Yes, please – and could I call for a taxi? We're in a bit of a hurry.'

'I'll take you, lad – where do you want to go?'

Cary decided to tell the truth. 'To Eton?'

'Eton? Like the College?'

'The same.'

A big grin eased across the farmer's face as comprehension dawned. 'You're at the school, aren't you? You've been off on a jolly.'

'We're both at Eton, actually,' Cary said. 'Lily here is one of the housemasters' daughters. We had a sudden urge to go to the seaside.'

The farmer led the way through to a traditional farmhouse kitchen, with a flagstone floor and a toasty kitchen range. Two hams hung from the ceiling. The farmer's wife, not nearly as suspicious as her husband, got up from the table to welcome them, while two shy daughters watched with wide open mouths as Cary and Lily drank tea and told the story of their ludicrous adventure.

'Pity we never thought of doing that when we were at school, eh, Ann?' The farmer slapped his thigh.

'They've still got to get back!' Ann said.

'They have, they have – but let them finish their tea first.'

The farmer, Mick, took them out to an old Land Rover and, as they drove off, the girls and their mother furiously waved at them from the kitchen window. Lily sat in the front passenger seat, and Mick insisted that she went through the whole story again, and how long had they been dating, and were these excursions a regular thing?

He was chuckling to himself all the way to Eton, and it was only when he was about to drop them off that he mentioned the money.

'Who'd have thought I've got a couple of Etonians in my car – no-one would ever believe it! But that explains why you've got all that cash in your pocket – suppose it's fairly standard for Eton kids to have 500 quid cash in their back pocket.'

'In case of emergencies,' Cary said.

Mick dropped them off close to the athletics track, and said he'd have the Mini out to the farmyard by noon the next day, ready for the AA to pick up. Cary offered him another £100 for the ride, but Mick wouldn't touch it.

'After a story like that, you can have the ride for nothing!'

He waved and headed off into the dusk and, just like that, the adventure was over and Lily and Cary were safe back at Eton, and in time for supper, with no-one any the wiser. They did what they did so naturally at times like this. They kissed and gave each other a sweet hug.

'So,' Lily said. 'Your emergency fund?'

'For emergencies, yes.'

'Well, that was definitely an emergency,' Lily said. 'But it does mean you didn't give all your Sun blood money to The Project.'

'Please don't hold it against me, Lily, darling. It's not like the ring.'

'No, it's not like the ring.' She broke off and they started walking over the playing fields back to the school. 'What did we say? This whole thing will come tumbling.'

'It will?'

''Fraid so, Cary. All the *Sun* money had to go to charity, otherwise…'

'Otherwise what?'

She brought his hand to her lips and kissed it. 'We'll have a great fall.'

And Cary, in his turn, brought her hand to his lips and kissed her knuckles.

'If I've still got you in my life, then bring it on.'

And when you ask fate to bring it on, she usually delivers.

CHAPTER 37

I had been enjoying Windsor's high life, such as it was, courtesy of my mad-masters at *The Sun*. The previous night, I had taken a 'top contact' – girlfriend Amanda – out for supper in The Cockpit and, rather than going back to her flat, we'd spent the night in a luxurious suite at the Castle Hotel, where, or so my mad-masters believed, I was doing essential prep-work for the biggest day in the Eton calendar: The Fourth of June.

Eton's Parents' Day used to be quite an event in the Society calendar, when squads of workmen would set up marquees, so the upwardly mobile could show off their darling sons to best advantage. By the time Prince William went to Eton in 1995, all the marquees had been banned, and the flash folks had to slum it with – the sheer vulgarity of it! – a picnic on a rug!

That was of no concern whatsoever to me, as I had a most leisurely breakfast with Amanda. For me, there was only one item on the day's agenda and it was an absolute beauty.

For the moment, however, there was another slice of toast to be buttered and a lot of papers to be read. Amanda, devil that she was, had not even bothered to dress for breakfast and was wearing a sky-blue kimono and tan Ugg boots; the other hotel guests thought she was positively *shameless.* With ruffled bed-hair coiling around her shoulders and an air of spectacular depravity, it was difficult to tell if this, this hoyden, was even wearing anything underneath her kimono. (She wasn't.)

On the table between us were ten of the morning papers. Amanda preferred the broadsheets, while I always dived straight into the tabloids; first *The Sun*, for the thrill of seeing how the subs had mangled my stories, and then *The Mirror*, to read Bain's latest piece of mischief. I grinned to myself – because today, I was going to be at my old school and on my old stamping grounds, and Bain, God rot him, was in for a right royal shafting.

Grubby, festooned with camera gear, shambled into the hotel dining room. He was wearing a grey suit, the better to blend in with the Eton parents – though for some reason, Grubby made the suit look more like a rumpled smock.

'Morning, Amanda.'

He kissed her on the cheek and offered me a huge paw before helping himself to coffee and joining in the delicious ritual of reading the papers, occasionally commenting on a story, or scribbling a note, but generally reading in a mutually agreeable silence – well, is there any other way to have breakfast?

Though the great and the good would not be arriving at Eton till 11am, I would be in position long before then. I kissed Amanda goodbye, she with a lascivious hand to my cheek, and patted Grubby's shoulder.

'Fingers crossed.'

We'd run through the plan the previous day, and it would probably work, it was bound to work; in fact, there was hardly anything that could go wrong, but still I had this tight ball of tension in my stomach – exciting, invigorating, and ever so slightly terrifying.

I was wearing my very finest suit, a bespoke Prince of Wales check that had been given to me by my father as a birthday present. Coupled with a white shirt and a lilac waistcoat, I was at one with the world of Eton starch. Out of roguery, I was even wearing my Old Etonian tie, black with thin blue stripes. It was the first time I'd ever worn the thing, but then OE ties do make quite a statement: 'Made in Eton and proud of it'.

What a gorgeous morning and, with a scoop in my hands,

and with my girlfriend patiently awaiting my return, what a day to be alive! I meandered over the Windsor Bridge and spied an apartment I had once known in another life. My piano mistress had once lived there. It had ended badly, as all first loves tend to do. I'd never seen her again. I wondered whether to go down the street to look at her old front door, but decided against it. Some memories are best left undisturbed.

I walked up the High Street, every shop-front so ripe with memory – Rowlands the tuck shop, and Tom Brown the tailcoat-makers, and New and Lingwood with the white shirts and the hellish collars. I stopped outside Hills and Saunders, the school photographers. The window was devoted to pictures of Etonians in all their glory – house pictures, team pictures, and pictures of Eton's various peacock elites. There was a funny little man in the window, bald and with thick-rimmed black glasses, who was dusting down the photos. He gave me a jovial wave with his feather duster.

I walked past the Chapel and the School Office, and crossed the road to the flower-seller by The Burning Bush. Because it was Parents' Day, the boys were allowed to wear buttonholes. I bought a red rose and threaded it into my buttonhole. In a mad moment, I thought of going back into The Timbralls to see Cary and Mr Fleming, but that would have been a catastrophically bad idea – and how was young Cary getting on, anyway? I hadn't heard much from him since he'd got out of hospital. And how on earth was Cary spending all the money? At the last count, I'd given him over £50,000!

As I ambled past Prince William's house, I had this prickling sense that I was being watched. I stopped, looked back. Just on the other side of the road, I saw another of my Eton contacts, that strange old man in his tweeds, who liked to be called Mickey Mouse. He appeared to be speaking into a walkie-talkie. We saw each other at the same moment and simultaneously turned on our heels. He went off in the other direction but I still couldn't get it out of my head that I was being followed.

I was heading for Eton's Drawing Schools, where, like any other art lover, I would admire the schoolboys' pictures. But there was only one picture I wanted, Prince William's picture. As soon as I found the picture, I'd call up Grubby, who would glide in like any other Eton parent and take a couple of pictures of the young Prince's daubings.

Once I was done at the Drawing Schools, I planned to visit the School of Mechanics to see if Prince William had knocked out anything in wood or metal, or perhaps even silver. Grubby would again do the business and, by lunchtime, I would have filed my story on this rising new talent in the art world. By 2pm, I'd be done for the day, and would be heading over to the Christopher for a well-deserved lunch with Amanda and a bottle of their very finest white wine. And after that... we might go back to the hotel for a little nap before dinner at the most expensive restaurant I could possibly find. Oh, to be a Sun staff reporter with an exclusive story and limitless expenses!

Except I couldn't shake off this twitching uneasiness. Instead of heading direct to the Drawing Schools, I took a detour past the Fives courts. I emerged onto the Parade Ground. The Drawing Schools were much larger than I remembered them, stretching the length of the far end of the Parade Ground. Just like all else that Eton so graciously offered its boys, the Drawing Schools were vast, acres of windows, studios to take your breath away.

The Drawing Schools had only just opened and I was one of the first visitors. The lady at the reception was on the phone. I gave her a cheery good morning and dived into the paintings. I'd never much been one for art, but I diligently did the rounds, examining every single picture that was on display until, after 40 minutes, I found what I was looking for; a white triangle on blue and, beneath it, a little card with the beautiful words, 'By William of Wales, aged 13'. It was an okay picture, nothing special, but a proud parent would have been more than happy to have had it on the kitchen wall, and –

'Is it a boat – or do you think it's the dorsal fin of a shark?'

I winced when I heard the voice behind me. How the hell – how the hell? – had he found me?

I turned round and there was the grinning coxcomb himself, with an Olympus Twin Sure Shot in his hand, and already firing off shots at William's picture.

'You couldn't move a bit, old cock? You're in the way.'

I moved to the side. 'What an unpleasant surprise,' I said.

'I hoped it might be!' Bain said, still chewing on his damn piece of gum, and with this foul smirk plastered all over his face. 'What do you think of my get-up? To me, it says, Summer Garden Party.'

I scowled. Bain was wearing a creamy suit with a peculiarly noisome Paisley pattern tie and an even more noisome buttonhole. The whole ludicrous outfit was topped off with, God help me, brown and white co-respondent shoes and a Panama hat.

'You look like a clown.'

'You do say the sweetest things!' Bain crowed. 'The red carnation sets it off so beautifully.'

'It's not a carnation, you idiot, it's a chrysanthemum!'

'Aren't we the botanist?' Bain hummed to himself as he went up close to the picture and took another shot. 'Now, what do we reckon – flash on or flash off?' He fiddled with the settings. 'Well, you know what, Kim! I'll try it both ways, and leave the clods at head office to decide what they like best!' He fired off another couple of frames, this time with the flash on. 'And that's that, job done.'

'If you don't mind my asking, how did you find this place? How did it even occur to you to come here?'

And Bain just stood there, hands in his pockets, happily chewing on his gum, Panama hat tilted jauntily on the back of his head.

'Do I mind you asking?' he said, gold eye-tooth glittering in the sunshine. 'On the contrary – I'm thrilled beyond belief that you asked! And what's more, I'll tell you! How did I know to come here, now, to this exact spot? Sheer rat-like cunning! And I'll tell you one more thing – you're going to love it!'

A couple of parents came into the room, talking quietly, respectfully, as if they'd just entered the Holy of Holies.

'Amaze me,' I said.

'Not having the luck to be an Old Etonian, and not really knowing the turf, I reasoned to myself last night that there was bound to be one person in this world who knew what he was doing, and that would be the saintly Kim. So I was up early doors, very early doors, and while you were doubtless having a leisurely breakfast with Amanda, I was prowling around the one place you would absolutely have to walk past – that bush thing. Then, when you did walk past, and after you'd had your little chat with the flower-seller – she sold me this, this... CHRYSANTHEMUM! – and all I had to do was follow you here! Very foxy around the Fives courts, weren't you, you rascal, but soon enough, I worked it out! Kim's on his way to the Drawing Schools, and why's he on his way to the Drawing Schools? Because he wants to get a snap of Prince Billy's pictures!' He held his hand up. 'No need for applause!'

I felt like I was being forced to swallow a large mouthful of glistening gristle. I put my hand to my mouth and rubbed down to my chin, as if to stem the expletives I wanted to yell at Bain. I choked and swallowed.

'It always gives me the utmost pleasure chatting to you, Bain, but I'm afraid I'm just a little busy—'

'Off already?' Bain unwrapped another piece of pink bubblegum and popped it into his mouth. 'Can I give you a word of advice, Kim?'

'Please – I can't think of anything I'd enjoy more.'

'Don't know whether you've ever come across one of these things before,' he said, wagging the Olympus Twin in my face. 'It's called a camera. Very, very complicated to work, but I'm sure, given enough time, you'd get the hang of it. You just point and press the button and, lo and behold

– you've got yourself a picture!' He poked me in the midriff, before strolling out. 'It's all very well you blunts leaving the pictures to the monkeys, but sometimes it can be extremely useful to be able to take a picture yourself.'

Bain walked over to the receptionist and gave her a chummy leer. 'Sorry to bother you, but this chap—' he jerked a thumb at me '– he's from *The Sun* newspaper – and he will soon be sending over Grubby, a very grubby photographer, to take a snap of Prince William's picture. I'm sure you'll know what to do.' Bain fluttered his fingers at the receptionist.

I gaped a moment before following him outside. Bain was standing at the top of the steps, staring at a map of the College.

'That was pretty low – even for you,' I said.

'We mustn't let ourselves be ruffled by these setbacks.' Bain was still examining the map. 'I'm off to the School of Mechanics. Wouldn't it be great if William had made his mummy a silver bangle? Just the sort of heart-warming exclusive we love to see splashed all over the front page of *The Mirror*.' He took a step towards me, brushed a speck from my lapel. 'I'd ask you to show me the way, but…' and here he gestured towards the Parade Ground, where three men were hurrying towards us '…I can see you will be otherwise engaged.' He grinned and blew a large pink bubble. 'Tinkerty tonk, old cock. Do please send my special love to Amanda when you next see her.'

He scuttled down the steps and darted off towards the Fives courts. I was about to follow, when I heard a cry.

'Hi! You! You on the steps! Stay where you are!'

The gowned man in the middle was obviously a beak, though the two men either side of him, in suits and dark ties, looked just a little too muscly to be teachers.

With my left hand on my hip and my right arm loose and jaunty, almost balletic, I sashayed down the steps.

'Why, Mr Moffatt,' I said. 'Good morning to you.'

Mr Moffatt stopped two yards away from me; he seemed to have brought along a couple of Prince William's bodyguards for company. He sniffed and looked me up and down from head to toe.

'Are you completely without shame?' he said.

'No,' I smiled. 'I don't ever feel ashamed. If that's what you mean. Do you ever feel ashamed?'

'And wearing an Old Etonian tie too! You are the limit!'

'Perhaps even over the limit, Mr Moffatt.'

'That is all beside the point. I want you off the school premises immediately and, if you enter any school buildings, I will have you prosecuted for criminal trespass.'

'Criminal trespass? I don't believe I've ever come across that one before. Is it bad?'

'Yes – it will be very bad for you.'

'Is this the way you treat all Old Etonians?'

Mr Moffatt turned sheet white with rage. 'Only the ones who work for *The Sun*!' he said. 'Get out of my school and don't ever come back!'

'And you were always such a nice Latin teacher – one of my favourites.'

'Leave this school immediately!'

'Can I say one thing – those pink tassels on your loafers are simply... to die for! Wherever did you—' I was cut off by the appearance of the receptionist.

'Oh, Headmaster!' she said.

'Mrs Ramsay?'

'Is this man really from *The Sun*?'

'Unfortunately, he is.'

'Apparently, he's going to be sending a photographer here.'

'Very good point, Mrs Ramsay, thank you so much.' He turned to the two bristling security men. 'I'd like a guard put next to Prince William's picture – and I'd like another guard in the School of Mechanics.'

'Very good, sir.'

'And as for you,' he said to me. 'I hope never to see or hear from you again!'

'But won't you be at the school reunions?'

'Get out of my sight!'

And, having baited the man enough already, I did just that, but though it had probably been a score-draw against the headmaster, my mad-masters were made of much tougher stuff and, unless I did some incredibly nifty footwork, they'd give me an absolute kicking. Not only had I signally failed to land my much-touted Royal exclusive, but I had handed it on a plate to *The Mirror*. The woes, the woes of being a Sun staff reporter!

* * *

While Cary's parents were traipsing around Windsor, and discussing that simply *frightful* woman from the breakfast room, Cary was talking with Ian Fleming. They were discussing a large and very official letter he'd received that morning.

Fleming scanned the letter and chuckled. 'You've only been and gone and done it!'

'When the master says to trust in God but tie up your camel, then the wise pupil listens.'

'Very Confucian of you, Cary, but I still didn't think you'd actually do it!'

'Of course you didn't.'

Cary was sitting at his burry, while Fleming was lying on the bed, languidly propped up on a nest of pillows. He took his third puff of a cigarette and stubbed it out on a saucer.

'But applying for something like this! You're the first Etonian to do it!' Fleming said, still shaking his head. 'You'd better make sure it's properly hidden.'

Cary took the document and tucked it under the faded grey rug by the bed.

'Brilliant!' said Fleming. 'No-one would ever dream of looking there.'

'Why would anyone want to search my room?'

'Says the boy who's spent the last nine months selling stories to *The Sun*!'

Cary grinned as he tied his bow tie. 'Probably be quite a story.'

'Quite a story? It'll go right round the world!' Fleming was going through his theatrical routine of lighting up another cigarette. 'If, that is, you see it through.' Fleming studied his lighter. 'I used to think I smoked because I was addicted to the nicotine. But I now believe that what I was actually addicted to were the little routines I performed before I lit up.'

'You make quite a show of it.'

'It was wonderful during negotiations,' Fleming said. 'They'd make their offer, and I'd be there, biding my time, lighting my cigarette and, before you knew it, they were so rattled that they'd upped their offer – and I hadn't said a word.' He admired his slippers as he crossed his ankles. 'Seeing Lily today?'

'I doubt it,' Cary said. 'I'll be traipsing round with my parents.'

* * *

Lily was experiencing a most unusual Parents' Day; she was seeing nothing of her parents. Arctic and his wife had to spend their Fourth of June talking to the Farrer boys' parents, dutifully feigning interest in the chitter-chatter about the Farrer boys, their lives and their futures.

It was sunny and the house cocktail party was being held in the Farrer garden. Lily's mother and father were on duty from 11.30am, and would then lunch with some of the leavers and their parents. Lily was to be left to her own devices until 4pm, when she would join her parents to watch the Procession of Boats – but she had much better things to do with her time than visit Eton's various exhibitions. She was going to play Fives with Fredster Campbell – and she was going to beat him, and then she would be top of the ladder and Eton's Queen of the Fives court and, although Lily had felt a little queasy during breakfast, she was now feeling fine.

She had arranged to meet Fredster by the Slab at 10.30. She was wearing a white pleated tennis skirt, short, and a white top, all quite irresistibly wholesome. Fredster, when he arrived, had scrubbed up well; in fact, was almost over-scrubbed. His hair was slicked back and there was the usual fug of Aramis aftershave. He held the door open for Lily, couldn't help but admire her lissome legs as she walked out.

'Where are your parents, Fredster?' Lily asked. 'Why aren't they here?'

'They've gone to the Parents' Day at Marlborough,' Fredster said. 'My brother's there.' He laughed. 'I couldn't be happier! I'm going to play Fives with you.'

Lily already had her Fives gloves on. She juggled the ball back and forth. 'How are you going to take your beating?'

'I'm going to take it like a man.'

'Won't the other boys object to having a girl at the top of the ladder?'

'They're rooting for you,' Fredster said. 'There were a few boys who didn't like the thought of being beaten by a girl. But you've beaten everyone in sight – respect.'

'Thank you.' Lily said. They were walking down Judy's Passage and she was aware that their shoulders had touched; Fredster was very aware. It was electric. 'I like it that I started at the bottom of the ladder,' she said. 'I got to know more of the boys in Farrer.'

'We could team up to be the school champions!'

'I've got to finish you off first.'

'As the actress said to the bishop.'

'Insolent toad.'

Fredster slipped on his Fives gloves, stole the ball in mid-air and paddled it between his hands. He had a feeling of heady excitement; Lily was, quite simply, the most beautiful, the most desirable, the most exotic, the most sexy girl he had ever known – and now, here he was, alone with her, walking with her past the library, and soon they would be playing

Fives, and if – if – he played his cards right, she might even go out for lunch with him.

They walked into the School Yard where boys traipsed with their parents through Eton's old bits; the Lower School, the Chapel, the Cloisters.

'How are you getting back home?' Lily asked.

They had the Fives court all to themselves.

'I'll just get a train to Winchester after Absence.' Fredster took off his blazer and laid it down on the cobbles.

'So, why are you at Eton while your brother's at Marlborough?' They started to warm up, gently scudding the ball against the side of the Chapel. 'Wouldn't it be a lot simpler if you were at the same school?'

'My youngest brother George is due to go to Winchester!'

'Three different schools?' Lily laughed. 'Your parents must be mad!'

'They just love spending their weekends shuttling from one school to the next.'

They started the game. A few boys and parents came over to watch; most had never seen a girl playing Fives, and certainly none of them had seen a girl as proficient as Lily. She could have been making life difficult for Fredster by sending the ball over to the Pepperpot, but instead, she gave him the run-around, with dinky drop shots by the wall before sending him scurrying backwards to the far edge of the court. Sweat dripped from his red face. She looked like she'd barely stepped onto the court. In no time at all, he was two games down.

'Want some water?' he asked.

'Thank you,' she said out of politeness.

He offered her a bottle of Volvic. She had a swig and returned it to Fredster; he drank and wondered what it would be like to kiss her.

The last game was over in minutes. Lily started going for her shots, landing the ball plum in the Pepperpot, or smacking them to the corner. Fredster only won two points.

He smiled. He'd always known he was going to lose. He'd always dreamed of this moment.

'Congratulations, Lily,' he said. 'You're the best.'

He held out his arms and, because Lily was happy, and because she'd let her guard down, she went in for a hug. Fredster's dull antennae completely misread the situation and, instead of giving her a quick hug, he went in hard to kiss her on the lips.

Lily recoiled. 'Fredster!' she said.

'A celebratory kiss?'

'No!' Lily said. 'Certainly not!'

'I thought you liked me.' His face crumpled, suddenly transformed back to his urchin self.

'Not like that!'

'Oh, well – can't fault a guy for trying,' Fredster said, putting on his blazer.

'I wouldn't try that with any other girl, I can tell you,' Lily said.

They stood by the buttress. 'Have you already got a boyfriend?'

'Not that it's any of your business, but I do.'

'So, when and if—'

'Don't even go there, Fredster,' she said, holding up a warning hand. 'It's not happening today. It's not happening ever.'

'Never say never, Lily,' Fredster said.

'I'm saying never,' Lily said. 'Thanks for the game.'

She walked away but ruined the effect by being sick on the cobbles. She was used to it by now. She'd been throwing up for the past week.

* * *

Cary wished he could actually have enjoyed his parents' company. A lot of Etonians seem to be having genuine fun with their parents – joshing with their dads, clinging to their mums' arms as they wandered down the pavement.

But Cary was finding it a grind. His parents had stumped up to his room and sat awkwardly on the sofa, while Cary served them tea. It was a low sofa, and you either had to loll back on the pillows or perch on the edge and lean forward. His parents were perchers.

After five minutes of pit-a-pat, his father, wearing his best three-piece suit, a brown pinstripe, came to the matter in hand. 'Your A-levels are in a fortnight.' He placed his cup and saucer on the ground next to his feet. 'Where are you going to university and what are you going to read?'

'I haven't decided yet,' Cary said. 'I'm going to take a year off.'

'But you can still get a place at university – why can't you do that?'

Cary drummed his fingers on the desktop. He'd known this conversation was coming, and it was turning out every bit as badly as he'd thought it would.

'I don't know where I want to go, or what I want to do,' he said. 'I want a year to think about it.'

His mother, Penny, nervously twisted the small diamond engagement ring on her finger. 'But Cary, darling, why can't you at least get a place somewhere? Mr Ormerod says you could walk into any university. And, if you change your mind in a year, then you could do something else.'

'You're cracked, boy!' his father said. 'You need to get a degree – and all you want to do is fart around!'

'I wouldn't call it farting around,' Cary said. 'I've spent my whole life jumping through hoops. I want to spend some time outside the hoops.'

'All these advantages you've had!' his father said, so excited that he kicked his teacup over. 'The very best education that money can buy! And all you want is to loaf on a gap year! That's gratitude!'

'I'm sorry.' Cary brought his fingers together and made a decisive tap on the table. 'I suppose it really depends on whether I spend my life doing what you want me to do, and doing what the teachers expect me to do – or whether I spend it doing what I want to do.'

'But you don't know what you want to do!' Penny said.

'I certainly know what I don't want to do,' Cary said. 'I don't want to be sitting more exams, just for the sake of it.'

Anthony had had enough. 'Come on, Penny.' He had to rock forward a couple of times before he could stand up. 'Let's go and have a drink with this damn tutor. See what he's got to say about it.'

Cary helped his mother up. 'Ormerod's all for it,' he said.

'Poppycock,' Anthony said, opening the door and stumping out.

Penny wiped away a tear and shook her head. 'Oh, Cary,' she said. 'What's happened to you?'

'It's all good,' he said, and he gave her a hug because that was what she needed. 'I'm finally beginning to find myself.'

* * *

The showdown, when it came, was quite unexpected. Everyone was tetchy. Cary had spent the afternoon sparring with his parents and, as for Lily, she was not only sick, but sick with worry about what the future would hold. Her parents, meanwhile, had drunk too much at lunch and both had a headache.

They were all walking back from the Thames, having watched that great Eton event, the Procession of Boats. For well over two centuries, the school's elite Eights have dressed up in their very fanciest rig, monkey-jackets and white trousers, and with the most fragrant flowers laced into the brims of their boaters. Some of the coxes even dressed as full Admirals, complete with fore and aft hat. The Eights rowed down the river and, when they reached the crowds, they all stood up, including the cox, and when they were all standing, and when their oars were quite vertical out of the water, they waved their boaters, and the flowers fell into the water, and it was quite archaic, and oddly magnificent. But the crowds were only there for one thing and, this year, it had actually happened; one of the rowers had started to lose his balance, swaying from side to side, and then he'd infected the other oarsmen and the boat was rocking, properly rocking, and suddenly she'd gone, and the crowd, already baying, let out a cheer of sheer ecstasy, and the cox and all eight of the crew, a moment ago so very splendid, had been transformed into bedraggled rats as they paddled towards the riverbank.

Arctic, who'd had a hand in training the crew for the Procession, was livid.

'The number seven went over on purpose!' he said to Tor. 'He took the rest of them down with him!'

Lily didn't care. She just wanted to get back to her bedroom. She wanted to see Cary. She wanted to tell him the news. She didn't know how he'd take it.

They were walking back from the Thames meadow, Arctic still fulminating about how the Eight had fallen in the river, when quite by chance, Lily and Cary saw each other. They did what came naturally. They did what every instinct was urging them to do, and she needed it, and Cary knew she needed it, and, as all the crowds of parents and schoolboys swirled and eddied around them, they gave each other a long, hard hug, and Lily burst into tears of relief. Cary was with her and everything was going to be all right.

Their parents, who had been dickering away about the Procession of Boats, gradually became aware that they had lost their children. They stopped, they turned, and they saw Cary and Lily in a tight clinch; more than a clinch. They were kissing each other.

'That's better,' Cary said.

'Much better,' Lily said, and they kissed again and, though they were in a crowd of hundreds, they only had eyes for each other.

Lily dabbed at her eyes and smiled, laughed, and with their arms around each other's waists, they started sauntering back to the school, and it took them both a few moments to register that they were being watched by their parents. Arctic was beside himself with anger – his daughter, his very daughter, kissing a boy in full view of the entire school! Anthony and Penny were shocked, but Lily's mother, Tor, once she'd got over the initial surprise, had recognised Cary and she was really rather pleased.

'Mum, Dad,' Cary said. 'I'd like to introduce my girlfriend, Lily.'

Anthony dickered, but Penny did at least have the good manners to say, 'Nice to meet you.'

'And this is Cary,' Lily said to her parents. 'He's my boyfriend.'

Tor went straight in. 'Lovely to see you again, Cary,' she said, and then, because she knew it would irritate her husband, she kissed Cary on the cheek. 'How did I know that my daughter would like you?'

'Hello again, Tor.'

'You've been dating for some time now,' she said impishly. 'In fact... you've been seeing each other since before I met you at Mr Ormerod's supper party, haven't you?'

'Very perceptive of you,' Cary said.

'And very perceptive of you two to keep it under wraps.' Tor gently squeezed Cary's earlobe between thumb and forefinger and gave him her first genuine smile of the day.

Arctic was going through a whirling jangle of emotions. It was disgusting enough that two teenagers should be openly snogging each other on full display to the entire – *entire* – school; beaks, pupils, parents, the whole lot were witness to this most revolting of spectacles, but that it should be his own daughter, Lily, who was hugging and kissing and mewling over this cocksure Popper was beyond belief. And she'd lied to him! Not once, not twice, but repeatedly, for months – had been seeing this, this ne'er-do-well for months and months and, of course, they'd started copulating with each other, and she was only 16, dammit, and it was not only against the school rules but the very rules of nature. And then he realised they'd still got their arms around each other in a quite repellent public display of affection, and boys were looking, and boys were nudging each other, because the news was spreading fast that Lily, the only girl in the school, his daughter, was now spoken for—

'Take your hands off each other!' Arctic said. 'Can you not control yourselves? You are on school grounds and it is the school's Parents' Day!'

Cary disengaged from Lily. 'Of course, sir. We just got a little carried away.'

'Carried away!' Arctic said. 'That's a fine term for it! Brazenly kissing my daughter! You are utterly without shame!'

'I'm sorry you feel like that, sir,' Cary said.

'Yes, I do feel like that, as any normal, respectable father would feel to see his daughter necking in public – and to realise that she has been lying, lying to me for months—'

'You do over-react, Daddy,' Lily said. 'It's actually quite normal for 16-year-old girls to start dating their schoolmates.'

'Do I have to remind you, Lily, that this is not any bog-standard Secondary Modern – you are a pupil at Eton College, the only girl in the entire school—'

'No, you do not have to remind me of that,' Lily said, taking Cary's hand, and feeling the squeeze of his fingers. 'I am reminded—'

'Stop that!' Arctic screeched, now quite red in the face, and if Eton's pupils had not previously been aware that there was a hubbub by the bridge, they certainly were now. At least a hundred boys and assorted parents had stopped to watch. 'Stop that right now!'

'Why?' Lily said. 'What's it matter if we hold hands?'

'Just stop it! School rules expressly forbid it!'

'Sorry to butt in, sir,' Cary said. 'I think you've just made that up.'

'How dare you!'

'What about those boys – and those boys?' Cary said,

gesturing to the rabble of sniggering boys who'd surrounded them.

At least eight of them had started holding hands, and now that they'd got the gag, they were all holding hands and, very soon, it had turned into a large ring of 150 hand-holding boys, and all loving, adoring, every moment of it, such that they would treasure that day, and that moment, for the rest of their lives. First, the boat had gone over – and now this! Lily's mother, Tor, was, of course, also thoroughly enjoying herself, though Cary's parents, rather more retiring, were wishing that the ground would pleasantly open up and swallow them; why did Cary have to make such a scene?

'Stop that!' Arctic shouted.

'I think, if you carry on like that, sir, they're all going to start kissing each other,' Cary said.

'Lily, you are coming back home with me right now,' Arctic said.

'I don't think so,' she said, shaking a little, but quietly reassured by Cary's calm presence next to her; she felt like she always felt when she was with Cary. If he was there, then all would be well.

'Lily!' Arctic said. 'You are coming back home with me! Now!'

One of the bystanders, Arctic couldn't tell which one, called out, 'Daddy's gonna spank you!' and, within ten seconds, the whole mob of them had started up with 'Daddy's gonna spank you!' and were swinging their hands up and down, and poor Arctic had never seen anything like it, and had not the first idea how to win back control – not that he had ever had it.

'You will hear more of this, young lady!' he said, forcing his way through the mob, all of them laughing at him and still chanting, 'Daddy's gonna spank you!' Never, never in his life had he experienced such a humiliation – and at the hands of his own daughter, no less. He was not, for the moment, sure as to what exact punishment he would mete out to Lily, but there would be consequences; there would be consequences.

CHAPTER 38

When he'd started out as a newspaper photographer 30 years ago, Henry Borden had dreamed of working on Fleet Street, and of travelling the world, and of taking pictures of the world's most glamorous women. But that was not how his life had turned out and, after five years of grubbing around on a weekly newspaper in Slough, he'd thrown in the towel for the soft, easy life of a school photographer. It wasn't the most exciting life you could imagine, but it was easy, regular work. It paid the bills. His wife was happy; happy-ish. True, he did miss the thrill of the newsroom and the occasional scoop, but those days of taking exclusive front-page pictures were long, long gone; just so much ancient history.

He'd joined the Eton photographers, Hills and Saunders, 25 years ago, in 1971, and had worked his way up to being a full partner. The work was spectacularly unchallenging. He took pictures of Etonians in all their various garbs. In the winter, he took pictures of the rugby players, and the Wall Game players and the Field Game players and the football players and, in the spring, he did more of the same. But his busiest time by far was in the summer, when he took pictures of the rowers and the cricketers and the athletes and the Fives players, and the swimmers and the water polo players and, basically, every single activity you could think of, from Scottish country dancing to stargazing.

There was one other set of pictures that Henry had to take in the summer, and that was the house photos. Henry would spend a whole week visiting Eton's 25 houses. The smallest boys would sit cross-legged on the grass at the front and, behind them, sitting on chairs, would be the housemaster and his wife, if he had one, and the Dame and ten or so of the senior boys. Behind them, another row of boys standing and, behind them, a final row of boys standing on chairs. In the centre of the picture, in pride of place next to the housemaster, would go the silverware, all the glittering cups and trophies the boys had won during the previous year.

Henry was rather disarming to look at, with this gleaming bald head and the most enormous thick-rimmed black glasses, but he had a wonderful knack with the boys. He'd josh them, banter with them, and the result was that, in his pictures, particularly in the house photos, the boys were nearly always smiling.

Henry enjoyed the week when he took the House photos – the housemasters, at least the nicer ones, would have him in for a drink and a chat afterwards. But this year, 1996, he was particularly looking forward to taking the house pictures, because, this year, he had the intriguing prospect of taking a picture that would almost certainly go down in history; he was taking Prince William's first house photo.

As it turned out, though, taking the royal house photo was a bit of a damp squib. William was just like any other new boy – smiley, eager to please, a little shy. He took his place on the grass in the front row, just in front of Dr Gailey, and, after a quip from Henry, gave the most picture-perfect smile.

Much more interesting were the two other houses Henry had to photograph that day. The first was at The Timbralls with that delightful chap, Ormerod, who always gave him tea and cake beforehand, and who always treated him to lunch afterwards.

The picture was unusual because one of the boys, a Popper who was sitting next to Mr Ormerod, had on his lap a framed picture of an Eton schoolboy. In front of him, sitting on the grass and leaning easily against his leg, was a very small boy with a toothy grin and very spiky hair; they were obviously good friends. The senior boy looked rather sad and, after a few moments, Henry realised he must be holding a picture of his dead schoolmate. After the picture had been taken, Henry gave him a consoling squeeze to the shoulder. The boy gave him a glum nod; there's not much to be said about the death of a teenager. It's always a tragedy and it's always ghastly.

But the most interesting house photo – by far – was in the Farrer House garden. As usual, the hatchet-faced housemaster barely said a word to him, but his wife was nice, gave him a cup of tea and a biscuit, and the Dame, Miranda, was just as lovely as she always was. There was one boy, obviously a rower because he wore stick-ups and white trousers, whom Henry did not take to at all. He was bossily marshalling the boys around, barking at the older boys and prodding the younger ones, but oddest of all was his behaviour with the girl. The girl was obviously the housemaster's daughter. She chatted to her mother and to the Dame, but there were two people she ignored completely. She would not even look at her father, let alone talk to him, and she also studiously avoided the senior boy in the white trousers. He responded by treating her with fake courtliness, as if she were a queen from another century. For all his antics, he might as well have been a ghost; she looked straight through him.

After Henry had taken the house picture, the girl got up from her seat next to her mother and, in a very assured manner, returned to the house; her father watched her walk away, then sat for a few moments, elbows on his knees, wondering what on earth the world had come to. And that was the last of Eton's house pictures of 1996, and that should have been the end of it.

About a week later, Henry was pottering around his shop on the Eton High Street, when a boy came in with a rather unusual request. He wanted copies of house photos – but not just of his own house, of seven other houses.

'My friends are in the houses,' he said. 'I want to have something to remember them by.'

'What a lovely thought,' Henry said, and then he remembered where he'd seen the boy before. 'You're in Ormerod's house, aren't you?' he said. 'You had the picture of your friend.'

'I miss him.'

'Must have been awful for you,' Henry said. 'Let me see about getting you those pictures.'

Henry went through to the back office and dug up the relevant house photos. A photo of the scholars sitting outside the College, a photo of Farrer House, with the girl and the grim father, and a photo of the boys from Angelo's and Goldolphin and Baldwin's Bec, and a couple of other houses, and then, last of all, a photo of the boys from Manor House with that nice Dr Gailey.

'And there we are,' Henry said. 'They're £13 each, so let's call it a round £100. How would you like to pay?'

'Cash, please.' The boy counted out the money in used twenties and, after a hearty 'Thank you,' left the shop.

* * *

Imagine, if you will, a Labrador, a very beautiful sandy-haired Labrador, that is lying by the fireside and contentedly licking its own gonads. This delightful dog is doing this, not because it especially enjoys licking its genitals, but because this is a part of its daily chores, ensuring that everything is hygienic and kept in general good order. (What a simply charming analogy, by the way – a dog licking its nether regions! I only hope it gives you as much pleasure to read as it has given me to write.)

It was just another pleasant morning in the *Sun* newsroom, and I was going through the journalistic equivalent of a dog giving itself a good lick-down; I was doing my expenses. Always a bit of a chore, but something that needed to be done every week; little and often was the way, because, otherwise, well, you'd suddenly be a month behind with your expenses, and a whole month's worth of expenses might prove to be just a little indigestible for the Managing Editor.

The Sun's expense forms were on green sheets of A4 paper and I'd racked up so many expenses during my Eton foray – the hotel, the lunch, the buttonhole – that I was already on my second sheet and, like that delightful Labrador by the fireside, I was not especially enjoying myself, but I did have that virtuous glow of knowing that another essential job was being ticked off my to-do list.

'What the hell are you doing?'

I literally jumped out of my seat. As was his wont, Spike had sneaked up behind me via one of the newsroom's side doors.

'Gosh, you gave me a shock,' I said. 'Do you have to do that?'

'You're doing your expenses??' he said. 'You're doing your expenses!'

Since I had two green expense forms in front of me and my desk was festooned with receipts, there didn't seem much point in denying it.

'Oh, yeah, that's right,' I said casually. 'Not much going on at the moment, so I thought I'd just get them out the way.'

'You what??' he said. (Just a small reminder – Spike's conversations were always peppered with swear-words; this one more so than most.) 'There's not much going on at the moment, so you just decided to do your expenses?'

'Only take five minutes.'

Spike picked up one of the green expense forms and started to read. 'This is from your botched trip to Eton!' he said. 'You got nothing out of it and you handed the exclusive to *The Mirror*!'

'Spike, it is true that, through no fault of my own, Bain got the story,' I said diplomatically. 'But it still cost me a lot of money. Sometimes, stories don't come off – that's just the nature of journalism.'

His apoplectic gaze returned to the expense form. 'I don't need you to tell me about the nature of journalism,' he said witheringly. 'What?? What?? Jesus H. Christ, you are taking the piss! A £300 dinner at the Cipriani with "a top Eton contact"?? You have got to be joking! You haven't come up with an Eton story in weeks!'

'I don't just take my contacts out for a meal when they've given me a story,' I replied primly. 'That would be cheap – mercenary.'

'The only contact you've got is one damn schoolboy, and you're hardly going to be taking him to the Cipriani,' he said. 'No, I know what you were doing – you took your girlfriend out for dinner, and you're now expecting me to pay!'

'My girlfriend?' I snapped. 'I wouldn't dream of it!' (How, how, had he known that I'd taken Amanda to the Cipriani??)

'I've had enough of this nonsense,' he said and, right in front of my eyes, he started tearing up not just the two green expense forms but also the receipts I'd so neatly lined up on the desk.

'Hang on, hang on!' I said. 'Those are legitimate expenses!'

Spike continued to tear up the receipts into smaller and smaller pieces – it would be hell trying to stick them all back together. He honestly looked like he was going to stuff them into my mouth or perhaps even into his own mouth.

'Let me remind you, Kim, about the nature of journalism,' he said. Tear-tear-tear went the receipts. 'When you bring in stories, then you can claim expenses.'

'That's not remotely the nature of journalism!' I said. 'I work my guts out for this newspaper and sometimes stories don't come off. *That* is the nature of journalism!'

'No, Kim, *this* is the nature of journalism!' He hurled the shredded receipts in my face. 'No stories equals no expenses!'

'What the hell am I supposed to do with all this?' I said.

'Put it in the bin, you idle tosspot!' he yelled. 'Don't waste my time with any more expense claims until you've brought me a story.'

All I could do was gape at him. You know what it was like? It was as if a delightful sandy-haired Labrador had been minding its own business, just diligently going about its morning ablutions by the fireside, and, for no reason whatsoever, someone had come up to that dog and had given it a savage boot up the backside! It hurt, I tell you, it hurt.

I picked up all the scraps of paper from the floor and put them into a drawer; it would have been impolitic to have started sticking them all back together in the newsroom.

Since I'd got nothing better to do, I started calling some of my few genuine contacts, though I already knew this was going to be a complete waste of time. When my contacts did have a story, they didn't tend to hang around.

And then – an honest-to-God jim-dandy. (That is: a miracle. Us professional wordsmiths do occasionally like to flex our lexicographical muscles.)

My pager vibrated and my spirits soared. It was Agent Orange – and the only time Agent Orange, or Cary as I now knew him to be, called up was when he had a story. I called the phone box where Cary was waiting, heard the good news and, in under one minute, was quite racing out of the office.

Spike, lounging by the news desk, watched as I tugged on my jacket. 'Where you off to?'

'Got to see someone,' I said – and, having learned my lesson from the failure of my much-trumpeted Eton scoop on the Fourth of June, I gave no further details.

'What – your girlfriend in Windsor?'

'I'm going to see somebody about a possible story,' I said, the very model of a consummate stand-up reporter. 'I'll try not to rack up too many expenses.'

An hour later, after a very brief meet-up at Waterloo Station, I was in possession of Prince William's house photo. But as I drove back to Fort Wapping, the picture lying next to me on the seat, I was not at all sure whether I'd got a scoop. I had the picture, but could *The Sun* even use it? Firstly, it went against the whole code of conduct that The Press had hammered out with the Palace when Prince William first started at Eton. Secondly, the copyright of the photo belonged to the school photographers, Hills and Saunders. If *The Sun* were to just print the picture without permission, then it could be expensive; get the Palace lawyers involved and it could be *eye-wateringly* expensive. Still – so not my problem. I was merely the humble Labrador, who was bringing the picture in to his master. It'd be up to Spike, who was editing the paper that day, what he wanted to do with it.

I took the lift up to the sixth floor and, as I entered Sun Country, I not only walked tall, I had a bit of a swagger. Spike spotted me immediately.

'What have you got?' he called.

'Just a picture of some kids,' I said. I plopped the picture on Spike's desk.

It took Spike a moment to realise what he was looking at, and then he started screaming at the absolute top of his voice, swearing mostly, and a lot of the F-word, but he did also pound me on the back and say, 'You beauty!' And that's really how I remember Spike – one moment, screaming at you till he was blue in the face and, the next, pumping your hand and saying you were the world's greatest reporter. Certainly kept us on our toes.

'What are you going to do with it?'

'We're going to clear the front page and we're going to clear the centre spread!' Spike chuckled as the picture editor bustled over to take a look.

'Ballsy,' I said.

'The ballsiest!' Spike said. 'Now, go and write the copy!'

Half an hour later, I was at my desk, writing up the copy for what would be a World Picture Exclusive. Because there was so very little to say, it was a story that called for great creativity. It was just a picture of Prince William with his housemates. The Prince was smiling and looked very happy. Somehow, I had to spin this out to 500 words.

I became aware that the back bench was stalking towards me. They were accompanied by News International's burly legal manager, Adam Findlay. Findlay was wearing a short-sleeved shirt, the better to show off his tattooed forearms; with his close-cropped white hair, he looked more like a bouncer than a lawyer, but that was often the way of things at *The Sun*.

I was soon surrounded by five men and one woman. I could smell the power. It wasn't a position I'd ever been in before. Around the newsroom, work ground to a halt. Calls were cut short so that everyone could watch the show. I stood up.

'Okaaay, Kim,' Spike said. 'How did you get hold of the picture?'

'I was given it by a contact,' I said. 'I believe he bought it from the school photographers for £13.'

There was a long pause. Findlay was weighing up the consequences of running the picture. The back bench held its breath. The legal manager's head tick-tocked. He pulled a face. He gave Spike the briefest of nods.

'Good boy!' Spike threw his arm round my shoulder and did a little jig of joy. 'Take your girlfriend out for dinner tonight, why don't you?'

'Thanks,' I said. The back bench dissolved. 'Anywhere in particular?'

'Take her where you usually take her,' Spike cackled, mercurial as ever. 'The Cipriani!'

I did indeed take Amanda to the Cipriani – she'd developed quite a taste for their Lobster Thermidor – and, at 11pm, loved-up and happy, we sauntered to Charing Cross station to pick up the first editions. The whole of the front page had been given over to Prince William's house photo, with the puckish headline, 'I Love It Heir At Eton', and there, in tiny ten-point, was my byline. Amanda squealed. For a few halcyon seconds, I savoured the moment – and then it was over. Things won are done, and stories written are nothing so much as tomorrow's fish and chip paper; journos' joy lies in the doing.

CHAPTER 39

Lily looked at herself in the bathroom mirror. She was up early. She was always up early these days. It was worry, and nerves, and not being able to sleep, and this terrible morning sickness and wanting to throw up and, when she did throw up, it was usually just a dry heave.

A month earlier, Lily had thought she might be pregnant. Then, over the next couple of weeks, feeling ever more queasy in the mornings, she'd thought it was likely. And now, she'd peed on the stick and she knew it; she was pregnant. Sixteen years old and pregnant! A trace of a smile flickered over her lips. She'd certainly be going down in Eton history; the first Eton pupil since 1444 to fall pregnant. The baby would be due in the early spring. If she had the baby. She didn't know what she wanted – lose the baby and continue studying for her A-levels and skirmishing with her father, and seeing Cary on and off until… until he found some other love, as he inevitably would. But there was a small whispering spirit inside her that wanted to keep the baby. It was part of her, it was a part of Cary, and the whole idea of aborting this ticking living thing revolted her.

She leaned over the sink and retched, but nothing came up. Her hair was wet with sweat and she smiled another trace of a smile – because, though her position was not great, she could also just about appreciate the ridiculousness of the situation. It had all come to pass just exactly as her father had feared. She had fallen in love with an Etonian and she was now going to have his baby. The tabloids, if they ever got hold of it, would go absolutely mental. She wondered if Cary would sell the story and was perceptive enough to realise that if Cary didn't sell the story, somebody else would. And more to the point – it was a story that would run. There would be the initial scoop: Eton Girl Pregnant! And then there would be all the follow-up stories; will-she-won't-she keep the baby, and then, if she did keep the baby, would she stay on at the school, and would the school provide a crèche, and would her father survive his subsequent heart attack?

And Arctic was a factor that loomed very large in Lily's musings. Her father, when he learned of it, would go absolutely stark staring mad. He'd pretty much lost the plot when she'd kissed Cary on the Fourth of June – but this! His daughter pregnant! The tabloids slavering! All of his very worst nightmares rolled into one – and wouldn't he just be so delighted at welcoming his favourite Etonian into the family? Mummy would probably be okay about it; no, she'd be great. She'd help look after the baby, no problem at all, and she was definitely a Cary fan.

Cary...

She hadn't told Cary. Though, knowing him, he probably already had a sense of it. But he was just sitting his A-levels – the first that morning, in two hours' time. Telling him that she was pregnant might prove just a little bit of a distraction. How would he take it? He'd be a trouper; he'd go along with whatever she chose to do. Though she did wonder... Perhaps he'd want to keep the baby. And what would happen then? How could he help her raise the baby if she was still at Eton? No – if she had the baby, she'd have to leave Eton, but what would she do, what would they do, how would they bring up the baby together? Cary certainly didn't have any family money, she knew that. Would she follow Cary to university, like some drudge housewife, to look after the baby while he studied? Or would he throw it all in and get a job – and what sort of job could an 18-year-old Eton schoolboy get anyway, and where would that leave her? She'd still be stuck at home, holding the baby.

Outside the bathroom, Arctic stood in his dressing gown and his practical leather slippers. He stood and he listened – and though he may have been obtuse, he was at least smart enough to understand the meaning of the sounds that were emanating from the other side of the door. His 16-year-old daughter was throwing up and, though there was a slight chance that it could be food poisoning, or perhaps even bulimia, he knew it was bad and he knew it was serious. She was pregnant. She'd been knocked up by that damn boy, Cary.

Arctic paced up and down the corridor as he, also, pondered his next move. But there was one matter about which Arctic was absolutely cast-iron certain. Lily would not be keeping the baby. No way. Not in a million years. The very thought of Lily keeping the baby was just… unconscionable! It'd be all over the tabloids, even the broadsheets, and then there would be his own humiliation, a housemaster who couldn't even control his teenage daughter. Reporters would be calling round to the house, asking him how he felt about his teenage daughter becoming the first Etonian in history to have a baby while still at the school.

Arctic's fingernails bit deep into the palms of his hands, but that wasn't good enough, that wasn't even remotely going to cut it and, instead, he hefted up a vase of plastic flowers and hurled it as hard as he could against the wall, where it shattered in a satisfying explosion of china and, for a second, made him feel a little better.

Miranda, snooping busybody that she was, poked her head out of her door – 'Is anything the matter?'

'Yes!' he said. 'Yes, there is. My daughter is pregnant.'

'She's told you, then?'

'What – don't tell me you already know?'

'Do excuse me,' Miranda said. 'I'm just going to get dressed.'

Arctic stalked back down the corridor, leather slippers

crunching on the broken vase. He could hear Lily gagging again. Well, it couldn't be helped; he'd have her down to the abortion clinic by the end of the week.

* * *

Cary may not have been informed of Lily's pregnancy, but he had a sense of it, just little things that had occurred in the past few weeks, not so very much in themselves, but, when they were all added up, they did tilt towards the fact that Lily was pregnant and that he was the father.

And it was fine, and they would deal with it, though he didn't exactly know how they'd deal with it. The timing could have been better. He was midway through his English A-level, discussing all things Romeo and Juliet, and, even with Cary's formidable powers of concentration, he was finding it difficult to concentrate. Lily was pregnant!

There were other things on Cary's mind. He didn't know quite what he'd expected would happen after he gave the Prince William picture to Kim the previous day… but *The Sun* had run with it. It was the talk of the school. The Headman was, as ever, livid. Quite the witch-hunt they'd set up to find the culprit who'd given the picture to *The Sun*.

Cary didn't worry about the Headman, who was nothing but hot air. If there was a danger, it was Mr McCreath.

And in this, Cary was quite right to be worried. That morning, Mr McCreath had received a most unusual phone call. The caller was a young man who refused to give his name, but who had identified himself merely as 'a friend of the College'. There'd been no pleasantries and this 'friend of the College' had cut straight to the chase; *The Sun*'s Eton agent was Cary.

'Cary?' McCreath had asked.

'That's right,' came the reply. 'The idiot who bust his leg on the assault course. Tinkerty tonk!'

Mr McCreath was surprised – but only for a moment. A

while back, at Christmas, he'd explored the idea that Cary might have been *The Sun*'s Eton agent. But then… things had come up. He'd been distracted, had other matters to attend to. Miss Robinson…

He'd always liked the boy, but… it made the most complete sense. Cary was on a scholarship and had no money – and, as was painfully obvious from his relationship with Lily, he didn't give a fig for the minor matter of school rules. He flouted the rules as he saw fit. Mr McCreath did not need long to mull it over. Of course Cary was the rogue Etonian. It had to be him.

He quickly checked the timetables, and found – pleasingly – that Cary was otherwise engaged that morning in the School Hall. Mr McCreath went straight round to The Timbralls and, after a brief conversation with Mr Ormerod, was led to Cary's top-floor bedroom.

The door was not locked. Eton's bedrooms were never locked. Mr McCreath stood on the threshold, inhaled, and as he was about to step into the room, he had a sense of a whisper – 'Get out of my damn room.'

Mr McCreath stood in the middle of the room and quietly took it all in. It was spotless, extremely spartan; Mr McCreath very much approved. Whatever Cary had been spending his Sun money on, it certainly hadn't been on himself. On the wall was a single poster – typical. The Italian Job. Lined up by the open windows were a lot of books from the School Library. There was a typewriter, of all things, on the desk of Cary's burry and, beside the lamp, was a framed picture of that boy Bruno, who'd hanged himself, and a very fine cut-crystal schooner. Mr McCreath picked the glass up to admire the tracery, and caught the unmistakable whiff of cherry brandy. McCreath sat on the bed and took it all in. He didn't know what he was looking for, but, using his twitching witchy senses, he instinctively knew where to look. Not in the burry, not in the drawers; actually, it didn't feel like there was anything much in the room at all. Out of habit, he toed over the grey rug by the bed, saw a piece of paper. When he read it, he was, of course, surprised, but he was also rather impressed. What a boy!

He tucked the piece of paper into his coat pocket and walked down the stairs to the ground floor and into the Timbralls library, fingertips trailing over the spines of the dusty hardbacks as he strolled through to Mr Ormerod's office.

'Funny room that Cary's in,' Mr McCreath said.

'Yes,' Mr Ormerod said. 'Ian Fleming lives there.'

'I'm not quite with you,' Mr McCreath said.

'It was Ian Fleming's old room.' Mr Ormerod brought up his hands as if in prayer, lightly tapping his fingers together. 'He still lives there, or so it is said; he exerts a quite powerful force on all the boys who stay with him. Gets them into all manner of scrapes. In the Eighties, one of Fleming's lads had a fling with his piano mistress.' He smiled pleasantly. 'Did you find what you were looking for?'

'Not yet,' Mr McCreath said shortly. 'But I think that boy's fling with the piano mistress is about to be knocked into a cocked hat.'

CHAPTER 40

Cary felt a taut tension in the tranquillity of The Timbralls, a close calm before the storm. He could sense it, though he could not tell when the storm was going to break.

Not that he needed to, but Cary was going through the motions of revising for the next day's History exam. And he asked himself – not for the first time – 'What's the point?' What was the point of good exam grades? So that he could get into a good university, and could then get a good seat on the middle-class Gravy Train, so that he, in his turn, could send his children to a smart school, so that they too could be put through the Eton mill – and though this comes to us all in the end, Cary was only 18 years old, and already he was asking himself that most unanswerable of questions: Why?

And as his eyes flicked over pages of tedious Tudor history, which, whether he learned it or not, would remain the same for centuries to come, he asked himself that question he had been repeatedly pondering – what's important? Lily was important; Lily was very important. In fact, she was far and away the most important thing in his life. The guys at The Project, whom he'd not seen so much of in the last half, they were important; and, in an odd way, Mrs Parker and Mrs Webber were important to him. It was bizarre, but he felt more of a connection with those two doughty cooks than he did with his own parents. And, as for exams and university and all the rest of the inspirational twaddle with which Eton had tried to stuff his head, Cary could not give a damn.

He'd quite like to talk it through with Ian Fleming, but Fleming had been strangely quiet that evening. Cary was fine with that. Fleming had spent the past year coaching, advising, needling and Cary felt about ready to go it alone. You're never going to be certain that you're ready to fly solo. But, at some stage, you have to take heart in hand. You have to go for it.

Cary checked his watch. It was gone 10pm and, just as he did most nights, he went downstairs to the Timbralls library to check his pager. Tonight, he was more than a little interested to hear how the College had reacted to *The Sun*'s front-page picture of Prince William. Cary put on his slippers. He was just leaving the room when he caught a glimpse of Fleming lying on the sofa. He was waving his cigarette holder. But it was what he said that was most striking.

'And here we go.'

Mr Ormerod had finished his night-time pottering and the house was silent. Cary padded down the three flights of stairs. He was still thinking about Fleming. And here we go? Sounded like something a TV commentator might say before a big title fight. Could be. What else could it be?

A single lamp was on in the corner of the library, but the rest of the room was quite dark and the bookshelves were hidden in gloom. Cary didn't need to look as he automatically stretched for The Fortunes of Nigel on the top shelf by the door. He knew something was wrong as soon as he touched it. The book was light.

He opened it and gawked at the cut pages, which were laughing at him. The book was empty – and the trap was sprung.

From the far corner of the room, the very darkest corner of the library, a figure emerged. It took Cary a moment to recognise him. It was Mr McCreath.

'Looking for these?' Mr McCreath held up the pager and the Cartier ring box.

As the storm finally broke, Cary did his best to recover his poise. 'Good evening, Mr McCreath.'

'Take a seat,' Mr McCreath said, gesturing to one of the

armchairs. He plumped himself down on the sofa and quietly gazed at Cary. 'You did pretty well.'

'I did?'

'Since you sold your first story to *The Sun* nine months ago, you have given me a pretty good runaround. But I got you in the end – shame it's happened during the middle of your A-levels, but that's the end of it.'

Cary nestled back into the armchair, still not sure how bad things were. How much did Mr McCreath know – was this a magnificent bluff?

'You're talking in riddles, sir.'

'Had a call this morning from some man who said you were *The Sun*'s Eton mole,' Mr McCreath said, eyes not leaving Cary even for a moment. 'Or should I call you Agent Orange?'

Cary twitched, only a little, but enough. Who'd made the call? It was Bain, without a doubt, getting his own back for the Prince William picture.

'Agent who?'

'And do you know the funny thing was that, until I had that call this morning, I hadn't believed that you could be *The Sun*'s mole. But then I only had to think about it for a minute. It couldn't be anyone else. It could only be you.'

He crossed his legs and leaned forward a little to hitch his tweed trousers at the knee; now that he had trapped this rogue Etonian, he was going to make the most of the denouement. On the side-table next to him was a bottle of Glenfiddich, a small jug of water and two tumblers. Mr McCreath had placed them there an hour earlier as he'd been getting the lie of the land.

'Will you join me in a glass of whisky?' Mr McCreath said.

'I'd love one, thank you, sir.'

Mr McCreath poured two healthy slugs into the tumblers. 'Water?'

'Please.'

Mr McCreath passed a tumbler to Cary. 'Cheers, Cary.' He raised his glass. 'You've had a good run.'

'Your very good health, Sir.' Cary took a tentative sip. He didn't normally drink whisky; it had quite a kick, but warming. He liked it.

'So, after I got the call this morning, I searched your room while you were in your English exam. I didn't find anything.' He took a long draw on his whisky tumbler and gave a smile of great satisfaction.

'No?'

'Except this.' From his breast pocket, he pulled out the piece of paper he'd found underneath Cary's bedside rug.

'Oh, that's where it went,' Cary said.

'You're only 18, Cary. You sure it's a good idea?'

'It's looking better by the minute.'

'You'd better have it back, then.' Mr McCreath handed the paper over. Cary folded it and tucked it into his pocket. 'I, of course, realised that the smartest boy in the school was going to be far too fly to leave anything incriminating in his room. So I walked about the house, I snooped in the boys' rooms, and I went into the bathrooms and the lumber-room. And, knowing that you enjoy cooking so much, I also had a good look in the kitchens, but none of these rooms really spoke to me.'

He poured himself some more Glenfiddich and then daintily topped up the glass with water.

'No,' he said, 'None of these rooms spoke to me, but this room, I had a sense of it. And you know what I thought to myself, Cary?' He chuckled and leaned forward. 'I thought that, if I had to hide something in here, where would I go? I would head straight for the most boring book in the room, and it did not take me very long at all to find Walter Scott's Fortunes of Nigel. I open it up – and what do I find but this pager and a very expensive Cartier ring.'

He paused to toy with the pager and grinned.

'One thing you might not know, Cary, is that your man from *The Sun*, Kim, has given me a pager too! It's identical to yours! Do you know what he calls me?'

Cary shook his head.

'He calls me Mickey Mouse!' He took another sip of whisky – what a good idea it had been to bring along the whisky. It would not have been nearly so enjoyable if he'd been dry. 'So that, then, Cary, is the case for the prosecution, and the Headman will be looking forward to hearing your defence tomorrow afternoon.'

'I see, sir. Is there anything more, or is that it?'

'That's about the sum of it, Cary,' Mr McCreath said, glancing at Cary's pager. 'Though perhaps you ought to take a look at this. It popped up an hour ago, while I was waiting for you.'

Cary took the pager and glanced at the message. He immediately got to his feet.

'I've enjoyed our chat,' he said.

'You'd better have your ring, as well.'

'Thank you – and goodbye.'

Cary darted out of the room and up the stairs. This was bad – this was very bad. Never mind that his Eton career was over; never mind about the A-levels. He took another look at the pager as he tore up the stairs. There was a single terse message.

'Lily's been locked in her room. She needs rescuing.'

* * *

Lily had been locked in her room since supper. Her father had come into her room without knocking and had demanded to know if she was pregnant.

There hadn't seemed any point in denying it.

'I am,' she said.

Arctic nodded to himself. 'And you're now going to have an abortion.'

'I'm sorry,' Lily said. She was lying on her bed, feet curled up beneath her. 'I don't think I heard a question mark at the end of that.'

'Because there is no question about it,' Arctic said.

'Is that so?'

'It is so,' Arctic said. 'You come here to my school, you fall pregnant with one of the schoolboys here? You've got your whole life ahead of you! You can't even think of having this baby.'

Lily eyed him speculatively. And then, quite suddenly, so suddenly that it was like the flick of a switch, she was surrounded by an aura of quite golden calm. She smiled at her father.

'I'll book you in for an abortion first thing tomorrow,' he said.

'That won't be necessary.'

'You've already booked it yourself?' Arctic said.

'Quite the contrary,' Lily said. 'I hadn't made up my mind – until now. But you have totally decided me. I'm going to keep the baby. Whether Cary stands by me or whether he doesn't, I'm going to have this baby – and I'm afraid, Daddy, that there's not very much of anything you can do about it.'

'Don't be ridiculous, Lily!' Arctic said. 'You'll be ruining your whole life – and for what? To have a baby! You can have a baby any time you please! Think of your A-levels! Think of your university career! And you'll be throwing it all away for a baby with some feckless schoolboy, who won't even remember you by Christmas.'

'That's as may be, Daddy,' Lily said and, now that the decision had been made, and now that she knew the path she would follow, she felt nothing but relief. 'Cary must, of course, do whatever he wants – he can stay with me, he can go and conquer the world, I'm not going to pressure him either way.' She smiled to herself. 'Though I would, of course, prefer it if he stayed around to be a dad. But either way, I'm going to have the baby – and you are going to become a grandfather.'

'But what about your Eton education?'

Lily let out a little laugh. 'To tell you the truth, Daddy, this Eton education isn't all that it's cut out to be – though I did get to meet Cary and, for that, I will always be grateful. But no, when I leave the school at the end of this half, I won't miss Eton in the slightest – not its classes, nor its teachers, and certainly not its damnable stiff-collar starchiness.'

The full horror of what Lily had said was slowly sinking in. She was going to have a baby! It would be the biggest scandal in Eton's history! The tabloids would go into a complete feeding frenzy.

'Lily, dearest Lily,' Arctic said, trying to soften his tone. 'I don't think you've thought this through. You can't have a baby.'

'You could not be more wrong,' Lily said. 'Not only can I have a baby, but I'm going to have a baby.'

'You've got to have an abortion.'

'I don't have to have anything – least of all an abortion. And, as far as I know, I'm 16 years old and you don't have much say in the matter.

'Lily – I am your father! I am telling you to have an abortion.'

'Well, Daddy, I've got news for you.' She let her hands fall simply into her lap. 'Those days of you bossing me around are over. I'm done.'

'But Lily – think of the disgrace! Think of the scandal!'

'I couldn't care less. I'm having the baby, that's that.'

'We'll see what you think about this in the morning, young lady – after you've had a night to think on it.'

'I can think on it for a week or a month and I still won't change my mind – I'm having the baby.'

Arctic was fast losing his temper again. He kicked over the chair by the desk. It crashed into the wall and one of the legs smashed.

Lily mildly watched him and gave a little sniff. 'Do you know, Daddy, I've never said this before, but you've got a simply vile temper.'

'I've got a lot to put up with.'

'Nonsense – you've got one of the cushiest jobs in the

world!' Lily said. 'An Eton housemaster, waited on hand and foot, people endlessly fawning over you. You know your problem, Daddy?' She fondly stroked her stomach. 'You've spent so long living in this goldfish bowl that you're not very good at dealing with failure.'

'I certainly failed with you, you young baggage!'

'Big time.'

It was those last two words that sent Arctic over the edge. He was a failure, not just as a father but as a teacher. He left Lily's room, slamming the door behind him – and then, when he was outside, he thought better of it. He opened the door again, retrieved the key to the new lock, and locked his daughter in her room before pocketing the key. Under the circumstances, it seemed the best thing to do.

CHAPTER 41

Ian Fleming was contemplatively smoking a cigarette on the bed when Cary returned to his room.

'I'll miss you, Cary,' he said.

Cary grinned at him. 'I'll miss you too, sir.'

'Just getting your things together?'

Cary pulled a duffel-bag down from the cupboard.

'Haven't got much. But I don't need much.'

He threw in a few clothes and his washbag. He scanned the books and the pens and the typewriter, but decided against.

'You'd better take your school uniform,' Fleming said.

Cary laughed at that.

'Why not?' he said, carefully folding his tails and his nicer waistcoat and his sponge-bag trousers. 'Never thought I'd wear them again.'

'You ought to look your best.'

'Very true.' Cary went over to the bed and shook Fleming's hand. 'Goodbye, sir – and thank you. Thank you for everything.'

He was about to leave when he noticed that Bruno's old schooner had been filled with cherry brandy. He picked it up to toast his mentor.

'To you, sir,' he said. 'And to absent friends.'

It could have been just the smoke, but it looked as if three tears were trickling down Fleming's face. He cuffed his cheek.

'Good luck, Cary – you've got an epic life ahead of you.'

'I hope so.' He gave a wave at the door and swung the duffel-bag over his shoulder. 'And Lily's going to be in it!'

Such a surge of happiness as he walked down the corridor to the fire escape. He knew what he wanted. He knew what he had to do. And, though he had no idea how it was all going to pan out, if he had Lily, then everything would work out more than just fine, it would work out brilliantly. He walked past Bruno's room – empty since Bruno's death – and gave the door a knock for luck. Dear old Bruno. He would have approved.

Cary slammed the bar down on the fire escape door. It was like a gun-shot. Barty warily emerged from the bathroom, huge brown dressing gown dragging on the floor. He smiled when he saw it was Cary.

'You off, then?' Barty said.

'I am.'

'You're running off with Lily, aren't you?' Barty said. 'If I had a girlfriend like Lily, I'd run off with her too. Will you stay in touch?'

'Course I will,' Cary said and impulsively stepped forward to give Barty a hug.

'You'd better.'

'How else will I find out about your latest hairstyle?' Cary stepped out onto the fire escape. 'Close the door behind me.'

The door clicked shut and Cary inhaled a deep breath of the crisp night air – Freedom! He'd done it. He was on his way. He mentally ticked off everything that had to be done. There wouldn't be any second chances. It had to be perfect.

He climbed onto The Timbralls' bins and onto the wall and jumped down into New Schools Yard, and then, after strolling through Cannon Yard, he set off for Windsor at a light jog. As he trotted down the High Street, and passed all the Eton shops for the last time, he felt an overwhelming sense of relief. This Eton Chapter was over; he was done.

The Mini – good as new after its scrape on the farm – was parked down a dingy cul-de-sac in Windsor. He tossed the bag into the boot and sedately drove out of Windsor, then took the long loop round to Eton's obstacle course. It was good to be back – to be saying goodbye to this place he'd come to know so well; which had nearly killed him. He climbed up the cargo net to the top of The Table and, as always, stood a while to admire the view.

Cutting the rope took longer than he'd expected. He only had an old pen-knife. One of Mrs Parker's Sabatier knives would have sliced through it in seconds. Funny to think how, six months earlier, the foul Maxwell had been stooped here doing the exact same thing. But Cary wouldn't change it – wouldn't change any of it. It was another link in the golden chain of his life and, if that one day had disappeared, how differently his life might have turned out... Pish and tush! Lily was always going to be part of his destiny, so all roads would lead to her.

He cut the last strand of the rope and tossed it over the side before climbing back down the cargo net. He hoped the rope was long enough; more to the point, he hoped Lily was up to it. He put the coiled rope on the passenger seat and drove back into Eton, past Sixpenny, past The Timbralls, past The Burning Bush and past all those other landmarks he knew so well. He parked up by Manor House, where the young Prince was asleep, and where the bristling CCTV cameras recorded his every movement. He slung the rope over his shoulder, and walked down Judy's Passage to Farrer House. Round the back, in the garden, he could see a few lights still on, but Lily's room was quite dark.

'Hello, old friend,' he said to the drainpipe at the side of the house. 'Didn't think I'd be seeing you again.'

He'd lost a little of his upper-body strength during his stay in hospital, but it didn't make any difference. One way or another, he was going to break her out, and then, when he did break her out... and, just as the last time, he lost his concentration for a moment, and his foot slipped on a patch of moss, and he slammed into the wall, not much of noise, but just enough to jolt Maxwell out of his witless revision by the window.

'Idiot,' Cary said to himself, but he was laughing too.

Next time – if there ever was a next time, and knowing his luck, there just might be – next time he climbed the drainpipe, he'd avoid that piece of moss.

He hauled himself onto the roof – what a night to be alive, the stars bright and the moon full, and a distressed damsel in need of rescue. He strolled along the rooftop to Lily's room and tied the rope around a chimney. Now – the part he had been most looking forward to. He dangled the end of the rope down to Lily's room and flicked it a couple of times against the window. The window opened and Lily looked up and, when she saw Cary, she just beamed.

'Cary!' she said. 'I wasn't sure you'd come.'

'Wouldn't have missed it,' he said. 'Mind out, I'm coming down.'

He slid down the rope until his feet were on the window ledge and then ducked into the room and into Lily's arms. They kissed and they kissed and, in between their kisses, they talked.

'So, your dad locked you up?' Cary said.

'Yes – I'm pregnant.'

Cary smiled and hugged her even tighter. 'I know you are.'

'How did you know?'

'I sensed it.'

'You know I'm keeping the baby.'

'And I'm going to be a daddy.' He kissed her and looked her in the eye. 'First, though, we're going to get married.'

'We are?'

'We're going to get married tomorrow.'

'But… but…' Lily was laughing and crying at the same time.

Cary had this extraordinary ability to confound her. She hadn't known how he'd react to her pregnancy – and now, here he was, not only embracing it but saying they were going to get married. They were going to get married – tomorrow! Cary would become her husband – tomorrow!

'I'm only 16,' Lily said. 'Can I really do that?'

'Not here, you can't,' Cary said. 'But we're not getting married here.'

'You're taking me to Scotland!' Lily said, shaking her head, still not believing this was happening.

'Mr Barne told me all about it,' Cary said. 'The Scots, so much more civilised than the English, have a number of different laws – and they even allow 16-year-old girls to get married without the permission of their dear daddies.'

Lily kissed him again. 'But don't we need a marriage licence or something like that?'

'What –something like this?' From his pocket, he pulled out that same piece of paper Mr McCreath had returned to him earlier that evening.

Lily studied it for a moment, saw Cary's name, saw her own name. 'How long have you had this?'

'Since I asked you to marry me on the beach.'

'I didn't think it would be so soon.'

'I did.'

'You're not just marrying me because I'm pregnant?'

'I'm not,' Cary said and enfolded her in his arms again. 'I'm marrying you because I love you and because I want to spend the rest of my life with you. The baby is just the icing on the cake.'

'And that,' and she kissed him, 'my darling Cary,' and she kissed him again, 'is the right answer.' And she kissed him one more time, entwining one leg around his knee. 'I'd love to make love, but I've got to pack.'

Lily started to get dressed – jeans and sneakers and a hoodie.

'Don't you have exams tomorrow?' she said.

'History.' Cary sat on her bed. 'Unfortunately, Mr McCreath has also discovered the true identity of *The Sun*'s Eton mole—'

'How did he find out?'

'Shopped by that guy from *The Mirror*.'

'Oh,' Lily said. 'I'm sorry.'

'While I was driving here, I realised something. I may be

good at exams – but I don't enjoy them. I'll be happy never to sit another exam for as long as I live.'

Lily was throwing a few things into a suitcase. 'Good,' she said. 'You're wasted in academia.'

'And you?'

'I was only sitting all those exams because that's what Daddy wanted me to do. And now, for the first time, I'm going to do what I want to do.' She went over to her desk, ducking to give Cary a quick kiss. 'Bring my makeup bag?'

'And your passport,' Cary said. 'And pack your nicest dress, that beautiful floral one you were wearing when you first found me shucking oysters.'

Lily smiled at the memory. 'I'm not the oyster-shucker, I'm the oyster-shucker's wife—'

'And I'm only shucking oysters, 'cos the shucker's lost his knife.'

Lily plucked the dress from her wardrobe and packed it in the bag. 'And will the groom be looking the part?'

'He will be doing his best,' Cary said. 'So, how did you manage to page me after your dad locked you up?'

Lily closed the top of the suitcase and clicked it shut. 'It was our darling Dame, Miranda. I slipped her a note under the door with your number and *voila*! Here you are!'

'Did you ever doubt it?'

'Not for a moment,' she said, and curled her arm round his waist and kissed him again; even though they had kissed a hundred times that night, she still wanted more. 'Shall we?'

Cary tossed the rope out of the window. It was three, four metres short of the ground, but not too bad.

'I'll go first,' he said. 'You follow when I'm down.'

He grabbed Lily's suitcase strap and swung it over his shoulders.

'Fun, isn't it?'

He took the rope and braced his feet on the window ledge.

'Everything with you is fun.'

Lily leaned out of the window to look down at him. She

gave him a little wave and he smiled at her, and she smiled at him, and she was still smiling when the fire alarm went off, and it was so sudden, so shocking, that Cary lost his footing and banged into the wall. He fell the last few metres and landed flat on his back and the air was punched clean out of his lungs.

* * *

Like all idiots, Maxwell had been revising till late, late into the night, as if this last-minute cramming would somehow help him make sense of his incomprehensible physics course. Having failed to get any grasp whatsoever on theoretical physics in the last two years, it was unlikely that, the night before his exam, he'd suddenly get the hang of it. But, still, he pored over his textbook, mumbling over line after line of gobbledygook which, as far as Maxwell was concerned, might as well be written in Linear B. Why, why did he pick Physics for his A-level, rather than something simple like Theology or Geography? But no, he had to listen to his stepfather, who'd certainly seemed happy enough when Maxwell had picked Physics and who would certainly be extremely unhappy when he saw the result of Maxwell's Physics A-level.

He heard a muffled bang from outside the room. He switched off the light and opened the window, just in time to watch Cary heave himself up onto the rooftop. He sat by the window and watched and waited and, two minutes later, he saw Cary climbing into Lily's room. He tapped on his teeth with his fingernails. Now, how was he going to fix them? Run along to Arctic's quarters and tell him that Cary had climbed into Lily's room? Could badly backfire. Set off the fire alarm now? No – he wanted them caught in the very act. So, he sat in the darkness, watching and waiting and, eventually, he was rewarded by the sight of Cary climbing back out of Lily's window.

Maxwell sprinted out of his room and down to the far end

of the passage. He elbowed the fire alarm and Farrer House exploded into life with the din of hammering bells.

* * *

Cary landed badly. Not as badly as when he'd fallen off The Table, but he was winded and his newly healed leg was twinging with pain. Please don't say he'd have to go back to hospital. Lily was looking straight down at him, was saying something, but he couldn't hear her over the noise. He gingerly got to his knees and stood up; his leg was painful but he could just about walk on it. He gave Lily the thumbs up. She climbed out of the window, leaned back on the rope – and then she just froze.

Farrer House was quickly coming to life, every light in the house switched on, every door opened. In a matter of moments, the boys would come streaming out into the garden – and God knows what would happen then, if Arctic caught his daughter.

'Lily, dear,' he called up. 'Come on – you can do it!'

'I'm terrified!'

'You'll be brilliant!'

'Are you okay?'

'Just dandy,' he said. 'Please get down here! We've got a wedding to get to!'

She looked down at him. 'I wouldn't do it for anyone else,' she said. 'But I'll do it for you.'

Slowly, very tentatively, she started to abseil down the three storeys. Cary nodded his approval.

The garden door boomed open and the first of Farrer's boys exited the house and walked out into the garden. It was Fredster, in dressing gown and slippers. First, he saw Cary – and then he spotted Lily on the rope. Another boy joined him – and then another and another. Lily was brilliantly lit against the wall.

For a while, the boys watched in silence, and then Fredster called out, 'You can do it, Lily!'

More boys joined in – they may not have known that she'd been locked in her room by her father, but they could certainly see she was trying to escape, and they were all rooting for her. She was a Farrer girl and she was getting away and they loved her for it.

'Come on Lily!' 'You go, girl!'

Lily got to the very end of the rope and let go and fell straight into Cary's arms. The boys cheered. She gave them a little curtsy and a wave.

'Bye, bye, boys!'

Arctic had just emerged from the house. He couldn't think what was going on – first the fire alarm, and now all the boys whooping. It only needed a second to take it all in – the rope hanging from Lily's window, and there was Lily herself, running across the lawn with that damnable boyfriend hobbling behind her. Arctic took off after them.

'Hi! You!' he shouted. 'Stop! Stop that!'

Lily didn't even pause. She got to the wall, kicked against it and, in one smooth movement, pulled herself up. She sat on the wall and waited.

'Come on, Cary darling,' she called. 'You can do it!'

'I'm terrified!' he called back and, even though her father was hard on his heels, he was laughing for the sheer brazen hell of it.

He could have chosen a slightly less conspicuous way of taking his leave of Eton than being chased across a lawn by his prospective father-in-law and in full view of his girlfriend's – no, his *fiancée's* – cheering housemates.

He got to the wall but, with his dodgy leg, it wasn't so easy to climb.

'Take my hand,' Lily said, leaning down.

He grabbed her hand, her arm, and she pulled and he all but crawled over her to get onto the wall. A huge bellow of approval came from the Farrer boys. Arctic lunged for Lily's foot, grabbed it, but she kicked him off and, a moment later, Cary and Lily were both over and away. Arctic tried to follow, but in his creaking leather slippers, he couldn't get any purchase on the wall. He let himself out through a side-gate. He hurried round the corner and, there, in the distance, a long way off down Judy's Passage, he could see Cary hobbling along with his arm round Lily's shoulder.

Arctic tore after them. He didn't know what he'd do when he stopped her, probably just give her a cuff round the ear and frogmarch her back to Farrer. He ditched the flapping leather slippers and ran after them barefoot. He was definitely gaining, would catch them in no time, but then, agonisingly, as he emerged from the passageway, he saw they were no longer on foot. They were in a car, a Mini, its rear lights twinkling red in the darkness, and Arctic conceded his defeat with a howl of impotent rage.

CHAPTER 42

The next day, I was loafing in Fortress Wapping when I was handed one of the great scoops of my life – Eton's only girl had eloped with her boyfriend.

'Let me get this right.' I scratched at the back of my neck. 'You've run off with Lily – and you're going to get married this afternoon?'

'That's right,' Cary said cheerily. 'Like to come to the wedding?'

'Would I like to come?' I swallowed. 'I'd love to come!'

'See you there, then,' Cary said. 'Should be in by about tea-time.'

'I'm on my way!'

I charged off to the back bench to give the good news to the mad-masters. What a scoop, what a scoop! And this story would run for ages! First, there'd be the wedding, then he'd have the honeymoon, then the baby – and along with all that, there'd be the outraged parents and the outraged Headman. This. Story. Had. Legs!

I swung out of the News International gates and, although a good dutiful reporter would now have headed for the north, I was neither good nor dutiful, and instead headed west to pick up Amanda. Well, who didn't love a good wedding, particularly one where the happy couple were actually in love. Oh, what a cynical brute I have become.

So, while I took this mild detour to pick up Amanda, and while Grubby my photographer was diverted to Scotland,

Cary and Lily were having the most leisurely of breakfasts at an M25 service station…

* * *

Cary and Lily had spent the night at a Travelodge and woken up to the unexpected delight of being in each other's arms. They had already celebrated their wedding day in the traditional manner – because they could, because they were in love, and because it was most definitely the right thing to do. As wedding days go, things could not have got off to a better start. No stress, no twitching bridesmaids, no seating plan, no last-minute nerves, it was just the two of them, alone and in love.

Arctic sat disconsolate on Lily's bed. She was gone. His pregnant daughter had run away – run away in full view of the entire house – and his humiliation was now complete. He kicked at the carpet. How could she have done this to him? His Lily, now not only pregnant but she'd jacked in her education, her exams… She was throwing her whole damn life away for this wretched boy and, before you knew it, he'd have ditched her, and Lily, stuck with the baby, would be left to face a lifetime of menial drudgery – well, what else could you hope for if you left school at 16?

Arctic gave another petulant kick at the rug. How had it come to this? He, a teacher, wasn't even up to the job of controlling his own daughter? And as for his wife, Tor, far from being supportive and loyal, she'd been simply vile to him – had told him last night that he was an A-grade idiot, who had brought this entire catastrophe upon himself, and, when he'd tried to say that he'd only wanted what was best for Lily, she'd started shouting, telling him he'd been a useless husband and an even more useless father… and then Miranda had waded in – he, the housemaster, degraded and insulted in his own home. Well, he wouldn't stand for it and, this time, he kicked the rug so hard that it flopped over.

Arctic was dully aware that he was staring at the exposed floorboards. There was something not quite right about one of them. It was a little worn at the edge. He poked at the floorboard with his fingernail. It shifted. He flicked the edge, and up it came. There, lying between the joists, was Lily's diary.

He wouldn't normally have read his daughter's diary, but under the circumstances, Arctic felt no compunction whatsoever in reading the repellent thing. He sat on the bed, Lily's own bed, and read page after page of the most excruciating stuff imaginable. A lot of it he could hardly believe. Lily, his own daughter, had been rutting with that Cary boy all over Windsor, and all over Eton, and even in the hospital, and even on this very bed where he was now sitting! No wonder the silly slut was pregnant. There was page after unending page of the drivel, and it just got worse and worse – God's teeth, the unspeakable Cary had been the Eton mole selling stories to *The Sun*! With every entry, there was some new revelation to disgust him. They'd even driven off to the bloody seaside and Cary had asked her to marry him!

He slowly turned it over in his mind – and though Arctic was dull and brutally stubborn, he did have the wit to understand what Lily was now about. She was going to get married – probably today, that very afternoon. And, really, if you were 16 and you were looking to get married in a hurry, there was only one place to go: Gretna Green

No time even to change out of his Eton uniform, no time to pack a bag. He didn't bother to say goodbye to Tor – she'd only give him two fingers anyway – just bolted down the stairs to the Volvo that was parked out the back. With a good run, it would take about five hours; he'd get there by around 4pm, probably too late, but, for Lily's sake, he had to give it a try. Marrying that damn boy would be the most disastrous decision of her life. Lily might not see it that way now, but one day she would, and she would thank him for it, and he owed it to her, as her father, to do everything, everything in his power, to put a stop to it. First, stop the wedding, and then, after everyone had calmed down, try to talk some baby sense into Lily – make her see reason, for Christ's sake!

* * *

The first to arrive at Gretna Green were Cary and Lily. This little village is the first Scottish town north of the border and, for over 200 years, runaway brides have been getting married in the smithy. Gretna's original smithy is still there, relatively unchanged, still with its anvil and its old blacksmith's hammer. But more recently, Gretna has become a large commercial operation, with hotel, function rooms, a restaurant and even a souvenir shop selling horseshoes and wee anvil key fobs.

Hand in hand, Lily and Cary walked over to the office, where a genial woman was making herself a cup of tea. She was whistling cheerily to some piano music coming over the speakers. She saw them and smiled.

'It's Gretna Green's theme music,' she said. 'Handel's Harmonious Blacksmith. Can't get enough of it. On a good day, I am the harmonious blacksmith.' She got some milk from the fridge. 'Like a cup of tea?'

'Love one,' Cary said.

'Thank you,' said Lily.

The woman, perhaps in her sixties, perhaps a little older, had bright blue hair and a remarkably unlined face; she was called Moira. She eyed them for a moment, raised a quizzical eyebrow.

'I think this might be my lucky day.'

'You do?' Cary said.

'I do,' Moira said. She got a couple of extra mugs from the cupboard and poured the tea and milk. 'I've been doing this job for over 20 years. It's the best job in the whole world. But in all that time, I have never married a pair of runaways.'

'Is it that obvious?' Lily said.

'Don't often get a couple of teenagers driving in like you have, and just walking straight into my office – so yes, I reckon you want to get married.'

'Today?' Lily said.

'If you've got the paperwork, darling, I will marry you any time you please. Have you?'

'We've got the licence,' Cary said. 'We've got the passports.'

'Yes!' said Moira. 'And have you really eloped? Please say you have.'

'We have eloped.'

'Genuinely?' said Moira. 'You're not just saying that to please me?'

'We ran away from school last night,' Cary said.

'Lovely,' Moira said. 'Any particular reason why you're in such a hurry to get married?'

'Lots of reasons,' Lily said. 'But mainly because we're in love.'

'And that, my dear, is the very best reason of all,' Moira said. 'We can go to the smithy right now, if you like.'

'We've got to wait for a friend,' Cary said. 'Can we rent a room for the night?'

'You certainly can, young man.'

'The honeymoon suite?'

'Where else?'

Cary takes their bags up to the suite. It has spectacular views over the rolling Dumfries fields, as well as the most enormous bed they've ever seen. They're laughing, it's so big.

'It's as big as a trampoline,' Lily said. She kicked off her shoes and started jumping up and down on the bed. 'Make love now or make love after?'

'Obviously, both,' Cary said. 'Though we wouldn't want to keep the man from *The Sun* waiting.'

'A quickie,' Lily said. 'How quick can we make it?'

'A very quick quickie,' Cary said. 'Come here.'

* * *

I poured five glasses of Vintage Krug from the Magnum I'd just bought from the hotel bar. We were sitting at a pub trestle table in the garden; the girls had immediately recognised each other, and had fallen into each other's arms.

I raised a glass.

'To the most beautiful couple I have ever seen,' I said – and I wasn't wrong there.

Lily, blooming in her floral dress, a dash of lipstick, hair simple. She was as naturally beautiful as the lily of the valley; anything more would have been a diminishment. Cary was in his school uniform. There are many disadvantages to Eton's old-fashioned uniform, but for weddings, it is stand-out perfect. He'd got the lot – starched stick-up collar, immaculate white bow tie, a white rose in his buttonhole, elegant tailcoat piped with braid, and the silver buttons just gleaming on his black waistcoat; could have been a pin-up for Bride magazine.

We chinked – 'Cheers!' as Grubby stalked round the table, taking pictures of the happy couple. It was, without a doubt, the easiest, the very jolliest wedding I had ever been to.

'So, let's take it from the top,' I said. 'I want to know – and the readers of *The Sun* will want to know – why you have eloped.'

Cary shrugged, looked at Lily. 'Will you – or shall I?'

'I will,' she said. 'I'm pregnant. My father wanted me to lose the baby. When I refused, he locked me in my room last night. Cary came and rescued me – and here we are.'

'Aren't you supposed to be sitting your A-levels or something like that?' I asked.

'At this moment, I should be sitting my History exam,' Cary said, and then revealed one other minor detail from the previous evening. 'They found out I'd been selling you stories. Bain told them. I doubt they let expelled boys sit their exams.'

'Oh,' I said, momentarily confounded. 'I'm sorry. We'll make it up to you.'

'I'm happy with where I am.' Cary took Lily's hand and kissed her knuckles.

He might have said more, but there was a commotion coming from over by the car park. A Volvo had swept in at speed, gravel flying. A burly man bristled in a grey suit.

'Would this be your father?' I said.

Lily turned round. 'It would.'

'It's all going to kick off then,' I said. 'You up for it, Grubby?'

Grubby was already taking pictures of the man as he marched towards us.

'I forbid this!' he called. 'I forbid this to happen!'

'Forbid what to happen?' I said.

'Who are you?'

'I'm Kim,' I said. 'Glad you could make your daughter's big day.'

The man turned on Grubby. 'Put that camera down – stop taking my picture.'

'Don't you want to appear in *The Sun* tomorrow?' I asked.

'You're from *The Sun*!' He turned on Lily. 'You called in *The Sun* newspaper?'

'We did,' Lily said.

'I think they're clearing the front page,' I said, much enjoying the man's discomfort. 'One question, though – how do you feel about your pregnant 16-year-old daughter getting married?'

'You're a disgrace – to Eton and to journalism,' he said, before turning back to Lily. 'Lily – you cannot get married. Not here, not today, and certainly not to this boy, who has spent the whole of the last year selling stories to *The Sun*.'

Lily took a long pull on her Champagne glass. 'You keep using the word "cannot", Daddy,' she said. 'It's a mistake.'

'I forbid you to get married.'

'Daddy, dearest, you've spent a lot of time telling me what I can't do. You've told me I can't have a baby – when I absolutely can and will have a baby. And you're now telling me I can't get married – when I can do that too.'

'God's teeth!' he roared. 'It makes me mad! Now, you

listen to me, Lily! If you get married, then, by my soul, I will disown you. I will have nothing whatsoever to do with you.'

'How very dramatic,' Lily said. 'You ought to go on the stage, Daddy.'

'I mean it – and what's more, I will do my utmost to stop this wedding, to block the door, to disrupt the service. I will do everything, everything I can, to wreck it. You cannot get married.'

Cary was just sitting quietly next to Lily, monitoring this strange man, who was Lily's father. He'd been holding Lily's hand underneath the table. Now, he fiddled with his waistcoat pocket before taking her hand again. Lily looked at him thoughtfully. Cary nodded and she grinned.

'But you're wrong, Daddy,' she said. She brought her left hand up from underneath the table and fluttered her fingers in her father's face. On her ring finger glittered a Cartier Tank ring, 18-carat gold topped with a square-cut citrine. 'Not only can I get married, but I am married. Cary is my husband.'

Her father was so angry, he looked like he might hit someone – hit Cary, hit Lily. He was rendered entirely speechless.

'Glass of Champagne to celebrate?' I asked.

'No,' he said, this raging force just as suddenly spent. 'No – damn you, damn you all,' and, with that, he was gone, striding back to his car, and striding – at least for the moment – out of Lily's life.

We all looked at each other in complete silence. Lily admired the ring on her finger. 'I'd forgotten how pretty it is.'

'You wear it well.'

Lily tugged the ring off her finger and returned it to Cary. 'Nice work.'

'Couldn't think of any other way to get rid of him.' Cary tucked the ring back into his waistcoat pocket. 'Time to get married?'

Lily turned to Amanda and me. 'Will you be our witnesses?'

'I would love to!' Amanda said, bursting into tears because, at heart, she was the world's biggest softie.

Moira led the way to the old smithy, not so very different from how it was 300 years ago; white walls and low black beams, and all upon the walls were the blacksmith's old tools. You walked into the smithy and you could sense all the adventure and all of the drama that had happened there, in that room, at that very anvil.

'You're sure about this?' Moira said. 'This is for keeps.'

'More sure than anything,' Cary said. 'I've found a keeper.'

The pair stood, holding hands by the anvil, just beaming as Moira took them through their vows.

When they'd all but finished, Cary asked, 'Could I say something?'

'Of course,' Moira said.

'These words were written by Bertrand Russell – and, for me, they sum up how I feel. "Today, I marry my best friend, the one I have laughed and cried with, the one I have learned from and shared with, the one I have chosen to support, encourage, and give myself to, through all the days given us to share. Today, I marry the one I love."'

Lily's eyes were teary bright. 'And, today, I marry the one I love,' she said, swinging his hand in hers. 'May I say something to Cary?'

'Please do.'

'It's a blessing – an Apache wedding blessing. I learned it at school, six years ago; I was only ten years old. I never dreamed I'd be using it.' They held hands, beaming and crying. 'From this day forward, Cary, you shall not walk alone. My heart will be your shelter, and my arms will be your home.'

Cary slipped the Cartier ring onto Lily's finger.

Moira hefted the hammer. 'As a blacksmith binds together two strips of metal that have come from the fiery furnace, so I bind you, Lily, and you, Cary, together, for now and all time.' The hammer clanged and the anvil rang, and our spirits soared. 'I now pronounce you man and wife. You may kiss the bride – as I hope you will be kissing each other for many decades to come.'

Cary leaned in to Lily and they kissed, tender, sweet; my days, what a privilege it was to have been there, and to have witnessed this most beautiful couple, deliriously in love and getting married, not a penny to their names but rich in love and, in the end, that's really the only thing that matters.

CHAPTER 43

Of course, we love that beautiful conceit of 'love'. But, as Mrs Parker was so very fond of telling Renton, 'Love doth butter no parsnips.' Cary and Lily being married and heels over in head in love was great, it was fantastic, and it dominated the news for weeks and weeks – for, after all, who doesn't love the idea of two Etonians falling in love and eloping to Scotland? And, when their daughter was born, they were in the papers and the glossies for another week or two and, I suppose, if they'd wanted to, they could have become 'celebrities', those vacuous people who have somehow elbowed their way into the public's consciousness and who have become famous for being famous.

Cary and Lily had much more interesting plans. They'd dreamed up the idea when they were camping on their honeymoon in the Highlands. Cary liked cooking; he was great with people; he adored working at The Project. What if, rather than just cooking meals for the homeless, he trained those poor souls how to cook; and how to wait at tables; and, for those with the charm, how to be a personable Maître D'? Maybe, if Renton and Fergie were up for it, they could turn The Project's main hall into a restaurant; train up Windsor's down-and-outs; with just a small slice of luck, you'd be giving them far more than a meal. You'd be giving them a career.

Fergie and Renton were delighted – especially when they learned that Cary had lured both Mrs Parker and Mrs Webber away from The Timbralls kitchens. Finally, finally, the safe in the office could be opened, and they could start spending some of Cary's ill-gotten Sun money. Not that they spent very much, as most of the painting and decorating was done by Cary and Lily. But they did have to buy in new tables and chairs, as well as crockery, cutlery and thick white linen tablecloths. The Project restaurant might have been staffed by the one-time homeless, but from the get-go, Cary insisted it was going to be classy – the very best white napkins, knives and forks that had heft, top-quality salt and pepper mills from Peugeot and fresh flowers daily on every table. They spent a fortune on candles. Windsor's waifs and strays were still catered for in the morning, at breakfast, and in the late afternoon in their own annexe off to the side, but gradually, their numbers dwindled. Having been trained up by Cary, and Mrs Parker, and Mrs Webber, they almost all of them took wing, finding jobs in hotels and restaurants in Windsor and in London and, eventually, all over the world.

Because The Project was a charity that was run by the homeless for the homeless, Cary was able to strike a deal with the local supermarkets. Instead of throwing out food that was past its sell-by date, they'd give it to Cary, who'd scratch and sniff and taste and decide whether it was genuinely past its sell-by date or whether it was altogether edible; in fact, probably delicious. (Except for the seafood, which always had to be straight from the sea). First thing in the mornings, he'd tour the supermarkets – now in a white van, rather than his brown Mini – and would pick up all the food that would once have gone straight into the skip. Back at The Project, Mrs Webber would usually be finishing off the breakfast, and the sous-chefs – under the strict eye of Mrs Parker – would be prepping for lunch and dinner.

Lily supervised the laundry, while Renton and Fergie could almost certainly be found in the office, drinking tea and rolling on the floor with the baby.

Within one month, The Project became the most popular restaurant in Windsor. The quality of the food and the service helped, of course. But, thanks to their elopement, newspapers wanted to write about them and people wanted to read about the next chapter in their lives – would they, could they possibly even make a go of it, or would they crash and burn, exactly as their parents had predicted? The Project restaurant even got a spread in *The Sun*; I took Amanda there after they'd been open a week and, even though Matty was so nervous he knocked a glass of red wine into my lap, the charming Maître D', Lily, more than made up for it with a bottle of Champagne on the house, so I gave them a glowing five-star review – and, coincidentally or not, The Project was packed thereafter.

The turning point, however, came seven months later, in the spring, just after Lily had her first child. She was the brisk Maître D' that evening and had already greeted a number of old friends, including Mr Ormerod and Mr Barne, who loved The Project so much that they sometimes ate there three or four times a week, quaffing red wine in the corner as they nudged knees under the table. Also dining there, perhaps surprisingly, considering all that had passed between them, were Mr McCreath and his – ahh, how shall we describe her? – his girlfriend? His partner? His *inamorata*? No – I think we shall label Miss Robinson with the Scottish term that she most enjoyed. She was his bidey-in, and they had taken to visiting The Project on Friday nights; if the weather was fine, they would sit outside on the patio, where they would kiss over their coffee, and marvel at how Cary, the one-time scourge of Eton, had become such a dear friend.

A middle-aged man came into The Project – followed by a now not-so-very-small boy. Behind them, Lily caught a glimpse of a chauffeur polishing the side-mirrors of a black Bentley.

'Barty!' Lily threw her arms around the boy and kissed him on the cheek. 'How you've grown!'

'It's finally happened!' Barty said, his voice deep, then suddenly cracking. 'Got any sisters?'

'Thankfully, Barty, I have not,' she said, turning to the middle-aged man. 'You must be Barty's father.'

She gave Sir Archie a warm, confident handshake, which was not so very unusual in itself, but was a little unusual in a 17-year-old girl. Barty's father may have been bald and prosperously pudgy, with sleek tufts of hair above his ears, but he exuded that indefinable but oh-so-sexy quality: Power. Sir Archie was very pleasantly surprised. His son had badgered him into having dinner at The Project – 'Teaching a Trade to the Homeless' – but he'd not really been looking forward to it. He'd rather expected to be visiting some grubby soup-kitchen, there to eat food cooked by ex-cons and served by tattooed waiters. But instead... He sized up the main hall, with its tasteful Eton and Windsor prints on the walls, and its low-lights, and the little vases of flowers that twinkled in the candlelight. It was tasteful, and efficient, and the linen and the napkins were crisp to the touch, and, as for the Maître D' – he'd seen her in the papers, wife of Cary, no less – she was utterly charming, so no wonder Barty was besotted with her.

Barty asked for a glass of lager shandy, while Sir Archie ordered his favourite drink, a Bellini. Sir Archie watched the barman prepare the drink. The barman – Joe, as it happened – looked the part in a white Nehru jacket with gleaming gold buttons. He grated the skin off a peach, juiced and sieved, and topped the peach juice up with Bollinger. He gave it a final swirl with a vintage swizzle stick and placed the two drinks on a silver salver, bringing them over with a bowl of nuts and a bowl of olives, and – for Barty – a bowl of Hula Hoops.

'Saw you making the Bellini,' Sir Archie said. 'Never seen anyone grate the peach before.'

Joe smiled. He had a bandage on his neck that did not quite cover his tattoo. He could have done with a little work on his teeth, but for all that, you could have slotted him behind any bar in the world.

'The boss had a whole night with us making Bellinis,' Joe said. 'We tried a lot of Champagnes, and we tried a lot of ways of making the peach juice. And, after we'd had about ten, we all decided they tasted better with the skin in.'

'I'd better try it, then.'

The Bellini was coral pink, a tempting thread of bubbles trailing to the top. It was in a handsome goblet rather than a flute. Sir Archie took a small dubious sip; not bad. And another sip; actually, not bad at all. He savoured the Bellini – just the most extraordinary combination of bubbles and alcohol and peach juice. And Joe was right; the peach skin added to the flavour. You could really taste the peaches.

'Absolutely delicious,' he said.

'Thank you, sir.'

'If you don't mind my asking, what do you hope to be doing in ten years' time?'

'Me?' Joe said. 'I'd like to be making Bellinis in Venice—'

'In Harry's Bar?'

'Yes, sir.'

Sir Archie had another sip of the Bellini, and then, to hell with it, he knocked it back.

'I'll have another one, please,' he said. 'By your boss – you do mean Cary?'

'Yes, sir – he's brilliant.'

'And he's only 19?'

'And nice with it. You'd never guess he'd gone to Eton.'

The waitress, Minty, took their orders. Barty wanted steak and triple-cooked chips. Sir Archie wasn't sure about the fish.

'Your *Fruits de Mer*,' he said. 'How fresh is the fish?'

'Doesn't get any fresher, sir,' she said – what an extremely glamorous young lady – she certainly wasn't going to be homeless any time soon. 'Cary picked it up from Billingsgate Market first thing this morning.'

'He must have been up early.'

'He gets in at five to pick up the best fish.'

'I'll have the *Fruits de Mer* then, please,' Sir Archie said. 'Can I have some of your chips, Barty?'

'No, you cannot!'

'And some chips too, please, Minty.'

'Would you like any wine, sir?'

Sir Archie snapped the leather menu shut to put her on the spot. 'What would you recommend?'

'With the *Fruits de Mer*? Well, we all had a wine-tasting last month, and Cary had us trying all these expensive ones – first time I've ever spat, I can tell you, sir – but you can't beat the £40 bottle of Pouilly-Fumé. We've got more expensive ones; Cary went over to the French vineyards and picked them up himself, but the Pouilly-Fumé is a first-class wine at a really great price.'

'I'll have that, then.'

Minty brought the wine over, proffered the label to Sir Archie and, when she was given the nod, snapped out her waiter's friend and confidently pulled the cork. She poured a little taster, and Sir Archie approved – really rather good, he'd have to buy a case – and, as Barty chatted merrily about Eton, and about how he'd just broken the school cross-country record, and how, next year, if he was lucky, he'd be getting Ian Fleming's old room, Sir Archie glanced at the other diners. The place was packed. And how happy everyone looked, particularly the staff, all of them exuding a quiet confidence and quite obviously loving their jobs.

The *Fruits de Mer* was magnificent. Sir Archie didn't think he could eat even half of it, but after he'd tried an oyster, and dipped a lobster claw into the melted garlic butter, and snapped open a langoustine, greed got the better of him and he finished the lot. And the chips, the so-called triple-cooked chips, Sir Archie didn't know what Cary had done to those potatoes, but he'd never tasted better.

By the time Minty cleared away the empty plates, Sir Archie was feeling pleasantly, muzzily, replete. She brought the menu and, no, he was full, he couldn't touch a thing more, when, out of the corner of his eye, he noticed they were only serving his all-time favourite, Raspberry crème brûlée, and how could he resist?

Twenty minutes later, the bottle of wine now finished and the pudding-plate licked clean, the kitchen doors swished open and the manager himself, still in his apron and long-sleeved jacket, entered the restaurant. There was a lull in the conversation, and Cary grinned and pulled off his cap and, in all his years of fine-dining, Sir Archie had never seen a show like it. It was nothing short of the arrival of Father Christmas. Like a seasoned politician, Cary systematically worked the room, shaking hands and kissing cheeks, with not a single name forgotten. Following behind Cary was Joe with the drinks trolley, glasses down below, and, on top, an array of spirits and stickies. Unless Sir Archie was very much mistaken, they were giving away free drinks to everyone in the room.

At length, this conga of merriment wound its way to Sir Archie's table.

'Sir Archie,' Cary said, shaking Sir Archie's hand and giving Barty a hug. 'I don't know if you remember me, but you were once kind enough to give me a lift in the pouring rain.'

'I remember you well, Cary.'

'Tempt you to a glass of Armagnac – on the house? Or perhaps some brandy?' Cary gestured towards Joe's drinks trolley.

'I'd love an Armagnac, thank you, Cary,' Sir Archie said. 'Are you done for the day – can you join us for a moment?'

'I'll just finish serving the drinks; it's a little ritual we have,' Cary said.

'Why do you do it?'

'We get much, much better tips!' Cary said, polishing a large brandy balloon and producing a bottle from the lower shelf.

He went to the next table, where Mr Ormerod and Mr Barne were happily working their way through a bottle of port.

'Good evening, sir,' Cary said. 'May I borrow your corkscrew?'

'Of course, my dear boy,' Mr Ormerod said, extracting his grandfather's Laguiole from his very snug waistcoat pocket.

Cary pulled the cork and, before he returned the Laguiole to the delighted Mr Ormerod, he gave it a kiss.

'It's a long story,' Cary replied to Sir Archie's quizzing eyebrow, before pouring a healthy double.

Sir Archie happened to notice the very plain bottle, and couldn't quite believe it. 'May I see the bottle?'

'Of course, Sir.' Cary handed it over.

There was nothing flash about the bottle, the label scuffed and peeling at the edges. Sir Archie goggled. It was a 1923 Bas Armagnac des Chais de Francis, bottled by Darroze! He'd heard tale of this particular Armagnac, but had never dreamed he'd ever get to taste it – least of all in a restaurant run by homeless people. Simply unbelievable!

'Where did you get this?' Sir Archie asked.

'We were given it by a very generous supporter,' Cary said. 'I was saving it for a special occasion.'

Sir Archie took a delicate sip – notes of apricot and plum jam, and, and, was that oak? – he closed his eyes in quiet ecstasy. This. Was. Heaven.

A few minutes later, Cary pulled up a chair and joined Sir Archie and Barty. He'd brought along the bottle of Armagnac and a cut-crystal schooner for himself. It was Bruno's old glass, his favourite glass, the same glass that, a lifetime ago, he'd refused to smash in the Tap fireplace. He poured the Armagnac and held the glass up to the light to admire the beautiful tracery on the bowl, the girl and the boy chasing and chasing through their field of vines.

'Your very good health,' he said, sending up a silent prayer for Bruno.

And now, with Sir Archie thoroughly hooked, Cary slowly reeled him in. I don't know quite how he did it, but what I do know is that the original suggestion came – or so he would later believe – from Sir Archie himself.

'This is brilliant!' Sir Archie said, now on his third glass. 'You've got the talent, my firm's got the money – we've been crying out for a charitable venture like this! We're going to train up homeless people! We're going to give them skills for life – we're providing a fantastic service and, at the end of it all, we'll get a damn good meal.'

'It's a great idea, Sir Archie—'

'Call me Archie, dammit!'

'It's a great idea, Archie!'

'We are going to roll out The Project all over the UK! But you have to head it. If you head it up, we'll fund it.'

'I'm only 19,' Cary said. 'Are you sure I'm the right guy?'

'I've seen what you can do!' Sir Archie said. 'Look at what you've done with this place – it's staggering!' Sir Archie had another tipple of the Armagnac, studied the bottle again. They'd already had half the bottle! 'You, Cary, are the only person to head it!'

Cary was in that delicious position of a fisherman who, after months of plotting how to bring in the big fish, had finally caught his king salmon, and had played it, and had reeled it in, and now there the big fish was, hook tight in its jaw, beautiful rainbow scales shining in the sunlight as it slipped so very easily into the net.

'It would be a pleasure, Archie.' He topped up their glasses, and gave a very small glass of Armagnac to Barty. 'To bringing The Project to Britain.'

'To The Project,' and they chinked and, from the kitchen, there was a small but quite riotous detonation; Renton and Mrs Parker had been agog as they'd watched the whole scene from the kitchen windows.

'He's only been and gone and done it!' Mrs Parker shouted.

'Played for and got!' Renton said. 'We're going global!'

And, though Cary was still very much trying to concentrate on Sir Archie and the Armagnac, he found he was just a little distracted by the racket that had erupted from the kitchen. Perhaps they'd also been dipping into the drinks trolley, because it seemed to him that all of The Project staff, including Lily, were dancing around in a circle and, in the centre of this giddy whirl, he even fancied he caught a glimpse of Mrs Parker kissing Renton on the lips – though there was so much kissing going on at that particular moment, it could have been anyone.

Ah, yes – yet another perk of being an Etonian. You get all the wonderful education, the self-confidence that borders on cockiness, and then, the most delicious icing on the cake, you also get to mingle with other Etonians, who can sometimes be persuaded to open the doors to their very rich daddies…

* * *

Renton's face was a picture of concentration as he put the finishing touches to the cake. It was a remarkable fruit cake, three layers, and a full 18 inches across. Mrs Parker had made it a month ago, Renton her devoted sous-chef, and, for the past three weeks, he had been feeding it sherry. The cake had now been assembled and, as Mrs Parker watched, hawk-like, Renton deftly piped the icing, not a tremor in his fingers; in fact – not a single thing for Mrs Parker to complain about.

'Not bad, Renton,' she said. 'What are you piping in the centre?'

'A picture of The Project.' He switched funnels. 'And, above it, I was going to pen the words, "Home Sweet Home". Does that meet with your approval, Mrs Parker?'

'It does, Renton. It does,' she said.

Over by the oven, Fergie was lifting out a ham. He'd been up since four in the morning, boiling it, and then peeling off the skin and layering on the molasses and the cloves. There hadn't been any need for Mrs Webber to get up with him to help with the ham – it was really only a one-man job – but she'd come down all the same and, while Fergie had been bringing the ham to the boil, she'd put the tea on and made a start on the napkins, which she liked to fold in the shape of dainty pixie boots. When the ham was on a gentle simmer, they'd quietly let themselves out of The Project. The streets were deserted, and they had all of Windsor to themselves. It was their very favourite time of day, walking hand in hand past the Castle and watching the sun come up in Windsor Great Park. But no time for lovey-dovey-ing now – even though Renton had just given Mrs Parker a sly kiss on the cheek – no, indeed, it was all hands to the pump. Funny that the restaurant – called, simply, The Project – was closed for the day, and yet they were all having to work harder than ever.

The tables had been arranged in one long line down the diagonal of the main hall, so that, at a pinch, they could sit all 70 of the guests. It was still doubtful whether some of the guests would be able to swallow their pride and turn up. (Arctic, for instance, had been a no-show at the first Christening AND the second one.)

But there was a chance, quite a good chance, that Arctic would turn up to this Third Christening, because how long can a father hold a grudge against his darling defiant daughter? Well, in Arctic's case, quite a long time – five years. But there comes a stage where you have to admit that, yes, your daughter's marriage hasn't worked out so badly, and yes, your ne'er-do-well son-in-law might actually be doing rather well for himself and, more importantly, that he makes your daughter happy, and that's really the only thing that matters. So, with only some very mild goading from his wife, Tor, Arctic had soaked it up, and had even bought his latest granddaughter a handsome silver rattle from Tiffany's.

Anthony and Penny, having a very leisurely breakfast together at the Castle Hotel in Windsor, had come to terms with their son's elopement much more speedily. It had helped that, while they adored Lily, they were completely besotted with their first grandchild, Victoria. They'd been fearful, of course, about how Cary and Lily would cope with marriage; where they'd live, what they'd do, how on earth they'd cope with each other, let alone a new baby wailing its way through the night. I don't know why it came as such a surprise to them, but Lily and Cary didn't merely survive in some mealy hand-to-mouth way. They flourished.

So, as Anthony and Penny ate their stewed prunes, they had much to be grateful for: their son, their daughter-in-law, their three – THREE! – grandchildren and, what's more, Cary's charity was doing really rather well, and had been receiving lots of write-ups in the papers! The only (mild) vexation was that young man sitting across from them in the hotel dining room, surrounded by newspapers and canoodling disgustingly with his houri girlfriend who – for God's sake! – now appeared to be performing a partial strip-tease over her fried English. The brassy young man caught sight of them and then had the effrontery to saunter over.

'Hello!' he said. "It's Cary's parents, isn't it? I believe I'll be joining you at the Christening!'

Anthony goggled, but Penny quickly recovered – 'You must be one of the godparents,' she said.

'And there are a lot of us.'

There were a lot of us. Lily and Cary could have gone along with tradition and given their third child, Juliet, just the usual three godparents, but – as you will have gathered by now – they couldn't have given a fig for tradition. These friends were like family to them, and so, by making them godparents, they were making them part of the family. Mrs Parker and Mrs Webber (who had still retained the names of their first husbands) were obviously godmothers, both for the third time; Renton and Fergie were godfathers, and Fergie, when he'd been asked by Lily, had been so overcome that he'd burst into tears and had howled like a baby; and Mr Ormerod and Mr Barne, who had by now – thankfully – come out, they were godfathers also, both for the second time; and Miranda, just flown in from Nicaragua, or was it Guatemala, she was to be a godmother; and Amanda and I – who did have the quite major scalp of having been the only people to have been invited to Cary and Lily's wedding – were to be godparents; and the last of Victoria's godparents was to be Barty Pleydell-Bouverie, whose growth spurt, when it had finally happened, had been simply monstrous, like a giant Titan arum plant from Sumatra, which does nothing for years and years and then, suddenly, out of nowhere, produces the world's biggest and most foul-smelling flower (it smells of corpses), such that Barty was now 6'5" and, from being a scrum-half, had been promoted to full-back and, in his time, had been the fastest full-back in Eton history.

As for Lily and Cary, they were up in what had been their temporary home, but which suited them so very well that it had become their permanent home. They lived with their three children in the attic above The Project, though, after the birth of Victoria, the ladder in the bathroom had been replaced by a staircase. They'd thought about partitioning off various parts of the attic, but preferred it open-plan, and even all slept together on a bed that was fully six metres long (three mattresses pushed together on top of a dozen old pallets). And you might think they never get any privacy, but their two older children now roamed around The Project at will, and every single person they met, whether it was Renton or Mrs Webber or Tor (who could hardly be kept out of the place), just showered the toddlers with hugs. Never in your life have you seen such happy, contented children. At this moment, while Lily and Cary were getting ready, all three children were being looked after by Minty and Jazz, who had saddled up Matty and Joe and turned them into kiddy-ponies. Round and round the office they went, spurred on by their riders, and by the great yowls of laughter, and never mind that Matty and Joe were scuffing up their shoes and their new suits; if the kids were happy and their girlfriends were happy, then nothing else even remotely mattered.

Cary, now 23, is no longer a boy; he is a man. He looks over at Lily, who is just pulling on her dress.

'Zip me up?' she says.

He goes over, kisses her on the neck. Thanks to the dormer windows which Cary set into the roof two years ago, the attic is flooded with light. Their home stretches the length of The Project and it is airy and spacious; open the door and you are out on the rooftops. Cary takes Lily's hand and leads her out to their little private garden, where there are herbs and shrubs and a sand-pit for the children.

Hands are starting to wander. They look like lovers who are still in the first flush – you would have not a clue, not an inkling, that they've been married five years and they have three children.

'So, where are you off to next week?' she asks.

'Edinburgh.' He kisses her cheek. 'Then Glasgow. And then I'll be seeing our new Project in Aberdeen.'

'How long till the Christening?'

He breaks off from her lips to check his watch, a cheap no-nonsense Casio. 'Over half an hour.'

'Plenty of time,' she says and, like two beautifully synchronised dancers, they each move to the other's rhythm. 'Inside or out?'

'How will the tourists be able to see us if we go inside?'

'You're so thoughtful like that, Cary darling.' Lily holds her arms up. 'Unzip me?'

They move to the sun-lounger. There is an umbrella, which will at least partially hide them from the tourists' cameras, and, easy as anything, they are back in harness.

'Time for the emplacement?'

'The emplacement of the condom?' Lily giggles. 'That still makes me laugh.'

'I can fetch one.'

'Let's take pot luck.'

And they kiss and roll and writhe, and the lover on top is now the lover beneath, and the sun beats down and, if they close their eyes, they could be basking on the beach of a Greek island.

'How many children do you want to have?' he asks.

'As many as I can get!'

'Are we talking a football team?'

She purrs, contented, sated, quite deliriously happy with life. 'I've always preferred rugby.'

They lie side by side, snug on the sun-lounger, and drink in a view that they will never tire of; the Castle towering above them, the Thames below and, off into the distance, spiking on the horizon, the finials of the College Chapel.

'Odd, isn't it?' he says. 'I spent my whole time trying to get away from Eton – and now I'm living right next door to it.'

She turns her head and nibbles at his lips. 'And I spent my childhood doing everything I could to get away from my parents – and now I can't keep my mother out of here.'

'If we don't look out, your father will be joining her.'

'He might even take his tie off.'

'He'll just have to join the babysitting rota, like everyone else.'

And the clouds scudded over the Castle Round Tower, and the Thames eased on its way to the sea, and the flags fluttered over the College Chapel, all just as it had been for over five centuries, and who would have thought that so much love and so much joy could come from a rogue boy selling stories to *The Sun*, but that, my dears, is just the way it happened.

HISTORICAL NOTE

Almost all of this story is true – and I should know because I had a ringside seat.

In September 1995, when Prince William donned his Eton tails for the first time, Buckingham Palace did indeed strike a peculiar deal with the British press: After the Prince's first day at Eton College, there was to be a complete news blackout on anything at all to do with William's education.

But though Britain's tabloids couldn't write anything about Prince William, they were still ravenous for any stories at all about Prince William's teachers and his schoolmates.

The first big Eton story came from a 17-year-old pupil. He called up *The Sun* to say that two Etonians had been caught drunk in the grounds of Windsor Castle.

That story was the next day's front-page Splash. The tipster was duly paid and, in short order, *The Sun* established itself as the go-to paper for Eton stories.

How do I know all this? Because once, a long time ago, I was a Sun staff reporter; an even longer time before that, I was a pupil at Eton. Rather unbelievably, I shared classes with not one, but **two** Prime Ministers – the British Prime Minister Boris Johnson and also the Prime Minister of Thailand, Mark Vejjajiva. (There was also, more pertinently, an acned lad in my English class, Darius Guppy, who went on to be jailed for fraud; Eton is a very broad church.)

Like most Old Etonians, I used to keep absolutely mum about where I'd been to school; ditto *The Sun*, after I quit

Fleet Street in 2000. The subjects of both Eton and *The Sun* were a couple of jaw-droppers which, when they came up in conversation, could provoke quite a spicy reaction. Some people get very hot under the collar when they meet a former Red Top reporter, and those same worthies can get equally excited when they meet an Old Etonian. You can only imagine the exponential levels of rage that are reached when they come across that full double whammy of loathsomeness: an Old Etonian Sun reporter!

These days, I am more circumspect. Both Eton and *The Sun* are a part of what I am. And they are both, dare I say it, utterly brilliant training grounds for life… though in rather different ways.

The Sun, when I worked there in the 1990s, had several Etonians on its books. I was their spriggish 30-year-old handler. I bought these boys their coffees and their hot chocolates; I spun their tips into front-page news; and, in and around the cafes of Waterloo Station, I would give them the most immense wads of used £20 notes.

Most of the stories in Eton Rogue are true. The story of the Charterhouse headmaster who used to hire a school-age call-girl – that happened in 1995; the story of the Etonian who hanged himself on his dressing-gown cord occurred in 1999.

Amongst my tipsters, there was one Eton schoolboy who was head and shoulders above the rest – and that, of course, was Agent Orange. I only hope that this story has done him justice.

There is one other very minor matter I'd like to address.

I do appreciate that it must seem utterly fanciful to have included Ian Fleming's ghost in this story. And yet… to a rare few, this character will ring very true.

When I went to Eton in the late 1970s, I was lucky enough to be housed in The Timbralls. In my final year, 1982, I was even more lucky to be given Ian Fleming's old room. For a boy who had been addicted to James Bond since the age of seven, this was the most unimaginable thrill. Fleming died, at the age of 56, just three weeks before I was born. And now, there I was, sleeping in Fleming's old room, perhaps in his very bed – the same room, with the same walls, the same windows, where the seeds of James Bond had first been planted.

Not that I was quite the scamp that Cary or Kim were, but at times, at night, lying awake in bed, I could sometimes believe that the old master was actually talking to me. More than likely, they were just my most whimsical dreams, but a small part of me likes to think that a pinch of Fleming's spirit still lingers in that third-floor room, still occasionally giving counsel to those boys in need of it.

My Eton career was staggeringly unsuccessful. I was one of the many mediocrities who never achieved anything of note. I never won any prizes, never picked up any of those glittering silver cups, never picked up any awards; save one.

In my final year, by some extraordinary fluke, some divine jiggery-pokery, I landed Eton's journalism prize. I was not awarded a cup, but a brick of wood, to which had been attached a most unlifelike bronze owl. This prize was named after an Etonian who went on to carve out a quite brilliant career as a journalist. It was called The Fleming Owl.

THE Sun 22p

£100,000 REPLAY

SEE PAGE 21

Sun ROYAL EXCLUSIVE

DRUNK ETON BOYS BREAK IN WINDSOR CASTLE TO SEE QUEEN

CAMILLA FAMILY BLASTS CHARLES

Fury after he reveals fling

Agent Orange's first Sun Splash

THE Sun

32 PAGE FOOTBALL MAGAZINE

IT'S FREE WITH Sun NEXT WEEK

SEE BACK PAGE

Charlie Kray on £78m cocaine charge

WORLD PICTURE EXCLUSIVE

I LOVE IT HEIR AT ETON

£20,000 LUCKY NUMBERS AND £1MILLION

And Agent Orange's final scoop with The Sun.

ACKNOWLEDGEMENTS

When it comes to acknowledgements, some idiot authors list just about every single person they know – as I did in my last novel *Palace Rogue*.

This is moronic for two reasons. Firstly, by listing over three pages of names, you dilute the whole "thrill" (such as it is) of being included in the acknowledgements in the first place.

Secondly, you're absolutely bound to leave several people off the list. And they will take very grave offence. ("He's listed over 500 people, and I don't even get a b****y mention!")

Last time round, I contrived to miss out several of my nieces and nephews. What a dolt! So may I now attempt to make amends to "The Bloods" by thanking Evie Costello, Kit Lloyd Parry, Stellan Lloyd Parry, Isobel Wilson and Will Wilson. Cheers, ya filthy animals!

In *Eton Rogue*, then, I adopted a much more cunning method of paying tribute to my friends: I've named a load of characters after them. Sometimes the descriptions tally, sometimes they don't. Generally speaking, the more odious the character, the higher that I hold them in my esteem.

These friends include: Anthony Alderson; Simon Alterman; Jonathan Barne KC; Miranda Bennett; Harry Borden; Alison Boshoff; Moi Costello; my nephew Fred Coles; my nephew Max Theodore Coles (MTC), who in this year of 2024 is actually in Eton's Lower Sixth [I'm sure, Maxwell, that this novel will do you no end of good in currying favour with Eton's Cheeses!]; my cousins Joe Coles and Matt Coles; Tor Crawley; my accountant Roy Davis, James Fergusson; Adam Findlay; Ann and Mike Jarman; Finn McCreath; Giles and Nicki Moffatt; James

Ormerod; Mrs Rosemary Parker; Archie Pleydell-Bouverie; Harry Barty Pleydell-Bouverie; Jazzy Pleydell-Bouverie; Mrs Victoria Webber; Fiona Wilson; and Caspian Woods.

Lastly, we must turn to two of my friends whose names have not just been filched but whose characters have been turned into the most grotesque parodies. These are Phil Hannaford and Charlie Bain. Phil Hannaford really is a Sun photographer, one of the best, and – to his friends at least – still answers to the name of "Grubby". As for Charlie Bain, he genuinely was an Old Harrovian staff reporter on *The Mirror*. We worked together for a month as tabloid consultants on *Die Son* in Cape Town. I have so enjoyed turning him into a scum-sucking monster. Just by the by, the year after *The Sun* had splashed with Prince William's house picture, Charlie pulled the same stunt for *The Mirror*. The blood-curdling shrieks of anger in *The Sun* newsroom apparently had to be heard to be believed. I, however, was 3,000 miles away at the time, having become *The Sun*'s New York Correspondent, there to write about Bill Clinton's trysts with Monica Lewinsky.

I'd like to thank: Lord Russell for his kind permission to use the glorious wedding vows that were written by his grandfather Bertrand Russell.

My housemaster at Eton, Michael Meredith, still as cheery as ever, still bestriding Eton's libraries. (He even put my first novel, The Well-Tempered Clavier, in pride of place in the College Library. What a gent.)

My publishers at Legend – Lucy Chamberlain, Tom Chalmers, Lauren Wolff-Jones, and my editor Annie Percik.

In my last two years at Eton, I was lucky enough to have two girls in my English class, Abby Eaton and Emily Bourne (Boris Johnson also happened to be in the mix). When I was writing up Lily's adventures, I did my best to channel these two Etoniennes.

My parents, Bob and Sarah – still, amazingly, yet to be consigned to an old people's home; my brother Toby; and lastly, but by no means leastly, my sons Dexter and Geordie and my wife Margot.

I thank you all!